THE BOY WITH

ONE MILLION SOCKS

James Warwood

(Starring a boy who gets into a lot of trouble,
also bunny rabbits, stale biscuits, pigeons,
wheelbarrows, smoke bombs, a bad guy,
advanced mathematics, paper aeroplanes, tasers,
carrots, thugs, tea bags, mild risk of death
by a nuclear meltdown, and a few
juicy sneezes.)

THE BOY WHO STOLE ONE MILLION SOCKS

Produced by Curious Squirrel Press

Paperback ISBN: 978-1521382240
Hardback ISBN: 979-8797006114
Ebook ASIN: B071K9S2SC

Cover art & illustrations by James Warwood
Edited by Anna Bowles
Interior design by James Warwood

www.cjwarwood.com

Give feedback on the book at:
me@cjwarwood.com

Second Edition

for my wife, Rebecca,
for her continued patience and encouragement
(and hugs)

1

AN
UNEXPECTED OBJECT

There was a boy called Seaweed. He had a serious
problem.

It was not the kind of problem boys normally face. He
did not have a spotty forehead or a squeaky voice. He
did not forget his lunch money or accidentally walk into
the girls bathroom. He was not allergic to peanut butter
sandwiches, nor was he the greatest sock thief the world
has ever known (well, not quite yet, but we will get to that
later).

His problem was much more . . . *explosive.*

Seaweed
(boy with a problem)

BOMB
(... said problem)

He was holding a **BOMB**

Top government scientists have a theory. They believe that holding a bomb that is seconds away from exploding is the most terrifying thing for a human to experience. Unfortunately, their theory remains unproven as none of the test subjects have been able to fill in the questionnaire afterwards.

Seaweed looked around. The annual Picklington Parade was in full swing. It was the one event of the year that everyone attended, even the local pigeons. The townsfolk had gathered together to celebrate the greatest invention of modern civilization – *electricity*. There were hundreds of fabulous floats sparking with limitless voltage parading through the high street. A thunderstorm of electrical brilliance rained down over the people. The crowd was mesmerised.

Nobody had noticed the boy holding a bomb. Nobody ever noticed him, and not through lack of trying. Seaweed was the only citizen of Picklington who thought that things could be different. He believed in global warming and carbon footprints and renewable energies. He believed we should look after our planet. He wanted to show his town how to use less energy, and perhaps then the Mayor would not need to build the new Nuclear Power Station.

So there he was, walking through the parade with a shoulder bag full of leaflets entitled 'Ten Easy Ways to Lower Your Carbon Footprint' folded into paper aeroplanes. That was how he came to hold the unexpected object. He had reached into his bag for a harmless piece of folded-up paper and pulled out an explosive.

Deciding they would prefer not to be a part of any hair-singeing experiment, Seaweed's forearm hairs uprooted and stampeded to safety under his armpit. Thankfully, his instincts kicked in. He bowled the bomb backwards, wore his shoulder bag as a helmet and did his very best impression of a shy hedgehog.

Everyone in the crowd was too distracted to notice. They were smiling and clapping and cheering and completely unaware of the rolling bomb. Seaweed clasped his bent legs and stapled his eyelids shut whilst his forearm hairs huddled together and said their goodbyes.

Then the bomb exploded.

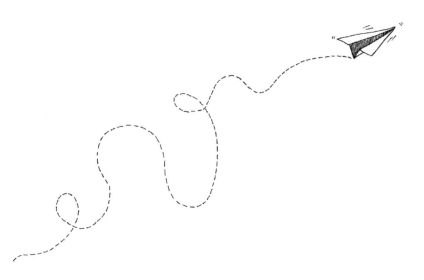

2

THE PICKLINGTON PARADE

The Mayor of Picklington watched the parade from the safety of his office.

He suffered from an illness called *Absolute Power* – a condition where the afflicted becomes addicted to the authority they wield over others (usually contracted by corrupt dictators of oil-rich countries and the occasional maths teacher). He oozed the many symptoms like a snotty tissue.

Having governed the town for thirty years, his condition was now terminal. That was the problem; once you have been sitting on the throne of power for as long as he had, your bottom falls asleep, and your legs go stiff, and your fingernails get lodged into the armrests. In fact, it

Evil Glare
(with matching evil grin)

Srong, Menacing
Posture

Well-Developed
Hand Muscles
(For crushing his enemies)

Addiction to
Tea and Busicuits
(usually only seen in Math Teachers)

had reached the point in his condition where the Mayor believed he had *become the throne*, which in turn meant he could treat everyone else as his footstool.

His advisors sat respectfully around the boardroom table. The Mayor strode into the room, ignored his advisors' mumbled greetings and continued to once again stare down at the parade.

"I see you have done a fine job on security this year, Mrs. Jones," he commented. "Double the manpower, dog patrols, security cameras, very impressive work indeed."

Mrs. Jones straightened her back, but only slightly. Praise was always followed by praise-eating piranhas.

"But, as we all know, the star prize goes to whoever captures me a Carrot Bandit."

Everyone in the room flinched. Those two scary little words crawled under the advisors' skin and wriggled about until all their insides were thoroughly jumbled up. The Mayor, on the other hand, was completely unflustered. It took more than two little words to jumble his insides, mainly because he had a large amount of insides in the first place.

"Ladies and gentlemen of the Mayor's Advisory Panel," said the Mayor to his advisors. "Today is going to be a good day. Today I will strike back. Today I will show this bunch of amateurs that no one terrorises my town. Nobody can stop me from switching on my Nuclear Power Station in one month's time."

Since the Mayor had announced his controversial plans, a meddlesome group of activists had been causing trouble. It was controversial because he announced the major one-year project to build a Nuclear Power Station one month ago. He thought it was a good idea because he was using the promise of unlimited energy to become re-elected, and it was working. Picklington Lake, which had been bubbling away with a toxic green vapour hovering over the surface due to a disastrous radiation leak, strongly disagreed.

They called themselves 'The Carrot Bandits'. They were a sneaky bunch, always managing to ruin the Mayor's plans without being caught. However, he was a man well accustomed to vengeance. Evil anticipation flowed through his veins.

"But, sir, don't you think," muttered a wobbly voice behind him, "and I mean this with the deepest respect, that ignoring the Carrot Bandits' threats to sabotage the parade and endangering the public by not cancelling seems a bit, well . . . *immoral*."

The Mayor sighed. "Thank you, Mr. Dean. That'll be all."

The entire boardroom slouched a few inches. To the untrained ear, that sentence could be mistaken to mean the Mayor valued Mr. Dean's opinion or even appreciated it. However, may I point out that all the other advisors turned their heads towards the victim and mouthed 'it was nice working with you'. Mr. Dean sheepishly stood up, collected his things and reached for the door knob.

"Before you go, I could do with an extra pair of eyes on the ground. I can see the perfect spot right at the front that will do nicely. Now run along."

Everyone in the room gulped. The furniture creaked. The plant in the corner withered slightly. The condemned advisor scuttled off. The pigeons perching on the ledge outside courteously cooed to fill the silence. The Mayor congratulated himself with a satisfied smirk.

Suddenly, a paper aeroplane whizzed past the window. The Mayor traced it back to the source and found himself staring at a scrawny boy. Never before had the word scrawny been a more fitting description. The boy was the only person partaking in the parade on foot. Everyone else was using fossil fuels and the electricity provided, like good citizens.

He cast the insignificant boy aside and checked on his main attraction. At the centre of the parade stood an eighty-foot-high Plasma TV pyramid advertising his Nuclear Power Station's Grand Opening Ceremony one month from now. It was the light fantastic. The people of Picklington were absolutely awestruck.

The wonderful thing about propaganda was its overall ease and effectiveness. Simply advertise all the good stuff, neglect to tell anyone about the bad stuff, throw in some juicy lies and project it all on huge TV screens. The people of Picklington always believed every pixel, without fail. Nobody needed to know that the Nuclear Power Station had a list of safety problems roughly the size of his enormous belt. He also found that a catchy theme tune helped.

Out of the corner of his eye, he noticed something rolling away from the boy. Then there was a loud **B ANG** . . .

. . . followed by another **B ANG** . . . and another . . . and another . . . A chain reaction of explosions spread across the panicked crowd.

"Release the armed security team," growled

the smiling architect of chaos, "and make sure they capture the boy alive."

3

THE AFTERMATH

Seaweed opened his eyes.

He released the stale breath collecting in his lungs. Then he loosened the muscles in his legs and lifted the bag over his head.

Smoke, he was surrounded by smoke. A thick, smoggy, suffocating smoke. It was the kind of smoke that if you were peckish, you could spread it on a warm crumpet. The entire parade had been swallowed up by the thick smog.

"Smoke grenade!" shouted a hysterical woman.

"Get back, everyone get back," commanded a security guard pushing back the panicked crowds.

"Target acquired," said a voice through the smoke.

Seaweed caught sight of a floating Taser gun carried

by a floating hand. It was enough to make his kneecaps shake. So when he noticed several red dots appear all over his body, his kneecaps prepared for emergency evacuation.

"Oh," whimpered the target. "Well done."

"We don't take compliments from the target," said the same voice encased in the thick smog.

"Ah, well perhaps you might be interested in a complimentary paper aeroplane."

"We also don't take bribes, negotiate or discuss the weather with the target. We find, immobilise and capture."

"Fair enough, gotta catch the bad guy. You can't blame an innocent paper aeroplane salesman for trying to make a living in a smoke cloud, can you? I think I saw a group of screaming customers run that way, so I better be on my way."

"Put your hands on your head and lie down on the ground, now."

Seaweed immediately threw his hands in the air. "Wait, this must be a terrible misunderstanding."

"Put your hands on your head and lie . . ."

"But I didn't throw the smoke grenade. I'm just a kid. All I could manage was a gentle roll."

"Put your hands on . . ."

"Okay fine. But if you're insisting on the lying down bit, perhaps we could come to some sort of compromise, preferably something with wheels."

"Put your . . ."

"A skateboard perhaps, or one of those funny-looking trollies you get at airports to carry your . . ."

The armed security team fired. Seaweed ducked. Hundreds of thousands of volts pulsed through the air, and pretty blue flashes of pure electricity illuminated the smoke. It looked like a very entertaining light show, except for the agonising screams of grown men and women being tased.

Seaweed slipped through the thunderstorm. He had managed to skip over a twitching leg when he noticed something odd. The air surrounding him changed.

A pulse of electrical buzzing and humming vibrated the smoke-filled air in front of him. The buzzing made the streetlights flicker. The humming made the bins topple over. The vibrations scared the phone box on the other side of the road, so much so that it immediately dialled 999. He slowly walked forward until he bumped his head on something. The electrical humming stopped and was replaced by rumbles and shudders and tiny blue sparks shooting out in all directions, much like a spaceship taking off in a low-budget movie.

Suddenly, a man leapt off the Plasma TV Pyramid and ran as fast as his smoking bum could run. "It's going to blow," he yelled.

Seaweed turned and threw himself as far as he could as the pyramid burst into multicoloured flames. The explosion flung the boy further than any long jumper had ever jumped. He landed and rolled to the ground the same way sausages travel down hills. In synchronized chorus, the TV screens shattered into tiny pieces. A menacing black smoke billowed upwards, bullying the thinning smog from the grenades.

Everyone stared at the expensive bonfire. They all missed something fantastically odd, only witnessed by a boy lying bruised on the ground. A bunny rabbit appeared through the smoke, scanned the area for witnesses,

scampered through the crowds, thumped on a manhole cover and hopped out of sight.

That in itself is not fantastically odd. But I missed something. Something that was in the rabbit's mouth. Something that glinted in the midday sun with the bravado of the cat who stole the cream (from the cat that originally had the cream).

It was a grenade pin.

Before Seaweed could bewilderedly scratch that spot on your head specifically cornered off for bewildered head scratching, a bag was shoved over his head, and his hands were cuffed. As he was marched off, he heard something in the distance.

Somewhere high above him, a fist slammed against a windowpane.

4

THE INTERROGATION ROOM

When Seaweed woke that morning and opened his sock drawer, he had two choices: wear odd socks or wear no socks. He chose to wear the green, stripy sock and the one that had been in there since the dawn of time with a hole in the big toe.

He now regretted this decision.

You see, you may not realise this, but the problem with wearing odd socks is the jealousy side-effects.

Seaweed sat in a cold and damp corner inside of Picklington Police Station's coldest and dampest interrogation room. His left foot shivered with envy. This mould-infested, stale-flavoured, bone-chilling interrogation room was the perfect place for feeling sorry for yourself.

If you were to ask a professional colour expert to name the colour coating the walls, they would probably call it 'suicidal blue'.

Seaweed knew what he had to do . . . deny

EVERYTHING!

The fluffy little culprit who had bounced down the manhole earlier today would earn him an all-expenses-paid trip to the mental hospital with complimentary padlocked socks. His left foot may well see this as an improvement, but his dreams for a greener Picklington would be officially over. He knew what he had to do. He had to lie. He did not throw the smoke grenade, he did not destroy the Plasma TV Pyramid, and he definitely did not see any suspicious hopping.

The iron door clunked loudly and then painfully screeched as it slowly crept open. Nervous shivers ice-skated over his skin. Unforgiving numbness spread through his muscles. Capital punishment plagued his thoughts.

The bottom half of the darkened doorway suddenly turned into an old lady. She wobbled her way in carrying a large pile of folders with a plate of biscuits. "My name is PC Barbara. Our interrogations expert is at a tattoo convention for the weekend, so you've got me instead." She smiled sweetly and added, "Would you like a biscuit?"

Her old eyes were magnified by her old glasses, which were held in place by her equally old nose. She looked as scary as an asthmatic ant with a limp. Seaweed picked up a Jammy Dodger and took a bite.

"So then, young man, let's get started, shall we?" she said in a soft, elderly voice. "You are being charged as an accomplice to the Carrot Bandit."

Seaweed spat out a mouthful of mouldy crumbs. The Jammy Dodger was as stale as the contents of a mummified lunchbox. Taking no notice of the choking boy, PC Barbara reached up and plucked the top file from the pile, opened it and began to read.

"You are now the prime suspect in multiple criminal investigations. These include conspiracy to assassinate the Mayor of Picklington, intention to destroy the Nuclear Power Station, dumping nuclear waste in Picklington Lake, all of these threat letters addressed to the Mayor," she said as she waved her hand at the paper skyscraper, "and most recently the destruction of Council property, namely the Plasma TV Pyramid."

Seaweed was frozen solid. *Me . . . a Carrot Bandit?* thought the block of ice in his skull. *But I'm just a kid. The only evil plans I have ever created are the drawings in the back of my English book. Surely plotting ways to turn Mrs. Turnbuckle into a half-dragon, half-chicken grammar monster cannot be considered a criminal offence.*

He tried to articulate his thoughts, but all he managed was a pathetic bottom lip wobble. Using her finger to navigate the paper skyscraper, PC Barbara plucked a single sheet from near the middle. The old lady smugly slid the incriminating sheet across the desk into Seaweed's line of sight, as all smug interrogators like to do.

"Explain to me why your signature is on this petition against building the Nuclear Power Station."

Wobble.

"In fact, you're the only person who signed it, aren't you, Seaweed? Which makes me think it's your petition."

Wibble.

"And it just so happens you're the founding and only

member of the Picklington Energy Saving Society, the very same society who attended the parade earlier today."

Wobble wibble.

"And while interviewing eyewitnesses of today's attack, several people mentioned a scrawny little boy rolling something towards the Plasma TV Pyramid just before the first smoke grenade exploded."

Wibble-y-wibble wobble.

She kicked her chair backwards and slammed her hands on the table. "We know it was you, Seaweed. We know you're not the brains behind the attacks. So tell us, who is the leader of the Carrot Bandits?"

"It was a bunny rabbit."

A long and drawn out millisecond passed by, which gave Seaweed's face plenty of time to turn red with embarrassment. Halfway through the next equally slow millisecond, the iron door screeched open once again, only this time he instantly recognised the two figures standing in the darkened doorway.

"There you are," said his mum with enough fake concern to run for Prime Minister. She lifted her hand to her forehead and sighed with counterfeit love. "We were getting awfully worried."

Seaweed's eyes did that rolling motion, the one that people do when they've heard something one thousand times before.

"Damn that jet ski accident . . . DAMN!" shouted his father as he slammed his hand on the doorframe to add some drama.

His parents had been performing this double act their whole lives. Every time their green-minded son did something 'embarrassing', they'd tell this story. Seaweed knew it word for word.

"Please take a seat," said the policewoman in a politely stern manner.

"I must apologise for my son. He suffers from a rare mental condition," said his mother as she leaned in and whispered, "He thinks he needs to save the environment."

Seaweed buried his head in his arms as she went on. "While I was pregnant, I almost suffocated and died. We were at the beach when a jet ski collided with the inflatable banana I was on and catapulted me into the air." She paused and choked on her words, pretending her memories of suicidal fruit were too much.

Seaweed's father placed his arm around his wife's shoulders and sprinkled his vocal chords with a pinch of regret. "Why did I book a beach holiday in Blackpool . . . **WHY?**"

Dabbing her eyes with a tissue, she expertly blew her nose the way only a distraught mother knows how and continued. "When the lifeguard dragged me out of the ocean, I was wrapped from head to toe in seaweed. It took three minutes to bring me back to life, but by then it was too late. The seaweed had already done the damage."

Seaweed had never been able to figure out how much of this convincing lie was complete nonsense. For as long as he could remember, everyone called him Seaweed. It was meant to be a nasty nickname, but he rather liked it. His mother had always held an unnatural grudge against bananas. He had googled Blackpool once and quickly realised why his dad regretted the decision. He was one hundred percent certain of one thing: his parents were ashamed to have an eco-minded, vegetable-loving, environmentally-friendly son.

While the amateur dramatic society quietly sobbed, PC Barbara cleared her throat loudly. "If you are quite done, your son is being charged as an accomplice to the Carrot Bandits."

The necks of two opportunistic parents snapped into alignment. "I knew it," chirped his mother. "He's always been a danger to society with his door knocking and endless protests and ridiculous conspiracy theories. Lock him up before he does any more damage to our beloved town."

"We'd be happy to drop off his toothbrush in the morning," added his father optimistically.

Whilst the negotiations continued, Seaweed slowly slipped further and further under the table. There might be mouldy chewing gum under there, but at least there were no parents. The sound of metal chair legs scraping across unforgiving concrete jolted his body into attention and silenced the room. The policewoman (known to her colleagues as *the stale old biscuit* for all the obvious reasons) walked over towards the doorway and turned to face the dysfunctional family.

"Unfortunately, we don't have any hard evidence. No one has been able to find the grenade pin, and the security cameras were mysteriously turned off during the attack, so Seaweed is free to leave."

She walked to the door and looked over her shoulder. Her stare focused on him and him alone. Suddenly, his childlike innocence was yanked away, and in its place sat a paranoid twitch wrapped in a bow.

"Beware, young man. We'll be watching you."

5

THE CARROT BANDITS STRIKE AGAIN!

Hiding in a port-a-loo and protecting himself with the plastic toilet lid, a security guard hid from the sounds of carnage outside. The feeling of warm pee dribbled down his leg and into his sock.

"Buster, hold it in! You're supposed to be my fearless guard dog."

The terrified face of a dormouse covered Buster's usually menacing mug. Even his whimper sounded more like a dormouse than a Rottweiler's growl. The soggy-socked security guard gave his trusty guard dog a reassuring chin scratch.

Then a sixteen-tonne, solid-steel wrecking ball collided into a digger (which didn't make the kind of sound that

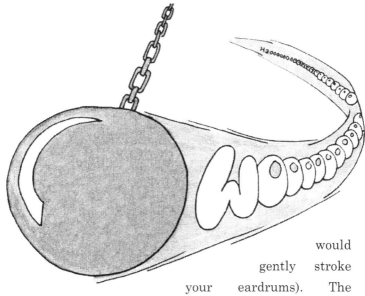

would gently stroke your eardrums). The deafening screech of metal striking metal smacked the walls of the port-a-loo. The hiding guards jumped out of their skin. Buster head-butted the soap dispenser while the security guard kicked the taps off the plastic basin. The end result – two shivering piles of foam.

The wrecking ball continued its flight of destruction, gliding past the mangled digger and onwards through the newly built cooling tower for Picklington's Nuclear Power Station. Hundreds of thousands of gigantic concrete crumbs crashed to the ground. Now a dust cloud stood tall while the cooling tower was somewhat flat and spread evenly across the construction site.

"How am I going to explain this to the Mayor?" shivered the panicked guard.

Silence fell. Then one more **WOOOSH** flew past the port-a-loo, making the plastic walls wobble. He heard a loud crash, which was followed by the familiar smell of rich tea biscuits. He quickly added, "And how am I going to explain to the construction workers that their stockpile of biscuits has been demolished?" He turned to his shivering guard dog. "I am a dead man."

The port-a-loo door swung open, revealing the wrecking ball's masterpiece: a lumpy sea of concrete and biscuit crumbs. Before the security guard and his dog could even blink, they were pounced upon, tied up, blindfolded, gagged, dragged, hung upside down and lifted up into the air by a crane. Even though they were blindfolded, they could tell this demolition crew were no fools; they were the real deal. They smelt organized; they reeked of revenge, and every single move stank of cold-blooded, merciless, ruthless criminals.

No one could help them. They were the only ones at the construction site, except for a few startled pigeons. Sweat trickled down the security guard's forehead as the crane winched them higher and higher. He counted the seconds till the droplet of sweat hit the ground.

One . . . two . . . three . . . four . . . plop.

His mouth instantly dried up at the thought of hanging hundreds of feet in the air. Gulping felt a lot like swallowing a tiny cactus. The sounds of muffled whimpering drifting into his left ear could only be coming from his pathetic guard dog. Feeling a little tingly behind the eyes from the blood sinking into his skull, he let out the loudest shout for help he could muster.

"Hmmmmmmmlp, Hmmmmmmmmmmmmmmmmmlp, Hmmmmmmmmmmmmmmmmmmmmmmlp."

You would be surprised how comical an upside-down

security guard sounds when he has a carrot taped over his mouth.

6

CLEANING THE RABBIT HUTCH

Children all over Picklington were playing video games or jumping in muddy puddles or annoying their older sister by hiding her mobile phone. Seaweed wasn't doing any of those things. He was grounded.

No one messed with Seaweed's mother. Centuries of hardened reincarnation had seen to that. He had thought long and hard and decided she had been on the ultimate reincarnation rollercoaster ride: Egyptian Slave Master, Roman Tax Collector, Viking Butcher, French Executioner, World War Two Tank Driver, and finally reborn as his mother. Although there was no hard evidence for every single rebirth, it certainly explained why she cut his sandwiches with such precision.

Fortunately for Seaweed, she was also obsessed with the game *Candy Crush*. She played it constantly on her mobile, tablet and laptop all at the same time. Sneaking off was made even easier seeing as his father spent his Saturdays sat in front of hundreds of TVs watching every single TV channel all at once. (If you are wondering how he managed this, he sat on a swivel chair in the middle of the lounge with TVs mounted on all the walls including the ceiling.)

And so, with a clipboard in one hand and a handful of leaflets in the other, Seaweed hit the streets of Picklington like every other Saturday.

Knock knock.

"Would you please sign my petition against the Mayor's decision to build a new Nuclear Power Station?"

Knock knock.

"Would you sign my petition against building the Nuclear Power . . ."

Knock knock.

"Would you sign my petition against . . ."

Knock knock.

"Would you sign my . . ."

SLAM!

Knock knock.

"Free Mars Bar if you sign here."

Long pause.

A large woman smelling of yesterday's sweat stood in the doorway. She paused, then loosened her grip on the door handle. Her belly rumbled, but her left eyebrow would not be as easily persuaded. The suspicious eyebrow slowly filled with helium and floated to the top of her forehead.

"What's the catch?"

"No catch, ma'am. All you have to do is sign here," said the little door knocker, cunningly dangling his chocolatey bait.

Seaweed looked past the woman and saw the same thing as he did in every home in Picklington – an untamed sea of cabling and plugs. It looked like several rainbows had shone through the front door, dismantled themselves on the floor and formed a knotted, multicoloured mess. A 36-way extension cable core poked out the top. How were there so many electrical appliances in the hallway alone? Looking at this plughole of energy wastage made him sad, and slightly dizzy.

"There's something 'bout you that's awfully familiar." The woman looked him up and down as if she was inspecting a suspicious looking vegetable. "Have you ever been on TV?"

"Nope, I'm ordinary. Nothing different or interesting or unusual about me. Here, you can use my pen."

The TV was on full volume in the background. ". . . this just in," announced the news lady in her neatly folded British accent. "The Mayor's stolen Rolls Royce has been found at the bottom of Picklington Lake. Although it is too early to tell, the police suspect this to be the work of the notorious Carrot Bandits, who were responsible for dumping nuclear waste in the lake . . ."

The woman scratched one of her many chins. "Aren't you the kid from the parade, the one with those annoying leaflets?"

"What, me?" Seaweed said as he stuffed his leaflets in his back pocket. "Course not, I hate leaflets. I mean, seriously, who actually reads them these days? That kid is such a killjoy saying stuff like 'one heated toilet seat is enough; anymore is a waste.'"

"Hahaha," chuckled the woman. "I wish I could invite him in to see my downstairs toilet." She opened a door to reveal seven heated toilet seats piled high. Seaweed's left eye twitched.

The TV continued, ". . . since the construction of the Nuclear Power Station began, there have been numerous attacks, the most recent of which was the destruction of the main cooling tower and the Picklington Parade smoke bombing. Meanwhile, the Mayor has insisted the plans to open the Nuclear Power Station next month remain unchanged. In other news, the town is experiencing a shortage of socks due to high levels of shoplifting, home robbery and warehouse theft . . ."

The woman's eyes scanned the boy's clipboard. It was a very quick glance as the page was empty apart from a scribbled title, 'Say No to Picklington Nuclear Power Station', with one lonely, childlike signature below.

"It is you. You've got that scrawny look of someone who eats his greens. Nice try, but the Mayor is right. This town needs that Nuclear Power Station, and there is nothing you can do to stop it." She snatched the chocolate bar and slammed the door so hard the hinges did double somersaults.

Seaweed stumbled into the garage, exhausted by

another unproductive day. All this door knocking and leaflet dropping and signature collecting was grinding him down. He felt like a street cleaner in Noah's day whose only tools were a mop, a bucket and one of those little yellow signs to warn people that the floor might be a bit wet.

He navigated his way through piles of broken and discarded electrical appliances and collapsed next to the rabbit hutch. He then pulled his most prized possession from his pocket. For as long as he could remember, he had had his wooden cup-and-ball game to keep him entertained. Having grown up in the energy-wasting capital of the world, it had become an important reminder to him – fun does not need a plug. He flicked his wrist and landed the ball in the cup on his first attempt, just like always.

"Good afternoon, Thumper."

His pet rabbit bounced around his wooden cage, excited to have some company.

"Have you ever wondered whether your life has purpose?" asked Seaweed. "Whether sitting in a rabbit hutch all day, eating hay and occasionally weeing in the corner, isn't your true calling? I've always believed that I could, you know, do something good in the world. I also thought that by now I'd have achieved something," he mumbled as he looked at his feeble petition. "Maybe I'm wrong. Maybe I'm being stupid and should climb down from my cloud, crawl back into my rabbit hutch and play computer games all day. What do you think?"

He looked behind him and scratched his head. The rabbit hutch was empty. He looked behind the pile of broken toasters, under the ancient printers, in between the collection of classic TV sets and inside every disused microwave but didn't find a single grey hair. Thumper had tumbled into a magician's hat and completely vanished.

Something bounced into view from behind a toaster. It was Thumper, and he was holding a catapult. Seaweed's jaw immediately unlatched itself and hung from his head like a fleshy hammock.

The bunny rabbit then loaded the catapult, stretched it back and fired.

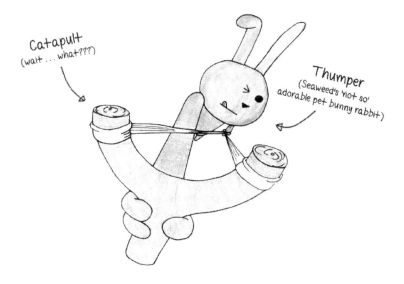

Catapult
(wait ... what???)

Thumper
(Seaweed's 'not so' adorable pet bunny rabbit)

7

IN THE
MAYORS OFFICE

The Mayor of Picklington sipped his cup of tea and listened for some half-useful advice from his so-called *advisors*. He was fat, bald and as cold-blooded as a dead lizard. Just by looking at him, you could tell this was the sort of man who owned a fluffy white cat and stroked it while he sentenced people to life imprisonment in a shoebox. When he smiled, his advisors marked it on a calendar.

The Nuclear Power Station's security guard reluctantly opened the door and slowly walked inside the Mayor's office. A group of pigeons scuttled closer to the window for a better view.

"Explain to me . . ." the Mayor took a brief moment to

glance down at his notes for a name, ". . . Derek, how a security guard whose single purpose was to guard my new Nuclear Power Station was found hanging from the very same wrecking ball that destroyed it?"

"Well, sir . . . it was very dark . . . and I was outnumbered . . . and . . ."

"As much as I enjoy the stuttering excuses of a doomed employee, let's fast-forward to the fun bit, shall we?" The Mayor stood up and revealed to the boardroom a half-eaten carrot. "It seems that poor Derek, whilst failing to do his minimum wage job, ate the only piece of evidence we had to catch the Carrot Bandits."

As the Mayor walked past his advisors, you could hear stomachs clenching and toes curling and one or two bladders leaking.

"It seems I owe our guest an apology. I am asking him these trivial questions when he's come to finish his dinner. It's no use to me anymore, so out of the kindness of my heart you may finish eating this priceless piece of evidence for your lunch." The Mayor rolled the half-eaten carrot along the table and leaned in to deal the final blow.

"Don't eat it all at once, as this carrot is also your redundancy pay."

Derek felt that familiar, instinctive reflex in all humans to suck his thumb. Without making eye contact, he muttered his thanks, grabbed his carrot, walked out the  door and didn't stop walking until he was in his mummy's cuddle.

The Mayor smoothed the creases over his round belly and turned to his terrified advisors. As he glanced past the window, the group of pigeons dropped their popcorn and scuttled out of sight. The only possible way to make this moment even scarier would be for distant screams to echo from an underground dungeon.

"Triple the security at the construction site."

"But, sir, don't you think we should consider postponing your plans, at least until the perpetrators have been caught?"

"They don't seem to be slowing down. We've just been informed by PC Barbara that they've stolen a lion from the local zoo."

"And now the public know about the nuclear waste that was dumped in the lake by the Carrot Bandits, they may start asking questions about whether your Nuclear Power Station will be run safely."

The room filled with mumblings, mutterings and murmurings.

The mumblings and mutterings immediately stopped, whilst the murmurings had to be gagged, stuffed in a pillowcase and sat on by a trembling advisor.

He looked as furious as a raging bull on Red Nose Day, but deep down he loved it. He loved the shouting and screaming and scaring his advisors into an early grave. He especially loved lying, having pushed the barrel of nuclear waste into the lake himself, and he considered framing the Carrot Bandits for it one of his greatest achievements.

The Mayor bellowed away the silence. "I don't pay you to worry. In fact, I've forgotten why I pay you at all. Triple the security as I said, and double the workers at the construction site."

"Where are we going to find more workers?"

"Reassign those workers from that other construction site."

"You mean the Orphanage," murmured a muffled voice from underneath an advisor's bottom.

"Perfect. I don't care if the Nuclear Power Station is safe or not. All that matters is that I'm re-elected. We need to send a clear message to this amateur bunch of vegetarian troublemakers. The Mayor of Picklington will not be scared into submission. My glorious Nuclear Power Station will be built on time, and nobody can do anything to stop me."

The Mayor stormed out of the boardroom and walked straight into a lion. Around the beast's muscular neck was a piece of string dangling a very well-known knobbly orange vegetable. The next word to come from the Mayor's mouth was a swear word, followed by a ferocious roar, quickly followed by the sounds of the Mayor leaping out the window into a thorny bush.

8

A VERY DIFFERENT INTERROGATION

It is not generally recognised that bunny rabbits have a natural aptitude for advanced mathematics, especially in the field of angles.

The invention of maths dates back to the Ancient Egyptians, or so we assume. Humans had to write funny little squiggles on papyrus to calculate simple sums at around the same time rabbits were using complex algebraic equations and interdimensional geometry to pass the time. Many consider Archimedes to be the father of maths and one of the greatest mathematicians of all time. And it is no small coincidence that he had a pet bunny rabbit and would often leave the hutch door open and come back the next morning to find a head-scratching equation solved with fragments of hay and little droppings surrounding it.

In fact, bunnies are far more intelligent than dogs, monkeys and even dolphins. Once you give it some thought it makes sense. You don't see bunny rabbits fetching slippers, or testing shampoo, or back-flipping in front of a crowd of humans for a kipper. That's because their ancestors quickly worked out that the best thing for an intelligent animal to do was to make sure the human race didn't find out about it. So they settled for a simple lifestyle and in return get stroked at petting zoos and occasionally get the chance to poop in their owner's hand.

There was one particular bunny rabbit, the one wielding a tiny catapult, who happened to be a mathematical pioneer in projectile weaponry. He was also affectionately named Thumper. His owner, who was currently standing on a netted trap, began to negotiate with the armed fluff ball.

"Now Thumper, let's not do anything we might regret."

Thumper was thinking, *With a circumference of 4.3 millimetres and an estimated mass of 0.361 newtons, this pellet will require 197.82 joules of potential energy to reach the paint can with enough velocity to . . .*

"Just put the catapult down, and I'll scratch that spot behind your left ear the way you like it."

. . . Let z = potential energy required from the catapult. Let v = velocity of pellet. Let d = distance between paint can and trap trigger. Let t = time. Let y = curvature of the pellet. Let bingo = force required to trigger the trap . . .

"Now hop in your cage like a good bunny rabbit, and I

promise I'll forget this ever happened."

. . . Divide y^2 by $(z + td^3)$, which gives us the proposed point of maximum impact, which we'll call the 'sweet spot'. Therefore, multiply y to the power of sweet spot = bingo!

Thumper pulled back the elastic to z and released. The pellet pinged across the garage and with pinpoint accuracy knocked a paint can off the shelf. A sequence of noises and movements followed which were too complicated to explain, but the end result proved Thumper's mathematical equation was one hundred percent correct.

From his upside-down swinging-from-side-to-side view, he watched in horror as hundreds of bunny rabbits suddenly hopped into view. When you see a gathering of bunny rabbits, you would normally think of words like innocent, cute and harmless. None of those words are currently appropriate.

Seaweed stared at the group of bunnies, and they stared back.

"Hello, Seaweed. Hope we aren't disturbing you." Out from the shadows emerged a figure. It slowly walked towards him, revealing the owner of the voice. Seaweed blinked. It was a girl. She was small and pretty-looking with glasses and a laptop. She looked completely harmless, except for her smile. If fly swatters could smile the moment before impact, they would smile like she did.

"Show him," murmured the mysterious girl. "Show him everything."

The rabbit army moved in unison. Lying before him was a line of neatly placed items. A rabbit hopped and landed

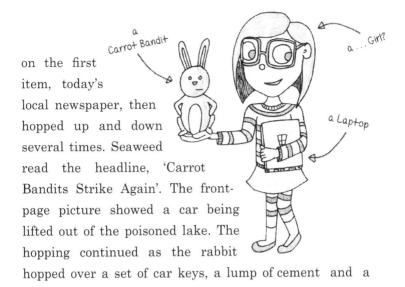

a Carrot Bandit

a . . . Girl?

a Laptop

on the first item, today's local newspaper, then hopped up and down several times. Seaweed read the headline, 'Carrot Bandits Strike Again'. The front-page picture showed a car being lifted out of the poisoned lake. The hopping continued as the rabbit hopped over a set of car keys, a lump of cement and a clump of yellow fur.

Seaweed scratched his bottom, forgetting he was upside-down.

Then the rabbit hopped into the arms of the girl. She stroked it lovingly, then plucked something from the fluffy white tail. It was small and shiny and looked like a hair pin. All of a sudden, the entire contents of Seaweed's brain rejumbled into horrified alignment . . .

They were the keys to the Mayor's sunken Rolls Royce.

That was a chunk of the demolished Nuclear Power Station cooling tower.

That was a clump of fur from a lion recently broken out of the zoo.

And the biggest shock of all: that was the missing smoke grenade pin . . . he had been captured by the infamous Carrot Bandits!

Seaweed looked up. Every single bunny rabbit in the garage was now wielding a carrot. A hundred tiny daggers slicing through the air as they were violently unsheathed. It sounded much like the Fruit Ninja sound effect when slicing through a pineapple. Their innocence drained away. Righteous anger was staring at him now.

Seaweed screwed his eyeballs tight shut. Hundreds of tiny thuds followed . . . then silence . . . followed by more silence.

He reopened his eyes. He was hovering, but not over a gruesome crime scene. No blood, no pain, just a hundred or so bunny rabbits and the girl pointing towards the wall behind him. He awkwardly swung himself around until his dartboard came into view. Impaled by a hundred tiny daggers was a picture of Picklington Nuclear Power Station, and the Mayor's face was barely visible, as he was given the same treatment.

Relief washed over him, closely followed by an unfamiliar emotion. They wanted what he wanted. For the first time in his life, he was in a room filled with like-minded peo . . . *bunny rabbits?* So they were not like-eared, like-nosed, like-teethed or like-pretty-much-anything. Why should that matter? It didn't matter to her, and neither did the illegal stuff. He basked in the moment. It made him feel warm inside. It made him feel justified and hopeful and strengthened all at the same time. Finally, he had someone to sign his petition.

"Would anyone like to sign my . . ."

The sound of footsteps reached Seaweed's ears. The hoard of bunnies turned towards the door and drew another deadly carrot.

"Seaweed, did I hear something unusual happen?"

screeched his tyrannical mum. She was close to reaching a high score on *Candy Crush* on her mobile whilst playing Beethoven's Fifth Symphony on *Piano Tiles* on her tablet. Just as she was about to reach the door handle, Seaweed blurted out some letters that would hopefully form words that would hopefully form a sentence.

"Don't carrot in."

"Pardon?"

"I mean, don't come in. Thumper's escaped."

"Oh, have you looked on the pile of microwaves where he usually hides?"

He glanced over to the microwave pile and saw several bunnies aiming towards the door and one glaring directly at him poised to strike.

"Yep," he quivered.

"Well hurry up and don't waste too much time; your chores list isn't getting any shorter." The footsteps walked back into the house.

Suddenly, the net dropped to the ground with a thump (it was Seaweed who made that noise, not the net, and if you want proof you'll need to wait three to five hours for the bruising to appear).

"We've been watching you for some time now, Seaweed," said the girl as the rabbits surrounded him. "My name is Pank and we are the Carrot Bandits. We are not the criminals everyone thinks we are. The Mayor was responsible for poisoning Picklington Lake by illegally dumping nuclear waste, not us, and if we don't stop him he'll do it all over again. And it just so happens that we could do with your expertise."

He smiled. For over two years he had been on his own: campaigning, marching, door knocking, and petitioning. He had had no help, collected no signatures, received zero pats on the back and achieved nothing. Now he had an opportunity to do something meaningful, to fight back, to make a real difference.

He spotted a box in the corner of the garage. It was his box, a forgotten project he had never managed to complete. His parents had never warmed to the idea of energy-saving light bulbs. Perhaps it was time to find out how many bunny rabbits it took to change a light bulb.

Thumper hopped into his lap. The bunny's big eyes looked up to him, awaiting his response.

"You've got a deal, but first I need you to do something for me."

9

MISSION
SWITCH-A-ROO

Seaweed crept down the stairs.

He crept as every child does when sneaking out of their room after midnight, with a rebellious grin plastered across his face.

Treading lightly was easy for him, more so because he was wearing all the odd socks in his sock drawer. Before reaching the final step, he paused to shine his torch around the narrow hallway. It was empty apart from a spider, who until now was enjoying a peaceful night's sleep.

Disturbing one spider's beauty sleep was worth the success of the mission at hand. He crept to the front door, unlocked it and slowly let the moonlight seep in. Pointing his torch to a bush across the street, he flashed the light three times and waited. The bush rustled. Two figures emerged, one small and the other even smaller. The dark figures silently stampeded to the door.

"What took you so long?" asked Pank as she slipped through the crack in the door.

"Shhh, keep your voice down. You don't know my mother like I do; I had to be sure she was fast asleep before we could get to work." Seaweed closed the door gently. "Did you remember to bring them?"

Pank rolled her eyes. There could have been other signs of annoyance, but Seaweed could only see two eyes peeping through a black balaclava. She swung her shoulder bag into her hands and lifted the front flap to reveal the energy-saving light bulbs nestling peacefully together. There was also another balaclava.

"This is for you," she said as she threw it at him. "If you work with us, then you gotta look like us."

He glanced down and was greeted by his pet, Thumper. The bunny was wearing one too, only he had two extra holes for his ears.

"Now let's get to work."

The covert unit moved from room to room and replaced every light bulb in sight. Working as a team filled him with a tingling sensation. He was fighting for the planet's survival, and at last he was making some progress. Admittedly, energy-saving light bulbs were a small victory, but a victory nonetheless.

"This is the last one." The three of them bent their necks

backwards to look at the hallway chandelier. "Wow. I've never seen so much fake crystal surrounded by so many light bulbs in my life."

Seaweed smiled. "I know. When I open the front door at midday, the sun squints." "Well then," chuckled Pank, "you certainly left the best till last."

She rested the torch on the floor, floodlighting their target. Hidden among twisted metal and plastic droplets were a herd of sleeping sixty-watt light bulbs. Seaweed climbed onto Pank's shoulders for the final time. Thumper clambered up both of them until he reached the very top. The rabbit set to work unscrewing dusty light bulbs.

As the last energy-saving light bulb clicked into place, a sleepy breeze blew by. It picked up a clump of dust from an old bulb, which cheekily floated around Seaweed's open nostrils. All of a sudden, a sneeze appeared at the tip of his nose and demanded to be released, immediately.

ACHOOOOOOOOOOOOO!!!

Pank instinctively did a forward roll and concealed herself in the darkened coat stand. Thumper dived off the chandelier, bounced on the torch, switching it off, and landed on the side table behind a photo frame. Seaweed wiped his nose. Heavy footsteps boomed from above.

Pank ferociously whispered to let go. Thumper calculated, from the decibel level and frequency of the footsteps, that his owner had five seconds to hide. Seaweed continued to dangle from the chandelier like a malnourished punching bag. The footsteps grew in weight and frequency.

Pank bit her lip. Thumper tucked his tail in. Seaweed held his breath and prayed they had woken up the right parent. The footsteps slowed and the weak step creaked at the top of the stairs.

"W-whoever y-you are, I have a b-b-baseball b-bat and I'm not afraid t-to use it," quivered a familiar voice.

Seaweed could smell the fear dripping from his father's forehead (the very same man who once locked himself in the downstairs cupboard for several hours because a spider was sighted in the neighbour's garden). They had won the parent lottery. The frightened voice spoke up with the authority and charisma of a doormat.

"I'm t-turning the light on now, so you b-better start r-running."

"I wouldn't do that yet," said a voice from the darkened hallway.

"Why n-not?" quivered dad.

"Because you need to scare us some more before you switch the light on," said another voice.

"D-d-do I?"

"Well, we know you're holding a baseball bat, but you haven't told us what you're going to do with it yet. So come on, make us shake with fear."

A short pause followed, in which the faint sound of a squeaky hamster wheel drifted down the stairs.

"I'm a little out of p-practice at th-threatening b-b-burglars, so if you could s-start me off, I w-would be most g-g-grateful."

The coat stand giggled.

"You know, 'I'll break your kneecaps you little toe rags' or 'you'll never walk again after my baseball bat is through with you'. That kind of thing."

"Oh r-right." Seaweed's dad cleared his throat. "You t-two should have b-brought a w-w-wheelchair along for this r-robbery because I used to be in my school's r-rounder's team, and although I always m-missed the b-ball, I had lots of p-practice at accidentally w-whacking my sh-shins, and I can tell you it r-r-really h-hurt."

If it wasn't so dark in that hallway, you would have noticed Mr. and Mrs. Tumbleweed and their children rolling between Seaweed and his dad on their way to the annual awards ceremony for the best family tumbleweed act.

"You're not very good at this, are you?"

"It's the n-nerves talking. Give m-me another g-go."

"I think you've just missed your chance."

"Please, s-sirs. I know I c-can do b-better. You'll be sh-shaking in your b-b-boots this time."

"Okay bozo, but let us give you a few tips first."

"Th-th-thank you, s-sirs."

"Never, ever thank a burglar! Slap yourself hard in the face."

SLAP!

The coat stand wobbled and a scarf fell on the floor.

"I feel b-better already. A-anything else?"

"Now then, keep your threats short and snappy. Don't babble on and on like a geography teacher. In fact, I have a better idea. A man of your appearance should play to his strengths, so forget talking altogether and act like an angry orangutan."

"Right, I m-mean . . . ook."

While this embarrassing display of parenthood was in full swing, a dozy and somewhat begrudging spider had scurried across the hallway floor and up the stairs towards two bare feet. If a spider wants its beauty sleep these days, it has to be proactive and do a bit of eight-legged tap dancing to scare the noisy humans back under their bedsheets.

"Beat your chest and blow a massive raspberry."

"Spppppppppppppppppppppppppp."

"I can't feel your anger. I did just steal all your bananas."

"Ook, Oook, Ahh, **ARGGGHHHHHHHH!**"

The deadly tingle of eight tiny legs shot up the orangutan's inner thigh. Seaweed's father screamed and started to frantically pogo on the spot. I have never tried bouncing like a pogo stick at the top of the stairs before, but you don't have to be the leading expert in pogo-ology at some overpriced university to know this is not a wise thing to do (but some insist on learning the hard way).

Bump,

    bump,

        bump . . .

THUD!

The coat stand wobbled. A photo frame fell off the side table. The chandelier swung from side to side. The front door opened and closed in a split second. A rather smug-looking spider settled back into its web for the night. Seaweed's father, who was completely oblivious to all this, clutched his ankle and wailed in agony.

Meanwhile, the bush across the street shook with laughter. Seaweed wiped a tear from his eye and congratulated his new colleagues. "Mission accomplished."

10

HIRING AND FIRING

Sinister footsteps echoed through the abandoned Council Offices. Cockroaches scuttled under the floorboards. Rats scampered in the opposite direction. Even the cleaners on the night shift took cover behind their hoovers and stuffed their ears with dusters.

The harrowing, loathsome, scheming creature had a sour taste in his mouth. He had not resorted to visiting the basement for some time as the Mayor of Picklington. It is a well-known fact that every evil genius needs their own secretive place for such things as plotting and planning and moustache twirling and general cackling in between flashes of lightning. So to say the Mayor had an entire basement for that kind of thing should paint a horrifying picture of his thirty-year reign.

His fearsome march kicked up a cloud of dust. Someone coughed, then wiped their glasses.

"Update," snapped the Mayor.

"Our police investigation has made some significant developments, sir," spluttered PC Barbara. Her short, elderly legs moved at double speed to keep up with her superior. "The lion investigation has unfortunately come to a dead end; no fingerprints were found in the cage. However, our forensics team has been studying soil samples from the carrot, and they have strong suspicions that their base of operations is most likely somewhere in Picklington Woods."

Strong suspicions. Is that it?"

"Your Rolls Royce driver's alibi checks out, and unfortunately, because the boy is a minor, the law says we cannot do any surveillance without hard evidence that he is involved."

"Anything else? Anything at all?"

"Well, our forensics team also mentioned the Bandits have a dandruff problem."

The Mayor rubbed his temples. "Oh Barbara, my old and trusted friend. I have a strong suspicion that your law-abiding police force are the wrong team for this job. At least our plan to frame the Carrot Bandits for contaminating the lake has worked delightfully. Everyone hates them."

"Yes, about that, sir."

The Mayor stopped walking. He looked very concerned. "What?"

"A man fell in last week. He has been taken to hospital.

I'm told the doctors are not sure if he'll survive the radiation poisoning."

Relief washed over his face like the Caribbean coastline. "Oh thank goodness. I thought you had bad news, but that's wonderful. Make sure the media mention that the police name the Carrot Bandits as the culprits, PC Barbara."

"Already done, sir."

"Splendid."

They turned a corner and descended further into the underbelly of the darkened basement. By this time all the cockroaches in the building had safely evacuated the premises. There were plenty of safer places for them tonight, such as the fireworks factory next door or the Dr. Martens boot testing facility. The Mayor and PC Barbara stopped once they reached a closed door.

"We will have to accelerate our plans. Are the candidates ready?"

"Standing in a line and ready for the interview, sir."

"And they've been briefed?"

"No blabbering, no handshakes, no jokes. Just one short sentence about why they deserve to be in your new personal assistant team."

"Excellent, shall we begin?"

The Mayor's steel toecap boot

collided with the door and as a result changed its status from closed to open very loudly. Most of the people inside the room jumped out of their freshly ironed suits. A small handful took little notice and continued to count cigarettes and crack their knuckles.

The Mayor stepped forward and pointed at the first candidate.

"I was the personal assistant to Mr. Grimsby, the CEO at Spam Foods Ltd, and was nominated for Assistant of the Year three years in a row," bragged a confident young man who stank of hair gel.

"Too slimy. Next."

"My knowledge of local government, impeccable organisational skills, and top-notch telephone manner make me the perfect woman for the job," said a smartly dressed lady with a smile that could hatch an egg.

"Too perfect. Next."

"Trunk," growled a large man who resembled an overweight gorilla. The hairy candidate then gave the Mayor a note written on a dirty napkin which read 'I chew bullets instead of chewing gum'.

"Excellent. You're hired."

"I graduated top of my class at Oxford University in politics and have since mentored several leading

politicians and written many journal articles," said a fresh-faced student with inch-thick spectacles and a herd of spots on his forehead.

"Too intellectual. Next."

"I arrived forty-five minutes early for this interview and prepared a PowerPoint presentation showcasing twelve ways I could improve your productivity," said a balding man with polished shoes, each reflecting off the other.

"Too shiny. Next."

"I just stole that guy's wallet, mobile phone and watch without him noticing," said a short, slender girl proudly dangling them for the Mayor's entertainment.

"Impressive. You're hired."

"Please, please hire me, sir. I've been unemployed for almost three years since you shut down the Recycling Plant. Me and my family are living off a can of beans a day," grovelled a desperate citizen of Picklington wearing odd socks.

"Don't care. Next."

"I can make a very tasty Frappuccino," quivered a nervous young man who had clearly borrowed his father's suit. "I only drink tea. Next."

"Well I have to say Mr. Mayor that I find your interviewing process highly insulting. I mean, honestly, how you can possibly assess the best candidates from one glance and a single sentence is preposterous. And who holds an interview at midnight? You haven't even asked to see any of our CVs let alone allowed us to . . ."

The final candidate in the line rudely interrupted the

man mid-complaint by grabbing him by his underpants and slinging him towards the fire exit. The man slid down the locked door like a squashed tomato. "Well, you did say it had to be a short sentence," smirked the muscular thug wearing an orange jumpsuit whilst swinging a set of chunky keys.

"That I did. Go on."

"I'm the reigning chess champion at Picklington High Security Prison."

"Splendid. You're hired."

As the down-trodden, light-pocketed bunch filtered out of the room, the Mayor gestured to his three new employees. He placed his briefcase on the table, arranged the numbers on the lock until they clicked and revealed a solitary folder.

He looked at his three new employees. "Congratulations. As you may have heard, the Carrot Bandits have been getting in the way of my new Nuclear Power Station, until now. This is PC Barbara." The old lady smiled and brushed biscuit crumbs from her police uniform. "She will lead this underground operation. You will answer to her. While she makes sure the police don't interfere, you will take care of this very important task for me."

Trunk, Bishop and Vex leaned in. In bold red writing, the title on the folder read:

PRIME SUSPECT: SEAWEED

11

THE
GREAT SOCK ROBBERY

It was still midnight, or thereabouts.

The security guard passed the time by whistling to himself. He turned a corner and slowly walked towards the main gate of the warehouse. His guard dog quickly caught up wearing a mischievous grin, as all animals do after peeing on a manmade structure.

"That was a quick one, Buster." Buster trotted to a halt and began to scratch his ear. "Still nothing to report," said the security guard whilst swinging his baton. He scanned the main gate and noticed something odd.

He cautiously crept closer, pointing his flashlight towards the odd shape. Behind the metal fence slept a motionless body wrapped up in a patchwork, tattered-at-every-seam sleeping bag. A rickety wheelbarrow sat beside the pavement dreamer. With professional pride, the security guard whacked the metal fencing with his baton, shone the flashlight at the end which most resembled a head and lowered his voice.

"Oy, you. This is private property. I want you gone after my next fifteen-minute patrol, or you'll be sleeping in a prison cell for the rest of the night."

Without warning, Buster pounced at the fence and barked ferociously. The entire fence shook with metallic fear. If the fence had a bladder, it would be raining iron filings over a five-foot radius. All the while the sleeping bag lay motionless on the ground.

"Come on, you dumb mutt. This one's harmless," said the security guard as he dragged Buster away from the fence and whistled as he walked out of sight.

For a few moments, nothing happened . . . after the eighth or ninth moment, lots of stuff happened.

The wheelbarrow suddenly erupted with bunny rabbits wearing balaclavas. Several bunny rabbits wielding high-powered crossbows hopped to the ground. The patchwork sleeping bag burst open revealing Seaweed clutching something tightly.

"Seaweed, the dog has gone. You can let go of my legs now."

Seaweed shivered. Pank rolled her eyes. Meanwhile, the bunny sting operation formed a pyramid and cut five circular holes in the security fence, each fifty centimetres in diameter.

"You do remember our roles in this heist, right? I'm the lookout and you're the getaway driver."

Seaweed shivered again. Pank drummed her fingers. Five high-powered crossbows fired clotheslines at the roof of the warehouse. The arrows bullseyed their targets thanks to an ancient mathematical formula the bunny species perfected centuries ago. (In fact, if you were to point a powerful magnifying glass at a bunny rabbit's eyeball, you would see a protractor etched into the back of their retinas.)

"Would you get a move on? I can hardly see anything from down here."

Seaweed attempted to move, then shivered instead. Pank wriggled about a little. A rabbit high above them cut the phone line to the guard station while five others, who had shimmied up the clotheslines, shot the arrows carrying the clotheslines back through the security fence.

"This is pathetic. I do hope that whatever's going on inside your head is worth it."

Seaweed was stuck in a loop. Not the good kind of loop, like a hula-hoop or a conga line or an all-you-can-eat buffet table. He was trapped inside his head, and his moral

compass was spinning out of control. This was new territory for him, you know . . . *law-breaking.* By now the ingenious clothesline heist was fully operational, with freshly manufactured socks dangling from clothes pegs travelling downwards. It was an impressive sight to behold, especially when you considered the paws responsible.

"Great, and now I'm starting to lose the feeling in my toes. Could I get some help over here?"

Seaweed shivered some more. Pank checked her watch. Several pigeons had gathered on a lamppost to watch the show. Thumper broke ranks, hopped over to his owner and thumped him very hard on the big toe.

Seaweed's arms immediately unlocked, his body jolted upright and his jaw firmly clamped shut. A yelp of agony hurtled into his mouth with such force that his teeth played duck, duck, goose. His law-breaking pet glared up at him and pointed his ears to the wheelbarrow.

"Thanks, um . . . what's that one called again?" asked Pank.

"Thumper, and now I know why," said Seaweed whilst hopping on his good foot.

"Right, thanks, Thumper. I suggest you hop over to your position before your pet does another little demonstration."

Seaweed obediently hopped towards the wheelbarrow. It was already halfway full with socks. He locked his hands onto wheelbarrow handles and sucked in several deep breaths of the cold, prickly night-time air. By his count, they had already broken three laws: damaging private property, breaking and entering and stealing.

The disturbing thought of the police interrogation room, painted suicidal blue, and PC Barbara's selection of stale biscuits caused his breathing to double.

"Calm down over there," whispered Pank. "We're professionals, you know."

"Oh, so I suppose you've broken into plenty of warehouses before."

"Depends. Define 'plenty'."

"Pardon?"

"Well, if by 'plenty' you mean hundreds of warehouses, then no I haven't, but if you mean somewhere between ten and fifteen different sock-related burglaries ranging from houses to superstores, then yes, I have."

"Oh," puffed Seaweed. "Sorry, but this is my first."

"Just try to remember the bigger picture. Changing those light bulbs was a lot of fun, but this is where the real work happens. You're a Carrot Bandit now. No one else cares that this Mayor is using the environment as his doormat. You remember what happened to Picklington Lake, right? The Mayor cannot be trusted. Did you know he has already cut down forty percent of the woodlands? We are trying to stop an unsafe Nuclear Power Station from destroying the rest of our town, not save money on your parent's energy bills."

"I know, I know . . . but *socks* . . . Why are we stealing socks?"

"Beats me," shrugged Pank. "I was going to ask you the same question. My pet bunny, Peanut, told me you're the expert." Pank pointed towards a white lady rabbit with large, floppy ears and a bushy tail. Seaweed gasped. A piece of balaclava fluff lodged into the awkward bit between the gullet and the tonsils.

"Yep, that's why we recruited you. You've got valuable skills that are vital to the Carrot Bandits' master sock plan, apparently."

Cough . . . "Me?" . . . *splutter*. . . "Valuable?"

"I know. That's exactly what I said, followed by 'really?' and 'are you sure?'"

"But," . . . *awkkkkkkk*. . . "that doesn't make any sense."

"I said that too. Uncanny. Me, on the other hand, I'm valuable." She patted the thin bag on her back and smiled. "Can do anything with a laptop and a Wi-Fi connection, me. Who do you think disabled the security cameras at the parade and downloaded the blueprints to this warehouse and is working on ways to sabotage the Nuclear Power Station's electronics? That's right, because of me they didn't catch you rolling that grenade on camera. Anyway, we've got a job to do now. You can thank me later."

He stared at his new colleague as she winked and skipped away. He couldn't help it. He never expected to fear and admire someone in equal measures, so to point out that that person also had pigtails was rather embarrassing.

Three minutes of silence passed. The wheelbarrow was almost full. Seaweed had been distracting himself with his wooden cup-and-ball game. He could not shake what Pank had said. He was valuable. He had something important to offer. He was, according to Peanut, a leading expert on socks.

"Psst, Pank. Over here."

"What is it?"

"When I was very young, I ate a sock. Well, *nibbled* would be a better description. That can't be it though, can it?"

Suddenly, every single floppy ear stood to attention and turned in the same direction. Bunnies glided down the clotheslines dangling from coat hangers and jumped into the one-wheeled and two-legged getaway vehicle. It was time for a fourth law to be smashed into tiny pieces: assaulting a security guard.

OY THIEVES!
STOP RIGHT THERE!

By the time the last letter escaped the security guard's mouth, Buster was already halfway to reaching the sock thieves. The ferocious dog leapt at the fence and barked with the strength of a bulldozer. The security guard arrived huffing and puffing shortly after.

Seaweed was frozen to the spot. He could not move a muscle, not even the teeny-tiny ones in his little fingers. The security guard regained his breath, loudly and slowly.

"Did" . . . *deep breath* . . . "you see" . . . *deep breath* . . . "which" . . . *deep breath* . . . "way the" . . . *deep breath* . . . "thieves escaped?"

Droplets of hope echoed inside Seaweed's head.

"Err, that way," mumbled Pank as she pointed behind

her towards a darkened alleyway.

"Thanks," . . . *deep breath* . . . "now you two better" .
. . *deep breath* . . . "scram before the" . . . *deep breath* . . .
"police arrive."

The security guard grabbed Buster by the collar and
dragged him away from the fence. "Take this" . . . *deep
breath* . . . "and get yourselves a cuppa." He reached into
his pocket and threw some spare change through one of
the freshly made holes in the fence. "And if you see any of
them" . . . *deep breath* . . . "blasted thieves," . . . *deep breath*
. . . "be sure to let me know."

Seaweed's legs remembered their one and only job: to
run away. He jump-started his legs and pushed off. The
wheelbarrow squeaked under the weight of multicoloured
cotton and bunny rabbits as he gained more and more
speed.

WAIT!
STOP RIGHT THERE!

The forceful command demanded complete obedience.
Seaweed slammed on the brakes and almost fell into the
wheelbarrow. Pank skidded to a halt with a little more
grace. A flashlight lit the backs of their legs. Footsteps
slowly moved closer and closer. The sound of a crossbow
being loaded rattled inside the wheelbarrow.

"Before you go, I'd better take a closer look at that
wheelbarrow," said the security guard, having finally caught
his breath. "I'd be a pretty lousy security guard if I let you

go
that
easily,
wouldn't
I?"

The
flashlight
moved towards
the area that,
although must
have been the
comfiest place in the
whole of Picklington,
was also the hiding place
for the recently stolen goods.
Seaweed braced himself.

"Aha, I knew it," smiled
the security guard. "That's a
Wheelbarrow Grandmaster. I've got
one of those
too.

"If that

squeak begins to annoy you, just loosen that bolt at the front, give it a couple of drops of oil and she'll be as good as new. Now run along."

Seaweed and Pank obediently followed his orders and along they ran. Sirens and flashing blue lights passed them by as he tilted the getaway wheelbarrow and turned a corner at speed. Just as they were in the clear Seaweed noticed something.

It was something he could not ignore.

Without warning he suddenly changed course.

The wheelbarrow bounced off the curb as they crossed the road. Seaweed reached into the wheelbarrow and pulled out the thickest pair of socks he could find.

Then he quickly tucked them underneath a lady sleeping on the side of the road, threw the spare change he was given in her paper cup, and pushed off into the night.

12

THREAT LETTER

It was a normal morning at Picklington Council Offices:

- The office staff were working extremely hard to do as little as possible.
- The managers were discussing each other's weekend activities and sipping fresh coffee.
- Norris the tea lady was blowing the dust off the biscuits.
- The local pigeons were perched in their usual spot.
- And the Mayor was systemically torturing his advisors at the morning meeting.

The Mayor slowly paced up and down the boardroom beside a row of empty chairs. His freshly polished shoes squeaked with every step. If you did not know any better, you might have thought the soles of the Mayor's shoes were made of sandpaper and the floorboards were made of hamsters.

"You all know why you are here," bellowed the Mayor to the room of empty chairs. "It is now two weeks to the local election, and we are currently five weeks behind schedule. My Nuclear Power Station has to be fully operational for the Grand Opening Ceremony the day before the election. The people of Picklington must witness my wonderful creation for my victory to be sealed in their minds."

A breeze slithered into the boardroom from the open window. He turned around and continued to talk to himself. "You all know how much I hate to repeat myself, so I will say this only once. It is your job to ensure I win this election. If you succeed," said the Mayor with a carefully measured amount of gratitude, "you all get to keep your jobs. If you fail," this time said with an unmeasurable amount of premeditated torture, "you all get to keep your jobs."

"Mrs. Perkins," said the Mayor to an empty chair. "Have you written my speech for the Nuclear Power Station's Grand Opening Ceremony?"

"Yes, sir. Typed, printed and on your desk, sir," bragged a strained voice from outside the window.

"Mr. Chan," said the Mayor turning to another empty chair across the table. "Have you bribed the Nuclear Welfare Committee yet so all those silly little safety inspections will go smoothly?"

"Yes, sir. We've paid all the right people and blackmailed the others so that your Nuclear Power Station will pass all the checks," spluttered a different voice from outside the window.

"Mrs. Sharma, have you threatened the Construction Company with legal action if the Nuclear Power Station is not ready for the opening ceremony?"

"Yes, sir," answered the out-of-view, red-faced advisor. "They are working unpaid overtime as you graciously suggested."

"Mr. Williams, have your team distributed the posters and flyers for the opening ceremony?"

No one answered.

The Mayor suddenly leapt onto the mahogany boardroom table. The entire room seemed to bend under the weight of his anger. The pigeons, who had been watching the whole time, edged backwards. "Thank you, Mr. Williams. I have been meaning to practise my aim with the newest golf club in my set, and you have just given me the perfect opportunity."

The sound of nervous shuffling drifted in through the window. "But sir, wait. We've tried everything."

"The golf club is called *The Rocket*. The man in the shop assured me the golf ball will catch fire if I hit it at the perfect angle."

"We've tried delivering in the morning, at night, in disguises, by helicopter, but they always manage to stop us."

"I will have to do a half swing, but I can add some extra

power to the shot by . . ."

"It's the Carrot Bandits, sir. It's all their fault."

The Mayor's exhausted advisors, who had been dangling from a flagpole outside the boardroom window for over ten minutes, began to whisper their frustrations amongst themselves. The Carrot Bandits were a sneaky bunch. Not only had they been disrupting Mr. Williams and his team in promoting the Nuclear Power Station's Grand Opening Ceremony but they had been wedging their unwanted vegetables everywhere. The office photocopier was a fine example.

Suddenly, a golf ball pinged through the open window. Milliseconds later another high-pitched noise galloped out from Mrs. Perkins's mouth as a high-speed blur cracked her knuckles. Four seconds later there was a loud splash, followed by more splashing and gargling noises.

The Mayor poked his head out the window and bellowed, "Well don't just wiggle about like a

COPY-TRON 1000

circus seal, Mrs. Perkins. Get back up here now. I don't like people wasting my time. Mr. Williams, you'd better go and help her."

"Of course, sir." Mr. Williams dutifully plugged his nose and let go.

The Mayor continued as if this was a normal day in the office over the splashes and gargles seven floors below. "While we are on the subject, I received another threat letter this morning."

The Mayor opened the envelope and read aloud.

Deer Mayear,

Bee warned. Our treats are aboat to becum reel. Cansill the Opuning Ceremoni and dee-comb-ish-shone the Powa Stayshone. Otterwise we wil disstroy yor rep-u-tay-shone and embrace u infont of the hole of Pik-call-ling-tone!

Yors, The Carot Bandates.

He waved the letter in the air. "Well then, my advisors. What do you make of this?"

No one answered. Then, for fear that the Mayor may have another golf ball in his pocket, one of them suggested, "Well, their vocabulary is certainly getting better."

"Their grammar's improved as well," another added nervously.

"Perhaps they've been getting English lessons."

"Maybe we could introduce a new tax on private tuition."

SHUT UP YOU IMBECILES!

shouted the Mayor as he slammed the t(h)reat letter on the table. His nostrils flared like a bull who had misplaced his favourite nose ring. "Isn't it obvious? Do I have to spell everything out? These amateurs are building momentum, getting stronger and stronger and becoming more and more ambitious. They are no longer an annoying little pest; they have become an established weed. So the question is, how do you kill a weed?"

"You pull it out, sir," answered Dr. Simmons , whose arms were now considerably longer than they were ten minutes ago.

"Incorrect, Mr. Simmons. Goodbye."

The Mayor walked around the corner of the table whilst rubbing his hands together. "An established weed such as this must be given the space to grow. It must flourish without the fear of demise. Once the leaves are large and green, and the roots are fat and complacent, and the ground is loose and moist . . ."

Splash.

". . . you plunge your sharpened spade into the earth and turn its world upside down. You pluck every single leaf, every single root and every single tiny hair from its life force, chop it into tiny pieces and . . ."

Gargle, gargle, gasp.

". . . throw it into the flaming furnace of eternal

damnation and watch it burn until there is nothing left but ash."

The exact same thought popped into the minds of each and every advisor. They were all thinking a slight variation on the 'why did I choose this profession again?' question many adults ask during their lifetime. At least they were getting plenty of fresh air.

The Mayor picked up his briefcase, straightened his tie and headed for the door. "Inform Mr. Williams to commission a TV ad, radio commercial and website banner to promote the opening ceremony. Mr. Johnson, double the security, and Mrs. Geoffrey, clear all my lunch appointments. I'm going down to the basement."

13

DOOR KNOCKING WITH A DIFFERENCE

Seaweed approached another house. The last time he approached this house he was giving away his homemade leaflet, asking for signatures and offering what he considered to be valuable advice. What he didn't realise at the time was that walking up to the people of Picklington with a leaflet about recycling was like taking five bouncy balls to fight Goliath.

This time it was different. This time he had help. This time he did not want any signatures, unless they were autographed socks.

Walking towards the front door, Seaweed noticed a big red sticker in the front window. It was in capital letters with a bold font and an unnecessary amount of punctuation.

NO DOOR TO DOOR SALESMEN!!!

SO TURN AROUND AND BOTHER SOMEONE ELSE!!!

He grinned to himself. This one was going to be too easy.

Knock knock.

"Are you interested in buying . . .?"

The door slammed shut, well almost. A boot was wedged in the doorway. The boot's owner protested, "But, sir, don't you want to hear what I'm selling?"

"No, I do not want to hear about whatever rubbish you're selling. Why don't you tell my front door about it instead? It's a very good listener."

"Well, perhaps this free glossy brochure full of discounted cleaning products might change your mind."

"Jolly good, my front door is always telling me it's due for a good clean," said the man as he fumbled about for something sharp and pointy to stick through the crack in the door.

"And let's not forget our amazing voucher booklet worth over £300, which could be yours if you make a purchase today."

"Marvellous, that'll make an excellent sponge."

"If you close the door, you'll also miss out on the chance to win a once-in-a-lifetime all-expenses-paid trip to Disneyland for the whole family."

Suddenly, the door flung open revealing a red-faced man in his wife's fluffy pink slippers. As he opened his mouth to bark at the pretend salesman, he revealed what remained of his teeth, which I would describe as unemployed.

"Now listen here, you money-grabbing, cold-blooded, good-for-nothing . . ." The man paused once he realised he was speaking to an empty doorway. Meanwhile, several grey blurs shot past the fluffy slippers unnoticed.

"I'm down here," chirped Seaweed. "Would you like to see today's special offers?"

Several odd noises followed:

- The opening and closing of clothes drawers.
- The complex calculations needed to demolish the washing line.
- The yowling complaints of a cat being restrained to a radiator.

The disgruntled homeowner was too busy to notice he was being robbed as he searched for a pen and paper. "This is outrageous. Employing an underage worker. You should be in your dressing gown watching Saturday morning cartoons right now. I want the name of your superior and their phone number. I'm going to make an official complaint."

Seaweed smirked as this truly magnificent stalling tactic presented itself. "Certainly, sir. Who would you like to speak too?

"Your manager."

"He's on compassionate leave from the last complaint he had to deal with."

"Then I'll speak to anyone in the senior management."

"Sorry, but they have all been demoted by the CEO."

"So then, I'll have to speak to the CEO."

"You could try but he's celebrating his recent promotion," said Seaweed holding back a giggle. "We were all surprised too, but I suppose he calls the shots, so why not create a new role which requires a larger pay cheque and an even bigger office chair."

The man hung his head whilst massaging the area of the adult brain which deals with outwitting children. It was somewhat underdeveloped compared to the throbbing purple vein on his forehead. Having noticed this unsettling development, Seaweed decided it was time to wrap this one up. He stomped his foot three times.

"Just give me the main switchboard number, and I'll talk to whoever picks up."

"It's been switched off."

"Why?"

"The entire building is being fumigated by the janitor."

"Um, does the janitor have a direct line?"

"Yes."

"Finally," said the man as he began to talk like a movie villain. "I've found the poor unfortunate soul I shall crush. What's his number?"

"Oh, he probably won't answer his phone. He's not really fumigating the building. He's actually playing poker with the cleaning staff." Seaweed smiled politely. "And you didn't hear that from me."

The man's face turned a dark shade of purple. Clearly the throbbing vein had decided to take the rest of the day off. Meanwhile, several grey blurs whizzed through the open door carrying full sacks from a successful heist.

"Oh, forget it. I'll send an email instead!" The man slammed the door so hard the hinges got headaches.

The sun was low in the sky. Even the sun seemed exhausted from a hard day's work. Seaweed had knocked on every door in the street. Back when he was knocking on doors and asking for signatures, he felt as deflated as a bouncy castle at a cactus's birthday party. Today he felt different. It was a different kind of exhausted. Although his bones creaked and his muscles ached and his armpits had developed their own ecosystem, he knew he had accomplished something.

He leaned on the gate and stumbled around the corner. His father's wheelbarrow was waiting for him with an unwelcome hand rummaging around.

"Oy, I hope you're not stealing any socks from Team Seaweed?"

Pank flinched, then threw her hands behind her back. "Course not. I'm no cheat."

"Good. We're on for six straight victories against Team Pank, you know."

Pank removed her hand from behind her back and pointed a purple, woolly sock at her competitor. "Nobody likes a cocky winner," huffed the sore loser as she threw the sock back into Seaweed's wheelbarrow.

The sock thieves collapsed beside their wheelbarrows. Pets are more intelligent than we think. For example, they instinctively sense when their owners' laps are vacant (even goldfish, they just choose not to act on this information). Two tired bunny rabbits hopped into their owners' laps and made themselves comfortable.

"Thumper, you've certainly earned yourself a good belly scratch, my friend," praised Seaweed as Thumper willingly accepted his reward. "But we still have no idea why you and your friends need so many socks?"

"I had another thought last night," commented Pank. "Perhaps the bunnies are planning to ransom the town's socks in return for votes against the Mayor. Then another local politician would win the election and might decide to scrap the Nuclear Power Station."

"But none of the other politicians care about the

environment. All their policies are about taxes and house prices and other boring stuff."

"Well, whatever the Carrot Bandits are planning, we haven't got long. The Grand Opening Ceremony is tomorrow morning." Pank sighed. "Did I ever tell you why I joined? You've got your eco thing, but do you know my story?"

"No," said Seaweed as he suddenly realised how little he knew about Pank.

"Me and my dad used to fish on Picklington Lake every weekend. I used to love sitting in the boat, the breeze in my hair, chatting for hours and occasionally catching something for dinner. Then one Saturday my dad slipped and fell in. At first I laughed so hard I dropped my fishing rod, but when he started vomiting and lost all his hair and was rushed into hospital, I was scared he wouldn't make it."

Seaweed didn't know what to say, so he said nothing and put his hand on her shoulder.

"Even the doctors were worried. Radiation poisoning is a deadly sickness. It was my dad who discovered that nuclear waste was dumped in the lake illegally. Everyone else may have forgotten, but I haven't. Fortunately, the radiation sickness is wearing off and he is starting to recover, but it was a close one." Pank wiped her eyes and looked at her friend. "We are going to make sure it never happens again."

Seaweed smiled and nodded in agreement. Without thinking, he reached into his pocket and pulled out his cup-

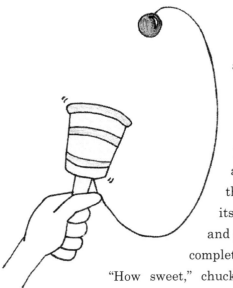

and-ball toy.

"Psst, Seaweed. Look."

Seaweed looked in the direction Pank's finger was pointing. Both Thumper and Peanut were staring at the ball. Their eyes followed its path falling out of the cup and gliding back in. They were completely mesmerised.

"How sweet," chuckled Pank. "Sometimes I forget they are just fluffy little animals with tiny brains."

What they failed to notice was that behind them was a row of bunny rabbits peering over the edge of the wheelbarrow. Some were scribbling calculations down on notepads while others were discussing mathematical formulae.

Seaweed, Pank and the row of bunny rabbits all failed to notice a pair of binoculars close by. It was poking out of a bush and pointing in their direction. (And what the mysterious binoculars failed to notice was above them all perched a group of nosey pigeons.)

"We better head back", said Seaweed. "We wouldn't want anyone to notice what we're doing."

There was movement on his lap. Thumper hopped up onto the wheelbarrow and rested his paws on the edge. The rabbit looked ready to sail into battle on a ship made of justice, righteousness and cotton fibres.

"Alright, Thumper," conceded Seaweed. "One more house."

14

WHO IS THAT IN THE BUSHES?

There was something lurking in the bushes. To be more specific, there were multiple things lurking in multiple bushes.

To be even more specific, the bushes were very unhappy about this. How would you like it if something invaded your personal space, made themselves at home for the afternoon and bent a few branches in the process?

The bush on the left was swollen to twice its normal size. The bush on the right seemed to be hanging over the edge of the pavement and growing slightly every time someone walked past. The bush in the middle stood unnaturally still, even for foliage. To the average pair of eyes, it did not look as suspicious as the other two, but it was that very

same observation that made this bush the most suspicious of them all (and the binoculars were a bit of a giveaway too).

The boy across the road was currently talking to a door about cleaning products. The swollen bush on the left suddenly began to shudder.

AHHHH

A hand poked out of the bush on the right, holding a tissue. Another hand, which was larger and much less agile, emerged from the middle bush and snatched it.

AHHHHHHHH

The tissue appeared again, this time on the left-hand side of the middle bush. Then a gigantic hand with fingers the size of baby legs emerged from the swollen bush and grabbed the tissue. It quickly withdrew inside and sneezed.

AHHHHHHHHHHHCHOOO!!!

"Why did we bring him again?" questioned Vex.

"Protection," reminded Bishop, who continued to keep

his eyes firmly pressed against his binoculars. "Anyway, no one chooses to have hay fever. Ain't that right, Trunk?"

"Trunk," whispered Trunk.

The enormous crook with a single-word vocabulary clearly understood their situation. He had not cracked his knuckles once or punched the closest object or even laughed to himself when he broke something. He simply sat as still as he could and watched the boy.

Footsteps approached. The bushes went completely still, apart from the bush on the right, which leaned forward in anticipation. As the unsuspecting pedestrian walked past, the contents of his pockets mysteriously vanished. The pedestrian did not notice the magic trick performed by the shrubbery and continued to walk away from his personal belongings and around the corner.

"What can you see through the binoculars?" asked Vex as she inspected her new acquirements.

Bishop scanned the house. He could see an angry person at the front door arguing with Seaweed. Through the upstairs window, he saw clothes being thrown in every direction. Then he glanced towards the alleyway, where he caught a glimpse of a washing line collapsing in the back garden.

"Just the usual."

"This spying business is sooooooooo boring," moaned Vex. A nearby pigeon cooed in agreement. "The kid and his rodents are doing the same thing over and over and over again. Can't we just go and pound them yet?"

"Trunk," whispered Trunk supportively.

"How many times do I have to remind you both? We need to wait until they're all together, in one big group. Capture the leader and scare the bunnies skinless so they all scatter. That's the Mayor's plan. Would you like me to write it down on a nail and hammer it into your thick skull so the message sinks in?"

"Hurhurhur."

"Shut up, Trunk," scowled Vex.

"Trunk," he whispered apologetically.

The door across the road slammed shut and reverberated throughout the neighbourhood. The boy, however, seemed completely unflustered as he walked around the corner and joined the girl. Bishop, however, had the binoculars fixed on the wheelbarrows.

"What I don't understand," speculated Bishop, "is how these kids are controlling those fur balls? They seem to follow their every command." Right on cue two bunny rabbits hopped out from the wheelbarrows and leapt onto their masters' laps.

"Beats me," said Vex. "What I've found in my time as a criminal is that there's nothing a little bit of harmless torture can't solve."

"Trunk," agreed Trunk, who seemed excited by this prospect.

The boy and the girl stood up and moved their wheelbarrows to outside the next house. You did not need a pair of high-powered binoculars to work out this homeowner had an obsession with garden gnomes. There were five gnomes fishing in the pond, seven climbing up the drain pipe, eleven watering the flowers, three pushing mini wheelbarrows around the lawn and one rather unfortunate gnome positioned on top of the bin. The little thieves began to walk up the driveway while the bunny rabbits moved into position.

"Come on, I've seen enough of this already. We'll report back to PC Barbara and return in the early hours of the morning in case an opportunity emerges. Now let's go."

As the trio slowly reversed from their hideout, staying out of sight, a knocking on a front door could be heard from across the street.

Knock knock.

Good evening. Would you be interested in talking to us about gnome insurance?"

15

THE
INITIATION CEREMONY

Seaweed gripped a baseball bat.

He was standing in the Picklington Woods. The early morning chill seeped through Seaweed's slippers. His pyjamas dreamt of radiators and airing cupboards.

It was that time in the early hours of the morning that no one believes actually exists. The limbo between midnight and dawn. It's a cold and dark and eerily quiet period of time. No one dares to venture out from their warm beds, which in turn makes it the perfect time for a Secret Initiation Ceremony.

On the ground directly in front of Seaweed lay a toaster. The shiny metal glinted in the candlelight. Seaweed looked around. He was encircled by the Carrot Bandits, each holding a lit candle. Pank was not here.

His drowsy brain was still processing what time it was. He knew that today was the day of the Nuclear Power Station's Grand Opening Ceremony. Several important questions impatiently formed a queue:

- What am I doing here?
- Where is Pank?
- What are the Carrot Bandits planning?
- Where am I?

There was one final question with an obvious answer:

- What is the baseball bat for?

Locked onto his target, Seaweed lifted the baseball bat above his head and swung downwards. The toaster's brutal execution echoed throughout the woods. His forearms tingled from the impact, his shoulder joints temporarily blacked out, and his eardrums considered writing a formal complaint. The toaster definitely came off worse.

Seaweed received a round of applause. The bunny rabbits thumped their back feet on the ground in delight. The bunnies had got it right. Doing the right thing sometimes means you have to break the law. So most of the people of Picklington were wearing odd socks, and his parents were now missing one of their seven toasters, big deal. That was what you called collateral damage . . . a means to an end . . . a worthy sacrifice for something bigger and revolutionary and radical.

He gave a modest bow. As his head lowered towards the

ground, he spotted a tiny dagger disguised as a carrot on the ground.

This was it. Time to stop the Mayor. Time to save the town from themselves. Time to make his dreams come true.

He was now a member of the Carrot Bandits.

"Is it time yet?"

"Yeah, how many toasters have to die before we pounce?"

"Trunk!"

Someone sighed. "Did your grandmas forget to teach you something called patience?"

The three thugs scratched their heads. It was obvious there were several words in the question that needed explaining. Bishop was the first to embarrass himself. "I don't think I have a grandma."

"Yeah," agreed Vex. "Your parents adopted you from the zoo."

"Hurhurhur ," laughed the hairy mass of muscles.

Well, the only thing your grandma taught you, Vex, was how to cheat at bingo."

"Be quiet you idiots," said PC Barbara without breaking her concentration, a skill she had perfected over years of corruption and knitting jumpers. "We wait until the kid drops the weapon. Then we make our move." She paused to sharpen her tongue so that the next four words were underlined. "Wait for my signal."

The pained metallic cry of a dying toaster echoed through the woods, quickly followed by hundreds of bunny rabbits thumping the ground. Seaweed dropped the baseball bat and bowed.

Three sets of muscular, impatient legs twitched. One authoritative, wrinkly hand sprung into the air.

"Wait for it."

The bunnies broke ranks. A handful hopped towards Seaweed while the others hopped into the darkness. The boy was swarmed by bunny rabbits. It looked like he was wearing a living fur coat. Every so often a tape measure could be seen. They were taking every type of measurement known to the animal kingdom: waistline, inside leg, even bottom circumference.

This is the perfect distraction, thought the three knives clenched between three sets of teeth. They readied themselves in preparation to make a fur coat of their own.

"Wait for it."

The ground began to wobble slightly. It was distinctively different to the shudder created by the bunny rabbits thumping. It was smooth and oddly comfortable, like bouncing on custard. Then something gigantic and round and highly unexpected rolled into view.

"It's show time, boys."

Three sets of knuckles cracked loudly.

Seaweed picked up his initiation gift.

He grabbed it by the handle. It felt oddly familiar: the wooden surface, the smooth carving, the flaky varnish. He lifted the object for closer inspection to discover it was actually his cup-and-ball game.

How odd. He had spent hours perfecting his cup-and-ball skills throughout his childhood. How can this be an initiation gift when he already owned it? Why give him this?

Suddenly, he was covered from head to toe in bunny rabbits. His vision went blurry and everything was in greyscale. There are certain animals you do not want to be swarmed by: killer bees, piranhas, elephants wearing stiletto shoes. Being swarmed by bunny rabbits felt as though he was hugging an Inuit's wardrobe.

As they leapt off one by one, Seaweed stumbled about. Then he bumped into something and fell on his bottom. Seaweed rubbed his eyes, brushed the dirt off his pyjamas and looked for what had knocked him off his feet. Then he rubbed his eyes again and looked upwards. Then he rubbed his neck so that he could look upwards-er.

As the little ball dangled by his side, Seaweed stood staring at the gigantic ball made of socks. It was the size of a semi-detached house with an extension at the back and double garage to the side. It was both an awe-inspiring and spine-chilling sight.

Everything clicked into place inside his head:

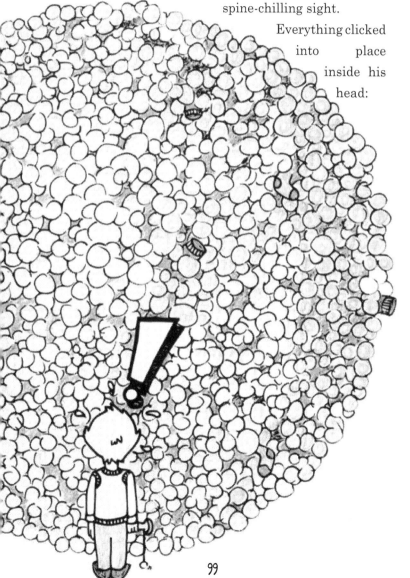

- This gigantic ball of rolled up socks was the ball.
- The Nuclear Power Station's cooling tower was the cup.
- He was the weapons expert.

Seaweed took a brief moment to panic.

The rabbits must have thought this would stop the Nuclear Power Station. Except he knew that after it stopped working there would be emergency sirens, and after the emergency sirens there would mass panic, and after the mass panic there would be an explosion, and after the explosion there would be an enormous mushroom cloud of radioactive ash, and after all that there would be no people or bunny rabbits or Picklington . . .

JUST ONE MASSIVE CRATER

When something horrific happens, like when you realise you have joined a group who in a matter of hours will cause a nuclear disaster and kill thousands of people, your brain assumes that nothing worse could possibly happen next. Interestingly, more often than not the opposite happens (at least in all the exciting books).

"I told you I'd be watching you, Seaweed."

He turned around to see PC Barbara and three unsightly thugs walking towards him. They were the pedigree of criminal lineage, apart from the big hairy one, who looked of primate descent. They were most definitely the kind of thugs who punch first and punch even harder later.

"Imagine my surprise to see you here," continued PC Barbara, "surrounded by hundreds of bunny rabbits all following your orders. You are a clever little boy, making everyone think the parade was an accident when you were the criminal mastermind all along. I must say, I'm impressed."

Seaweed was speechless.

"And to think you and your bunny hoard came this close to ruining the Grand Opening Ceremony of the Mayor's Nuclear Power Station. What exactly where you planning to do with this . . . well, I'm not even sure what it is."

PC Barbara paused for a response, and when she realised she was not going to get one, she slowly and purposefully reached into her bulletproof vest. Seaweed flinched. He had watched enough gangsta movies to know what happens next. The tiny hairs on his forearm, well-practised at the emergency procedure, assumed the brace position.

She pulled out her weapon. It was a ziplock travel bag containing several crushed biscuits. "Would anyone like a biscuit before this gets ugly?"

The big, hairy one could not contain his excitement any longer. He ran full force towards Seaweed and the bunny rabbits. Bishop and Vex followed knife in hand. Seaweed braced himself. The bunnies hopped. PC Barbara munched on a chocolate bourbon.

The fight was over in under a minute. Trunk was an

unstoppable force. Vex was a blur. Bishop was a brute. The bunnies fled and Seaweed was left behind dangling upside down.

"Rabbits aren't as loyal as you thought, are they, Seaweed?"

"But you don't understand," pleaded the red-handed and red-faced boy. "It's not me, the bunnies are planning to . . ."

"Save your breath kid," threatened Vex as she slowly pressed her knife against his neck. "I'm no cop. I don't care for your excuses. What I care about is that we don't have no orders for bringing you in alive."

Seaweed buttoned it.

"Yeah," added Bishop as he circled his prey. "The Mayor only mentioned finding the leader of the Carrot Bandits. He never said to bring him back in one piece."

"Trunk, hurhurhur," agreed Trunk.

Seaweed re-buttoned it, as an added precaution.

The sound of crumbs being brushed off police uniform interrupted them. "That would be unwise. We still need him."

The three thugs loudly huffed and puffed. After all, why become a thug if you do not get to do thuggish things, apart from the good pay of course. PC Barbara ignored them and slowly walked towards her next sentence as old ladies do. "You'll get your chance, but first the Mayor wants to see him."

16

LOCKED UP

Seaweed had discovered many things during his imprisonment, four things to be precise:

- Being tied to a chair, gagged, blindfolded and locked up is no fun.
- Basements are cold on the toes and unwelcoming on the nose.
- He was going to need thicker pyjamas for prison.
- Waiting for a nuclear explosion, knowing there was nothing he could do to stop it, was the worst kind of torture imaginable.

Seaweed tried to think like a rabbit and calculated the chances of PC Barbara and her thugs locking him inside a nuclear bunker. The percentage in his head started with zero and was followed by a decimal point and many more zeros. Perhaps this is all a big hoax. Perhaps the giant sock ball will not work. Or maybe the bunny rabbits will call it quits and go back to munching grass and innocent hopping.

There was no sidestepping the horrifying truth. PC Barbara and the Mayor thought he was the evil mastermind, the ruthless leader, the puppet master who planned everything. They thought that because he had been caught, the bunnies had lost their leader and disbanded. They thought that when the Nuclear Power Station was switched on at the opening ceremony in one hour, the Carrot Bandits would do nothing.

Seaweed heard voices approaching.

". . . can't believe it. So it was the little brat all along."

"Oh I know, the youth of today."

"What was his name again?"

"Seaweed, sir."

"Interesting. Sounds like some kind of silly gang name to me. He probably wants money, they always want money."

"Don't worry, sir. We caught him and his accomplice before they could do any real damage."

Seaweed winced. So they had captured Pank too.

"Yes, well done PC Barbara. I knew I could count on my most trusted and corrupt police constable. No thanks, I'm watching my figure."

"Suit yourself," munched the familiar voice.

"Be sure that my three favourite employees get paid. I suppose they're out celebrating their big prize catch."

"No, sir, I sent them out to buy more teabags."

"Excellent. Now then, I think it's time I welcomed our guest."

The door opened. Two sets of footsteps entered. One set lightly pitter-pattered across the floor like a finalist in the Elegant Footsteps Competition. The other set loudly stomped around the room, leapt onto the judges' table and stamped on their fingers. The blindfold was yanked away.

"Greetings, leader of the Carrot Bandits," said the Mayor of Picklington with an infinite amount of smugness.

Seaweed looked around. He was surrounded by mops and buckets and paint cans and toilet paper and every kind of cleaning product imaginable. He had been imprisoned in the janitor's cupboard.

"I understand you've been running a highly illegal extracurricular activity out of school hours, young man. I won't lie. The disruption you've caused has impressed me. The car in the lake, the lion, the smoke grenades, the demolition were all ingenious moves. In fact, if I wasn't so annoyed, I may have offered you a job." He leaned forwards so that Seaweed could smell the cold-hearted revenge on his breath. "You've had your fun, Seaweed. Now it's my turn."

Seaweed suddenly noticed the Mayor's hand reaching for his pocket. The sweat on his forehead rippled with fear. The desert in his mouth turned into quicksand. As the Mayor's hand slowly emerged from the pocket, his body plummeted to sub-zero temperatures. Closing his eyes was his final solace.

A tickling sensation appeared under his nose and above

his upper lip. It slowly moved across his face, curled around his cheek and then disappeared. Seaweed opened his eyes and discovered a permanent marker pen hovering above his nose.

"It was all I could find on short notice," confessed the Mayor, smirking to himself. He turned to PC Barbara. "I trust you have made adequate preparations for his interrogation." The old policewomen took the pen and nodded. The Mayor then stared into Seaweed's eyes. The white bits seemed to glint with delight while his pupils began to grow, eclipsing all hope in the room. "I don't care how much pain you cause, how much mess you make, how much taxpayers' money you waste. I want to know everything."

Seaweed noticed something moving in the background. It was PC Barbara's police hat.

"I want to know how he managed to catch, train and control a horde of bunny rabbits to do his bidding, and most importantly, where they are hiding so I can skin them alive one by one."

The hat suddenly lifted upwards revealing a bunny rabbit and several stationary objects. It was his pet, Thumper.

"I want to know every single detail about their failed plot so that if my new Nuclear Power Station begins to fall apart, I can deliciously frame the Carrot Bandits all over again. Only this time we'll have two red-handed culprits for the front page."

Without making a sound, PC Barbara calmly lifted the

permanent marker pen to head height. The bunny took the pen and started to write something on a piece of paper.

"And be sure to lock them away for the rest of their miserable lives. How does that sound, PC Barbara?"

Thumper quickly replaced the pen onto its cap, then dropped the paper into the spare hand of the old lady and disappeared under the police hat. "Wonderful idea, sir," said PC Barbara while patting the Mayor on the back. "Don't forget your pen, sir."

The Mayor straightened his back, took his pen and turned around to leave. "Thank you, PC Barbara. You're a credit to my police force. Now then, I've got an opening ceremony to speak at and a local election to win."

17

LUCKY ESCAPE

"**Y**ou must be wondering why I'm helping you, Seaweed."

Stunned silence.

"And how I've managed to deceive everyone, including you."

More stunned silence.

"And you might also be curious as to why there was a bunny rabbit under my hat. But before all the long explanations, would you be a dear and offer an old lady your chair? I've been standing all morning, and my feet are bitterly complaining about it."

Seaweed closed his mouth and looked down. The rope that had bound him to the chair was lying on the floor with frayed and gnawed edges. A bunny rabbit was hopping joyfully around his feet. It leapt onto his lap, bounced on his knee and licked his nose. It was Thumper.

Pank burst through the door. Peanut was happily sitting on her shoulder. "Did I miss anything?"

Seaweed and PC Barbara swapped positions and then swapped stories. She explained how a long time ago she was high up in the same political party as the Mayor, until she voiced her concerns about environmental matters. She was immediately demoted, and that was when the bunnies approached her. She retrained in the police force and had been working for the Carrot Bandits ever since. She was their mole.

"So, when you interrogated me at the Police Station after the parade . . ."

"Young man, we would have had enough evidence to lock you up and throw away the key if I hadn't shredded half your file."

Seaweed shivered at the thought.

"One thing is for certain," commented Pank. "We've all been recruited because we are against the Nuclear Power Station."

"Darn tootin', young lady. That thing is a disaster waiting to happen." PC Barbara took off her hat and shook it in anger. Several clumps of grey hair fell out (it was impossible to tell whose). "We're here to do important jobs. I've been distracting the police, slowing down the Mayor's plans, feeding false information and creating cover-ups. What about you two? What have the bunnies asked you to do?"

"Um . . . well . . ." They looked at each other and confessed. "We've been stealing socks ma'am." Their heads and shoulders drooped towards the floor, as the law of confessions advises of the guilty. Seaweed realised PC Barbara was currently wearing odd socks, like most of the people of Picklington, and sunk into the ground a little more.

"Well I never. I thought my sock drawer had looked rather empty recently."

"We're both really sorry," said Pank. "We wouldn't have done it if we'd known what they were planning."

"Have you been stealing tights as well?"

"It doesn't matter. Don't you see? The giant sock ball . . . *it's a weapon.*"

"Well I'd still like my tights back. They're not cheap you know."

"But, PC Barbara, we've helped them build a terrible thing."

"An old lady without her tights is like a cup of tea without a saucer, like an armchair without a matching footrest, like a game of bingo without the jolly, fat man at the front."

The old lady was stuck on repeat. Clearly, she needed some time to grieve her loss, but Seaweed and Pank lacked the time. Seaweed reached into his pyjama pocket and pulled out the little wooden game. Pank kicked the chair leg and pointed towards the little ball. It glided through the air and landed in the cup.

The whites of the old lady's eyes lost their glossy shine.

They turned a dull grey at the sudden thought travelling to the tip of her tongue. "Oh . . . golly gosh . . . but don't they realise that . . . that . . ."

"That blocking the Nuclear Power Station's cooling tower with a giant sock ball will cause a catastrophic nuclear explosion and destroy everything within a hundred-mile radius?"

Seaweed, Pank and the policewoman looked at the little bunny rabbit that was currently rummaging around the cleaning cupboard shelves. Pank sighed, "I don't think the bunny rabbits have a clue."

Seaweed was currently more concerned about the crooks. How were two children, an old lady and two bunny rabbits going to escape from three hardened criminals? They needed a plan. Seaweed glanced around the cleaning cupboard until a bottle came into view.

"And to think my tights collection is going to contribute towards the end of Picklington."

"Not if we can stop it," protested Seaweed. "And I've got the perfect plan for when your three friends come back from the shops."

Five minutes later the thugs arrived. The door to the Council Office basement was unlocked, thrown open, then slammed shut. Vex didn't bother locking it. Why bother when they weren't planning on staying for long?

"Remind me one last time why we've gotta go?"

"It's simple," said Bishop whilst packing up their various thuggish belongings. "You've both been involved in plenty of jobs, right?"

"Yeah."

"Trunk."

"And how many of 'em have involved a group of suicidal bunny rabbits, a power-mad Mayor and an unsafe, half-built Nuclear Power Station that is about to be switched on?"

"None, except this one."

"Trunk."

"And would you both agree that I'm the most experienced criminal in the room?"

They both looked at each other, then nodded.

"Then I say we're leaving, right now. We'll take the cash, leave the stuff we don't need and go."

"But Billy the Jackhammer is coming over to play poker tonight, and he owes me three hundre—"

"No buts. It's time to go! We can find another job in another town for another . . . Wait, did you hear that?"

"Hear what, Bishop?"

The three thugs looked around the room. They were alone. No one in sight, except for the kettle. "See, I'm starting to hear things," muttered Bishop, "things hopping around in my head. Look, when a job starts to turn sour, you leg it and don't look back."

"You need to calm down, Bishop. How about a cup o' tea? You always feel better after a nice brew."

The three thugs sat down. They stirred multiple spoons of sugar into their cups and drained them in one big gulp.

"Lovely cuppa. Is this a different blend?"

"No, the same one as always."

Just as Bishop picked up the bag and headed for the door, something rolled through the crack in the door. The three thugs instantly recognised the rolling object and leaped under the table.

BANG!!!

Smoke filled the room. The thugs coughed and spluttered under the table.

"Nobody move," threatened a voice through a crack in the door. "Listen closely. Do what we say or you'll die a slow, painful death." Then the door swung open and smoke poured out of the room to reveal the kids wearing gas masks. "Got any questions?"

The three thugs unfroze. "Oh thank god, it's just those little brats. How did you two escape from the basement?"

"You're asking the wrong question," said Pank through the gas mask. "You should be asking yourselves what kind of smoke you have been inhaling."

Thumper landed onto the table. The rabbit dropped the grenade pin and then hopped into Seaweed's arms in no less than three mathematically faultless hops. Attached to the pin was a label covered in more danger symbols and toxic warnings than a rat-catcher's knapsack.

Trunk could not read, but he understood what the picture depicting an upside-down rat with its legs pointing upwards meant. He clenched his giant hands into fists and launched himself towards the bunny rabbit. He only managed to get halfway before his legs gave way and his stomach grumbled loudly. Vex and Bishop's stomachs replied. Then all three stomachs began to harmonise with one another.

"Arrggh." Bishop tried to stand up but only managed a slight wobble. "No, you're lying. You don't look like the type of kids who could gas three grown adults to death."

"You're right. But I reckon *she* would."

PC Barbara and her familiar smell stepped into view. She too was wearing a gas mask along with her cunning smile underneath.

"Trunk," groaned Trunk.

"I agree with Trunk. She definitely would."

"Oh, shut your mouth, Vex." Bishop turned to the traitor. "You betrayed us. Do you want to know what I do to traitors? I skin them alive and feed 'em to . . ."

"I wouldn't finish that sentence," interrupted PC Barbara, "if you'd like to know where I've hidden the antidote."

Trunk lay on his back clenching his belly. Vex fell off her chair dramatically. Bishop's face had turned a pale shade of yellowy green. "Antidote? Oh, my stomach. It feels like it's about to explode."

"That's just your imagination," scoffed Seaweed. "You've got plenty of other stuff to worry about before your insides explode. First of all, you'll lose the colour in your face."

They all looked at each other's colourless grey faces and began to sweat.

"Then you'll sweat uncontrollably until you become dangerously dehydrated."

They all lifted their arms in the air to reveal huge sweat patches. They wriggled towards the sink.

"This particularly nasty brand of biological weaponry makes drinking water kill you even quicker."

They stopped wriggling.

"And that's when your stomach will explode."

"Ooo, will it be painful?" questioned Pank.

"Extremely."

"Alright, you've had your fun. Now tell us where the antidote is."

Seaweed stretched out his arm and opened his hand. "First throw us the keys to your pickup truck."

Vex frantically rummaged through the bag, flung the keys. "Now spit it out!"

"There are two tablets on the chairs you tied us to." He smirked. "You better hurry up."

What happened next was a truly comical display. There was shoving and swearing and, I am sorry to say, lots of loud farting. As the noise of the three thugs rushing down the corridor grew quieter, Seaweed congratulated his comrades.

"That was brilliant thinking to turn the heating to full power, Pank."

"Thanks, it was all your idea in the first place."

He reached into his pocket and pulled out an empty bottle of powdered constipation medicine called 'The Blockage Buster'. Judging by the amount of what they thought was sugar in their tea, they were going to need a lorry load of toilet paper.

"You did remember to leave two of your biscuits for them to find, right, PC Barbara?"

"Actually, I left one. Two would have been a terrible waste, don't you think?"

Thumper interrupted their conversation by looking directly at PC Barbara purposefully. She looked puzzled, then shook her head and smiled.

"Oh right, of course." She winked at the bunny, "It's time to make a very important phone call."

18

BLADDER CONTROL

The Mayor of Picklington reread his speech one more time.

[Wave and smile to the crowd. Wait for applause to die down]. Ladies and gentlemen of Picklington *[pause for silence].* I have been your Mayor for almost thirty years, and in that time I have cut your energy bills by over half, considerably increased your daily energy allowance and made the Picklington Parade of Electricity a public holiday for the whole town *[pause for roaring applause].* You are all gathered here today to witness another momentous achievement. Today is the day that, once again, your Mayor proves he is the best choice in the . . .

He paused. Snatching the pencil from behind his ear he

scribbled on the page, then continued.

. . . Today is the day that, once again, your Mayor proves he is the **ONLY** choice in the local elections. You asked for your very own inexhaustible, cheap source of electricity to power your every need, and today is the day you will have it. People of Picklington, I give you *[pause and raise hand over the big red button]* your very own Nuclear Power Station. *[Hit the button, watch the fireworks, smile and clap]*.

He leaned back on his chair and grinned. The man believed, with all his blackened heart, he would easily win the local elections. Even if the voters did not tick the right box, he knew the right people who would happily recount the ballet boxes with a heavy back pocket. His Nuclear Power Station only had to run smoothly until he was announced as the new Mayor of Picklington, for the sixth consecutive election, and then there would be plenty of time to deal with nuclear meltdowns and radiation leaks and all that trivial stuff.

The security was on the highest alert. Even though the Carrot Bandits were on the run and their leader was imprisoned, the Mayor was still extremely paranoid. He had been taken to a secure location. The entire building had been swept by the armed security team. Guards armed with tasers were posted at every possible entry point. It was just him, a chair, his speech and a jug of water.

The Mayor spared a thought for what lurked in the basement of the Council Offices. The cunning little bandits who had caused him multiple migraines were currently having their insides remodelled and their outsides redecorated while the bits in between watched in horror awaiting their turn. His trademark smile, all crooked and vulgar, filled his face at that deliciously evil thought.

Fancy Watch

He looked at his wristwatch . . . Only three minutes had passed.

He looked at the water jug . . . It was empty.

Empty Jug of Water

He gently pressed his bladder . . . It was full.

The Mayor slowly raised himself from his chair, taking extra care not to startle his bladder. Suddenly, the only door in the room flung open and hundreds of security guards stormed in.

The Mayor's (Full) Bladder

"Excuse the intrusion, sir. We've received intelligence that our location has been compromised. We have to leave immediately."

"But we're not due to leave for another thirty minutes."

"Thirty-two minutes and fifty-seven seconds actually, sir," said a security guard as he hustled the Mayor through the corridor and out the fire exit.

"But I haven't finished practising my . . . Oy, watch where you put your hand."

"Sorry, sir. This is rock-solid intel, sir. PC Barbara informed us herself."

"But I'm bursting for the loo," pleaded the Mayor as they shot past a large and welcoming bush.

"There's no time, sir. Get in."

Twelve identical cars with blacked-out windows pulled away, then peeled off in different directions. The Mayor buckled his seatbelt and gripped the door handle as the car sped off. They turned left, then hard right, then entered a roundabout. The engine roared. The wheels squealed. The Mayor's eyeballs bulged. The car slid sideways and accelerated towards the town centre. Speeding through the streets of Picklington, the car suddenly screeched to a halt.

"Darn road works," yelled the driver.

While the enraged driver beeped the horn, the Mayor unclenched and exhaled. Once the internal reservoir finally settled down, he heard the faintest noise outside. He pressed his nose against the window and saw something horrifying, something he would not be able to un-see, something that would trigger an irreversible chain of events.

He saw a bunny rabbit having a lovely wee.

DRIVE! shouted the Mayor as Mother Nature called

his name (which was Terrence, if you are wondering).

The driver's foot hit the floor. The road block snapped in two. The bumpy ground and many obstacles slowed down their escape. The Mayor looked to the right and noticed a group of bunnies hopping from puddle to puddle.

"Eek! Stop the car by those toilets."

"Sorry, sir. Security policy number seventeen states that under no circumstance can the passenger leave a moving vehicle. It's for your own safety."

The Mayor clamped his hands firmly against his ears as the car passed the long row of port-a-loos. Each of them flushed at the exact moment the car passed by. He grasped and pulled the door handle wildly. "Unlock my door, **NOW!**"

"Sorry, sir. Security policy number three states that vehicles must be locked while in transit."

"Then pass me an empty bottle."

"Sorry, sir. Security policy number fifty-seven states that no potentially dangerous objects are allowed in the vehicle."

Mayor bit his bottom lip in an attempt to distract himself from the inward tickling. "Just get me to the opening ceremony as quickly as you can."

"Sorry, sir. Security policy number forty-one states that when driving off-road, I must drive at safe speeds to ensure the safety of the passenger."

THEN GET OUT OF THE ROADWORKS YOU BUFFOON!

The car burst through another set of barriers and re-joined the road. With the roadworks out of view, the Mayor collapsed in his seat with his legs knotted together. "Now then, to my Nuclear Power Station and step on it."

"Sorry, sir. Security policy number nine states that you should never arrive early to an appointment in case you are ambushed, and security policy number seventy-two states that when transporting the Mayor, you must remain inconspicuous to the general public. So we are currently two gentlemen friends going on a pleasant drive to get the car washed."

The handbrake creaked as the car stopped. Giant, spinning bristly tubes began to engulf the car, and water jets blasted from all directions. The driver opened up his morning paper. The Mayor added another lip to his bite, buried his head deep into the foot well and tried his best to imagine he was on a nice stroll through the Nevada desert eating a packet of cream crackers.

19

THE PIGEONS ARE WATCHING US

Picklington town centre was empty, apart from one solitary pigeon.

Re-election is no easy task. You have got to force the entire town to grind to a halt, throw an unforgettable opening ceremony, herd all the voters through the front gate and remind them they have one extremely electable man to thank. Simple plan, wouldn't you agree?

Except simple plans like this one often overlook simple creatures, like meddling children and bunny rabbits and this inconspicuous little pigeon.

You may not have realised, but pigeons are definitely up to something. Think about it:

- They are everywhere.
- They blend in.
- They are always within earshot.
- And if you have the time and patience, you might catch a glimpse of a notepad tucked under one wing and a pencil under the other.

Being a pigeon is surprisingly boring, so they developed espionage and notetaking skills to pass the time. Everyone needs a hobby. So the pigeon, who was enjoying having the town centre to himself for once, waited.

Footsteps broke the silence, followed by the slam of a car door. The reconnaissance pigeon sprang into action and flew towards the disturbance to collect whatever information was being spilled.

"We've already lost time fooling those thugs. Let's get going . . . Wait, why am I in the driving seat?"

"You've always been the getaway driver," reminded

Pank.

"But wheelbarrows don't have an engine." They both looked at PC Barbara.

"Don't look at me. I can't drive," she said as she pulled her knitting needles out from her police jacket. Meanwhile, the pigeon had landed on the edge of the truck, scuttled into earshot and pretended to look for discarded chips, as his reconnaissance training had taught him.

"But we're just kids. We can't drive."

"Poppycock! When you're the only person who can stop something terrible from happening, you can bend the rules. I should know, I am a policewoman after all. And believe me, you don't want me behind the wheel. I had my licence revoked last year."

"What for?"

"Crocheting behind the wheel." She stared at Seaweed and Pank as she continued to twizzle and loop material around her knitting needles. Her serious face clearly expressed her strong belief: crocheting should never be a criminal offence.

Pank snatched the keys, thrust them in the ignition, turned them hard and grabbed the gearstick. Thumper and Peanut hopped into the foot well and lunged towards the pedals. Seaweed gripped the steering wheel. PC Barbara put on their seatbelts and continued to crochet. The engine roared into life. Pank thrust the gearstick into drive. Thumper hit the floor. The rev counter hit the red zone. The tyres screeched. Seaweed gripped the stirring wheel even harder, so much so that the engine's mighty rumbles loosened his toenails.

"Which way is it?" screamed Seaweed as he turned a narrow corner and knocked over a bin.

"Just follow the signs," replied Pank.

"But which ones?"

"The ones that smell right."

"Eh?"

"Well, I don't know. Follow your nose. That's what my dad always says when he doesn't have a clue where he's going."

Seaweed crossed his eyes. "What does it mean if my nose is currently dribbling?"

"Um . . well . . . from which nostril?"

"Left."

"Then turn left."

He turned hard left and joined a busy road. They had found the traffic leading towards the opening ceremony, and it was approaching fast.

BRAKE!

Peanut thumped on the brake pedal. The pickup truck skidded and screeched to a halt. Smoke rose from the battered engine. Seaweed stumbled out of the truck and collided with the tarmac. Pank landed on top of him, followed by Thumper and Peanut.

PC Barbara stuck her head out the window. "Darn Saturday traffic. You just can't get anywhere at the weekends without warming a car seat in a traffic jam, can you?" She was wearing a freshly knitted scarf and matching mittens. The unflustered old lady looked at the smoking bonnet and then at the traffic ahead.

"Oh my, you'll have to go on foot from here. Now run along with your little pets, and I'll catch you up. My leg's a little stiff from the journey. Chop chop, you know what will happen if you're late."

Meanwhile, another survivor of the near-crash stretched his wings and shakily took off. He drifted across the traffic and landed on an electrical line. There was a group of pigeons watching hundreds of humans sitting in the traffic jam.

"Rough day, eh, Melvin."

"Awful. You see the wreckage down there?"

"The smoking pickup truck?"

"Yep. Those two Carrot Bandit kids were at the wheel. I'm telling you, Bert, rabbits should never be allowed to operate human machinery."

"Save it for the bimonthly meeting," commented a nearby pigeon.

"Well at least you've been for a ride." Bert waved his wing across the traffic jam. "This lot are a boring bunch, queuing up politely so they can congregate around the big concrete thing."

"That's just it. I've finally uncovered the Carrot Bandits' plot. The rabbits are planning to . . ."

"Hold it, hold it. Let's do this properly. Trevor, go take over surveillance in the town centre, and the rest of you help me debrief Melvin."

One pigeon flew off while several pigeons shuffled

closer. Melvin cooed about what he had overheard while smoothing down his wonky feathers. One driver looked over towards the racket and complained about those dirty rats with wings. Thirty to forty pigeons subsequently noted the registration plate in their notepads for later.

"So the little activists have become bandits," sighed Bert.

"There goes your escape-to-France-in-a-hot-air-balloon-made-out-of-socks theory, Cindy."

"I wasn't that far off," scoffed Cindy.

"Those poor kids have been indoctrinated. They're faceless soldiers for a fundamentalist ideology that has corrupted their ability to objectively make rational decisions."

"That's what happens when you hang around with bunny rabbits."

Right then," said Bert. "Suppose it's time for us to get out of here before things get messy."

"Wait. It's not too late," squawked Melvin. "Look over there. They are trying to straighten all this out."

The blurry speck way off in the distance was Seaweed, Pank and their pets. They were running towards the Nuclear Power Station, full of purpose and determination and a niggling feeling that they didn't have a clue what to do next. That did not matter. It was the very fact that they were running towards the imminent danger zone that had caught Melvin's attention.

"What's your point?" chirped Bert.

"Well, look at them. They know they're running towards

a huge ka-**BOOM**. Yet there they are, running towards it. They may have willingly joined a group of criminal bunnies, but they're running in the right direction now. So I've made my decision. I'm going to fly over there and do more than just watch. I'm going to help."

The group of pigeons gasped.

It's important you understand something. The pigeon civilisation has built their existence around one fundamental law: don't interfere, just watch. The laws around perching rights and chip distribution were often disputed, but the entire pigeon community were in complete agreement when it came to helping other species. Do not do it. Except now it seemed that one pigeon wanted to make an exception.

The pigeons perched silently. Their expressions were blank. Then Burt broke the silence with hysterical laughter. The rest of the pigeons joined him, causing the electrical wire to wobble.

"Good one, Melvin. Help the kids . . . Do more than just watch . . . You're hilarious. So, what shall we do with this new information then?"

"The local news channel always tips generously."

"How about the Mayor? He'll give us the good stuff for this."

"What do you think, Melvin? You collected the intel. How d'ya think we should use it?"

No one answered. Bert leaned forward and saw a gap in the wire where Melvin was perching. He then tilted his head towards the Nuclear Power Station and saw the familiar outline of a pigeon flying towards it. The cogs turning inside his tiny pigeon brain creaked. However, the cogs regained their normal function when Bert realised exactly what they should do.

"Well, I suppose someone should go and watch Melvin. Any volunteers?"

20

A SPEECH
TO REMEMBER

At the back entrance to the Nuclear Power Station there was a blacked-out car going through a series of time-consuming security checks. While several security guards were sweeping the car with bomb detectors, a bunny rabbit switched on a nearby sprinkler. The floppy-eared rebel squeaked, which is roughly translated to a human chuckle.

The Mayor of Picklington was due to give his Grand Opening Ceremony speech in two minutes. He should have been straightening his tie, glancing through his notecards and practising his election winning smile. Instead, the Mayor was chewing his tie, ripping up his notecards and biting his tongue. The man had enough wee stored inside his bladder to sink a battleship.

Meanwhile, the people of Picklington were waiting. A large crowd had formed around a stage at the foot of the cooling tower. The big red button stood on the stage next to the microphone, waiting to be pressed. A low-lying cloud of irritation hung over the crowd. Some people tapped their feet, others bickered to a neighbour, and one particularly grumpy woman cursed a small child barging past her.

"Oy, watch it, kid."

"Sorry, ma'am, pardon me, has anyone seen my pet bunny rabbit?"

Seaweed and Pank decided to split up. The plan was simple. He would find the weapon and Pank would find the control room. As soon as they arrived, Thumper hopped into the crowd and vanished. Seaweed had been searching for over five minutes. It was much easier for a little bunny rabbit to navigate through the holes and cracks of an agitated crowd. He was losing valuable time.

Suddenly, the crowd erupted in cheers and yelps and wild applause. The Mayor had finally arrived, and he was dancing up the stairs of the stage. The cheering slowly died down as the Mayor reached the microphone. Although Seaweed couldn't see anything, apart from the floor and several backsides, he could hear that something was amiss.

"Pe-**OOO**-ple of Pickling-**EEK**-ton . . ."

The Mayor paused, then wriggled on the spot like a vertical caterpillar.

". . . I have been your May-**AAH**-or for almost four

yEEEEEEars, and in that t-TIE-ime I have . . ."

He paused again, this time to uncross his eyes.

". . . cut your en-UUUUUURG-gy bills by half, in-CRY-creased your daily energy allow-OOOOW-ance . . ."

Everyone in the crowd, having been encouraged to overconsume energy by the Mayor for over twenty years, was recording the speech on their fully-charged smartphones. Well, everyone except for Seaweed. He had a giant sock ball to stop. He tripped on a stray shoelace and tumbled out of the crowd. Staring at him through a security fence was Thumper.

A welcoming port-a-loo swung open at the side of the stage. "Just vo-ERRRRRK-vote for me," yelped the Mayor as his beautifully crafted speech was thrown over his shoulder and his hand slammed the big red button.

Fireworks erupted from the stage. Confetti canons exploded in every direction. Every colour of the rainbow filled every corner of the sky. Smoke began to drift from the Nuclear Power Station's cooling tower. Every single eyeball in the crowd was mesmerised.

In the excitement of the moment, no one, not the crowds nor the security guards, noticed three very important plot developments:

- The Mayor was waddling into an ambush.
- A small boy was crawling underneath the safety fence into the restricted area.
- A crack was forming in the concrete tower.

Well, that's not entirely true. Perching high up in a nearby tree sat two pigeons on the job.

"Well, neither of us saw this coming."

The two-pigeon surveillance crew chirped in agreement. They had watched as a bunny rabbit splinter cell covertly entered the port-a-loo an hour ago. Now they watched as the very same port-a-loo pogoed on the spot.

"Those bunny rabbits really know how to ruin human plans, don't they? Ambushed in the port-a-loo, clever stuff. Hope you're still making notes, Betty."

"Course I am, Frank."

"Ooo, don't forget to note down that humans are easily distracted by bright, colourful bangs in the sky."

"That's more an observation than an important development."

"Over there, look. The Carrot Bandits have finished tying up the entire security force to the rear of the big grey hollow thing."

"Noted that down over a minute ago."

"Plus that kid and his pet rabbit are now making their way through the restricted area towards them."

"I ain't blind, Frank."

"And make sure you add that the big grey hollow thing is starting to crack."

"Oh, thanks for pointing that out. I hadn't seen that extremely important development because I was too busy pruning my feathers."

"Sorry, Betty, just trying to be thorough."

"Oh, well in that case, I'd better write down that Frank

just lost a chest feather."

"Ouch!" The ruffled pigeon hopped ninety degrees to the left and lifted his wings in an aggressive way. "That was uncalled for. You know it gets draughty in that area this time of year. I think it's time I made the notes and you did the watching."

Betty spat out the chest feather. "You'll have to come get it, baldy."

The two surveillance pigeons broke their gaze on the scene below and scuffled for control of the notepad. Wings flapped and claws scratched and more than a couple of feathers were sacrificed in the scuffle. Meanwhile, another slightly larger and more authoritative pigeon landed on the branch.

"Oy. Who's watching the humans while you two are scrapping?"

"Bert. We were . . . just . . . err . . ."

"Frank had a scratch he couldn't reach, so I was . . ."

"Save your excuses for later. Just tell me which direction Melvin flew past?"

An exclamation mark, followed by a question mark and one of those squiggly little things drifted over the two pigeon's ruffled heads.

"Frank was in charge of watching."

"Well, Betty was distracting me."

"If you hadn't been stating the obvious, maybe you would have seen Melvin fly past."

"Shut up, the pair of you," squawked Bert as he banged their heads together. "He's over there."

Melvin was circling around the Carrot Bandits. He was drifting lower and lower towards the ground.

"Holy plumage," shrieked Betty. "He's flying into the restricted area!"

"He hasn't defected, you know, joined the bunny rabbits, has he, sir?"

"No, lads, it's far worse than that."

What you must remember is that pigeons are unforgiving, resentful creatures. They had not forgotten the good old days, back when they were entrusted to carry important messages from noble kings to gallant knights, when they would risk their lives flying over no man's land and battlefields. Then telecommunications was invented. Pigeons were cast aside, forced to scavenge on the streets and fight over scraps. Replaced by thousands of miles of phone lines and invisible radio waves and big, shiny satellites that can send messages a million times faster without asking for any birdseed in return.

Fortunately, they've been able to make a living in the surveillance business, but they had not forgotten. Melvin's actions went against every rule in the notepad. The three pigeons watched as the renegade glided towards a soft landing pad and touched down.

"Holy taxidermist," screeched Frank. "He's landed on the giant ball made from those things the humans put on their feet."

"But the bunnies are going to shoot it into the big grey hollow thing with Melvin on it and then . . . um . . . What will happen then, Bert?"

Bert looked blank. "Err, I think it will just stop working," lied the pigeon.

"Well that's a relief. I was beginning to think it would turn into one of them big, colourful bangs the humans were staring at and kill us all."

"Nah, don't be so theatrical, Frank," chirped Betty. "Melvin must have wanted a closer view for when the kid and his pet reach the Carrot Bandits. All about surveillance, right, boss?"

Bert didn't answer.

"He's a clever pigeon that one, always willing to fly the extra mile. He would have been a fine carrier pigeon."

"Oh look, the kid and his pet have almost reached them. They have only got a few more fences to hop."

"Well, write it down then."

"I can't, you've got the notepad, you birdbrain."

"Oh perfect, another brilliant observation from Frank, the master observer. Maybe you should write it down on a piece of paper and deliver it too."

While the dysfunctional reconnaissance team squabbled for the second time, a dilemma coiled itself around Bert's conscience. He knew Melvin wasn't there to collect intel. Melvin had discovered the true dangers of the big grey hollow thing. He knew that if someone didn't do something, then all the humans and all the pigeons and all the bunny rabbits would soon become piles of dust.

He was there to help.

21

THE
BIG FLING

The concept, design and construction of the giant sock ball was nothing short of a modern masterpiece. It was a magnificent achievement, especially when you acknowledge who built it.

At this present moment in time, the person who could appreciate it the most was Seaweed. He had managed to sneak up undetected and was knelt at the foot of the monolithic weapon. His pet rabbit seemed very pleased with himself as he watched his owner untie the pantaloon bungee cord.

"Just a few more and then we can alert the guards."

There was no answer, but of course, Seaweed did not expect one. Perhaps a mathematical formula for calculating the curvature of the earth, but not a normal response.

"I must say, I'm really glad you're helping me. Not just because you're my pet but because it means you understand that destroying life is wrong, no matter what the cause."

Again, there was no answer. Although this time it was because Thumper had been ambushed by his comrades and was currently being restrained to the giant sock ball.

"It gives me hope that maybe, when you explain everything to all your friends, all this can be forgotten, and you can lead them with pride into a more peaceful and diplomatic future."

Thumper tried to squeak a warning to his owner as his not-so-peaceful friends surrounded him with pointy daggers. Unfortunately, the squeaks were somewhat muffled by the frilly pink sock that was respectfully used to gag him.

"I know that abandoning your plan will mean we'll lose this battle against the Mayor, but we haven't lost the war just yet. There'll be plenty of opportunities to plan campaigns and write angry letters, and did I mention I'm very experienced at door kno . . . *OUCH!*

Blood dribbled down his ankle. Seaweed leapt to his foot, the other one of course. The horde had encircled him and were closing in. The bunnies did not seem angry, or even slightly annoyed at his sabotage attempt. They were simply trying to get his attention with a friendly stab in the ankle. Seaweed noticed that there was something familiar in the way they looked at him. He was sure he had seen it before, on his history teacher's face, as if to say, 'Ah, there you are lad. I don't mind that you're late, but take your seat quickly before I get to the interesting bit'.

Seaweed thought that perhaps now was a good time to admit to himself, while he was gagged and tied to the giant sock ball in the star position, that the bunnies never really considered him to be a weapons expert. In fact, it turns out that for the predicted trajectory of the sock ball, his body mass, proportions and aerodynamic qualities matched the deadweight needed to plug the concrete tower in one direct shot. This, as I am sure you can imagine, made him feel rather insignificant, and a little motion sick. But I would like to add that the rabbits, who were preparing to launch a deadly weapon that would most likely destroy the entire town, did have the kindness in their little hearts to bandage Seaweed's foot with a stripy green sock.

He scanned the area for a speck of hope. There were several bunny rabbits patrolling the area. Others were repairing the bungee cord. One bunny was perched on top of the cooling tower, drilling a hole to attach the bungee cord of pantaloons to the target. The security guards were heavily guarded and paralyzed by the bizarre experience.

How did he ever think he could make a difference?

Lying atop the giant sock ball Seaweed wiggled and wriggled and squiggled every cell in his body. Nothing. He didn't move a millimetre. This was it. He had his one chance. There was nothing else he could do. At least, he thought to himself, there are plenty of less comfortable ways to die: hippo stampede, starvation, all-day poetry recital, hot poker up your rear end. There was much comfort to be had in the thought that, in Seaweeds case, the silver lining of death was rather comfy.

Seaweed listened closely. He could faintly hear the low-frequency humming of nuclear activity. He could hear hundreds of tiny feet dragging him and the sock ball slowly backwards. He could hear the stretching of the bungee cord. He could hear, and also feel, something small wriggling nearby. It would seem that Thumper had protested and was left to the same fate as his owner.

Then something entirely unexpected happened: a historical event, a selfless act of reconciliation, a momentous turning point in world history . . . a pigeon helped a human being.

Melvin stuck his head into the sock ball and re-emerged with a single sock in his beak. He had been doing this for around ten minutes without anyone noticing (except for two surveillance pigeons and their infuriated boss). Melvin discarded the sock and shuffled over to the boy to continue his painfully slow rescue. After plucking away seven more socks, a human hand emerged, followed by an arm, then shoulder and finally a head.

Seaweed gasped for clean air. He turned his head to thank his rescuer and was greeted by two tatty wings, dull grey feathers, tiny purple nostrils and the smell of floor. The little pigeon hopped about and cooed happily.

"Thanks, but snapping the bungee cord would have been the best thing to do."

The little pigeon glared at the boy and cooed bitterly.

"It's not that I'm being ungrateful," continued Seaweed,

"I just think that if I was a pigeon in your situation, I would have . . . **OUCH**. Watch it. I've only got ten of those!"

Melvin was more interested in his rescue plans than impolite conversation. He hopped over to a wriggling lump and plunged his head downwards. Seaweed contributed as best he could. Moments later Thumper sprung up into the air taking several socks with him.

The three escapees smiled at each other.

For a brief moment, they cherished the company. They felt as though they could have been sitting in the park together enjoying a lovely picnic or relaxing in a field after an afternoon stroll. This temporary fantasy was rudely interrupted by the terrifying reality of what they were sitting on. It was not a comfy picnic blanket, nor was it a field of grass and wildflowers. It was the largest collection of stolen socks in the history of humankind rolled into a gigantic ball, which in the next few seconds would be catapulted towards the Nuclear Power Station.

And that was the last non-blurry image each of them saw.

22

IN THE CONTROL ROOM

The Nuclear Power Station had been bubbling away for around two minutes.

Inside the control room stood a gaggle of scientists. They were wearing white lab coats with several pens in their top pockets, each holding an important-looking clipboard. The entire control room was covered in blinking lights, buttons and those circular things with a red needle to measure some significant measurable stuff. Nobody said a word. They were all deep in thought.

Please do not be fooled. Just because someone has been to university for half a century and now has a fancy title and a sparkling-white lab coat does not mean they know what they are doing. All it really means is they are the ones qualified to make the mistakes.

They had been hired by the Mayor to reassure the public that the Nuclear Power Station was in safe hands. Truth be told, none of them knew what all the blinking lights and wobbly red needles actually meant. It would be unprofessional to admit this to each other, so they continued to stare intently. Some of them scribbled scientific nonsense on their clipboards, others chewed the end of their pen, and a small group in the corner quietly discussed the possibility of sneaking out to watch the fireworks.

"Well then," announced the oldest and wisest looking scientist. "I think we can all agree that everything is in working order. No catastrophic disasters here. Well done, team."

The scientists patted each other on the shoulder and shook hands.

"My wife made flapjacks to celebrate. Help yourselves. You've earned it."

He opened the tin and placed it on a table. The scientists looked at each other and smiled. Staring is hungry work after all.

Suddenly, the outside wall shook and a loud thud echoed down the cooling tower. The ground shuddered from the impact. It sounded like the meteorite that wiped out the dinosaurs sixty-five million years ago had come back to check up on the holiday home it had made. Then everything went wrong all at once. The warning sirens sounded. The flashing lights changed to red and blinked at double speed. The tin of flapjacks was knocked off the table. The red needles in all the circular things began to wobble towards the bit that said 'danger'.

Scientists like to disagree with each other, but there is one thing they all agree on: when the blinking lights turn red and the warning sirens start, it's time to run for it. The eldest scientist blocked the exit and bellowed.

"Stop. Remember we are scientists, not school children."

The stampede of panicked lab coats stopped and caught their breath.

"We all know what has to be done. This nuclear facility is our responsibility. Someone must stay behind and attempt to shut down the main reactor."

The scientists looked at each other nervously. Their faces were glowing red, partly because of the warning lights but mainly because none of them knew how to shut down the main reactor. If it were up to them, this control room would be nothing more than an on-off switch, a comfy chair and a fancy coffee machine.

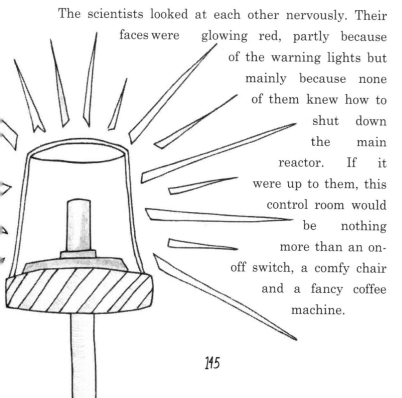

One scientist, the youngest of the gabble, climbed on top of the table and bellowed at the top of his shaky voice. "We are scientists. We are the people who have dedicated our lives to the pursuit of science. Right now that pursuit is leading us back into the control room. With our collective intellect, we can stop this disaster. So I am going to stay here because I am a true scientist. Who will join me?"

The rest of them stood in stunned silence. None of them had ever witnessed such bravery in a laboratory before. Unfortunately, most scientists are not motivated by bravery such as this. They are motivated by staying alive for as long as possible.

"Well volunteered, Dr. Simmons."

"I'll name my firstborn after you."

"Remember to cover your eyebrows if there's an explosion."

"A piece of advice," said the eldest scientist. "If in doubt, try praying. You know, keep all the bases covered." He turned around and walked through the door to join the group of deserters. Just as the metallic door closed, Dr. Simmons glimpsed something big and blurry **WOOOOOOOSH** past. Then the door slammed shut.

He walked up to the door and pressed his ear against it. He faintly heard the distant screams of his colleagues, having been catapulted off into the distance.

"Yeah. There's something very satisfying about seeing a bunch of humans thrown into the air by a giant sock ball," smirked the pigeon called Betty while surveying the frenzied scene below. Humans were running in every direction and screaming for help while the giant sock ball wildly swung back around. "Be sure to note down where each one landed."

"Well, three of them splatted against the big concrete thing."

"There's a few of them dangling from tree branches over there."

"That one is still in flight, look."

Both pigeons turned their heads as the human wearing a white lab coat plummeted back to earth and landed on a big pile of leaves.

"Good shot."

The bunny rabbits don't seem to be enjoying this as much as we are. They created this masterpiece and they're not even watching."

"They're all huddled around some paper, scribbling weird-looking symbols and wiggly lines."

"What do you think all those pointy objects are for?"

"Probably some kind of scratching implement."

"Oh look, here it comes again."

The giant sock ball seemed to be gaining momentum, not losing it. It was a breathtaking sight to behold, pure mathematics in motion. It collided with the wooden stage and spun off. Thousands and thousands of splinters erupted from the crash site.

"So why don't we like the big concrete thing again?"

"Well, we don't like humans. And no one likes how they treat nature. So we don't like anything they do or say or make, especially big concrete things."

"But we like those doughy circular things the humans make, you know, with the little sprinkles on top."

"Yeah, but . . ."

"And those delicious little green slices they throw out of their burgers."

"True, but we really shouldn't . . ."

"And cold chips."

"Okay fine. With the exception of human food, we hate everything they do, right, Bert?"

The pigeon called Bert hadn't said a word for the past two minutes. He had kept his eyes fixed on the giant sock ball, or more specifically on the three blurry passengers hanging on for dear life.

Remember, Bert has a pigeon brain. If he had a human brain he would have seen the little boy and immediately attempt to save him, and in doing so make things worse, then blame everything on the government. If he had a monkey brain he would have seen the swinging object and immediately joined in. If he had a rabbit brain he would be looking for a pattern in the sock ball's trajectory and working out formulae to predict its collision course. Bert's pigeon brain was paralysed, caught in a tricky dilemma.

Meanwhile, the giant sock ball was beginning to slow down. Of course, the two talkative pigeons had noticed this, along with some other interesting developments.

"The rabbits are on the move. And look, the annoying human has found the microphone in the rubble. I hope he has something more interesting to say this time."

Groups of humans were huddled together for protection and hiding behind anything that had so far survived the sock ball's rampage. The Mayor shouted things into the microphone like 'there's no need to panic', 'highly skilled team of scientists' and 'remember to vote for me'. The two pigeons glanced downwards to check on the so-called highly skilled team of scientists.

"I didn't realise balancing on a tree branch was a skill."

"Hang on a second. We mastered that skill ages ago. Maybe we would make good scientists."

"I dunno about that. I quite enjoy just watching stuff all day."

"But that's all they seem to do. And think of the perks. More respect and more responsibility, fewer hours and much less paperwork."

"I do get claw cramp from time to time."

"Exactly, and just look at those beautiful white coats."

"Fancy."

If Bert had heard this conversation he would have knocked their pigeon heads together. Instead, he was staring at the giant sock ball and its passengers. He was paralysed by choice, and not the good kind. He had to choose who would live and who would die.

Then something genetic happened. The very same strand of DNA that had snapped inside Melvin earlier that day began to weaken inside Bert.

What if the pigeon community stopped watching and started to help? Everything would be different . . . happier . . . maybe even better . . . for everyone.

Maybe pigeons still have something to offer?

Maybe they could help humans again?

Regain their former glory?

Be helpful.

SNAP

"Imagine the look on those smug dove beaks when we fly past the fountains wearing a coat like that."

"Plus they've got really big pockets to keep your notepad and pen."

"Chips as well. Don't forget the chips."

"Yes, yes. So here's the plan. I'll tickle their feet with my tail feathers until they fall to the ground. Then you two can swoop down, take their coats and meet back up here. Got it?"

"Got it."

Only one pigeon answered.

"Do you want to hear the plan one more time, Bert?"

Both pigeons leaned over and saw an empty space where Bert had been perching a few moments ago. The branch was still wobbling slightly.

23

PRAYER
OF DESPERATION

Billowing black smoke poured from the Nuclear Power Station's cooling tower. The thick streak of polluted smoke stretched across the sky like a dirty smudge on the landscape. It was a nerve-racking sight. Any unfortunate onlooker who happened to be close by knew they were looking at a pre-/present-/post-disaster rolled into one.

(You now have my permission to gulp.)

One such onlooker was Seaweed, although in his case the words front-row participant would be a better description. The giant sock ball, which he had been clinging to with his pet bunny rabbit and new pigeon friend, was delicately balanced on the very rim of the cooling tower. Rewind a minute earlier and their circumstances were considerably better.

They were dangling on the giant sock ball as it came to a stop. Their heart rates were slowing down, their sweat glands were taking a quick breather and their bladders were celebrating a dry pair of underpants (which is more than can be said for the Mayor's bladder, which was currently slumped in the corner of his abdomen and shivering from post-traumatic stress).

Seaweed then noticed something.

"Why is that massive tree bent over backwards and pointing at us?"

Well, he would have said all those words if he had the chance. He managed to say three of them before the bunny rabbits who were holding back the tree released it.

The rabbits then hopped around the wobbling tree for a better view of their home-run, slam-dunk, knock-it-for-six hit. The giant sock ball soared upwards, bounced from one rim of the cooling tower to the other and then rolled around the edge to finally come to a stop.

There are certain perks to owning a pet rabbit. They are friendly, sweet and never ask if you have finished your homework. After a long day, you can have a nice little cuddle, then release it into your older sister's bedroom. They are adorable, well, most of the time when they are not stealing or sabotaging or about to cause a nuclear catastrophe. Even their poo is quite cute.

Another perk that Seaweed had never appreciated until today was the rabbit's natural ability at balancing. Without

Thumper, all three of them would have plummeted into the cooling tower and dissolved in the violently bubbling nuclear liquid. Even though the chances of this particular life-threatening situation happening to you are 1 in 100,000,000 I am sure you would agree it is worth owning a bunny rabbit, just in case.

Seaweed glanced down at the scene below. Everyone was running towards their cars, jumping in, starting the engine and then crashing into whatever was in front. It looked like a disorganised carpark after a monster truck show had driven through. A single bead of sweat dribbled down his nose and dropped off the end. It disappeared from sight as it plummeted down the one-hundred-foot drop. They were so high up the little bead had probably evaporated along the way. *Lucky little sweat bead*, he thought.

The faintest of sounds drifted into his ear. A quiet, squeaky noise and a soft, squawky one. Thumper had been muttering quietly for some time now and so had Melvin. They certainly were not communicating with each other, or with themselves. Seaweed noticed their eyes were both tightly closed and their faces were screwed up.

No, surely not.

Animals don't pray, do they?

Seaweed was not a traditional believer. The last time he prayed, he distinctly remembered hitting a wheelie bin, although perhaps that was unfair on God seeing as he was travelling at forty miles per hour with a bunny rabbit sitting on the accelerator pedal. If you're going to test God, don't involve animals, human machinery or those wheelie bins with a wonky wheel. That was an unfair test for any deity to prove themselves.

He was, however, a believer in staying alive. Therefore, three prayers were most likely better than two. He closed his eyes and awkwardly prayed.

Hi . . .

Too informal.

Sir . . .

Too official.

Heavenly Father . . .

Too weird.

Almighty creator of the universe, ruler of the heavenly realms and commander of the angelic armies, whose power and wisdom and glory far surpasses my puny and insignificant existence . . .

Too fancy.

Dear God . . .

That'll do.

I'm gonna talk to you whether you like it or not or don't care or don't even exist. In fact, I'm rather hoping that

maybe you'll do more than listen and give me a hand down here. You do remember me, right? I'm the kid who's named after a weed and gets bullied for growing vegetables and once tried to build his own wind turbine. We both know how that ended.

Seaweed realised his prayer was not getting to the point quick enough. He brushed aside his doubt, locked it in the broom cupboard of his mind and gave faith a chance.

Anyway. I like our planet. It's amazing. Soon it's going to become darker and poisoned and radioactive thanks to me. All I've ever wanted to do was help, but it looks like I've made things much worse. If you do love your creation and if you do love us humans, even though we've made a mess of everything, please do something . . . anything . . . Save us, please.

A sudden gust of wind blew them off balance. The giant sock ball rolled into the cooling tower and plugged it up. The three intercessors collapsed in a heap. Seaweed noticed a small group of tiny specks hopping up and down on the spot in celebration.

Oh marvellous. This was exactly what I meant.

24

TIME TO CIRCUMVENT

The control room inside the Nuclear Power Station was still shuddering. Some lights that were flashing had stopped while others had been flashing so violently they had popped. The young scientist who was left behind knew this was a very bad sign and, to compensate for this, squeezed his eyelids even tighter.

Please, please God. Do this one thing for me. I'm not asking for much, just for the Nuclear Power Station to miraculously fix itself and not blow up causing a deadly radiation leak that will kill everything in a twenty-mile radius.

The young scientist had already reread every single button, lever and twisty thing several times. Unfortunately, none of them said 'press to make everything better'. He sighed and then walked into the centre of the room, where he had decided was the best place to be when it happened. He lay down next to the message he had scratched into the floor. The message read 'I wanted to be a dentist!' At least this way, when future generations who had mastered less complicated and more environmentally-friendly ways of making energy dug up his remains, they would know that the life of a nuclear scientist was his second choice. He closed his eyes and thought about tooth decay and mouthwash.

All of a sudden, the control room door burst open. A small girl with pigtails in her hair and a laptop tucked under her arm ran into the room, closely followed by a bunny rabbit. There was no time for introductions. She leapt over the exasperated scientist, plugged her laptop into a control panel and began hacking into the security software.

"Excuse me. Don't you know this is a restricted area? Only scientists with the proper security clearance are allowed in here."

Pank ignore him and continued to type at lightning speed.

"And you are definitely not allowed to bring your pets and unauthorised equipment to . . . to err . . . do whatever it is you are doing."

She did not stop. If anything, Pank's fingers seemed to type even faster. It looked like she had twice the amount of fingers. The scientist shuffled over to the laptop screen. Numbers and letters zoomed up and down and left and right.

"What exactly are you doing?"

"Listen, it's really hard to shut this thing down by hacking into the mainframe server and manually overriding the security protocol to divert all the power away from the main reactor while some bozo is asking stupid questions. So shut your mouth."

"Wow. That all sounds really scientific, and I should know; I've got a degree. If you need any help, anything at all, I'm ready."

"Actually there is something you could do."

"Excellent. How can I help?"

"I'm starving. Are those flapjacks homemade?"

"They are," said the scientist. "My boss's wife made them."

"And where is your boss?"

He looked towards the door and shrugged his shoulders. "He's probably buying a plane ticket to Hawaii."

Suddenly, steam burst into the room and everything began to flash at the same time.

"Oh no. The system's jammed."

"I'm sure I saw an 'unjam button' around here somewhere." He ran around the room frantically until he found and pressed it with professional pride. The shredder made a strange noise and spat out some confetti.

Peanut thumped her back foot with all her might. Both humans in the room looked around to see the bunny rabbit hopping up and down pointing her ears towards something. Pank and the scientist walked over for a closer look. The lever read 'Circumvent the Main Reactor'.

It is well known, among scientists, that the word *circumvent* was a made-up word. Somewhere along the centuries, the real meaning of some scientific words had been forgotten. All that was left was a bunch of words, like *circumvent* and *dermatologically tested* and *superconducting quantum nuclear device*, that no living scientist understands.

They stared at the lever. The scientist then pushed the girl back. "Stand back, young lady. This is a job for a scientist." He took a deep breath and did what all good scientists do when faced with a difficult task. He gave himself an inspirational pep talk.

"Okay, Trevor. This is it." He wiped the sweat that was pouring down his face and straightened his tie. "All you need to do is pull a lever. Don't think about all the terribly painful ways this could go wrong. Just do it." He paused again to wipe away more sweat with his trembling hand. "Right, time to show this lever what seven years of academic study, a degree in applied sciences with honours and a master's in nuclear physics can do."

Meanwhile, Pank shrugged her shoulders at Peanut and pulled the lever. The scientist fainted.

"What?" said Pank. "It's just a lever."

25

HOW DO YOU LIKE YOUR SEAWEED? BOILED, CHARGRILLED OR INCINERATED?

Seaweed, Thumper and Melvin were frantically pulling the sock ball apart.

Sock by sock.

Unfortunately, it was not making the slightest bit of difference. It would take them weeks of non-stop plucking to dismantle the Carrot Bandits' plan. No amount of polite reasoning was going to persuade a Nuclear Power Station to delay blowing up by a few weeks.

The sheer volume of socks was unfathomable. At a

guess, there were close to a million socks, ankle socks, tights, leggings and the odd set of long johns stuffed inside the cooling tower. (For a more accurate amount, please consult a bunny rabbit.)

The vibrations beneath them were building. What had started as a gentle wobble quickly grew into a heavy rumble and was now an earthquake's tremor. It was much like standing on top of the belly of a giant who had skipped breakfast, lunch and dinner and was now staring longingly at you.

Two floppy ears suddenly stood to attention. They looked left, then right, then leaned down to inspect the new noise coming from below, then turned towards Seaweed. An important message took off, glided through the atmosphere and made a perfect landing on the human brain runway . . . *Thank God, the main reactor is being circumvented.*

Seaweed paused mid-plucking.

Circumvent. That was an unusual word. He knew what 'circumstance' meant, but not 'circumvent'. He then noticed a high-pitched whistling noise getting louder and louder. It didn't sound very good to him, but if Thumper was hopping about, he decided that it must be good news. Seaweed noticed that the pigeon had also stopped plucking and was flapping its wings and cooing happily.

Thumper then stopped hopping, sat on his hind legs and prepared for the circumvention. The pigeon copied. Seaweed continued to look confused. How did a bunny rabbit and a pigeon have a greater understanding of the English language than, well, the one who could actually speak, write and comprehend the English language?

The tremors were now strong enough to wobble a plate of jelly into a coma. The high-pitched whistling was deafening. Seaweed could barely stand up, and walking would definitely end by roly-polying off the edge. He crawled on his hands and knees towards Thumper and shouted above the deafening screech.

"Um, excuse me. I seem to be the only one who does not know what the word circu . . ."

Then, as if the Nuclear Power Station took pity on him, Seaweed was given a first-hand demonstration.

"Listen pal, I think I'd remember if I ordered a giant bouncy castle!"

"Well you should have told me that before I inflated it. *Pal.*"

"Can't you see we're in the middle of a major crisis?" yelled the irate security guard.

The bouncy castle man continued to ignore the flashing sirens and panic-stricken people running to safety, reached into his van and pulled out his daily schedule. "It says here on my clipboard: one bouncy castle for a Mr. B. Birdseed at Picklington Nuclear Power Station next to the big concrete thing. Go on, take a look for yourself. It even says in the comments section, 'the biggest size you've got'. So, including the inflation cost, delivery and the one hour hire

fee, that'll be five hundred big ones."

High above them there was a huge explosion. It sounded like the pop of a cork shooting out of a champagne bottle, only a thousand times louder. Hundreds of thousands of socks began to rain down from the sky, but they did not notice, as they were too invested in their argument.

"So let me get this straight," said the security guard, rubbing his temples to ease the pressure building in his head. "You expect me to pay you for hiring this bouncy castle, which I did not order and no one is going to bounce on."

Just as the security guard said his last word, something landed on the bouncy castle and bounced off in three different directions. It was too blurry to tell what they were, but I have certainly never heard a sock scream or seen a sock with floppy ears or felt a sock flap its wings.

"What was that?"

"Ah ha! Something bounced on the bouncy castle," remarked the bouncy castle man, "which means your cancellation and refund is no longer valid."

"You didn't say anything about a cancellation and refund."

"Well you never asked for the form. It's all here in the contract."

"Give me that," snapped the security guard as he snatched the wad of paper. "Hang on, it says here you get a 'no obligation one bounce satisfaction test' before the customer loses the right to cancel the purchase."

"I know, but that was not one but three bounces." The man smugly adjusted his belt buckle. "After working in this business for over forty years, I can hear every single bounce, and I definitely heard three separate bounces."

While they continued to argue over the small print, the three bouncers were rocketing through the air. The smallest one of the three extended his wings and glided towards a group of pigeons.

"You fool. You flea-ridden, feather-plucking, meddlesome fool."

Melvin landed on the branch and spat out several cotton fibres. Two pigeons hopped over excitedly to congratulate their brave co-worker.

"You stopped the big concrete thing from blowing up."

"You're a hero, Melvin."

"Oh stop it, both of you. It was nothing. To be honest, I don't really know how I did it."

Bert stuck his disapproving peck into the conversation. "I know exactly how you did it. You broke our most important law. You helped a human being."

"Yeah, but so did you."

"How dare you suggest tha—"

"Then who ordered the squishy, bouncy thing we always see at children's parties?"

The feathers around Bert's cheeks puffed up. "Someone had to do something; you were going to fall. I could not perch here and take notes while you balanced on top of that thing."

"Thank you, Bert. You saved me."

"And don't forget that scrawny, meddling kid and his fuzzy pet. I saved them too."

"And how does that make you feel?"

Bert paused. He searched his feelings and found a distant and unfamiliar emotion lurking inside him. It was unlike anything he had ever felt before. It had lain dormant for years and had been awoken by this simple act of kindness. Years of inbuilt resentment and hatred had been washed away, leaving a rather pleasant, tingling sensation in his chest. He felt as light as a few hundred feathers.

"I feel great."

"Yeah, me too."

"I actually did something good, something worthwhile and positive and helpful, and the strangest thing of all is it feels right, as if I should do it again."

"I know. I've got goosebumps."

"We saved that human; we both did. We should be ashamed of ourselves. Our Perching Licences should be revoked, and we should be banished from all the water fountains in the country. Except I don't care because it was worth it. That kid is going to live a long and happy life because of us."

"Um, boss," squawked Frank awkwardly. "It was a very good speech and all, very inspirational. Only, pardon me interrupting, sir, look at the kid now."

Seaweed had begun to nosedive back down to earth. The boy was flailing about like a ragdoll and heading for the remains of the wooden stage, which after being hit by the giant sock ball was now extremely jagged with lots of sharp pointy bits.

"Oh dear. Well at least he lived for another few seconds."

26

LAWS
OF GRAVITY

The laws of gravity are straightforward.

Actually, for Seaweed they are straight downwards.

If something is dropped from a height, it will fall to the ground. If that something is squishy and prone to breakages, you will probably need a dustpan and brush. If that something is a boy, he will be screaming at the top of his lungs.

Seaweed was demonstrating the laws of gravity with excellence. Mother Nature herself would have awarded him a ten out of ten for perfect technique. Unfortunately for Seaweed, there is no rabbit-infused mathematical formula to reverse gravity, but not through lack of trying.

(One such rabbit, affectionately named Mrs. Cuddles by her seven-year-old owner, dedicated her life to beating the laws of gravity in between pretend tea parties.)

As the ground moved closer and closer, Seaweed braced for impact.

There was movement at ground zero. Hesitant people slowly crept out from their hiding places. No one was quite sure whether the lovely fireworks and the inspirational music and the giant sock ball of destruction and the warning sirens and the big explosion shortly followed by a downpour of socks were all part of the Nuclear Power Station's Grand Opening Ceremony. Needless to say, they were all on high alert in case that was only the first act.

A metallic door burst open. The crowd gasped and recoiled, like a nervous spring. Out stumbled a traumatised scientist. You could tell he was a scientist because of the lab coat. You could tell he was traumatised by the wonky angle his glasses were sitting on his nose.

A proud little girl skipped out of the very same door. She guided him towards the splintered stage, dusted off the microphone and tapped it to check it had survived. She then nudged him to the front. "Go on, they need reassuring from an expert."

"Hello, is this thing still working?"

By the reaction of the crowd, the microphone seemed to have survived better than most.

"Thank you all for your patience while I and my wonderfully brilliant colleague here resolved some minor issues. We decided to circumvent the Nuclear Power Station until these little teething problems have been fixed."

The crowd looked at each other. No one wanted to admit they did not know what the word *circumvent* meant, and so they all nodded in agreement that it was the sensible thing to do.

"There was never any need to panic. We had everything under control. Anyway, let's move on to the main event. Has anyone seen the Mayor? He was meant to do his big election speech twenty minutes ago and he doesn't like . . ."

"Look! Somebody do something!" shouted a hysterical women in the crowd. Everyone followed the direction of her finger and gasped at the sight of a small boy plummeting towards them. Panic erupted. Nobody knew what to do, least of all the person currently standing in front of the microphone.

At the back of the panicked crowd, there was an old lady

wearing a police hat barging through the crowd. "Pardon me, dear. Officer of the law coming through. Watch the needles; I could have your eye out."

PC Barbara had almost finished knitting her scarf, and barging through a crowd was not going to put her off. The ground beneath seemed to move around her, propelling her forwards and other people to the sides. It was a very strange feeling being forcefully shoved out the way by a tickling sensation just above the ankles.

"Mind out the way, me duck. Be sure to put that can in the bin later, young man. Oh I say, what a lovely pair of woollen gloves. I must remember to ask you for the knitting pattern later."

The polite crowd-barger reached the front of the broken stage. The scientist watched as everything he had been taught about the biological world turned into a pile of shredded textbooks. Hundreds and hundreds of organised bunny rabbits hopped onto the stage, rolled into fluff balls and formed a pyramid. His head tilted backwards as the structure grew higher and higher.

PC Barbara turned to the young scientist. "Could I please borrow your coat?"

"Eh . . . err . . ."

"Quickly son, I haven't got all day."

"Well . . . err . . . you see . . . this coat is only allowed to be worn by scientists who have passed their exams and paid the proper fees to the Royal Institute of Scientists. I am sorry, old lady, but unfortunately you can't borrow it."

"Thanks, and don't worry; I'm not going to wear it."

The scientist shivered. He did not notice that Pank had already slipped his lab coat off and thrown it up to PC Barbara.

"No problem, ma'am. Now go and catch my friend."

Pank and the scientist and the nervous crowds watched as the old lady ascended up the newly built pyramid without moving a limb. It looked as if the bunnies had installed a travellator into their pop-up pyramid. Once she had reached the top, she neatly folded up her knitted scarf and gently placed it in her handbag. With her hands free of wool and needles, she adjusted her glasses, then extended her arms outwards, creating a little white landing zone. She looked up to the sky.

"Forward a smidge."

The pyramid sprouted hundreds of tiny feet. They shuffled forward.

"A tad to the left."

They shuffled to the left.

"A tad more."

Shuffle.

"Perfect."

The crowd stood silently. A mixture of disbelief and hope filled the air. It was a lip-biting, stomach-churning, hair-raising, finger-and-toe-crossing moment. The young scientist distinctly remembered an old lecturer with a grey moustache and trousers hoisted above the bellybutton. He always used to say that putting your faith in something you do not understand was like having a lovely bubble bath and then sticking your fingers in a plug socket. He concluded his old lecturer had never actually tested his theory, crossed his fingers and gave hope a try.

The sound of screaming drifted into earshot.

27

THE
BIG CATCH

Seaweed plummeted to earth.

No one could watch. Everyone had their eyes closed. Even Frank the pigeon, whose job was to watch and then make notes, had his eyes closed. The one person who should have kept her eyes wide open was PC Barbara. Trying to catch a falling boy is quite difficult, so closing your eyes just before the big catch is probably not the best idea.

Fortunately, someone did have their eyes open. (Although I should add it was not through choice, as falling at one hundred and twenty miles per hour makes it very difficult to shut your eyelids.)

Seaweed tilted his body back on course.

Bullseye! The impact sent a powerful shockwave outwards. A wall of sawdust and splinters and socks and rolled up bunny rabbits pummelled the crowd. As they were much closer to the impact, Pank and the scientist were hit with the full force of the impact. They were now lying in a heap of splinters and bunnies twenty yards away from where they were standing a few seconds ago.

After the dust had settled, the crowd lowered their arms and stood up. The stage and surrounding area was covered in bunny rabbits. Hundreds of ping-pong-sized, bloodshot eyeballs stared at hundreds of grape-sized, bloodshot eyeballs, while perching on a branch one hundred yards away, there were eight raisin-sized, slightly less bloodshot eyeballs observing everything. Collectively, there were enough traumatised eyeballs to give an optician a heart attack.

Movement on the stage broke the stare-off. Everyone

held their breath. A police hat rose from the centre of the stage. Everyone looked at the lab coat in her arms. A leg was dangling out from one end. Another suddenly appeared, followed by two arms and a head. The boy slid out of PC Barbara's arms, landed on his feet and smiled.

Everyone let out their breath all at once, creating a euphoric chorus of cheering and whooping and whistling and thumping and flapping and chirping. Seaweed and PC Barbara walked to the front of the stage to wave and smile awkwardly. The cheering grew even louder.

"What are they all cheering about?"

"Not a clue, dear."

"Perhaps the Mayor is standing behind us," suggested Seaweed.

They cranked their necks over their shoulders. Behind them was nothing but shattered wood and dazed-looking bunny rabbits.

"Nope, suppose it must be for us then."

Seaweed had a thought. It was the kind of thought that instantly crystallised into a perfectly formed diamond perching on the end of your tongue. "Don't people who stand on a stage in front of a microphone and a cheering crowd usually make a speech?"

"Well . . . yeah . . . I suppose they do, dear."

"Maybe you should say something, you know, something inspiring."

"Why me?"

"Well, you are the hero of the day."

There was a creak as her ancient forehead slowly

wrinkled. "I am?"

"Yep. I almost fell to my death, but you caught me. You saved my life."

"Golly gosh, that I did."

"And let's not forget you are the ex-councillor who was robbed of becoming the true Mayor of Picklington thirty years ago."

"Good heavens, I suppose I am."

"All these people have come to hear an election speech," nudged Seaweed. "So go on, this is your chance. Give your speech."

PC Barbara unwrinkled her forehead, wiped the dust off her hat and nervously walked up to the microphone. She stood on the tips of her toes to be heard.

"Ladies and gentlemen of Picklington . . ."

". . . Oy, that's my election speech."

The Mayor sat bolt upright. He had been lying on the stage unconscious until those words rang through his ears. He stood up, forcefully. Eighty percent of the blood in his body had risen to his enraged face. The rest seemed to be pulsating around his throbbing, outstretched finger pointing directly at PC Barbara.

"How dare you stand in my place and give my speech in front of my voters. You're fired. Now move aside."

He waded through the stage without bothering to check what it was he was wading through. He pushed PC Barbara aside and grabbed the microphone. The red-faced Mayor reached into his splintered jacket and pulled out his crumpled speech. He then waved, as his speech instructed, and spoke in his election voice.

"Ladies and gentlemen of Picklington *[he paused, even though everyone was already silent]*. I have been your Mayor for twenty years, and in that time I have. . . *[He paused again, this time because he realised something was sitting on his head.]*"

The Mayor arched his arm to investigate the unknown headwear. Dangling upside down a few inches away from his nose was a bunny rabbit grinning back at him. It too was dangling something. It glinted and glistened in the sunlight. He suddenly became aware of numerous sharp and pointy daggers surrounding him. His election speech derailed with the elegance and grace of a fully grown rhinoceros falling down the stairs.

AAAAAAAAAAGRH . . . EKKK . . . URRRRRRRRRRRRRRR RRRRRRRRRRRRGGGLE . . ." CREAK . . . . . . THUD . . . "WOOOO-NOW-I-HAVE-ONLY-GOT-TWO-OF-THOSE . . . . . . MUMMY . . . . . . THE FRYING PAN IS ON FIRE. I REPEAT, THE FRYING PAN IS ON FIRE . . . I SAID THE STUPID FRYING PAN IS ON FIRE!"*

*Please follow the word-by-word commentary

below to understand what just happened.

AAAAAAAAAAAGRH – the Mayor screamed when he realised he was face-to-face with his tormentors, the Carrot Bandits.

EKKK – the bunny rabbit squeaked having been dropped on the floor by the Mayor.

URRRRRRRRRRRRRRRRRRRRRRRRRRRRRRRGGGLE – this noise did not come from the Mayor's mouth. If a swimming pool could talk this is what they would say if it sprung a leak.

CREAK – as Pank knelt behind the Mayor a floorboard creaked with delight at what was to come next.

THUD – using both hands, Seaweed pushed the Mayor with all his might, and, thanks to Pank, he fell with a mighty thud.

WOOOO-NOW-I-HAVE-ONLY-GOT-TWO-OF-THOSE – these panicked words were directed at a mischievous bunny rabbit who had chosen the Mayor's little toe as a hostage.

'MUMMY' – the Mayor felt the leak reach his socks.

THE FRYING PAN IS ON FIRE. I REPEAT, THE FRYING PAN IS ON FIRE... I SAID THE STUPID FRYING PAN IS ON FIRE! – this sentence was the evacuation code.

His security guards rushed into action, scooped the Mayor off the stage and threw him in the back seat of his battered limo. The security team then continued the evacuation by pushing the wreckage towards the exit.

The crowd cheered as the Mayor slowly rolled away. As the crowd jovially waved the Mayor goodbye, PC Barbara stepped up to the microphone again. This time she actually did step up, as a mini stepladder made of bunny rabbits helped her reach the microphone.

"What I was about to say, before the Mayor rudely interrupted me, was that you deserve better."

Her voice wobbled slightly, but that did not matter. The crowd was ripe for the electoral harvest. They were already muttering amongst themselves about what could be better than a Nuclear Power Station. The general agreement was that whatever it was they all somehow deserved it, like the old lady said.

"I've served in the police for over thirty years and watched as Picklington has suffered under the reign of one corrupt man. His selfish policies have guided you down a destructive and wasteful path that has led to this Nuclear Power Station. I stand here today because I want change. I want to change our town into something better. But I do not have the power to do it. You are the ones who have the power to make that change happen."

The muttering grew louder as the crowd looked at each other. Change sounded like a good idea. Their excitement built at what this change was going to be. They shuffled closer and listened intently.

"I will be standing as a candidate for the Mayor of Picklington. Vote for me, and I will restore our wildlife and environment. Vote for me, and I will repair our children's education and broken tax system. Vote for me, and I will re-establish our libraries and playgrounds. I promise to regrow the fruits of a healthy society. Vote for me, and together we will bring Picklington back to life."

The muttering stopped. None of them had heard a genuine policy in a long time. Some people scratched their heads. Others got their phones out and searched for the meaning of the word *wildlife*.

Seaweed sensed the crowd's confusion. He could see their one-track minds grinding to a halt, but he had an idea for how to kick-start their engines. He barged to the front, tapped PC Barbara on the shoulder and whispered something into her ear.

She smiled and added, "And if you vote for me, I will turn the Nuclear Power Station into a water park."

The crowd immediately exploded with wild applause.

28

ONE YEAR LATER . . .

It was morning. Rays of sunshine poked through bedroom curtains all over Picklington.

A young boy rolled out of bed, stretched and walked towards to door. Except he did not make it to the door. Instead, he bumped his head on something. The corner of his open sock drawer left a nasty dent in the boy's forehead, though he did not seem to mind too much.

He had been waiting for this special day for a long time. The boy looked inside and discovered that all of his odd socks had been reunited with their soulmates. An orange, knobbly looking object poked through the cotton.

"Mum, Dad. Quickly, come look. The Carrot Bandits have been."

Sunlight barged through the iron bars of Picklington High Security Prison and poked the inmates awake.

"Remember the plan, boys," said a hushed voice. "Be on your best behaviour, persuade the probation officer you've become law-abiding citizens and get placed on probation . Then infiltrate Mayor Barbara's Advisory Council and report back to me."

Vex huffed. "How many times do we have to tell you? We like it here. Three square meals a day, great networking opportunities. Anyway, we've made our own plan."

The old Mayor almost snapped an iron bar like a twig. "What?"

"Yeah, our plan plays to our strengths," said Bishop. "You know, thuggish stuff. I'm going to explain to the probation service every single way I could escape. Then I'll probably grab a pen and stab the main one in the hand."

"Please don't. Wait, how about you tell me the escape routes instead," pleaded the old Mayor.

"I'm going to give them all detailed descriptions of their spouse and children," said Vex. "When they ask me how I could possibly know, I'll reunite them with their wallets, then smile in a mentally unstable way."

"No, Vex, don't do that," pleaded the old Mayor as he sunk to the ground.

"Trunk has got the best plan."

"Yeah, he really outdid himself this time."

"Don't tell me," sighed the old, deflated Mayor. "He's going to stand on the probation officer's toe like he did last time."

"That's what he wanted to do, but the poor bloke has run out of toes," explained Bishop. "So he decided to set his sights on new opportunities."

Trunk grinned, then leapt into the air and landed on his new opportunity. The sound of bones breaking, followed by the old Mayor's yelp of agonising pain, echoed throughout the entire prison.

The window in the Mayor's office was open, but for a very different reason.

The morning meeting (sometimes referred to as rehab by Mayor Barbara) was in full swing. It was the best place to be on a Monday morning, as positive contributions earnt you a biscuit. In her first year, the new Mayor and her two youngest advisors had made many changes. If you were to measure Mr. Jenkins's waist size, you would know that the biscuit tin was his favourite.

Mr. Jenkins nibbled the edges of a malted milk like a hamster. "Wonderful work, Mr. Jenkins. You should be proud of yourself. And Mrs. Collins," she put down her knitting needles and reached into the biscuit tin, "your suggestion to gift the children at the orphanage free passes to Picklington Water Park was very thoughtful. Are chocolate bourbons still your favourite?"

She grinned at Seaweed. They both knew exactly which biscuit was Mrs. Collins's favourite, along with everyone else's in the room. As the Mayor's Advisor for Environmental Matters, Seaweed had many important responsibilities. The best was supervising the decommissioning of the Nuclear Power Station, which overlapped rather neatly with its refurbishment. Who better to consult when planning, constructing and testing a six-hundred-foot waterslide spiralling around a cooling tower than a boy with a talent for falling?

Pank, the Mayor's Advisor for Technology, focused her time and energy on the Picklington Lake Restoration Project. I can happily tell you it was time and energy well spent. The townsfolk loved nothing better than walking around the tranquil lake and through the various nature trails in the woods. Last weekend, Pank's dad almost fell in for a second time reeling in a forty-pound rainbow trout.

The young girl cleared her throat. "Mayor Barbara, may

Mayor's Advisor for Environmental Matters

the new Mayor of Picklington

Mayor's Advisor for Technology

we present our proposal?"

Barbara slid a bourbon across the table, picked up her knitting and nodded. Seaweed and Pank stood up and walked over to a flipchart. Pank pointed at a complicated-looking graph.

"As you can see, the pigeon's and their attempts to be helpful is becoming increasingly difficult to manage." She directed her finger to a red line which travelled all the way to the top of the graph. "The number of complaints over the past month have skyrocketed. One pigeon reportedly stole a sandwich, removed the artery-clogging bacon, scraped off the fattening mayo and dropped it back into its owner's lap. Yesterday a group of them caused a ten-mile-long traffic jam so that a lost golfer could play his out-of-bounds ball from the motorway."

Seaweed kicked over the bin. Empty cans and plastic bottles rolled under chairs, and screwed up paper and chocolate wrappers covered the floor. "They are only trying to help but are actually creating a mess. We have the solution." He clicked a button and one giant word filled the screen.

"Recruitment."

The young boy cooed loudly towards the window. Then a group of pigeons flew in and engulfed the boardroom. After a couple of seconds, the pigeons landed on vacant shoulders and heads, revealing something truly surprising. Everyone gasped in amazement. The rubbish was neatly arranged in four piles.

"Ladies and gentleman," said Seaweed and Pank

together with professional pride. "May we present Picklington's new Recycling Litter Pickers."

Everyone stood up and clapped with great enthusiasm. In fact, Mr. Jenkins was so impressed that he did not even notice the white stain dribbling down his shoulder.

Picklington was finally a greener, happier place to live.

ABOUT THE AUTHOR

James Warwood is (usually) very good at writing about himself. So he would like to start by saying that this bio was written on an off day.

He lives on the Welsh Border with his wife, two boys, and carnivorous plant. For some unknown reason he chose a career in Customer Service, mainly because it was indoor work and involves no manual labour. He writes and illustrates children's books by night like a superhero.

Anyway, people don't really read these bios, do they? They want to get on with reading a brand new book or play outside, not wade through paragraphs of text that attempts to make the author sound like a really interesting and accomplished person. Erm . . . drat, I've lost my rhythm.

OTHER BOOKS BY JAMES WARWOOD

THE SKELETON KEYS CHRONICLES

Ruthless Pirates / Epic Monsters / Legendary Adventures

Book One: Monsters of the Sea

Book Two: Back from the Dead Red

Book Three: Admiral of the Black

TRUTH OR POOP

True or false quiz book series. Can you sort the fact from the fiction?

Book One: Amazing Animal Facts

Book Two: Spectacular Space Facts

Book Three: Gruesomely Gross

THE 49 SERIES

Non-fiction cartoon series full of helpful tips and laugh-out-loud silliness for getting the most out of life.

The Excuse Encyclopedia: Books 1 - 12 in the 49 Series

MIDDLE-GRADE STAND-ALONE FICTION

The Grotty Spoon: The Most Disgusting Restaurant in the World

The Girl Who Vanquished the Dragon

WHERE TO FIND JAMES ONLINE

Website: *www.cjwarwood.com*

Facebook Page: James Warwood

Twitter: @cjwarwood

Printed in Great Britain
by Amazon

Once

A

Killer

Also by Murray Bailey

★ previously entitled Secrets of the Dead

Once
A
Killer

Murray Bailey

Three Daggers
An imprint of
Heritage Books, Cornwall

For my wife, Kerry, my everything

ONE

Part of the thrill was uncertainty. He had control, she was in his power and he could keep on squeezing her neck.

And yet he supposed that a part of her brain still told her there was no real risk.

But life was risk. Life was a game. Without risk there was no excitement. Too safe and you may as well be dead.

That was his opinion anyway.

A breeze moved the white chiffon curtains, but their naked bodies were sheened with sweat. In Hong Kong, the humidity did that to lovers. Especially the vigorous ones.

The pulse of her blood against his fingers sent a shiver of excitement through him.

A moan came from her lips as an expulsion of air. More of a husky murmur than a proper sound. Her eyes closed in ecstasy.

Now he could see the neck swelling with trapped blood.

He squeezed some more.

Her eyes flew open and she stopped moving with his rhythm. Fear gripped her as her subconscious finally let go of the illusion.

He could kill her.

Now death became real; the ultimate rush.

She squirmed beneath him. He could feel her chest heave, saw her eyes grow large. It was like he was squeezing a balloon, the eyes swelling as he applied more pressure.

And then he stopped.

He removed his hands from her neck and placed one over her mouth as she started to choke.

"Shush!"

He pointed to his ear telling her to listen.

Footsteps. Someone was moving around downstairs.

She sucked in air, blinked and swallowed.

"Graham," she mouthed, before it came out as a hoarse whisper.

He nodded. Graham McGowan. Her husband.

He slid off her and rapidly pulled on his clothes left beside the bed ready, just in case.

She didn't move straight away. Her body was trembling.

He picked up her dressing gown, took her shaking hand and helped her dress. Her neck had red and white marks, and he pulled up the dressing gown's collar.

She blinked, nodded her understanding and took hold of the gown. Then she kissed him hard on the mouth. She drew a line along the six-inch scar on his chest and he put his hand into the gown, between her legs.

"You need to go!" she said, although she didn't move his hand.

Graham called out, "Barbara?"

They heard him coming up the stairs.

"Charles, go!" she hissed, and this time she moved back, freeing herself of his touch.

Charles Balcombe counted to five, cupped her face, kissed her and stepped to the window. He went through the translucent curtains and out onto the balcony. Three floors up.

The afternoon sun sparkled across the water. A property in Kennedy Town wasn't the most prestigious on Hong Kong Island, but there was a lot to be said for a view of the sea without Kowloon and the shipyards.

Behind him, he heard a knock on the door to Barbara McGowan's boudoir. Then her husband was in the room.

McGowan spoke and Balcombe could hear the suspicion in his voice. Of course he suspected her of infidelity. After all, why else would he be home, unannounced, at this time during a working day?

"You're looking flushed."

"You startled me, I was sleeping," she said unconvincingly. "You woke me."

Balcombe shrank away from the window and placed a hand on the railing.

Was McGowan going to come outside?

She said, "What are you doing?" Her voice was stronger, more confident now, indignant.

"Is there a man here?"

"No… darling."

Balcombe heard a door open. The bathroom? Then a cupboard. McGowan was checking the room. Three more seconds before he came out onto the balcony.

One.

Balcombe climbed onto the balustrade, his feet light, his hands relaxed.

Two.

A glance at the balcony ledge above. Leap and catch. His strong fingers clung to the balcony edge, his feet dangling.

Three.

The curtain moved. McGowan started to come out. Balcombe pulled himself up, his strength then momentum carrying him over the railing onto the balcony above.

Would McGowan look over the edge and up?

Balcombe's heart beat heavily as he waited.

It was almost a disappointment when he heard footsteps below receding into the boudoir. The husband couldn't imagine someone leaping from the balcony let alone climbing to the one above.

Balcombe turned and looked at his reflection in the French doors on this floor. Tall, lithe, rakishly good-looking, but he could have squeezed the life out of his lover this afternoon. He came so close, but that wasn't him. He didn't strangle women! No, he had to be more careful. He had to get the thrill without losing control.

He'd come to Hong Kong to escape. He'd changed his name. He'd changed his life. He had money and the island was full of frustrated wives looking for excitement. And he could give it to them. He had been giving it to them for three months now.

But was it enough?

He'd almost killed a lover today. He'd almost been caught by her husband. In fact, the possibility sent a shiver of pleasure through him.

Without risk there was no excitement.

But was it enough?

Could he keep this up?

After all, he was BlackJack and killing was his second nature.

TWO

Balcombe abhorred the repetitive, but life in Hong Kong was all about routine. For the upper classes anyway.

During the week, most of the male British ex-patriots worked long hours. They had important jobs in places like the Hongkong and Shanghai Banking Corporation or P&O or Butterfield & Swire or Whiteway & Laidlaw. They were merchants and bankers, lawyers and shipping brokers. They worked hard and they played hard.

If you were anyone you were a member of the Hong Kong Club—or aspired to be. So even when the British gentlemen weren't working, they were ignoring their pretty wives.

Friday was casino night. Saturday afternoon was the races at Happy Valley Racecourse. On Saturday evening there would be a party, and on Sunday Balcombe would go to church.

Since arriving on the island, three months ago, his only escape from this structure was his rock climbing. Whenever the feeling took him, he'd take the tram up to Victoria Peak and free climb the crags.

And then, of course, there were the liaisons. He made sure they weren't too regular, which also helped remind the ladies that the relationships weren't serious. He controlled who and when. Not too frequent, and he had five women on the go; bored, unappreciated wives, for whom Charles Balcombe was their occasional thrill.

Saturday night was the last before Christmas 1953 and the party was at the mansion on this hill owned by Sir Hugh Pretty. He thought he was a *Taipan* of old, a ruler of a Chinese empire rather than a shipping company. However, he was possibly the wealthiest man on the island and ensured that his guests knew it. Although Balcombe hadn't met the man.

Pretty tried to imitate the Great Gatsby with his lavish parties—extravagant but never vulgar. There were three hundred guests entertained by dancers and magicians. Tonight he also had a man dressed as a hunter parading two tigers on chains.

Balcombe noticed the big cats' eyes. The beasts were undoubtedly drugged, which was a shame. How much more dangerous would it have been to have deadly animals prowling at the event?

He took a fresh glass of champagne and strolled to the marquee. A top-notch jazz band played and he found his fingers tapping as he walked towards an acquaintance.

Roy Faulls was harmless enough and he had connections. Faulls had got the invite for the party and he should be nominated as a member of the Hong Kong Club next month. After three months he could nominate Balcombe.

They'd been together at the races that afternoon. Faulls had a foolproof strategy for betting on the horses. He placed money on the favourite to win. If he lost, he'd double his bid the next time. When he won, he'd start again.

How dull!

Balcombe bet on the outsiders. And he placed significant wagers; not on every race, just when the feeling took him. And fifteen hundred dollars made your heart thump. At twenty to one odds, a win made you leap for joy.

Faulls would never know that thrill. You have to take risks to experience life. Although the man did know that it was more fun in the crowd by the rails than in the stands: the noise; the smell of the earth and horse sweat; the buzz and thrum of the jostling bodies.

"Charles," Faulls said in greeting.

"Good band."

"Any sign of Sir Hugh?"

Balcombe shook his head. The man was a recluse. He threw extravagant parties but didn't appear. All part of his cultivated mystique, Balcombe assumed.

"Oh and congrats on your win today," Faulls said. "You're a bloody miracle!"

Balcombe smiled. He'd won over fifty thousand dollars betting on Golden Fleece at thirty-five to one. It meant that he was now only slightly down on his gambling returns. But gambling was the thrill. It wasn't about turning a profit. The Chinese knew this. They'd bet on anything, from which dog would win a fight to how much rain would fall within an hour. He knew that the taxi drivers waiting at Star Ferry Pier would bet on the passengers who would alight. They'd bet on the number of white men, the number of people wearing red, the number with umbrellas. Anything.

And they did it for fun, rather than the money. Balcombe suspected that being poor must make the thrill all the better for those taxi drivers.

Roy Faulls didn't understand that. He was a junior partner at Butterfield & Swire. He was comfortable and planned to move up the ladder. "Slow and steady," he would say.

Slow and boring, Balcombe decided. Still, the chap was inoffensive and one of the few other Roman Catholics from this high society crowd. And when required, Faulls could also provide a useful diversion: either distracting husbands or their wives.

"Isn't that Mrs McGowan?" Faulls said.

Balcombe had seen her watching a magician with a group, although he hadn't spotted Graham McGowan. Now Barbara was alone and looking his way.

Balcombe took a breath. Her wide eyes and a raised eyebrow suggested she wanted to speak.

Damn! Balcombe thought. After their liaison on Thursday afternoon, when they'd almost been caught, he thought she'd be more wary. After all, he'd been within seconds of strangling her to death.

Perhaps she'd seen him as he really was. Perhaps she was ending it—or worse, she'd involved the police.

"Intercept her, old chap," Balcombe whispered. Faulls grinned and stepped towards the advancing woman. Balcombe swivelled and was swallowed by the crowd. All the men were in black dinner suits, so he was sure to get away.

However, five minutes later he heard a familiar voice behind him.

"We need to talk."

Balcombe looked around to see Barbara McGowan right there. He took a mouthful of the canapé he'd just selected, to give himself time.

What was she up to?

When he spoke, he kept his voice light and low. "Mrs McGowan, how nice to see you." Then he glanced around, trying to give her the message that approaching him in public like this would be noticed. It was not how their liaisons worked. Secret messages would be exchanged, subtle hand signals would be made. Occasionally, there would be whispers as they passed. Never would there be a blatant meeting like this.

Again she said, "We need to talk."

Balcombe looked around again. "And where is Mr McGowan tonight? I haven't seen him."

"Oh, busy hobnobbing," she said dismissively. "You needn't worry, Mr Balcombe. No need to be afraid of me!" She laughed lightly and he guessed she'd been toying with him. "I have someone who would like to make your acquaintance."

Intrigued, he followed as she strode out of the marquee and was pleasantly surprised by the appearance of the young woman ahead.

Balcombe typically hooked and landed women in their thirties. However, the slim blonde in the burgundy evening gown looked younger. Maybe even younger than his twenty-four years.

Barbara McGowan pecked the blonde on the cheek.

"Darling, here's the young man I told you about—Charles Balcombe."

He took a proffered hand and brushed his lips on deliciously soft, scented skin.

"Charmed," he said.

She batted warm brown eyes. "Oh, I see you were right, Barbara. He is both good-looking and charming. But up to the job?"

"Oh certainly," Mrs McGowan said with a twinkle in her eye.

Balcombe continued to hold the introduced lady's hand. So Barbara McGowan was acting as a go-between, and with such a beauty! He spied the wedding ring on the other woman's hand.

"You have me at a disadvantage. May I know your name, Mrs...?"

"Grace Toogood," the blonde said. "Pleased to make your acquaintance."

He released her hand but maintained the contact with her deep brown eyes. Alluring and mysterious, he decided. He'd need to be careful with this one. Falling in love with a married woman would not do. Although he found his mind wondering what she looked like beneath the dress. Milky-white, smooth skin. Slim, not too thin. Breasts...

"Charles," Barbara McGowan said, snapping him out of his reverie.

He tore his eyes away from Mrs Toogood and focused on Mrs McGowan. Suddenly his lover seemed very ordinary indeed compared to the blonde.

She said, "I've introduced you to Grace because she's new to the island."

Balcombe smiled.

"And she's in need of your services."

Balcombe nodded.

"Your investigative services."

"I'm sorry?" Balcombe said, taken aback.

Grace Toogood said, "Barbara tells me you were an investigator."

The night air seemed to become warmer. Balcombe swallowed hard. This wasn't a subject for open discussion.

He told his ladies that he was operating for the British government, undercover—they liked the double entendre of that expression. They also liked the scars on his body. Some were injuries, broken bones and skin from falls, but seven were knife cuts.

In addition, he told his ladies that he'd been a detective. That part was true. He'd been a member of the elite Special Investigations Branch of the Royal Military Police—until he'd disappeared and changed his identity.

This, he said, was a secret. They weren't to tell anyone else. He was an investor who'd made his fortune on the stock market. That was his cover story. Nothing about the government. Nothing about being an investigator.

If the wrong person found out the truth, he'd have to disappear again. Or get caught.

Balcombe regained his composure and leaned close to whisper into Grace Toogood's ear.

"Barbara shouldn't have told you that."

"You're a secret agent, Mr Balcombe. And also some kind of special detective."

He winked. "I can't talk about it."

"But not connected to the police."

He shook his head. Definitely not connected to the police!

A serious look hardened Grace Toogood's eyes. "I need help," she said. "I need you to help me."

"Yes?" he said, still hoping this was a game, intrigued how this would progress.

She said, "Mr Balcombe, I need you to find my son."

THREE

When he'd arrived in Hong Kong, three months ago, Charles Balcombe had first stayed at The Peninsula hotel. Although luxurious, it was on the fringe of the docks, and so three days later he moved to the island. Initially, he stayed at the Peak Hotel, close to the crags where he could indulge his passion for free climbing. However, he soon found the hilltop location too remote for his liking and moved to rooms in a property off Queen's Road.

There was a string of first-class hotels opposite, the Connaught being the most prestigious. If he had to rate them, he'd put the Windsor Hotel at the top of the list. Why? Because he'd found that the ladies staying there were more amenable to his advances. Which was probably because they tended to be younger and their husbands less senior.

Balcombe sat at his window and watched the street. He could have afforded a view of Victoria Harbour. The big companies owned the prime locations along the front, before the wharf and its wall of warehouses. To get a view like the McGowan's had, you needed to live further out: west Victoria or even looking out over Belcher Bay.

The wealthy elite chose mansions on the hillside. While they gained with land and views, they lost the beating heart of the island.

Facing the mountains, Balcombe could watch the people on Hong Kong's first street. To his right, he could see the central market where the hustle and bustle of Chinese living started. To his left was old British colonial: City Hall, the Supreme Court, Statue Square, the cricket ground and the banks. And then came the Royal Navy port and the army HQ. Balcombe avoided them as much as possible. He'd changed his appearance—darker hair and a pencil moustache—and doubted that any of his ex-colleagues from Malaya would recognize him. But there was no point in taking chances on that score.

From his window, he watched ladies come out of the hotels, usually in pairs, and he'd guess which way they would go. Left or right?

The rickshaw boys lined up below his window were probably betting on it too!

He heard a noise inside his apartment. His cleaning girl shuffled through the next room. What was her name? Caihong. Yes, that was it. Most of the old men lusted after young Chinese girls. There were thousands of them. And largely available.

But Balcombe wasn't interested. At that moment he was intently studying a young woman wearing a cornflower blue dress as she came down the steps of the Windsor Hotel. She shook out her long fair hair before tying it back and covering it with a hat.

Not as pretty, but the way she moved reminded him of Grace Toogood from the party.

He looked up at the mountains. Clouds were gathering and the peak had been enveloped already. No good for rock climbing today. A shame, because he really wanted to clear his head.

Yesterday, Mrs Toogood had asked him to find her son. He'd joked that she wasn't old enough to have a child, and was then told the boy was twenty.

"Definitely too young!" he'd said, shocked.

She'd smiled kindly. "My husband's son from his first marriage," she explained. "Not physically mine."

She'd gone on to explain that they were concerned about him. He'd simply vanished on 14th December—five days ago.

"Just five months after I arrived here," she said.

"What do the police think?" he asked out of politeness rather than true interest.

"We can't involve the police."

Ah! Now he was intrigued. "Why not?"

Mrs Toogood swallowed uncomfortably. Her lips twitched, and he suspected she was looking for the right words. Balcombe waited.

Finally she said, "I can't talk about it. Mr Toogood wouldn't approve."

"I understand," he said, wondering what Mr Toogood didn't want the police digging into. Toogood had something to hide and thought it was more important than finding his missing son. It was also too sensitive to allow his wife to discuss it.

He waited to see if she would say anything, but she just calmly returned his gaze.

After a pause he said, "I must also ask for discretion, Mrs Toogood. Barbara should not have offered my services." He continued, explaining that his role in Hong Kong must not be compromised—an expression he used often. Providing detective services would expose him and his true role to people who shouldn't know. And that included the police. As such, Balcombe firmly but politely declined Mrs Toogood's request.

A crashing sound snapped his attention back to his apartment.

Caihong, the cleaning girl, appeared at the door and bowed. "So sorry, Mr Balcombe."

"You've broken something in the living room?" He immediately worried that it was the photograph. The special one. He'd been fifteen, standing beside his two climbing mates, the Roaches towering like shards of darkness behind them.

However, when he followed the cleaning girl into the living room, he saw the picture on the sideboard, intact. On the floor were broken pieces of porcelain. The rooms had come ready furnished. The smashed figurine wasn't even his.

Caihong quaked with fear. Tears brimmed in her eyes.

"I was... I was just dusting..."

He smiled kindly. "It's fine. It's fine." And to show her just how fine it was, he picked up the next statue and flung it to the floor. It shattered satisfyingly.

But rather than be relieved, the cleaning girl collapsed, great sobs wracking her small frame.

Balcombe stood over her, wondering what could be so terrible. Surely this was nothing to do with broken pottery.

He put a gentle hand under her arm and guided her into a chair, making "there, there" sounds, hoping to calm her.

However, once in the chair, Caihong put her head in her hands and sobbed even more.

All he could think to do was pour a glass of brandy.

She held it in a trembling hand, looked at the dark, shaking liquid, but didn't drink.

Balcombe waited. Eventually, without raising her head, she said, "So sorry, sir." Her voice still quaked.

"What's going on, Caihong?"

"Sir?" She glanced up at him, then away.

"You are far too upset for this to be about a broken statue."

She said nothing.

"Is it your boss? Is it a work problem?"

"No!"

He touched her arm and crouched so that his face was near to hers. In public, it wouldn't have been seemly to be so informal with the staff, but they were alone in his rooms and this girl was distraught.

"Tell me," he said softly. "Perhaps I can help."

"No one can help."

And then she told him a faltering story about her younger sister who had fallen for a boy. She'd thought him innocent, but he led her astray and then sold her to another man. A bad man.

She said that she had no one to turn to—no brothers, and her father was too sick.

"It would kill him to know that Meishan was in danger."

Balcombe took a breath. What had he got on today? There would be no climbing. He'd no appointments with his ladies—or anyone else for that matter. He'd planned to have dinner with a gentlemen's group tonight as his show of being one of the chaps, rather than the ladies' man he really was.

All he'd been doing was looking for lonely, pretty, married women. Well, now he had a different kind of challenge.

Balcombe took her other arm and held her so that their eyes met.

"Where I can find this chap?"

FOUR

Caihong blinked her surprise.

"I will reason with him," Balcombe said. "I'll persuade him to let her go."

Caihong blinked again and her face transformed, hope replacing despair.

Five minutes later, they were heading west on Queen's Road. The Chinese girl walked ten paces ahead as though they weren't together.

The street soon transformed into a Chinatown, and as a white man, he went from being in the majority to a minority within a hundred yards.

Street sellers crowded the pavements with goods and food. The air filled with the smell of boiled rice, roast chicken and spices. And then a few paces further it was pork he could smell.

Hawkers called and waved. They never pestered, which Balcombe liked about this place. Not like others he'd lived in.

He saw numerous policemen in their white uniforms and pith helmets. Chinese men controlling the public to ensure the white man was safe. At least that was how Balcombe interpreted it, and he knew others felt the same.

Caihong kept going west until the road split three ways. A traffic policeman whistled and beckoned to the drivers, adeptly managing the chaos created by the pronged roads, a mass of pedestrians and traffic.

The girl selected Jervois Street, the middle road of the three, which curved and seemed to become rougher and seedier with each pace. For the first time, Balcombe felt out of place as a white man. Then she turned right into an alley. Clothes ran on lines from building to building above him. It was a common sight, but this was a laundry.

"Here," the cleaning girl said, pointing to a reinforced green door beyond the laundry business. "The man has Meishan in here."

She stepped away as he knocked, but Balcombe beckoned her closer.

"It's him," she whispered, as a fat Chinese man answered the door. He had thinning hair, and Balcombe guessed him to be in his late forties.

The man bowed his head. "Sir?" At first he seemed confused, but then he noticed Caihong and his lips twitched in a small smile.

"Buying or selling, master?"

Balcombe glanced up and down the alley as though checking for police.

"Buying," he said. "You have a girl for sale?"

"I have four, master," the fat man said.

Balcombe felt his skin crawl. He knew this went on all over the world, but it was easy to ignore. Only when it became personal did the reality sink home.

"Show me," he said calmly.

Balcombe was led up a flight of wooden stairs and beckoned for Caihong to follow. She was needed in case her sister was here.

At the top was a large room with chairs. Balcombe guessed they were above the laundry and could smell the cleaning chemicals above the incense that presumably burned to mask bad smells. He could see the drying sheets hanging limply through grimy, part-open windows.

Balcombe was asked to take one of the four seats. Each had a fancy red cushion with gold embroidery. This was a viewing room: a place to check out the merchandise. The man disappeared through a door at the end, asking Balcombe to wait. After two minutes, Balcombe started to suspect the man had run. He was about to get up when the door opened and the fat man reappeared with a girl.

A teenager, Balcombe guessed, although rouge was dusted on her face, probably because this trader in human flesh thought it was what white men preferred. Maybe they did.

The way the girl teetered suggested she'd been drugged. She wore a loose-fitting silk gown providing glimpses of nakedness underneath.

Balcombe found his jaw tensing. He glanced at Caihong, standing to one side. The girl shook her head. Not her sister.

Balcombe stood. He found the disgust and anger easier to control that way. He breathed in and out and shook his head.

The Chinese man nodded his understanding and disappeared again.

The second girl looked almost identical; at least Balcombe couldn't see the difference: petite, young, long raven-coloured hair, make-up, a revealing sink gown and a look in her eyes that said she was drugged.

Balcombe breathed and waved the girl away.

The third girl was older, the fourth plumper. A descending order of appeal perhaps? Or maybe the trader thought the opposite. Whatever, each time, Caihong shook her head.

Not her sister.

The fat man looked crestfallen. "If the master returns next week, I get new girls."

Balcombe said, "Where do they come from?"

"China."

"Could I get one from Hong Kong?"

"Not the island. I arrange Kowloon... New Territories. If master tells me what he likes..."

Balcombe glanced at Caihong, who was looking increasingly uncomfortable and desperate.

"Do you have any other girls now?" Balcombe asked.

The man hesitated. He did have more. His dark eyes said so.

"Let me see," Balcombe pressed.

"She is taken."

"Let me see her."

"I—"

"Just a look," Balcombe said. "If I like her, then you will know what I'm looking for when I return next week."

The fat man's brow creased as he considered.

Balcombe added. "And I will pay you ten dollars now, just to see her."

"Twenty and she will be naked. She is beautiful."

Balcombe took a note from his wallet. "Just the ten."

When he disappeared through the door with the plump girl, Caihong interlaced her fingers, gripping so hard that the knuckles went white.

Would the next girl who came through that door be her sister Meishan?

It was. Balcombe knew because Caihong stifled a gasp.

The sister was taller than Caihong and looked even younger than the other girls, although the seller hadn't bothered to plaster her face with cosmetics.

Balcombe calmed his heart and breathing as the girl was made to turn around.

"Yes," he said. "That one will do nicely."

The fat man grinned. "From a good family. She is healthy and a virgin."

"How much?"

The man rubbed a stubbly chin as though considering, but he already knew a price. "One hundred dollars. Virgin." He grinned.

"All right." Balcombe pulled out his wallet again.

"No, no, no!" the man flapped. "Misunderstand. Not this girl. This girl is already sold."

Balcombe nodded. "All right, how much for this girl?"

The seller shook his head.

"Two hundred dollars?" Balcombe said.

The seller backed towards the door, opened it and pushed Meishan through.

"Three hundred," Balcombe said, and then regretted it. He'd no idea about prices, but he'd gone too far. The fat man's eyes screamed suspicion.

And then the man had a gun in his hand. It looked old, maybe pre-war.

Taking no chances, Balcombe raised his hands and patted the air. The international gesture for stay calm. I'm not a threat. "Not a problem," he said.

"No trouble?"

Balcombe forced a relaxed smile and backed away. "No trouble. No trouble at all. I was just very keen. She was just so perfect, I got carried away."

By the time he reached the door the fat man had relaxed but continued to hold the gun.

Balcombe grabbed Caihong and forced her ahead of him, down the stairs. She moved mechanically, her legs stiff and awkward. Once outside, he dragged her down the street.

"My sister! I can't leave her!"

She fought against his grip, but he wouldn't relent.

By the time they reached Jervois Street, she'd accepted they weren't going back. Her head was down and he could hear a low moan like a wounded animal's coming from her throat.

"Keep walking," he said, "and don't look back."

He found a café and ordered tea.

Caihong hovered for a minute, uncertain before turning to go.

"I need you to watch," he said.

"Sorry, sir?"

"When the sun goes down, I'll be here. You go back and watch the street. When you see the fat man leave the house, you come and get me."

"Sir?"

"I'm going back tonight, Caihong. And I won't leave without your sister."

FIVE

During the week, if not in the office, the dress code for the British was formal. In the summer months, they wore white. It demonstrated wealth, since they could afford the copious amounts of laundry. The custom probably dated back a hundred years.

In the winter they wore white shirts with suits of brown or grey. Unless they were attending a function.

Most of the time, Balcombe followed tradition, like wearing a bold-striped jacket and boater for the races, and black-tie for the evening. It was about fitting in, being accepted and not standing out.

However, that evening, he wore casual dark clothes. Instead of brogues, he had the black rubber shoes he used for rock climbing.

Balcombe had eaten dinner and read the newspaper in the café on Jervois Street. It was nine o'clock and he'd just decided to give it another half an hour when the cleaning girl appeared. Breathless and frantic, she told him that the fat man had locked up and gone.

Leaving a generous tip on the table, Balcombe jumped up and ran to the alley with the laundry operation. Labourers worked inside but the street was quiet. Light poured through the windows, but otherwise there was no street lighting, which left deep shadows and dark recesses.

He tried the green door. It was locked, solid and firm. It wouldn't be easily broken, however he'd already spied how he was getting into the property.

Asking Caihong to keep a lookout, Balcombe climbed onto a window ledge. After pulling himself up, he clung to the wall and worked his way along to a clothesline. With a better grip, he then swung across to reach a second-floor window. Within seconds he was over the edge and inside the viewing room. The incense burners had been extinguished and the bitter scent of fear seemed to hang in the air.

Balcombe hurried to the end door and found himself in a corridor with numerous doors feeding off it. Six doors. The first door was open. The others were shut. One with a bolt across.

He looked in the first room and noted a reasonable-looking bedroom. There was a vanity unit and dressing table. Balcombe guessed this was the fat man's room and where he cleaned up the girls, gave them the gowns and applied make-up.

Balcombe quickly moved on and opened the first door. He held his breath, unsure how horrific his next vision would be.

It was a cell-like room with a bucket toilet and a mattress. A girl lay naked, curled up, hugging her knees.

Wide eyes pleaded with him. Not Meishan. This was girl four, the plump one.

"It's all right. You're safe now," he said, hoping she'd understand his tone if not his words.

Putting a gown over her shoulders, he helped her stand and then led her to the corridor and viewing room. Then he went back and opened the other doors.

Each time he said the same words, then covered them and led them out into the viewing room.

Meishan was in the last room. The bolted one.

Like the other girls, she hardly knew what he was doing as he helped her to her feet and wrapped a gown around her limp body.

He guided her into the room. The other girls stood, huddled in the far corner, scared, unsure what to do.

Balcombe took Meishan to the stairs and one step at a time to the bottom.

The heavy door unlocked easily from the inside and he opened it to the passageway.

Immediately, Caihong dived through, grabbing her sister, hugging, crying and laughing at the same time.

"We must go." Balcombe pulled her away. "The others. Can you take them all to safety?"

Caihong nodded. "I will try."

Balcombe darted back upstairs and again told the girls they were safe now. He told them to hold hands, and in a line, they went carefully downstairs.

Opening the front door, Balcombe checked the passageway and waited for someone to flick a cigarette stub away and disappear into the laundry. Then he shepherded them outside and pointed away from the route they'd taken to get here. Further into the alley. Further into darkness.

He shut the door and joined the slow human train shuffling along the passage. At the end, they turned left and right until they were on a busy street.

Balcombe corralled them into a dark doorway and stepped into the road. Within seconds he'd hailed a taxi and got it to the kerb.

Whether the driver thought anything strange about six girls cramming into his cab, Balcombe didn't know.

Maybe he often picked up inebriated, semi-dressed girls at night.

As Caihong squeezed in last, he handed her a bundle of cash. "Take them home."

There were tears in her eyes as she bobbed her head and thanked him.

"What will you do now?" she asked as he shut her door.

He shook his head. "You don't want to know. Just make sure they are safe."

SIX

Chen Chee-hwa chuckled to himself. The gods were smiling. The planets were aligning. He'd spent the evening on a boat in the harbour playing mah-jong. An invitation-only game. One with high stakes. And he'd won big time.

His fortune was changing. Last month he'd had his future read with the *Kau Chim* sticks. It couldn't have been better! He'd been told to paint his front door green and it had been the start of his good luck.

Next year would be the year of the horse. His year. Today was the 20th of December. The 20th was his lucky day. December was his lucky month. So today was his luckiest day of the year, and it was true. The hundred dollars in his pocket—his winnings— confirmed that.

He called for a rickshaw. He'd travel home in style, like a snobby, colonial Brit. He deserved it.

After he barked where he was going and then told the kid to pull harder, he thought of the tall man who had visited today.

Three hundred pounds! He should have accepted. The man who had already bought her might have forgotten what she looked like, or Chee-hwa could have said she'd turned sick and had to be disposed of. For a second his good mood was soured as he cursed himself for not thinking fast enough. He shouldn't have been suspicious. Some Brits had no idea of the price of things. Three hundred for a girl! Maybe he should put the prices up.

Maybe he should tell the original buyer that the price had gone up. Could he pull that off? Would the disgusting, lascivious white man agree?

"Yes!" Chee-hwa said out loud. He could do it. After all, his luck had turned.

It all seemed to start when Chee-hwa had recruited the good-looking boy. The pretty girls fell for his words. He was brilliant at luring them, teasing them and finally drugging them so he could hand them over to Chee-hwa.

Or was it because he'd painted the door green?

Whatever, he could now see a prosperous future. This latest girl was the start of big business. Where had she come from? Did the pretty boy get her from Kowloon? Chen Chee-hwa reminded himself to insist that the boy never got them from the island or the Sham Shui Po district where the gang operated.

"This way!" he barked at the rickshaw boy who almost missed the turn. "Fool!"

Once on the right road, Chee-hwa returned to his thoughts. Three of the other girls came from the gang. He bought from them and sold them on. But they were inferior merchandise. Not like the beauty he could sell for three hundred. Yes! He would sell the new girl for three hundred. If the disgusting one wouldn't pay, then Chee-hwa would find the tall chap who had come today. He would agree to sell to him.

Hmm. Perhaps the price should be four hundred for the pretty girl.

Chee-hwa realized he was salivating. Gods! He could make serious money. His great grandfather had set up the laundry business and he'd lost it on a stupid bet. Very soon he would be able to buy it back. That would make his ancestors happy. And when he died, they would welcome him with cheers and praise. He had saved the family name. He had four children. Perhaps it was also time to have another son. A stronger one who he would influence more than his silly wife had influenced the others. Yes, that boy would take over the empire that he was going to build.

Chen Chee-hwa told the rickshaw boy to stop before the passageway. Once there, he handed over a few small coins.

"You don't deserve a tip—or even the full price," he said, paying less than the going rate. "Next time, work harder. That was the slowest ride I've ever had."

He grinned as he strode down the passageway, through the orange pools of light. Things were changing. The laundry business would soon be his. They were working inside—his future employees.

Standing in front of his green door, he touched the wood, felt the grain and thanked his ancestors. This was his day. Next year would be his year. Inserting the key, he heard the heavy lock turn. But what was that other sound?

Running feet?

As he started to open the door, he also turned towards the other sound. But before he could see what it was, a bull crashed into his back.

The blow made him stagger into the house. Not a bull, of course. A man! Chee-hwa started to fall, but a vice-like grip clamped around his neck, holding him up.

Who was this?

Had the criminal gang from Sham Shui Po decided to cut out the middleman? Was it the man who had stolen his laundry business, now steeling his girl-business? Or could it be Zhang, the man he'd had to borrow from last year? But he'd paid him back, double. Surely he didn't want more?

Chee-hwa struggled, tried to twist, see who it was, but the man was so strong. He could hardly move. Fingers dug harder into his throat, squeezing his larynx so hard that only a squeak escaped from his open mouth.

The man's grip tightened again and his body jerked.

Chee-hwa felt a pain in the back of his neck. A sharp pain like a bee sting. It made his throat feel hot, his skin dripping with sweat.

Or was it blood? Not a bee sting. He'd been stabbed in the neck.

Panicked, Chee-hwa struggled more and then gasped as the man punched him in the kidney. His legs were swept from under him and he went down, but the man flipped him so that he landed heavily on his back. The man was immediately on top of him, his grip still on Chee-hwa's throat.

This wasn't Zhang or the man who'd stolen the laundry business. The gang then? But he couldn't see the man's face. A big man. And all Chee-hwa could see were eyes through a mask.

He could no longer breathe. The man's weight crushed his stomach with the pressure of an overturned tram. And that iron grip! Who had fingers like that?

Calm! He told himself. Remember, he was lucky. The cut to his neck was just a scratch. It must be. This man wasn't going to kill him. If he'd wanted to take his life, Chee-hwa would be dead already.

He ignored the pain in his neck, the difficulty he had breathing, and tried to sign that he understood.

The attacker nodded, but his right hand was moving. And what was that discomfort in his solar plexus? Suddenly the pain was excruciating. Chee-hwa squirmed and thrashed. Gods! The man had cut his upper belly. And what the hell was that? It felt like a snake squirming in his chest.

His body felt hot and wet and he knew that blood was oozing from his chest. Despite the pain, he froze.

This was it. There would be no lucky year. No great business success. No prosperity.

He felt the beat of his heart against something foreign. Not a snake. The man was holding his heart within Chee-hwa's chest! Squeezing.

His heart was stopped and a shiver went through him, like none he'd ever known. Like his soul was tearing free of his body.

And then Chen Chee-hwa felt himself being sucked into oblivion.

SEVEN

"Father, forgive me, for I have sinned," Charles Balcombe said as he walked. He went to church but hadn't been to the confessional in years. He didn't believe in it. He believed in God all right, but as for the priest being a vessel for the Almighty? No. Man was just that: flesh and blood, human. Priests weren't special and they wouldn't understand.

He walked along Caine Road, the mid-levels street with big houses as well as the Victoria police headquarters and a synagogue.

The night insects buzzed and clicked. He smelled the trees that lined the street. He felt more alive than at any time in the past three months since arriving on the island.

After a killing spree in Malaya, Balcombe had changed his identity and fled to Hong Kong. He'd intended to change his ways.

Tonight he was cross with himself. He could accept killing the disgusting little man, but he'd lost control. He'd gone too far. Now he needed to talk with God.

When he arrived, the evening Mass had concluded and the English Gothic cathedral now only had a mere handful of people praying. They had spaced themselves out evenly, as though sitting too close to someone was a sin.

Balcombe walked to the front, knelt, crossed himself before Christ and then took a pew.

That night, he had felt the soul of a man—a bad man—leave his body. On the one hand, it was a sin to kill, but on the other, God understood punishment. After all, the Old Testament was all about the wrath of God.

A priest wouldn't understand that. He'd claim that vengeance was God's duty not his, but Balcombe knew that when he explained his actions God would understand. God would forgive him.

Charles Balcombe was the youngest of six— excluding the one who was stillborn. He, his four brothers and sister had been raised as Roman Catholics. When the baby was born dead, he thought his mother's faith would waiver, but it hadn't.

Nor did they deny Him when the two oldest brothers were killed in the war. But when his friend and hero died, young Balcombe had lost his faith. They'd been climbing the Roaches.

His friend was the real Charles Balcombe, although Balcombe now thought of him as Eric, which had been the boy's middle name. Eric was a year older and had taught Balcombe everything he knew about free climbing. He'd been ahead, on the overhang, when the rock came away in his hand.

Balcombe expected a sickening thud as his friend's body struck the ground, seventy feet below. However, the silent landing had seemed more awful than a crunching noise.

Balcombe and his other friend, Tim, hadn't given up climbing. They went most weekends, unless it was too wet. But without Eric to guide them, Balcombe soon got into trouble. He got stuck in the range's chimney. Tim couldn't help. He was below.

Young Balcombe couldn't go up, and after his hands started to tire, he could only see one way out. Give up and drop.

But he hadn't. He'd heard Eric's voice in his head, mocking. Telling him to fight. Telling him that fear was the thrill. Telling him that death reminded us that we were alive. Fear and anxiety may shout loudly, but without those, you cannot be truly courageous.

And somehow Balcombe had found a new grip and slowly eased into a new position. When he crested the chimney, he screamed into the wind. His body was charged with new energy. He was fearless. Death was to be faced and challenged.

From that day, he returned to God, because he had felt His presence. He'd also known Eric had been with him.

And young Balcombe had learned what he was.

He was a thrill-seeker and risk-taker. Because life was about danger. Take no risk and live no life.

But it wasn't until he killed a man just over a year ago that he'd found the true elixir of life. The other man had been a crook. He had a knife and would have killed Balcombe if he could.

They struggled and Balcombe got the upper hand. He'd thrust the knife into the other man's chest and pierced his heart. The jolt he'd felt from taking the man's life was incredible. Killing was all the more enhanced when the heart was involved, and nothing was more satisfying than stopping it from beating, holding the dying man's heart in his hand and feeling the soul depart.

Nothing.

He'd called himself BlackJack, partly because of the game but also with a nod to Jack the Ripper. Balcombe found mass murderers fascinating, always had. He'd studied Jack without realizing why, without appreciating their similarity. The man surely experienced the same rush.

Although there was an important distinction: the men BlackJack killed deserved to die.

Jack the Ripper had suddenly stopped killing. He'd walked away and left a mystery. BlackJack had tried to do the same. He'd almost been caught. He thought he could control his urges. He thought he could get his thrills in other ways. But he'd almost strangled Barbara McGowan and now he'd killed a Chinese man.

There was no remorse for the killing, because the fat man had been evil. Justice had been served. The little man wouldn't be treating young girls as chattels anymore. He had to die, and Balcombe's enjoyment of the kill was just a by-product. Wasn't it?

He asked God, but all he heard in response was the echo of feet as people left.

Balcombe crossed himself one more time, said a prayer for his dead brothers and Eric, and stood.

Cool air blew fresh up the hill as he walked home. The harbour twinkled like a moving bed of stars.

I can control the urges, he told himself. *I can control BlackJack, but I need a distraction.*

High society life wasn't satisfying. The gambling and dangerous liaisons were good, but he needed something else. He needed a distraction. He needed a challenge.

By the time he opened the door to his apartment, he had decided what he would do. Tomorrow he would see Grace Toogood.

He turned on the light and realized a piece of paper had been slipped under the door. He picked it up and saw one scribbled sentence. For the second time that night, Balcombe felt his heart pump pure adrenaline.

The note said: *I know what you did.*

EIGHT

Balcombe flipped over the note. Nothing else was on the paper.

I know what you did.

Who the hell had sent it?

Rushing outside, he stood on Queen's Road. Despite the late hour, the streetlights and hotel windows provided plenty of illumination. To the right was a mass of Chinese vendors and customers. To his left were the rickshaw boys, many asleep on their carts. Three gentlemen were laughing as they walked into the Windsor Hotel. A couple strolled towards the centre.

No one looked at him.

No one appeared suspicious or expecting him to appear on the street.

Then why send the note?

Returning to his rooms, he poured a large glass of single-malt whisky and sat in his favourite chair. Then he raised the glass to toast his friends in the photograph, Eric and Tim. It would be the tenth anniversary soon.

After a mouthful of the amber liquid and slow burn down his throat, he studied the note again.

I know what you did.

He'd immediately assumed that someone knew about BlackJack. Did someone see him kill the fat Chinese man by the laundry?

He'd been so careful, checking no one was about, but the passage off Jervois Street had wells of darkness. Doorways and bends where someone may have watched him crash into the back of the Chinese man and force him through the green door. After all, Caihong had waited on the street during the day and she'd been well hidden.

Did this unknown witness follow him through the streets afterwards and watch as he washed the blood off his hand and arm?

Perhaps they even followed him to the cathedral and saw him pray. Balcombe had a good memory and could remember the two people who had come into the church after him. He closed his eyes, sipped the whisky and pictured them.

The first had been a middle-class white man wearing a grey suit with a blue tie. He had neat, salt and pepper hair. His age? Late forties or early fifties. Tired, disillusioned eyes above a downturned mouth. Thin lips.

The second man had been Chinese. A labourer wearing brown pants and a grey shirt. About thirty years old, he was heavy-set and walked awkwardly, as though his hips troubled him.

Balcombe shook his head. Neither seemed a likely pursuer. Unless they were accomplished spies. Perhaps the Chinese man was faking his stiff hips.

Again Balcombe shook his head, finished his drink and poured another.

Why send the note and not go to the police?

What was their motive?

Perhaps this was a coincidence. Perhaps this wasn't about that evening. This could refer to his dangerous liaisons.

Could it be Graham McGowan, Barbara's husband? Balcombe took the gentleman to be a coward. It would be just like him to put a note under a door and run away, afraid of the confrontation.

Balcombe shook his head. No, a gentleman surely wouldn't scribble a note on a scrap of paper. If not McGowan, then perhaps one of their staff. A maid might have spotted him. She might have seen inappropriate contact and put two and two together.

That would make sense. The note was a threat. It wasn't something to report to the police, it was a secret they were willing to keep. Which would mean there would be another note. Whoever it was would eventually ask for hush money.

Satisfied that he would know the truth in the morning when he received the second note, Balcombe picked up the latest book he was reading.

It was about ancient Egyptian customs and rituals. He never read fiction. What was the point? His interest lay in history. And there was a fabulous second-hand bookshop in the markets where he'd bought a bundle of history books.

Balcombe's father never understood. He'd wanted his youngest to follow in his footsteps in the medical profession, ideally as a surgeon. He was retired by the time his youngest chose history as his specialist subject.

"History won't get you a professional job!" the old man had scoffed.

"Mankind has progressed because of history," Balcombe had snapped back, thinking he was clever. "We learn from history."

"Oh really? We learned from the First World War, did we?" his father had retorted, and that was the end of the argument.

But Balcombe had studied history, and afterwards he did the other thing his father warned him about. He joined up. But not as a grunt. Balcombe went to Sandhurst and became a military policeman. Then, because he had talent, he was assigned to Special Investigations. And he realized he was a natural detective. Still not a profession to please his old man, but a talent nonetheless.

Balcombe read a chapter on mummification. What particularly interested him was the practice of removing the heart during the process and then returning it to the body afterwards, whereas the other main organs were kept in Canopic jars. The Egyptians believed that the heart was the essence of the person, the *ib* part of the soul.

Balcombe had a book on the Mayans and Aztecs that spoke about sacrifice. Hearts were often cut out but in a ritualistic and reverent way. They knew. Like him, they had touched a beating heart, ended a life and felt the life force.

The Egyptians believed that the gods weighed the heart when someone died, determining whether they would continue to the afterlife or be devoured by the soul-eater. Balcombe liked that. He put the thought of the note out of his head. Tomorrow would reveal the truth.

He fell asleep with the book on his lap, dreaming of the fat Chinese man being devoured by a monster.

Charles Balcombe was wrong about the second note. By mid-morning, nothing had arrived. He'd been out to provide his accuser with the opportunity to leave one.

Pamela Amey, one of his ladies, had left him a signal. A tiny yellow ribbon tied to a railing outside her hotel. He replaced it with a black one. The yellow one meant she was inviting him to her room at 11am, and he'd accepted.

Pamela had shoulder-length, copper-coloured hair and looked amazing for her forty years. She also liked to play a game she called *gee-gees*. This basically involved playing the role of horses: a mare and stallion. Although he never commented on the unlikely scenario that the stallion should be equipped with a whip.

Afterwards, she lay on her front panting, her buttocks raw from the whipping. Then she flipped over and lit up a cigarette.

"Tell me about this one," she said, smoke pouring from her mouth as she touched a four-inch scar on his arm.

It was one of the seven knife cuts—from playing a game called first blood. As a teenager, he'd found a rough group who fought with knives: small penknives with tiny blades sharpened like razors. Draw blood and you won. No one was ever seriously injured, but he'd received six cuts before he'd become the best.

Pamela touched his first. The one on his chest had been the seventh and earned two years ago, playing the same game in Malaya—only the Malays used bigger knives. Balcombe had been drunk at the time and he never fought drunk again. Nor did he lose.

"What's wrong?" she asked after he told her lies about his scar.

"Wrong?"

She gave him a quirky smile and shook her head. "You weren't your usual self this morning, baby. Not gone off me already, I hope."

He laughed and caressed her thigh. "Not a chance."

41

"Then what?"

Of course, he couldn't confess to the killing, but he was still of a mind that this was about a liaison.

"I received a note," he said after consideration. "I think someone knows."

Panic flared in her eyes and she immediately stubbed out the cigarette. "About us? Does Clive know? I would just die if he burst in right now!"

"It wasn't specific, so I'm wondering if it's a prank," he said. "Or someone fishing, hoping to reveal a secret. They'll come asking for money next." He brushed her pretty copper hair from her cheek and kissed her. "Just a warning, perhaps. Your hotel room at set times is too predictable."

And so they discussed other signals and locations for their meetings, although he never included his rooms. His place wasn't an option for his liaisons.

She'd been right. He had been preoccupied during their lovemaking, but when he again found no second note pushed under his door, he decided it was indeed a prank.

Time to pay Grace Toogood a visit.

NINE

Balcombe rode in the back of a rickshaw up to Conduit Road to the Toogoods' house. It was on the mid-levels and where the almost-elite lived. Through the grand wrought-iron gate, he saw a Victorian mansion at the end of a drive. The Toogoods had a private car—something few islanders owned or required. The island was little bigger than a postage stamp, and anything worth a jot was along the three-mile stretch facing the mainland. However, the elite had Bentleys and Rolls Royces, for show more than practical use.

The Toogoods' car was a burgundy Daimler. He realized it was the same colour as the stunning evening dress he'd first seen Mrs Toogood wearing on Saturday night.

"Well hello," she said, approaching from the side of the house. "Admiring the motor car?"

He turned and couldn't help himself look her up and down. That afternoon she was wearing blue slacks and a cream silk shirt. He could see her bra underneath, and the well-fitted trousers confirmed that she was in good shape.

"Beautiful," he said, looking into her eyes. Her lips twitched, which he decided meant she understood the compliment was aimed at her. He wasn't normally so subtle, but he sensed this attractive young woman needed to be hooked and played before she could be landed.

However, that wasn't the main purpose of his visit, just a hopeful side benefit.

She started walking and he followed her into the house. They went along a walnut parquet-covered hall, past a staircase and grand rooms until they reached a kitchen. On the far side were patio doors opening out onto an immaculate English-style garden.

There were chairs outside and he presumed she was leading him to them. However, after a glance at herself in a mirror, she stopped.

"Oh, there's loose cotton at the back of my blouse," she said, mortified.

He'd noticed the tiny strand dangling from her collar.

"Would you be a darling and snip it off?" she asked.

There were kitchen scissors on the worktop so he picked them up and removed the offending strand.

She smiled demurely, as though he'd flattered her again. Then she continued into the garden and waited under the shade of a tree until he was beside her.

"So, Mr Balcombe, are you going to help us?"

"I'm still considering your proposal."

"Only considering?"

"I need to understand about the police," he said. "I need to know why they can't be involved."

She stopped, faced him and blinked a few times. "I'm sorry. I find this difficult to say."

"You'll need to explain if I'm to help."

She looked away and back. "Barbara says that you're trustworthy."

He said nothing at first. There was something illegal going on. Something that the police would be very interested in. He saw gardeners trimming bushes and digging soil.

She seemed to be waiting for him to declare his honesty. Or maybe she was just too uncomfortable telling anyone.

"You'll need to tell me," he said, "if you want me to find your husband's son."

She nodded then spoke quickly in a low voice. "What do you know about banking?"

"Assume very little."

"Mr Toogood is vice principal of the bank and it wouldn't be appropriate for him to be involved. And he's worried that Roger…"

"Roger being Roger Toogood? His son?"

"Yes."

"Has Roger done something?"

Grace's bosom rose and fell as she composed herself. "Roger works for the bank too, and employees need to be above the law."

That was a polite way of saying they shouldn't be criminals.

"Everyone should be above the law," Balcombe said.

"Bankers especially—not a doubt about their integrity."

"OK." He looked around the garden, giving her time to continue. There were trees at the far end, then a wall. He could see the forest climbing up the mountainside to the peak. Such an amazing spot. An English garden with a mountain beyond its walls.

"Drugs," she said quietly. "I don't know the facts, but Denis believes Roger has been involved with… illegal substances.

"And has run away?"

"We need to find him. Denis can deal with whatever the trouble is."

Balcombe thought about what she was saying. Drugs, especially opium derivatives, were everywhere. He didn't know how strict the bank was about their attitude to drugs, but he knew the police. They wouldn't be too concerned about Roger taking opium, but they would act if he'd been dealing. He didn't comment and they started walking again.

"Will you take the job, Mr Balcombe?"

He took another two paces.

She said, "You'll be well paid for your services."

"It's not about money."

She stopped again, turned and looked him in the eye. He saw a twinkle of mischief and he raised an eyebrow.

"Mr Balcombe, I hope you aren't suggesting something... something naughty?"

Of all the words she could have chosen, that one made him smile.

"Step this way," he said, walking behind a tree. They would be screened from the house. He didn't know if anyone was inside, looking out, but he knew no one could see them here.

He whispered, "Turn around and close your eyes."

As soon as her back was to him, he placed his hands on her hips, pulled his body next to hers. She made as though to pull away, but it was weak resistance and he held on.

"Mr—"

"You are beautiful." His breath was on her neck and he saw it flush. "I want you, Grace."

"Charles—" Her voice trembled as she exhaled.

"I'll make you scream. I'll make you feel alive. I'll make you feel desired."

She eased herself away, faced him and breathed in and out, slowly. She ran her hands down the sides of her slacks as a woman would do when straightening her dress. When they came away, he noticed her hands were trembling.

She raised a hand and wafted air into her face.

"My," she said breathlessly. "Barbara hinted that you were good. I had no idea…"

He said, "Do we have a deal?"

She took another breath, composing herself at last. "We certainly do. You bring back Roger and you can have"—she gulped as though embarrassed to say the words—"your way with me."

They looked into one another's eyes for a long moment before she broke the spell.

"Now you need to speak to Mr Toogood—Denis. But—"

"Don't worry," he said with a laugh in his voice, "I won't mention our arrangement."

"When he offers money, do accept," she said urgently as they walked towards the house.

"Is he here?"

"My man telephoned for him as soon as you arrived. I'm sure he'll be here by now."

And he was. Denis Toogood was waiting in a drawing room. There was a Christmas tree in a corner, covered with silver and mauve baubles. Toogood was wearing a dark buttoned-up suit with a severe tie and winged-collar shirt. His hands were clasped behind his back.

Despite Toogood's imposing presence, Balcombe had three immediate thoughts.

Balcombe was just wearing a casual white shirt and cream trousers. His shoes were brown and white brogues. And so his first thought was that he was underdressed. He regretted leaving his jacket at home.

His second thought was about health. It was an unseasonably warm day for December, but not so hot to explain the beads of sweat on Denis Toogood's forehead. His rush home was probably the only real exercise he'd had in years.

The third was that Toogood was even older than he'd expected. His son Roger was twenty, so he'd pictured Toogood to be around forty. The man looked no younger than fifty. He had a good head of steel-grey hair but the beard couldn't hide the sagging skin on his face and neck. He had tired but cold eyes. His fine suit showed a man who enjoyed his food and took little exercise.

Balcombe wanted to ask Grace Toogood why the hell she was with this old, unfit toad. But he didn't. Of course he knew. Denis Toogood may not be a *Taipan*, but he was vice principal of a bank. The man was loaded. Well beyond Balcombe's wealth. Toogood could probably buy half of Surrey back home.

The man nodded curtly. No handshake. "Mr Balcombe."

"Sir."

"Will you find my son?"

Balcombe said, "Mrs Toogood tells me that the police aren't to be involved."

"That's right." Toogood's tongue touched his lip, presumably because of the perspiration. "May I be certain of your discretion, Mr Balcombe?"

"Totally."

"I will pay you handsomely and won't tolerate any shenanigans."

"I'm an honourable man," Balcombe reassured the banker.

Toogood nodded as though considering. However, Balcombe knew it had already been decided. He was just not rushing things.

Balcombe said, "I will find your son and bring him home."

"And I will pay you one thousand dollars now." He held up a hand to prevent any argument at the large upfront payment. "For expenses and the like. I will create an account for you at the bank and transfer the money. You will be able to withdraw some or all of it by tomorrow morning."

Balcombe nodded his acceptance.

"And when you bring my son home safe and sound, I will transfer a final payment of twenty thousand dollars."

Balcombe couldn't help blinking his surprise.

Toogood said, "Yes, it's a handsome sum, Mr Balcombe, but it not only rewards your success but also buys your loyalty. Am I right?"

"Yes, sir," Balcombe said. However, the true prize was still Grace Toogood. Money didn't buy happiness. Of course it helped, but *the thrill* was far more important.

He pulled a small notebook and pencil from a trouser pocket.

"All right," he said. "I'll need a photograph and anything you can tell me to help find your son."

TEN

Detective Inspector Munro knocked at the morgue entrance.

"Babyface Munro!" a grinning man in scrubs said as he opened the door.

Munro blinked through his round spectacles. "Fai Yeung, I didn't... how long have you been back?"

"Yesterday. I was reassigned yesterday."

Munro hugged the other man, who had been his friend ever since he'd come to Hong Kong seeking his fortune. Everyone knew Munro as Babyface although few used his nickname since he'd been promoted. Yeung had coined it years ago and he was the only one who knew Munro's real name and that Munro was actually his given name.

Munro had never known William Munro, his Scottish father. His Korean mother's family name was Jo and he'd been raised as Jo Munro. When he'd applied to join the Hong Kong police force, a British official had written his name as Joe Munro, assuming Munro was his surname. And so, since he'd arrived in 1933, he'd been Munro.

"Forty years old, but you still have that babyface and you're as skinny as a starved cat."

Munro stepped back and assessed his friend. He was still solid, thickset with the neck of a bull, but the years were catching up with him fast. Yeung's eyes sagged and his hair was thinning.

"You look well," Munro said.

"And you're as good a liar as ever," Yeung said, laughing. "I hear you've been promoted to detective inspector. Congratulations."

"Dead man's shoes," Munro said dismissively.

"Still impressive, my friend—for an Asian, mixed-race or not. Me? I've only made it to *assistant* pathologist."

"Probably a mix up again. Someone assumed I was a Brit because of my name."

"That would explain it." Yeung nodded. "But I'm sure you're the real worker around here. I'm hoping for a bit more excitement after Macao."

"How's your wife?"

"Coping with the five children and happy I'm in Hong Kong."

"Because it's better here?"

"No! Because I'm here and she's there." Yeung laughed. "How's your knee? I see you're still limping."

Munro had suffered from the stiff leg for so long he was disappointed it was obvious. He didn't want to talk about it, because of the memories, so he shook his head and brought the conversation back to their work.

"You've looked at the body brought in yesterday?"

"Of course! What do you take me for, Babyface, a dozy fish?" He handed Munro a jar of Vaseline as he started along the corridor of the basement complex.

Munro could already smell the decay and gladly inserted a blob of the jelly up each nostril.

They went through a swinging door and there was a covered body on one of the four tables.

Yeung said, "In the New Territories all four of these would have bodies on. Mostly gang killings. I trust you're a better detective than your colleagues on the mainland."

"You're asking about my success rate?"

The assistant pathologist pulled the sheet off the victim like a magician performing a trick.

"Success at catching the actual killer or at putting some lowlife behind bars?" Yeung chuckled. "I suppose, either way, it's doing the country a service."

"Tell me about him." Munro already knew the young man had been found in the water off Taikoo Shipyard. He had no identification and no one from the Shipyard recognized him.

"Mature Chinese male aged between sixteen and eighteen. Been in the water for three to four days. Did I tell you I'd started a chicken farm?"

Munro tore his eyes from the pale, bloated body on the slab and looked at his friend. "No. Surely you're not—"

"Thinking of packing all this in?" Yeung said, jumping in. "Of course I am! I reckon I could make it big as a chicken farmer. Especially now... now I've made it, you mean? Assistant pathologist on the island?"

Munro did mean that, but his friend seemed less than impressed. He pointed at the dead young man.

"How did he die?"

"Drowned," Yeung said. "So, I was telling you about my chicken farm. I've bred some with three legs. Can you believe it? I'll make a fortune!"

Munro blinked at his friend. "Three legs?"

"You're supposed to ask what it tastes like."

"All right, what does a three-legged chicken taste like?"

"I don't know. I haven't been able to catch one yet!" Yeung guffawed.

"Still the joker, I see, Fai. Now tell me more about the boy on the slab."

Yeung shook his head. "You know your problem, Babyface, is that you don't have a sense of humour. It's necessary for this job."

"Tell me more about his death."

"I'm getting there! I'm getting there!" Yeung smiled. "The bruising you see is all post-mortem."

"Anything suspicious?"

"No. Probably a swimmer."

It was the general term for desperate people trying to reach the island. He might have swum, but more likely he'd lost whatever floatation device he'd been using.

Munro heard footsteps outside as someone came into the morgue.

"A shame," Yeung said, "I'd hoped my cases here would be more interesting."

A red-faced constable approached Munro, saluted and caught his breath.

"Take your time," Munro said to the man.

The constable nodded, breathed and finally spoke. "Sir, a body. A girl. Dead in a pig cold-store."

"Who's at the scene?"

"Sergeant Tam. He asked if you'd come at once, sir."

As Munro began walking, he called back to Yeung.

"Your lucky day, Fai," Munro said with irony. "Looks like your job just got interesting."

ELEVEN

Balcombe wrote down everything Denis Toogood told him. It wasn't much and he promised to keep Toogood apprised, either in person or by messenger.

Back on the lane outside the house, he flagged a rickshaw and asked to be taken to an address in east Victoria, beyond the army barracks.

The hood was up and he welcomed the cool shade as he settled on the seat.

The case sounded straightforward but would provide a good distraction. Plus, the likely relationship with such a beauty was a major added benefit.

"Hey!" he called to the rickshaw boy. "The centre. I didn't say the cathedral!"

The boy pulled into the cathedral's gardens.

"You received note, master." The boy spoke with a young voice and thick accent.

Balcombe sat upright. *The note!*

The boy stopped.

"Who have you brought me to meet?"

The boy didn't answer straight away but silently lowered the yoke. He didn't turn around, and Balcombe wondered if he didn't understand the question. Just a messenger.

Balcombe glanced around. He saw no one. What was going on?

"Who have you—" Balcombe started.

"Go into cathedral. Please," the boy said haltingly. "Sit in the rear pew on left, master."

The skinny kid had his head down showing deference. His clothes were too big and he wore a coolie hat hiding his face.

Balcombe continued to look around.

"Anything else?"

The boy paused. "Not... Do not turn around, master. No matter what."

Balcombe shook his head, got up and strode into the cavernous cathedral. The priest and some altar boys were at the front. There were a dozen people praying. Balcombe selected the end pew on the left and faced front.

"Do not turn around," a confident, gruff voice whispered.

"You sent me a message," Balcombe said.

"I sent *the* message."

Balcombe said nothing.

The voice said, "I saw you."

Balcombe tensed. Was this a shakedown? He'd heard of gangs jumping unsuspecting Brits. But here at a place of God?

"Don't worry," the voice said.

"What do you think you saw?" Which of his ladies was this about? Pamela Amey was the most likely, he'd convinced himself.

"By the laundry, last night."

Balcombe's pulse quickened. "The laundry?"

"I saw you kill the nasty fat man," the voice whispered. "I was in the passageway. Both times."

"Both times?"

"I saw you rescue those girls too. You went back and killed him. You forced him through the door, killed him and just walked away. Then you cleaned the blood off your hands and came to the church. You came here to pray."

"How much do you want?" Balcombe said, reaching for his wallet.

"I won't tell anyone."

Balcombe held up five dollars. The other man didn't take it. Balcombe held up another five. Then a ten.

Still no hand to take the money in his fist.

"Shall I leave it on the bench?"

There was no answer.

"You don't want money. What do you want?"

Still no answer.

Balcombe waited, took a breath and turned quickly. The money had been a distraction so that he could produce a knife in his other hand. But there was no one behind him.

Balcombe sprang from the pew and hurried outside.

He saw the skinny boy hurrying towards his rickshaw. There was no one else around.

Balcombe sprinted to the boy and snatched him by the collar just as he raised the rickshaw.

The boy shrank down. "Don't hurt me!"

"Who was it?" Balcombe snapped, his grip tightening, pulling the boy up.

"Me."

"You?"

"I won't tell anyone," the boy said in the same voice as Balcombe had heard whisper inside. There was no hint of an accent now.

"How much money do you want?" Balcombe said to the back of the boy's head.

"I was brought up to believe that money must be earned by hard work, master."

If only that were the way the world worked, Balcombe thought. "All right," he said. "So what do you want?"

The boy still didn't turn or look at him, but said, "Work."

"Work? You want work?"

"You can use me. I can be very helpful."

"I don't think so."

"Do you speak Cantonese, master? Mandarin even?"

Balcombe said nothing. He knew the odd word, but most people he came across spoke English.

The boy said, "And I am invisible."

"What do you mean?"

"Did you notice me last night? You did not. I was the one who took you to Jervois Street. I also picked up the fat one from the harbour and took him home. He didn't even pay me a fair rate for the ride. But I didn't care because I expected you to return. I waited. I saw what you did and followed you all the way—here and then home. You had no idea."

Balcombe's eyes narrowed. It was true, he hadn't noticed the boy before, and yet he'd clearly been around—close and watching.

"How do you propose it working?" Balcombe finally said.

"You use me for all of your transportation. You use me for translation. And, if necessary, you use me for spying because I can be invisible."

"And money?"

"You pay me at the end of each day. A fair amount."

"I could just kill you."

The boy shook his head, and for the first time, Balcombe caught a glimpse of a face beneath the coolie hat and black hair.

"You won't because you are a good man." He pointed to the church. "You believe in God."

"What's your name?"

"Prince Albert."

Balcombe spluttered a laugh, the tension of the situation suddenly gone.

The boy said, "I was raised by my grandfather, who was a royalist. He worshipped your king and queen. So he named me after the king. My grandfather thought it was his proper name. King Prince Albert."

"I can't call you Prince Albert."

"You can call me Prince." There was humour in the boy's voice… and something else.

"I'll call you Albert. Is that acceptable?"

The boy looked up. He had an effeminate face. "It is."

"Anything else you want to tell me?" Balcombe said, smiling.

Albert looked awkward.

"Then, Albert, please take me to east Victoria. Perhaps you'll tell me the other thing later."

TWELVE

Detective Inspector Munro looked past the hanging pig carcasses to packing boxes and the cluster of men at the back of the room.

Sergeant Arthur Tam had secured the scene and the photographer was finishing up. Munro waited until he was out of the way before walking to the rear and taking a good look.

The girl was wrapped in sacking and lying on the floor at the back of the long narrow room. He could see long black hair, the side of her face, an arm and the bottom half of a leg. From the look of her, he figured she was naked.

"No accident," Munro said to his sergeant.

"No. She didn't come in here to sleep and then freeze to death. Not by choice anyway."

"We'll see," Munro said, thinking of his pathologist friend. "Who found her?"

"A worker called Vang." Tam nodded towards four men who were watching them from the entrance. They were all skinny young men. Hard faces and hard bodies. "He's the one in the middle."

Munro looked at the man. Despite his skinny arms he was easily strong enough to carry the girl. But why? Why hide a body and then discover it?

Unless it was a cunning deception.

"What are you thinking?" the sergeant asked Munro.

"How devious it would be to discover your own murder victim."

The sergeant's eyes flew wide. "Then we should arrest Vang!"

Munro shook his head.

"It would improve your figures. And perhaps the man might crack. A few days in Victoria Gaol and we could get him to—"

"No!" Munro said, sounding more irritated than intended. He rubbed his leg. The cold was making his bad knee ache. Which, in turn, put him in a bad mood. At yet the day had started so well, seeing his old friend Yeung.

"I want the statements from all of the workers. Include those who weren't here yesterday. And get the body over to pathology."

The sergeant signalled for the removal of the girl, and then the two of them left the cold room and went to the office next door. A sweating manager, called Fung, sat upright in his chair as though just waiting for the police to return.

Tam said, "You gave the list of employees to my constable?"

"Yes."

Munro watched the man's eyes as they waited. The detectives wanted the manager to think they knew more than he did.

"Yes?" Fung said eventually.

"Why do you think someone would leave a body in your cold-store room?" Tam asked.

"I don't know."

"How did they do it?"

Fung looked perplexed. "What? Do you mean did they carry her there? How else?"

Munro watched Fung's eyes as he said, "You know she didn't walk in on her own accord."

Fung looked left and right as though searching for support, before he spoke. "No, I suppose she didn't."

"So, how?" Tam pressed.

The manager shook his head.

Munro said, "Who has the keys to the storeroom?"

"Just me." He pointed to the office door with his right hand and then the wall, which had a key hook. Munro noticed the man was missing his thumb, which made the fingers look like four pork sausages.

"There's an office door key," Fung said, "and one for the storage room."

"Is the room ever left unattended?"

"It shouldn't be. We'd probably lose a few carcasses if we didn't watch it."

"And yet someone carried a body in there."

Fung sighed. "It wasn't me."

"So, how did they get in and leave the body if you're the only one with a key?"

"I don't know how," Fung said, sounding more concerned. "All I know is that I didn't do it!"

THIRTEEN

Roger Toogood's rooms were off Queen's Road East just after the naval dockyards. There were four parallel streets starting with Gloucester Road on the coast and stretching almost a thousand yards. These streets were crammed with commercial buildings decreasing in importance away from the bay, after which was a wedge of streets between Queen's Road East and Johnston Road. The streets still had British names, like Anton and Gresson, but were packed with Chinese housing. There were some shophouses, but most properties were residential. This was where labourers lived. Not poor, but not well-off either.

So the fact that Roger Toogood lived here surprised Balcombe. He didn't know the area, but he saw few white faces and figured this was not the higher class location he expected for the son of a rich banker.

Albert had pulled the rickshaw two miles before he stopped on Spring Garden Lane.

Toogood Junior lived above a row of Chinese shops advertising acupuncture, medicines and something that, from the pictures, related to male sexual problems. The properties were less densely packed, and opposite was a small park where a group of people practised tai chi.

Denis Toogood had given Balcombe a key along with an apology, presumably because he was embarrassed about where or how his son lived.

"Keep going, down to the bay," Balcombe said.

Albert obliged and stopped at the dock where boys were jumping into the sea. Laughing and frolicking.

"Go ahead, Albert. Jump in and cool down."

Albert stepped away from the rickshaw and glanced at the boys having fun. They were all naked.

"Not today," he said quietly.

Balcombe grinned at the boy's awkwardness. "Shy, Albert?"

The rickshaw boy said nothing, looked at the ground.

"Ready to tell me the other thing?"

Albert looked up and Balcombe could see his guess was right. Albert was a girl.

"Why?" he asked. "Why pretend to be a boy?"

"I was raised like a boy and I can work as a boy." Her eyes were moist. "Please don't be angry."

"Why would I be angry?"

"Then please let me work for you. I'm as strong as a boy. I'm as good as a boy. I really am!"

Balcombe laughed. "You're probably better. No wonder you can be invisible. Now stop whining and take me back to Spring Gardens."

Once there, he left Albert outside, climbed the stairs and let himself in.

The rooms were surprisingly clean and reasonable. The windows provided good light and a view of Kowloon across the bay. There were four rooms: two living areas, a bedroom and a toilet room. There was no kitchen, which didn't surprise Balcombe. He was told the boy lived alone and presumably had no need for a kitchen.

There were paintings on the wall in the first room which looked Asian and expensive. The bedroom had quality white sheets and Roger's mammoth wardrobe had an array of fine clothes. So the kid wasn't without a few pennies. He just chose to live here. Balcombe also decided that the rooms were too clean and tidy for the usual single man, which implied a cleaning person.

He returned to the first living room, where he'd seen a long chest of drawers. There were three drawers with three cabinets beneath. On top were five photographs. Two were of planes: a Spitfire and a Zero. There was a young man, too small to make out but presumably Roger, standing by the Japanese fighter. The third photograph was of a school rugby team with a trophy. Roger looked about twelve in the picture.

The next photograph was of Denis and Grace Toogood on their wedding day. Roger stood to one side but without the same kind of smile as his father. The photograph was in an ornate silver frame, whereas the others had simple wooden borders.

The final photograph was of Roger and another boy in rugby kits, muddy and grinning.

Balcombe opened the back of the picture and read the scribbled inscription: *Me and John, November 1947.*

Two drawers were stuffed with papers and the usual detritus. Clearly the cleaner's role didn't include tidying the drawers. But the third drawer was virtually empty, containing just a handful of well-used stationery items.

Balcombe emptied the first drawer and went through the paperwork. Nothing jumped out at him. Most was written in English with some in Chinese. Generally, he thought these were receipts and other financial matters.

The second drawer had an address book along with scribbled notes that didn't make any sense to Balcombe.

Turning his attention to the address book, he noted the first section was packed with addresses, mostly in England. Was that relevant? Balcombe took a note that he should find out when the boy had come to Hong Kong. Had Roger been in England for some time? It would make sense that he went to boarding school there and that the names were old school chums.

At the back were pages of names. Girl's names but no addresses. There were two columns of numbers. The numbers increased down the first column. The second increased and then fell.

Balcombe studied the pages for a moment before deciding he couldn't interpret the numbers. It seemed that Roger liked to give girls a rating, possibly even betting odds. Did he bet on his sexual success with the girls?

The Toogoods hadn't been very helpful regarding Roger's friends. They'd given him one name: David Jones. He worked with Roger at the bank and Denis said Balcombe should question him. They said they also thought he had a friend with whom he went to the Happy Valley races, but they couldn't come up with a name.

There was a loose piece of paper between the pages. On it was a name and address. The name sounded Japanese. The address was further east at North Point.

The cupboards held old ornaments and other knick-knacks. At the back, beneath the almost empty stationery drawer, was a piece of paper. He pulled it out and saw at once that it was a newspaper clipping. Horse race details, with a red pen used to circle two names.

So Roger liked the horses. Balcombe hadn't seen the boy at Happy Valley, but then it was hardly surprising due to the number of punters. Plus Balcombe hadn't been searching for him then.

There was another piece of newspaper jammed further back. Balcombe eased it out. An obituary for someone called John Daily. Died of a broken neck playing rugby. He'd been eighteen.

Balcombe checked the top, which was torn, but it looked like the extract was from *The Times* of London and dated two years ago. So John Daily would have been about the same age as Roger. Balcombe picked up the photograph of the two boys in rugby shirts. It seemed likely that John in the photograph was the same one in the newspaper. Roger's friend had died playing rugby.

Balcombe took a moment, looking at the photograph but not seeing. His mind was on Eric. So he and Roger had something in common. Their close friends had died in sporting accidents.

He sighed and stuck the address book and newspaper clippings in his pocket. He saw nothing else of interest in the room and went into the second living room. He guessed this was the equivalent of his office or library.

In a bookcase there were two sections—fact and fiction—illustrating three interests. One shelf was only half full and Balcombe noticed dust. Again an area missed by a cleaner.

The first section of books concerned the Second World War. There were twenty or so hardbacks in various conditions covering the war in Europe and also in Asia. From the covers, Balcombe got the impression that Roger was into aircraft and Japanese military successes. This included five picture books written in Japanese.

The other factual books were about gambling: there were various titles about poker and strategies for winning at other card games. Judging by one entitled

The American Casino Guide and another called *Psyching Out Vegas*, Roger also had an interest in the United States.

Balcombe flicked through one called *Gamblers and Gangsters*, and wondered about the overlap.

The fiction reflected this fascination too, with a pristine copy of *The Gambler* by Dostoevsky. It had a bookmark and Balcombe opened it. There was an inscription written neatly and dated six months ago. It was signed *Grace, your devoted new mother*.

There were also well-thumbed cowboy novels. This interest was reflected by three framed posters on the walls. They were for westerns that had been screened recently at the cinema. One of them—*The Duel in the Sun*—was signed by Gregory Peck. Next to it was a hook where another picture or poster once hung. Balcombe wondered what had been there and why it might have been removed.

"All right," he said finally, stepping back and looking around the room. "I've got a good sense of who you are, Roger Toogood, but where the hell are you?"

FOURTEEN

Munro had the manager of the cold-store room escorted to the police station for questioning and another statement. Despite this, his gut told him the man was innocent. Of this crime at least. However, there was something he wasn't saying.

Munro sensed he was missing something obvious.

He rubbed his leg while being driven back to the station. Maybe the pain was psychological. If his friend, Yeung, hadn't mentioned it, maybe the memories wouldn't have come back.

It didn't help that the cold-store room was only a block away from where he'd been attacked. And where his wife Yan had been killed by a group of Japanese soldiers.

She'd looked at them the wrong way. She'd not shown respect and so they'd set upon her. Munro had intervened but it was too late. Their batons had smashed her skull and broken his fibula and kneecap. How many times had he prayed that the injuries had been reversed? He'd have given anything to take her place. The limp was a constant reminder. He'd failed his wife.

Arthur Tam sat in the back and said nothing. He was Munro's best sergeant, and, until recently, the same rank. He was perpetually grumpy but had a sharp mind and seemed genuinely pleased about Munro's promotion. Tam was also perceptive and undoubtedly knew the pig place was close to where Yan had been killed nine years ago.

"Sir," a clerk said as they entered the CID office. "We've just had a call about another body. There are men at the scene but—"

"I'll go," Tam said. "Where is it?"

"By a small laundry near Jervois Street."

"Suspicious?"

"Very."

Munro looked at the ream of paper on his desk. It would be twice as high later once all the pig cold room statements were in.

He shook his head, blew into the stale warm air then said, "Let's both go."

FIFTEEN

The shop beneath Roger Toogood's rooms smelled of incense and spice. Shelves covered two walls and were crammed with jars with mysterious contents and indecipherable labels. Chinese medicine, Balcombe assumed.

"Do you know Roger Toogood?" He shot the question at the wizened Chinese man behind a counter. The man looked like he had a bad smell under his nose, or he just didn't like English men.

The ancient man spoke.

A voice behind Balcombe said, "He doesn't speak English."

Balcombe turned and waved Albert closer.

"Ask him if he knows the young man who lives upstairs."

"No," the shopkeeper replied once he'd been asked in a language he understood.

Balcombe held out the photograph—the one with the two boys playing rugby—and pointed to Roger.

"Hai," the old man said. Yes.

"Upstairs," Balcombe said slowly while pointing at the ceiling. "Roger Toogood?"

"Hai."

Balcombe unfolded paper money and held it out.

"Ask him when he last saw Toogood."

After Albert asked the question, the old man looked thoughtful, like the bad smell had gotten worse.

"A week ago perhaps."

He reached for the notes, but Balcombe kept them out of reach.

"I need more."

Albert translated.

"What more?" the old man asked.

"What was he wearing when you last saw him?"

"Clothes."

Balcombe smiled. "Specifically?"

The old man shrugged. "Dark suit. I think he worked at the bank."

"Yes, he did," Balcombe said. "So you saw him leave for work a week ago?"

"Yes."

When nothing else was forthcoming, Balcombe said, "What about other people? Have you seen anyone else come and go from the rooms?"

"Another young man. Usually at night."

Balcombe decided to peel off one of the notes and hand it over.

"Describe this other young man."

"White-skinned with brown hair."

"How old?"

The old man shrugged. "Young. Not too young. Perhaps the same age as the boy." He pointed upward like Balcombe had earlier.

"About twenty?"

"Perhaps." A hand came out for another note, but Balcombe shook his head.

"More. I want more."

"He had one ear." The shopkeeper put a hand over his right ear to demonstrate.

"Anything else?"

"A man and a young lady came a few days ago."

"Describe them, please."

The shopkeeper gave a reasonable description of Denis and Grace Toogood. That made sense, the Toogoods had come looking for Roger.

Balcombe handed the man another note.

"Anything else?"

"They were upstairs a long time. And the woman came back later. It was dark. I had shut up shop."

"She came back alone? You're sure it was the same woman? Young, blonde. About this tall?" Balcombe indicated Grace's height.

"Yes. She was quick. In and out, but I saw her in the street light."

Curious, Balcombe made a mental note to ask her about the second visit.

"Anything else?"

The old man eyed the money in Balcombe's hand and looked like he was about to make up something to earn more cash.

Balcombe shook his head and handed over a final note.

"If you hear anything useful, I want to know. I'll pay you for real information."

"Why?" The old man scrutinized Balcombe with piercing, dark eyes.

"He is missing. I've been asked to find him."

"Is he in trouble?"

"I don't know."

"Is he coming back?" For a second the shopkeeper seemed eager.

Albert had a rapid exchange with him and the old man's expression froze like quick-drying cement.

She said, "He's hoping the rooms could be his. It's not uncommon for people to be moved in and charged rent for properties that are empty. Rooms on the island go for a premium."

The shopkeeper spoke again and asked for a contact address.

Balcombe wrote his details on a piece of paper and handed it to the man.

"I'll pay you well—very well if your information leads to the missing young man."

The old man nodded then pulled something from beneath the counter. Balcombe hadn't been able to read the man at all and tensed. But it wasn't a weapon of any kind. The man pushed a bundle of shrivelled brown roots across the table.

"For you," he said.

Balcombe picked it up and smelled it. He couldn't smell anything above the scented joss sticks.

The old man smiled and pointed to hand-drawn pictures of male organs.

Balcombe laughed. "I don't need—"

"Everyone needs it," the old man said, nodding sagely. "Shave a little into your tea, and whether you have a problem or not, you won't regret it."

★

A man in a dark blue suit watched the tall, well-dressed Englishman come out of the Chinese medicine shop. He'd gone into the boy's rooms, clearly spent time searching them before visiting the shopkeeper.

The old man knew nothing.

He will have told the Englishman about the parents visiting. He will have mentioned the friend, but he wouldn't have mentioned their arrangement.

Follow or…? The man in the dark blue suit watched Balcombe's rickshaw leave and then quickly popped into the shop.

"Charles Balcombe," the old man said grinning. "I got an address for you."

"Good." The man in the dark blue suit handed over the promised money and hurried out with Balcombe's address.

SIXTEEN

Munro stepped around the fat victim and went up steep stairs to the rooms above the laundry. Going up wasn't as uncomfortable on his knee as it would be descending.

He looked back and momentarily considered the impending pain before focusing on the crime. The dead man hadn't been attacked up here and then fallen down the stairs. There was only a little blood and it was all at the bottom of the stairs. His body wasn't twisted and crumpled, so he hadn't fallen. He'd opened the door to the attacker but what had happened next?

Despite the victim lying on his back, Munro had seen a little blood on the man's neck. There would be a wound on the underside, but a small one.

His shirt had been ripped open to expose a distended, hairy belly. Under his chest was a slash of red. More blood, but again not much. A thin line like a surgical cut. Not deep enough to cause massive blood loss. Deep enough to kill? Munro thought it unlikely.

The photographer would be here momentarily then they'd get the body to pathology—and hopefully some answers.

The dead man was a national, aged thirty-eight and called Chen Chee-hwa. A detective constable had confirmed the name by asking at the laundry business underneath. Apparently Chen had owned it until a year ago when he'd lost it in a game of mah-jong. A whole business! Some gamblers didn't make rational decisions while they were playing. They either couldn't believe they'd lose again or misguidedly thought they were about to be lucky. Munro knew he was unusual. He didn't believe in luck. Not the magical kind bestowed by ancestors or the alignment of numbers. Man made his own luck.

A detective would get lucky if he asked the right questions and found the right answers.

The answers found above the laundry were pretty awful. Chen had held people up here. And one got you ten, those people were young girls. Either directly for prostitution or to be sold into prostitution.

There were five rooms off the main one. There was a bolt on the last but they were all prisons nonetheless. The girls would have been drugged and afraid. If they tried to escape they would be killed.

Behind him, Sergeant Tam tutted then said, "Typical."

"Yes," Munro grumbled. They both knew the issue. The girls would have been more than fourteen years old and Chen Chee-hwa would have argued that the girls weren't held against their will. No crime committed then. Even if the police had known about his little operation up here they would have been powerless to protect the girls.

"Except for the lock," Munro said. "Why have four unlocked and one locked?"

"Maybe she tried to escape."

"Or she was valuable enough to risk imprisoning."

The sergeant nodded. "Brazen then. If we'd known…"

"I'm interested in the motive," Munro said examining the broken lock.

No sign of the girls told him that they'd been released. Or taken. Which gave Munro a motive. Which would explain the brutality of the murder.

He turned to his sergeant.

"Know of any gangsters who might kill like this?"

Tam screwed up his face, thinking. Or pretending to think.

Munro nodded and started walking. He didn't bother to say the name Chau Hing. The man was on death row in Stanley Prison for murder. He'd used a knife and cut out another man's heart. There were rumours that he was the executioner for a gang, although Chau had denied any further killings. He claimed to work alone, but everything about him said gang member. Not Triad, because he wouldn't have been captured so easily, but he knew people and had influence.

Yes, they'd start with interviewing Chau. That had the gang possibility covered.

Tam went down the stairs first. Munro followed uncomfortably.

A constable was standing guard by the front door. He was the same one who had conducted the initial interviews and got them Chen Chee-hwa's name.

If the girls hadn't been taken by a business rival that left the other possibility… The locked room might have held a local girl. Maybe she *needed* rescuing. Maybe this was personal.

"Check for any doctor who's recently reported a missing daughter." Munro nodded to himself. A doctor tracks down his daughter. Kills Chen and releases his girl and the others.

Tam said, "A surgeon in particular."

Munro was pleased they were thinking along the same lines.

The constable wrote in a pad and then looked up attentively, ready for the next instruction.

What was the name of the laundry business owner?"

"Lee Son Huang, sir."

"Right. Let's talk to him."

Munro cast another glance at the body in the hall before following the constable into the laundry.

"Was he a nice man?" Munro asked the laundry owner after being introduced.

Lee chuckled. Then caught himself and frowned.

"What was so funny?"

"We didn't see eye to eye. And no, he wasn't nice."

"Did you know about the girls he kept up there?"

"Of course not!"

Munro shook his head at the obvious lie. "Do I need to investigate your business to get you to tell the truth?"

Lee's eyes bulged. "No. Ha ha, no!" He smiled, pretending to be relaxed. "Yes, I knew about the young women. But he'd only recently started and it wasn't illegal—they weren't too young—otherwise I would have reported it."

"Have you had medical training, Mr Lee?"

Lee's eyes showed panic. "What? No, I don't need first aid—"

Munro shook his head at the other man's show of discomfort. This was no surgeon. Lee had thick fingers. He looked like he could hardly hold a chopstick let alone a scalpel.

"Did you see anything suspicious last night?"

"No, sir. I left at seven and came back this morning before sunrise. That's when—"

Munro cut him off. "Which of your staff were here after?"

"All of them. All night. We have—"

Munro cut him off and climbed onto a box. He looked down the long room full of white sheets in various stages of being cleaned. The place smelled of soap, starch and bleach.

In a booming voice, he said, "Which of you saw someone in the alley last evening?"

There were two men and three women. Five pairs of eyes swivelled his way and then down.

"I'll take you all down to the station if no one comes forward," Munro said.

Still no one responded.

"Last chance," Munro said.

A young man towards the rear put his hand up. Munro beckoned him over and stepped down from the box.

The man was naked from the waist up and looked like his skin barely clung to his bones. It was unnaturally white, like the sheets.

"What did you see?" Munro asked.

The man looked nervous. And he had a right to be. As many as five hundred citizens could be arrested in a single day and most for minor offences. They might not be able to convict the bad guys for forcibly taking or detaining a person but they could charge anyone with a spitting offence or pissing in the street.

"Come on, man," Munro said. "You didn't kill Chen, did you?"

"No, sir!"

"Then you've nothing to fear. Just tell us what you know."

The washer-man sucked in air to calm himself. "I saw Mr Chen come home last night."

"What time?" Tam asked too abruptly, and Munro patted the air to ensure everyone stayed relaxed.

The washer-man nodded and breathed. "About midnight."

"And afterwards?"

"Nothing until this morning." The young man looked at a fellow worker. "A few of us saw the pretty boy."

"Time?" Tam asked, now sounding irritated, presumably by the slow progress they were making.

"About six."

"Six thirty," the other washer-man said.

"Describe him."

The first young man described a teenager in considerable detail.

"How do you know him so well, eh?"

The first washer-man looked to his colleague for support then back to the detectives. "He comes often."

"He works for Mr Chen," the second man said. "We think he… we think he lures the young girls for Mr Chen."

The first one looked uncomfortable. "It wasn't illegal," he said quickly. "We would have reported otherwise."

The second one nodded vigorously. "They came willingly."

"How long did the pretty boy stay?"

"Seconds," the first man said. "We saw him arrive and then run away."

The constable leaned conspiratorially towards Munro and whispered.

"Sir, the boy they describe matches the description of the one who reported the murder."

Munro and Tam exchanged glances and nodded. The pretty boy had discovered the body then run. He'd found a traffic policeman, told him about the murder and then disappeared.

Munro said, "Name and address of this *pretty* boy?"
Heads shook.

"We honestly don't know," Lee said. "He'd not been working long and he never spoke to anyone here."

Munro looked at their faces and decided this was true.

"Last night," Munro said. "Tell me about Chen arriving home."

"Normally we hear him upstairs," the first washerman said.

The second added: "Walking up and about."

"But not last night?"

"No. No floorboards," the first said, glancing at the second man for support, and Munro wondered if they often heard other sounds too.

"I didn't hear anything."

Tam said, "And you weren't suspicious?"

"Perhaps he was drunk."

They asked a few more questions but learned nothing more from the men who had seen first Chen and then the pretty boy in the morning. Someone had visited in between and killed the fat man next door. Maybe they'd been waiting for him to come home.

Munro found himself looking into the eyes of the laundry owner, who seemed anxious.

"What time did Chen leave?"

"Leave?" Lee asked, giving himself time to think.

"We were told he *came back* at midnight, so he went out."

"After I left," Lee said. Munro decided that was true, although the manager was hiding something.

His awkwardness was saved by the second washerman, who said, "Nine o'clock."

Munro said, "So the key question is did you see anyone in the alley between the time he left and the time he returned."

Heads shook—including Lee's.

Munro waited but still no one was forthcoming.

"Right," Munro said, nodding first at his sergeant and then towards Lee.

"Right!" Tam growled. "Mr Lee, you are coming with us to the station. DC Wu"—he addressed the constable—"take statements from everyone else."

Lee's eyes were wide with desperation. "But I didn't see anyone! The only people I saw were earlier. A white man and a girl."

"What time?" Tam asked, already in the process of handcuffing the owner.

"Four-ish."

Munro shook his head. A white man, and too early in the day to be related to the murder.

"Anything else you'd like to add?" he asked.

Lee shook his head in desperation. "I don't know."

Tam cracked his knuckles. "A good beating will make you talk. Take this man away," he called, and beckoned two more policemen into the laundry room.

Munro and Tam followed them out.

"He's hiding something," Tam said.

"Yes."

"I'll get him to talk."

Munro looked up and down the alley. It would be surprising for a white man to come down here. Could it have been true? Was he here to sample Chen's goods?

He said, "Maybe, but it doesn't mean he's our killer, and you know…"

Sergeant Tam breathed out heavily.

Munro said, "You find out what Lee is hiding and I'll arrange the meeting at Stanley. We'll look into the possibility it was a gang and have a talk with your friend Chau Hing."

Tam snorted.

"A problem?"

"No," Tam said, but his voice betrayed the lie.

SEVENTEEN

"Where now?" Albert asked.

"Home."

"Already?"

Balcombe took a breath and shook his head, although the girl couldn't see him. She was pulling him west towards the centre.

"We agreed you would be my transportation and my translator."

"And spy," she added.

"But don't question me. Understood?"

Albert didn't reply, she just picked up the pace and he again marvelled at her strength and fitness, pulling a man twice her size in the heat of the day.

When she stopped outside his building, he told her to wait on the side road and stay there until he came for her later. Under no circumstances was she to follow him.

This time, when he said, "Understood?" she bobbed her head in obedience.

Thirty minutes later, after a wash, change of clothes and cup of tea, he slipped out and got another rickshaw.

★

The man in the dark blue suit found his boss sitting in his favourite chair looking out to sea. The man had a gin and tonic in one hand and a cigar in the other.

The boss hadn't been born in Holland, but he played on his Dutch heritage and deliberately spoke in accented English. He took a sip of his drink and squinted up at the younger man.

"Yes?"

"Sir, someone—a white man—visited the boy's rooms and is asking questions."

"Trying to find Toogood?"

"Yes."

"Who is he?"

"He's called Charles Balcombe, lives on Queen's Street opposite the Connaught Hotel. He's a socialite and a bit of a ladies man it would seem."

"Why is he looking for Toogood?"

Blue-suit shook his head.

"Then bloody find out, man!"

"Yes, sir."

"And don't waste time here. I want you following him!"

★

The sun cast long shadows by the time Balcombe got back from a tryst with another of his women. His mind had been elsewhere again. He'd been thinking about Roger Toogood and how little he'd discovered so far. However, he'd shaved some of the root into his tea and had been as astounded by the effect as the woman had been delighted.

He had to wait a further hour before the effects wore off. *Less root next time. Much less root.*

Albert was asleep on the rickshaw bench when he found her. He cleared his throat.

She jumped up, looking flustered.

"I didn't follow you," she said.

"Then why the expression?"

"What expression?"

"Guilty of something."

She bowed. "I'm sorry, I was asleep and—"

"It's fine," he said, knowing she shouldn't have been on the bench. He knew it wasn't seemly to sit in the same place as a lowly Chinese. But no one was looking.

She brushed it clean and he sat down.

"Where to, master?"

"North Point—if that's not too far for you?"

She smiled, then pulled her hat down like she was ready for business.

He was pleased that she didn't ask why they were going to North Point. They were going to find the girl from Roger's address book.

EIGHTEEN

There was a fairground at North Point. Balcombe could see the top of the white Ferris wheel against the backdrop of the mainland.

Albert didn't complain, but Balcombe was very aware that this was twice the distance they'd travelled before. If Balcombe hadn't had his afternoon delight, they could have continued on from Roger's place.

The properties were modern and of a style in keeping with the fair: low and white. There was none of the typical ornate or gaudy Chinese architecture. And none of the usual overcrowding.

The address was on a second floor overlooking the bay in a row of eight units.

A young woman answered the door when Balcombe knocked. The name he'd found on the loose paper in the address book was Emiko. He'd guessed she was Japanese and was right. She was dressed in cream silk trousers and a blouse with a floral pattern in black and fuchsia-pink. She was tall and elegant with a delicate face, like a porcelain doll.

He read surprise followed by suspicion when she looked at him.

"Emiko?" he asked.

"Yes?" she replied. He could hear the Japanese in her voice, but the English was excellent.

"May I come in?"

She said nothing for a moment and didn't move aside, one hand firmly on the door.

"What is this about?"

Balcombe produced the photograph. "I'm looking for a young man called Roger Toogood."

He thought she winced briefly and a lip twitched, but she said nothing.

"Miss?"

She shook her head. "Who are you?"

"My name is Balcombe. Charles Balcombe. I've been asked by Roger Toogood's parents to find him."

"Why have you come here?"

Balcombe waited a beat. Hadn't he just explained? Then he decided to say more: "Roger's address book had your name and address in it."

"Did it?" She shook her head.

"Miss…?" When she didn't add a surname, he continued: "How do you know Roger Toogood?"

"I do not."

"You don't know Roger Toogood?"

Her lips tensed. "That's what I just told you, Mr Balcombe."

"And yet, when I first mentioned his name, you recognized it. I saw the reaction."

"No," she said firmly.

"Why won't you tell me?"

"I cannot tell you what I do not know, Mr Balcombe. Good evening."

She started to close the door but Balcombe stuck his foot inside, stopping her.

"What do you know?" he asked through the remaining gap.

"Go or I will call the police!"

"Why did Roger Toogood have your address?"

"Police!" the young woman screamed.

Balcombe backed off and found he was staring at a now-closed door.

He turned around to see Albert at the bottom of the stairs looking up at him. There were others on the street. Maybe twelve within earshot.

Eleven people were looking at him. Presumably wondering why the woman had called "Police!", although no one seemed inclined to do anything about it.

Eleven people staring. One man not. A man in a dark blue suit. He was standing in the shadows and looking the opposite way.

Then he glanced and gave himself away.

Balcombe had been a detective long enough to recognize surveillance when he saw it. And the man looked familiar. Balcombe thought he remembered him from the street outside Roger Toogood's apartment.

At first, Balcombe pretended he hadn't noticed. Walking down the steps he turned in the opposite direction. And then, without warning, he sprinted across the road.

The blue-suited man bolted.

When he disappeared between rows of housing, Balcombe lost the man, but seconds later he spotted him again, heading for the fair. Music rose and swirled like a Pied Piper's lure.

Balcombe followed, running hard through the North Point fair entrance and then up a flight of steps to a terrace where people sat, drinking at round tables. Faces turned, voices were raised, but Balcombe's focus was purely on the other man.

At the end of the terrace, Blue-suit glanced back and confirmed Balcombe's belief: his size and speed hinted at Chinese ethnicity, but he was a tanned white man with dark hair. He was small and lithe and immediately disappeared from view.

Steps at the end of the terrace descended into the fair once more and Blue-suit darted across a moving carousel. The music was loud here as the carousel picked up speed. Balcombe skirted it and saw the other man disappear into a cluster of stalls: hoopla, hook-a-duck, coconut shy, tin-can alley.

Balcombe emerged at the foot of the Ferris wheel and a crowd of people. On the far side, he could see the dark-haired man bob and weave.

Balcombe pushed his way through the bodies and then past queues at candyfloss and popcorn stands. Then he pulled up. There was no sign of the fugitive.

Human instinct would have made Balcombe continue, but he didn't. He knew enough about chases to know that he should stop and look. If Blue-suit had continued running he might have changed course. He'd been going east and could have continued to the end of the fairground. But a switch in direction would be smart, and Balcombe figured it would be south since north led to the sea wall. South would be dumb because Blue-suit could find himself trapped.

However, Balcombe didn't turn south, he walked back towards the popcorn stand. He was breathless. The fugitive would be breathless. The man couldn't run forever. So the smart money said he'd find the opportunity to hide.

Not in the queues. Not behind the vendor stalls.

The Ferris wheel turned and there he was, crouching on the far side. The moment their eyes locked, Blue-suit was up and running. He went west, back the way they'd come.

Again Balcombe was restricted by the crowds. He charged through, with arms out front like an arrowhead, and shouting, "Out of my way!"

He was through more quickly this time, and weaving through the stalls, when a boy, no more than eight years old, stepped backwards with a duck dangling from a rod.

Balcombe tried to dodge him, slipped and collided with a woman. She screamed and continued to berate him as he helped her to her feet, apologizing. He raised both hands, said sorry once more, and started running again.

Beyond the stalls he stopped and scanned the area.

When he spotted him, Blue-suit was running through the fair's entrance and out onto the road.

Balcombe pushed himself hard for the hundred yards to the gates before pulling up, breathless. More people were streaming into the park now and he couldn't see any sign of Blue-suit.

"Did you see a man running?" Balcombe asked as he jogged up to Albert. She was waiting on the street, watching him with a bemused expression on her young face.

"Only you," she said.

"He was white-skinned with brown hair and wearing a blue suit."

"If I'd known, I could have been looking out for him," she said. "I just saw you sprint away from the house you visited."

"Someone was watching us."

"Blue suit, brown hair."

"A white man."

"I'll look out for him. There's probably only a few hundred who could meet that description."

He nodded; she was right. But the Chinese medicine man had mentioned someone similar, albeit missing an ear. Balcombe hadn't registered Blue-suit's ears. Could it be the same man?

"Have you been eating popcorn?" Albert asked in a light tone.

He frowned. "Pardon?"

She pointed to his jacket where a piece of popcorn stuck to his pocket. "And you smell of—"

"Enough!" he snapped, suddenly cross at her flippancy. "Take me back to the Japanese girl's place."

Immediately, Albert was the dutiful rickshaw boy once more. When they reached the row of properties, she let him dismount before standing with her head bowed.

"I have been impertinent," she said. "Forgive me, master."

He pointed to a shop that had *Money* written across the shopfront in English, and he supposed Chinese, with notes dangling from strings in the window.

Once inside, he waved Albert forward and showed the photograph of Roger Toogood to the lady at a desk. He knew what place this was. A grieving relative could buy things to *send* to their ancestors. This involved a burning ritual. Money was available. It looked genuine, but it wasn't legal tender. However, it could be used in the afterlife. Allegedly.

"Ask her if she's seen this boy."

Albert spoke Chinese and the woman answered curtly.

"No."

"He's called Roger Toogood."

"You are wasting my time," the woman snapped in heavily accented English. From behind her she grabbed a pole, maybe the handle from a broom. "Get out! I have customers. I am losing business!"

Balcombe stepped back and bowed then held out some paper money. "I will be a customer," he said. "What can I buy for this?"

The woman eyed him suspiciously before, as fast as a snake's strike, she snatched the money and exchanged his genuine note for a bundle of fake ones.

He said, "Now, have you seen this boy?"

"No."

"Roger Toogood?"

"No."

Balcombe gave her a piece of paper with his details on, and as he'd done before, said, "I'll pay you well— very well if your information leads to the missing young man."

The old woman continued to eye him suspiciously but nodded and took the paper.

Outside, Balcombe looked along the row of properties. There was no other shop.

"Where now, master?" Albert said.

He didn't answer. He'd decided to knock on the Japanese girl's door again.

NINETEEN

"Tell me about the girl from the cold-store room," Munro said, his voice deadened by the Vaseline up his nose.

"Between eighteen and twenty-two, perhaps," Assistant Pathologist Yeung said, whipping back the sheet. "I'd guess closer to eighteen. Not a virgin but never had a child. Five foot two. Seven stone three. In good health."

"Before she died."

"Ha! I see your sense of humour is improving, Babyface."

"I wasn't trying to be funny."

Munro looked at the markings on the girl's neck. When Yeung rolled the body he could see mottled skin around her buttocks and lower back.

"I'd say definitely an immigrant," Yeung said, returning the girl to her original position.

Munro nodded. He'd noted the weathered features, tough skin and broken nails. The girl looked like a peasant. Made her way from China to the New Territories, came over to the island. And was then killed.

"Murdered?"

"Strangled."

Munro nodded again. All obvious so far.

"Tell me about the marks on her lower back," he said.

"She was found lying, wrapped in sacking," Yeung said, "On her side."

"Yes."

"She'd been moved. The marks are blood pooling post-mortem. She was sitting originally and not at the back of that meat locker."

So she died somewhere else and was hidden in the cold room. That's what Munro had assumed.

The assistant pathologist continued: "So it makes time of death really hard to determine. Too hot or too cold and it messes with the decomposition."

"How long?"

"Between three days and a week."

"That's not helpful."

"It's the best I can do."

"Any clues?" Munro asked, starting to suspect this was yet another unexplained death without an obvious suspect. They'd questioned everyone who worked at the site, but he doubted any of them would be stupid enough to dump a body at work. The manager was nervous. His statements hadn't changed under pressure, but Munro sensed he was involved somehow.

Yeung put his hands close to the girl's neck.

"He strangled her with his hands." The assistant pathologist shook his head. "Big, strong hands but nothing unusual about it though."

"What can you tell me about the cloth she was wrapped in?"

"Standard cotton sacking." Yeung said, grunting.

"Notice anything unusual about it?"

"No."

Munro shook his head out of frustration. "Anything else you can tell me, Fai?"

"Did I say she wasn't a virgin? She'd had sex fairly recently."

"How recently."

"Between three and seven days ago." Yeung chuckled.

"Very funny."

"All right, my detective friend. I'd say she had sex within a few hours of her death."

Munro considered what he'd heard. "You think she might have been a prostitute?"

"I'm not doing your job for you, Babyface. You're the detective. I just point out the clues. Are we done?"

Munro took another look at the girl and shook his head.

Yeung covered her, swivelled to the second body and whipped back the sheet. Chen Chee-hwa the previous laundry owner, now a dealer in young women—or at least was until recently.

Munro wondered if his friend was going to make a connection between the two bodies, but he didn't.

"So, body two. Much more straightforward for you I think. Male. Five seven. Fourteen stones and eight pounds." He chuckled. "The bloating is natural. He was a bit of a chunker."

"Chinese heritage. A national," Munro said, meaning the man was from Hong Kong.

"Yes, clearly. Aged about the same as us, but with worse skin. He was also a nail biter."

"Is that relevant?"

"I don't know. I just point out—"

"—the clues. Yes, I know."

The assistant pathologist continued: "Time of death clearer than our frozen girl. This chap was killed between eleven and one last night."

Munro nodded and considered the witness statements. "Very good, Fai. Looks like it was exactly halfway between. He came home at midnight and immediately died."

"The wounds are ante-mortem, although the cause of death isn't immediately obvious."

Munro cocked his head, intrigued. He looked at the chest, which had been cut open and sewn back together by his friend. The cut beneath the chest hadn't been repaired.

Yeung said, "First, I'd like to point out these marks on his arms. He was held down or knelt on." He rolled the body so that Munro could see a puncture mark on the neck. "And then there's this cut. It's between the fourth and fifth vertebrae."

Munro had seen a small amount of blood on the man's neck at the crime scene.

"Access to the nerve cluster?"

"Correct, my babyfaced friend. But definitely not the cause of death." He let the body roll back and pointed to the slash on the victim's chest. When Munro had seen the body at the foot of the stairs, there had been blood, but not enough for a cut to any major blood vessel. He'd briefly wondered whether the man could have fallen down the stairs. But it didn't look like bones were broken.

Yeung confirmed that they weren't.

"Thoughts?" Yeung asked, watching Munro closely.

"Just a slash. There wasn't enough blood for it to be the cause of death. I thought the cut looked surgical."

"Could have been made by a doctor?"

It was Munro's second scenario—a man rescuing his daughter. He said, "Or someone else with medical training."

"Here's the really weird thing, I can't be sure." Yeung parted the slash across the chest. "The length is seven inches to the left, just below the sternum. I wondered why. Wondered whether something had been removed. So I opened him up."

Yeung hesitated, like he would before delivering a joke's punchline.

"And?" Munro prompted.

The assistant pathologist shook his head. "Most strange. Disturbing even."

Munro waited.

"I've never seen anything like it, Babyface. From the internal tissue damage, something foreign was inserted into his chest cavity. Your man here died of a heart attack, I think, but not from the shock of that foreign body. His heart was squeezed. Odd, but that's what it looks like."

Munro stared at the slash. "You're saying what? That the foreign object was forceps?"

"More likely a hand."

"How the—?"

"Here's my theory, and you can go along with it or you can dismiss it as crazy. I think a knife was jammed in his neck to paralyse him. I think he was then pinned down—someone kneeling on his forearms—as they slashed below his ribs. They inserted a hand and gripped the man's heart." Yeung shook his head again. His eyes were wide, as though he couldn't believe his own words. "Munro, I think whoever did this squeezed your man's heart until he died."

Munro looked at the cut and back to his friend's face. "Is that even possible?"

"Oh yes, it's possible. This isn't about the how, it's about the why—in my opinion."

Munro nodded. Why the hell would someone kill like that when a knife to the neck could have done it? This was definitely about the why. Why kill him that way? The killer had medical training, he was certain. But he was also strong and probably big.

"Which leads us to one more thing," Yeung said, his voice suddenly lighter, more relaxed.

"Yes?"

"The bet of course! Whether you will catch the killers—and I mean the genuine ones, not just any lowlife who can be accused."

"I'll catch them," Munro said.

"So how much?"

It was a common thing to bet on the outcome of investigations, and the debate went backwards and forwards until they'd settled on agreeable odds. The pathologist didn't expect the crimes to be solved. He clearly thought the girl's death was probably too old and the man's too bizarre. But Babyface Munro was a good detective and he had a feeling.

He was going to solve both of these crimes.

TWENTY

"I told you to go away!" the Japanese girl said through the door. "I *will* call the police."

Balcombe waited a beat before speaking.

"Perhaps you should."

The girl said nothing.

He said, "Someone was watching your place. I chased them away."

"Someone watching?" The door twitched open a few inches and he resisted the urge to put his foot in again.

Balcombe said, "Why did you lie to me?"

"Who said I lied?"

"You knew the name. When I said Roger Toogood, I saw it in your eyes."

She opened the door wider and she regarded him calmly.

She said, "You are a stranger. Your questions concerned me."

"Why?"

She gave a minute shrug of the shoulders. "You know why. Surely. I am Japanese."

Balcombe nodded. Some Chinese people still hated their island neighbours, couldn't forgive the atrocities committed in the name of war. Which was ironic because they were also popular as prostitutes.

He said, "I am working for the Toogoods. Their son is missing."

"How did you know that I lied before?"

"I saw it in your face. You covered it quickly, but you knew."

She let a smile pull briefly at the corners of her mouth. "Yes," she said, "I know Roger."

"How?"

"I was his teacher. He was learning Japanese."

That made sense to Balcombe. He'd seen the Japanese memorabilia and books.

"So Roger came here to learn Japanese?"

"Yes."

"Anything else?" He raised an eyebrow, implying there may have been more to the relationship. After all, Emiko was an attractive girl.

"No," she said calmly. "I was just his teacher."

"When was the last time you saw him?"

For a moment she looked thrown by the question and Balcombe wondered why. It wasn't a difficult one.

"Well?" he prompted.

"I'm sorry, I can't remember."

Balcombe waited, but nothing more was forthcoming.

Eventually, he said, "What can you remember?"

"Not much. He had a few lessons a while ago." Pause. "You say someone was watching. Why would they be watching me?"

"If you were more open with me, perhaps I could help," he said.

She shook her head. "None of this makes any sense. As I told you, I was his teacher and he came a few times. But it was a while ago."

"Is he in danger?"

"I don't know."

"Where might he be hiding?"

She shook her head again. "I really can't help you, Mr—"

"Balcombe." He handed her his details. "If you think of anything…"

"Of course," she said, and shut the door.

TWENTY-ONE

Chief Inspector Carmichael had his head down, reading, when Munro knocked on his door.

"You asked to see me, sir."

"How's the workload, Munro?"

There was a ceiling fan spinning in the chief's room. The morning's air was cool but Munro still enjoyed the fan's breeze for a moment before speaking.

"I could do with ten more men." He said it partly in jest, knowing he wouldn't be getting more resource.

Carmichael said, "You're behind on paperwork."

"I—"

Carmichael held up a hand, silencing him. "Don't make me regret promoting you, Munro."

"No, sir. I will act diligently—"

"And get results," Carmichael interrupted again. "Your predecessor didn't get bogged down with paperwork."

Munro knew why. Cases were classed as solved when they weren't. Criminals were either sent to court with insufficient evidence or, more frequently, charged with a minor misdemeanour.

He dismissed the conversation as soon as he left the chief's office. Worry about politics, and the important work wouldn't get done. He especially wanted to solve the squeezed-heart and cold-store room murders.

He was glad that Carmichael didn't know about Lee, the laundry owner. Tam hadn't needed to apply much pressure. The man's secret came straight out: he was with another man at the time. Tam had no doubt about their illegal relationship, but married-man Lee had an alibi for the evening and night.

"We could charge Lee for homosexuality," Tam said. They were on their way to Stanley Prison, the drive taking them through the heart of the island, past Happy Valley Racecourse and through The Gap that ran between the peaks of Cameron Mount and Jardine's Lookout.

"I've more important crimes to solve," Munro said. "Anyway, there's no hard evidence."

Tam grunted, staring fixedly out of the window.

They came onto the beautiful coast road going around Repulse Bay and onto the peninsula.

"There's something I've been meaning to ask you," Sergeant Tam began. "How do you do it?"

"How do I do what?"

"You've been promoted. Three weeks and now you're practically one of them."

Munro looked out to sea. There were at least forty boats out there, men fishing for their families. Beyond them, Munro saw white horses and crashing waves. The wind was picking up.

He knew exactly what his sergeant was alluding to. However, he'd decided long ago to keep his politics to himself. There was no point in questioning the authorities. That just singled you out as a troublemaker. The British were in charge and maybe, one day, that would change, but until then Munro's motto was to do his job as best he could and keep his opinions to himself. The attitude had served him well so far, although, after the Chief's comments, he realized expectations changed with the promotion.

Stanley Prison hove into view. It had originally been a fortress with a good line of sight both east and west. Then part of it had become an overspill for Victoria Gaol for a brief period before the Japanese invaded.

A perimeter wall had been built and for four years it had been used as an internment camp. Courtyards between barrack blocks had been in-filled with factory-like units: blank white walls and small barred windows. It now had the capacity for fifteen hundred prisoners.

"You know how many there are?" Tam grumbled as they walked along F Hall, following a prison warder.

Munro didn't respond, although he knew the answer.

The warder turned and threw back a comment. "Three to a cell at the moment."

"Overcrowded," Tam said.

They went through a door into what was known as the Print Room. Prisoners passing through here were fingerprinted to confirm identity. Munro and Tam merely signed a register.

The high-security hall was beyond and they were escorted into the interview room rather than walk down death row.

The chairs were metal framed with wooden seats. Neither the table nor the chairs were bolted to the floor. A risk, Munro had always thought, although there had never been any trouble. Punishment for misbehaviour was severe. Maybe brutal.

They waited.

The prisoner was brought in five minutes later. He shuffled with chains on his feet. His hands were also cuffed.

Chau Hing had a cocky look on his face and didn't have the same gaunt look of other inmates. His brown sack-like clothes fitted, rather than hung loosely from the more usual skinny frame.

"Sergeant Tam," the prisoner said as he dropped into the chair on the opposite side of the table.

Tam nodded calmly although Munro sensed his sergeant's tension.

"Sergeant Tam," Chau said again. "Still alive, I see. But for how long?"

"I'm not afraid of you, Chau."

The prisoner smiled again. "Oh, of course, not me. I can't do anything in here, can I now?"

Munro knew what he was implying. They both did. Chau had connections, had friends who would take revenge for his incarceration. It was something that all police officers feared. Retribution. Two officers had been murdered at the start of the year. Three men were in custody charged with the murders, although Munro wasn't convinced about the evidence against them.

Sergeant Tam had been Chau's arresting officer and would forever watch his back.

"Smoke," Chau said, and was passed a cigarette by a warder. Prisoners were allowed to smoke as a matter of course and could even request their preferred brand.

Chau put the cigarette to his lips and waited for it to be lit before sucking in and blowing a plume of smoke at the detectives.

"Now, what do you want?"

Munro pulled out a photograph of the squeezed-heart victim at the crime scene and slid it across the table.

Chau left his cigarette in his mouth and picked up the photograph.

"Who is he?"

"A dead man," Tam said sharply.

"Ha! You want me to help with something." Chau scrutinized their faces. "Yes, you do. You don't think this was one of mine. You want my help."

Munro said, "We want your help."

"Then get me out of here."

Tam shook his head. "You killed at least one man, cut out his heart, and for that you're going to hang."

Chau smiled. "Then I can't help you."

Munro said, "Tell us something—"

"And then what?"

"If it helps, then I'll get your sentence commuted to life."

"In an open prison."

Munro shook his head. There were no open prisons in Hong Kong.

Chau grinned as though he knew more than they did. "Lantau Island. The Prisons Department is converting Shap Long." He tapped his nose. "I know things."

Tam said, "So what do you know about Chen Chee-hwa?"

"So that's our victim's name!"

"Do you know him?"

The prisoner smiled. "Chen is a common family name."

Tam said, "I asked whether you know him?"

"Knew him, you mean." Chau looked at the photograph again. "He's not familiar."

The detectives stayed silent, waited to see if Chau would say anything else.

Finally the prisoner pointed. "Is that cut how he died?"

"On his chest. Yes."

Chau's eyes narrowed.

Tam said. "Most killers who use a knife slit the throat. Premeditated, cold-blooded murderers that is."

"You flatter me."

"Not really. Do you know any other killers who would—" Tam stopped himself. They'd previously agreed not to disclose too much and Munro was already disappointed that Chau now knew the victim's name.

The prisoner looked down at the photograph again. When he looked up, Munro detected a glint of deceit in the man's eyes.

"The man was cut in the chest, but that didn't kill him." He paused, presumably reading their reactions. Munro kept his face blank.

Chau said, "The killer stopped the victim's heart with poison on the blade."

The detectives stayed silent.

"Yes, I know a man who would do that."

Munro stood up. "You know nothing."

"I know the killer stopped the man's heart." His eyes narrowed. "He stopped the blood. Yes, that's what he did."

Munro said nothing.

Chau said, "I give you a name and you get me onto Lantau Island."

"Agreed," Tam said.

"Ng Yim."

"You have an address?"

"Give me a piece of paper."

The warder tore a piece from a notebook and handed it over with a pencil. For a second, Munro thought they'd made a mistake. Chau had a weapon. He could dive across the table and stab Sergeant Tam with.

Munro was still standing, and tensed, ready to react if the prisoner moved.

Chau laughed, licked the pencil lead and wrote an address on Ki Lung Street. It was close to Boundary Street, between Kowloon and the New Territories. He flicked it across at Tam then put the pencil in his pocket.

The warder quickly retrieved it, his baton raised, ready to strike should Chau resist. He didn't.

Tam took the paper.

Chau said, "Remember our deal."

Tam said, "I'll remember."

"Open prison."

"If your information proves useful."

"Oh, it will."

Tam stood up and the two detectives walked out.

"One minute," Munro said.

He stepped back into the interview room, leaving his sergeant outside.

Chau was standing, ready to leave by the other door. He turned, surprised at Munro's re-emergence. Then he smiled.

"Detective?"

"If anything should happen to Sergeant Tam," Munro said through clenched teeth, "then your time will be up, Chau. I will personally supervise your execution. You see, I know people too."

"Are you all right?" Munro asked as they drove back to Victoria.

"It makes me sick."

Munro said nothing.

"There are over a hundred and fifty men on death row."

"So I understand."

"How many were hanged last year?"

"Three."

"How many were hanged in fifty-one?"

"I'm not sure exactly. Ten?"

"Nine. And twelve the year before. You see the trend?"

Of course Munro knew the trend. The administration was tough on crime, but in the wrong way. Since the war, the population of Hong Kong had exploded. There were over a million more people now and crime had gone up disproportionately. One hundred and seventy thousand convictions a year, overcrowding in the prisons and plans to expand them rather than address the problems.

There were two issues in Munro's opinion: one was the arrests for minor offences, like spitting and unlicensed hawking. If convicted, the offenders might only spend three days in prison. Tough on crime? But at the other end of the scale was the second issue. Tam voiced it for him.

"The Commissioner and Governor are too weak. They're against capital punishment. God! I hear there's a commission to reduce corporal punishment too!"

Munro said nothing.

"If they want to stop the cane and cat-o'-nine-tails nonsense, they should be hanging more criminals."

"I agree the cat is antiquated—dates back to the old British Navy days."

"And don't get me started about the definition of criminal offences!"

Munro opened the car window and took a long breath.

"Like holding those girls against their will. Forcibly obtaining and detaining!" Tam said. "You and I both know they were prisoners, but the courts wouldn't agree. We'd have to prove it and we couldn't. So we get them on some silly lesser offence and before you know it they're out again."

Munro still said nothing.

"We need fewer civilian police and more detectives."

"Amen to that."

Tam swivelled to stare at his superior. "You agree?"

"Of course I do, but you can't change the law. You accept the failings and work within the rules. Unless you want to be Governor."

Tam chuckled, although there was little humour in his laugh.

After a long silence, he said, "I think I've had enough."

Munro looked at him.

"I've been thinking about quitting."

"And doing what?"

"That's the trouble, I don't know. The police and the prison service are my best options."

"Then best that you stick with the police."

"What do you think of our lead?"

"Ng Yim on Ki Lung Street?"

"Yes."

"I think it's bullshit," Munro said. "I think Chau took pieces of information we fed him, read our faces and guessed. And got it wrong. It wasn't poison that killed Chen. His heart was squeezed."

Tam said nothing.

Munro continued. "And the name and address he gave us won't be any use. We need a better lead. Perhaps go back to looking at doctors."

"What about the white man who visited earlier in the day?"

"Do you have any ideas about where we start looking for him?" Munro said without enthusiasm, knowing they had little to go on. "The Commissioner of Prisons matches the description, perhaps we should confront *him.*"

Tam laughed genuinely.

"Let's do that."

TWENTY-TWO

Tuesday dawned with a cool wind and a clear peak. Perfect climbing weather, Balcombe decided, but before he could leave there was a knock on the door.

"I'm Roger's friend," the young man on Balcombe's doorstep announced. "Mr Toogood sent me."

Denis Toogood said he'd arrange a meeting with Roger's friend but Balcombe had assumed it would be at the bank.

"You're his colleague, David Jones." The chap had fair hair and two ears, so this wasn't the man the shopkeeper had seen.

"Good morning, sir." Jones looked up and down, possibly confused by Balcombe's clothes—plus fours and rubber climbing shoes. "Is this a convenient time?"

"Come in," Balcombe said, and took the young man into the lounge.

Jones continued to look confused, although Balcombe suspected there was a hint of amusement as well.

"I was about to go climbing."

"Oh goodness. Sincere respect, sir. I have such a fear of heights. I can't even climb a ladder without getting nauseous. The most adventurous thing I've ever—"

"Stop." Balcombe raised a hand. The boy spoke quickly and Balcombe suspected he could talk for an hour without taking a breath. So he said, "What can you tell me?"

"About Roger?"

"Yes, about Roger."

"What do you want to know?"

"Where he is would be a good start."

The boy spluttered a laugh then choked it back. "Oh, you're serious. Well, of course, I don't know."

"You work with him?"

"Yes."

"You are friends?"

"Yes."

This wasn't working, Balcombe realized. When asked closed questions, the boy revealed nothing. He breathed out. "All right, David, just talk. Tell me what you know."

Jones talked about the bank and their department. He had worked alongside Roger since they'd started six months ago. He was diligent and aspirational. They socialized outside of work, playing the field for girls and horses.

"Do you work for his father?"

"Me?" Jones looked perplexed. It wasn't a difficult question.

"Well, both of you. You said you work together."

Jones smiled. "Oh, yes, of course, no. No, we don't work directly for Mr Toogood… well not directly. He's… Well, no."

Balcombe waited, but Jones just looked at him expectantly.

"Do you think Roger has run away?"

"I don't know."

"I heard a suggestion of drugs," Balcombe prompted.

"Ah."

"Is that why he's disappeared?"

"It could be. I mustn't talk about it." Jones swallowed hard. "It's illegal, you know."

"Tell me about the girls, David."

Jones relaxed and smiled again. "We like them. Roger likes girls."

"Any in particular?"

When Jones didn't answer straight away, Balcombe listed some of the names he'd seen in Roger's address book.

Jones grinned. "Yes, all of them."

"Is there a special one? Those names are from Roger's address book, but there aren't any addresses."

Jones shrugged and shook his head. "I wouldn't know addresses."

"What about a Japanese girl? Did he ever mention a Japanese girl?"

Jones shook his head again.

"A teacher? He was learning Japanese?"

"Was he? I didn't know that."

"Do you know any of his other friends?"

"Not really."

"What about someone with a missing ear? All I know is he's white-skinned with brown hair and a missing ear."

Jones shook his head.

Balcombe checked his watch. He could still catch the first tram to the peak.

"One more thing," Jones said. "Roger was worried about money."

"Specifically?"

"I don't know. I got the sense that he borrowed money or at least owed money to someone."

When Jones had nothing more to add, Balcombe thanked him for his time and the young man hurried off to the bank.

Thirty minutes later, Balcombe was alone and free climbing the Victoria Peak crags.

He began with thoughts cramming his mind, thinking about the Japanese teacher and the lack of information about the missing boy. Denis and Grace Toogood seemed to know so little about him. His best friend from work had little specific information. Was that normal? Granted, Balcombe was a few years older, but he realized he'd not been in touch with his parents for more than a year. They didn't know he was in Hong Kong. They didn't know his dark recent history. Maybe they thought he'd been killed.

Did the Toogoods think Roger was dead? It was a possibility, but surely they would be more desperate, more concerned if so.

As an MP, Balcombe had searched for missing men. Lots of times. And never once had they been found dead—except for when he'd killed them.

So the starting point was to assume Roger was alive and in hiding.

What was he hiding from? Perhaps that would be the clue to where he was hiding. Would he stay on the island or catch a boat off it?

Breathless and with a good ache in his muscles, Balcombe heaved himself to the top of the main crag. Standing, breathing the cool air and looking down at Victoria, he decided his next move. He'd trawl the shipping offices and check passenger manifests. But before that, he'd pay a visit to the bank and ask Toogood more questions.

Charles Balcombe walked into the bank foyer. A security guard beyond the revolving door gave him a respectful nod. A well-dressed white man entering the bank was not a risk.

At the concierge desk, Balcombe said his name and asked for an appointment with Vice Principal Toogood.

He'd expected to be taken to an office, but instead he was asked to wait in the public space. Aside from the security man, there were eight staff and three customers being served at the counter.

The air was cool and being circulated by four large fans on the ornate ceiling.

"Ah, there you are!" Toogood approached looking the same as yesterday, dark suit, a winged-collar shirt and tie. Although it was a warmer day, Toogood wasn't sweating. But then again it was cooler inside than out.

Toogood pointed to an open door. An office to the side of the foyer.

"Shall we?" It was a rhetorical question because Toogood immediately walked to the room. He waited for Balcombe to enter before shutting the door.

"Ah, Balcombe, you met young Mr Jones this morning?"

"I did."

"And what did you learn?"

"Not very much. Except a concern about borrowing money or owing it."

Toogood rubbed his chin, pondering.

Balcombe said, "But I went to Roger's rooms yesterday."

Toogood waited expectantly.

"You visited a few days ago. You and Mrs Toogood."

"Of course—looking for Roger."

"Did you learn anything?"

Toogood took a breath. "I thought you'd update me, Balcombe, not ask me questions."

"It's what investigators do, sir."

Toogood grumbled, then: "No. Nothing of any use."

"I have another question for you. Something that's bothering me."

Toogood looked dubious. "I've told you all I know."

"My question is: why wait for five days before finding an investigator. I understand you not wanting to involve the police, but surely—"

"My son is an adult, Mr Balcombe. It took five days before I started to become concerned."

Balcombe noticed a smile tweak at the corner of Toogood's mouth, which he thought was odd.

"Tell me about the money," Balcombe said. "Roger was short of money. Did he come to you?"

"He was always asking for money," Toogood said quickly. "He had an allowance and that was it. He'd ask for more, but I wanted him to learn responsibility. It's one thing to be a gentleman of leisure, but it's not going to be at my expense."

Balcombe nodded. His father had a similar attitude towards money. It had to be earned. If they only knew about his wealth now. They wouldn't be impressed, but he had far more than they or his brothers even imagined. And he didn't care.

"What did you learn at Roger's place?" Toogood said, snapping Balcombe out of his thoughts.

"I found an address book, but there aren't any local addresses, just names. Mostly girls."

Toogood smiled, presumably pleased with his son's interest in the fairer sex.

"But there was an address for Emiko."

Toogood's smile froze.

"I visited her and she said she taught Roger Japanese."

"A Japanese girl?"

"Yes. Could there have been more to it? I sensed she was lying."

Toogood looked away for a few seconds and then back. "Roger was fascinated by all things Japanese, particularly the military."

"I saw that: the books in his room. Japanese, military, westerns and gambling it would seem were his interests."

"Meet me in Statue Square at"—he looked at his silver pocket watch, which was unnecessary because the noonday gun had just fired—"Let's say at two o'clock."

And with that, the meeting was over.

Balcombe spent the next hour and a half asking about passenger ships.

At Marina House, he learned that there were roughly ten thousand ocean-going ships calling at Hong Kong a year—between twenty and thirty a day. However, most of these were cargo rather than passenger ships. There were three days between the last sighting of Roger and the Toogoods' concern that he was missing. During this time, there were only six ships that took passengers from the island.

Balcombe called in at the P&O Building, where staff didn't question his request to review the passenger lists. But he found that no one called Toogood travelled on the firm's ships in late December. He continued along the front to the Prince's Building and repeated the exercise at Thoresen & Co and Canton Ferries. Again there was no Toogood on the lists, but he discovered that more passenger ships had docked at Kowloon during the period. There were no records required for passengers taking the ferries to Kowloon so he wouldn't know if Roger Toogood had crossed to the mainland before catching a boat there. Balcombe knew he'd have to go to Kowloon and check more passenger lists.

With twenty minutes to spare, Balcombe visited Alexandra House and the passport and visa department. If Toogood went abroad he might have obtained a visa first. However, Balcombe was again out of luck. Denis Toogood had visas for China and Japan. Roger had none. Not issued in Hong Kong anyway.

Disappointed, Balcombe strolled the short distance to the square where the statue of Queen Victoria used to stand. It had been removed to widen the road so that the trams could run through. One side had become a car park and the other had a post-war prefabricated building: the PRO—public relations office. Behind that was the Supreme Court with its impressive dome. To Balcombe's right was the HSBC's headquarters, tall and imposing, set to the back in a subtle message of dominance. Balcombe wondered how real that impression was. Was banking now superior to the business of shipping or was it simply 'backing' it?

At a minute after two o'clock, Denis Toogood strode out of the bank's entrance and walked into the square. He was carrying a white envelope and wore a scowl on his face.

Three paces away, he stopped, his free hand clenched.

"Who the hell *are you*, Balcombe?" he snarled.

TWENTY-THREE

The vice principal of the bank breathed heavily.

Balcombe waited a beat then said, "What do you mean, sir?"

"I wonder whether you are a charlatan."

Balcombe's heart rate picked up. What did Toogood know? Surely his true identity hadn't been discovered.

Toogood continued to glower. "So out with it, man!"

Balcombe stood up straight, looked Toogood in the eye and said, "What are you talking about?" The indignation in his tone made Toogood doubt himself. Balcombe saw the uncertainty in his eyes before he caught it.

"I've spoken to the Governor," Toogood said, his confidence having returned.

Balcombe said nothing.

"He's a good, longstanding friend."

"What's your point?"

"You aren't what you say you are."

Balcombe shook his head. "What are you talking about?"

"You… you claim to be a government man. Well, the Governor would know—"

"Why?"

"Well, damn convenient claiming to be a secret agent from Whitehall!"

Balcombe shook his head. "Whoever told you that shouldn't have, sir. It was information shared in private. I do not advertise my true role in Hong Kong. And quite frankly, the Governor would not be informed of my presence."

"I don't believe you!"

"I don't care. I have a good mind to forget your missing son and just walk away." Balcombe said, although bluffing. The arrangement with Grace Toogood plus the distraction from taking another man's life meant he really wanted to continue.

Toogood said nothing for a moment.

"I'm a good investigator," Balcombe said, then for good measure added: "What other options do you have?"

"Will you find my son?"

"I'll do my best."

Sweat finally started to bead on Toogood's forehead. Balcombe could see the man thinking. Eventually he held out the white envelope.

Balcombe took it, curious.

"Five hundred dollars," Toogood said abruptly.

Balcombe opened the envelope and stared at the bundle of notes before meeting Toogood's eye.

"Why the cash? You said you were opening an account for me."

Toogood gave a curt nod. "It's open. The rest of the initial money—another five hundred—is there. I just feel happier knowing you have expenses in your hands."

"There was no need."

"Really?"

Balcombe looked at the man, trying to gauge why his attitude was so off. Did he suspect anything? Did he know about the arrangement between Balcombe and Mrs Toogood?

"Now I want real results, Balcombe."

"Rest assured—"

"And I don't want you to bother the Japanese girl again. Understood? She doesn't know anything."

Balcombe said nothing.

"Stop climbing rocks and start looking for my son… properly!"

TWENTY-FOUR

Munro liked to return to crime scenes. From experience, he found new insight could be gleaned or witnesses reveal new information. He'd return to the pig storage room soon, but for now it was a visit to the laundry where the fat man had been murdered. The owner, Lee, was still being held for questioning, despite his alibi. It was something Munro and Tam would use to increase the pressure on the staff.

Steam billowed from the doors with a smell like wet nappies. The same five staff were inside: the two washer-men and the women. On the left was an office with a glass door. Inside was another woman he hadn't seen before, sitting at a desk.

Munro signalled for Tam to head for the men while he opened the office door.

The woman looked up from her paperwork.

"Yes?"

"I need the room," Munro said. When the woman didn't immediately react, he barked, "Now!"

She scuttled out just as Tam appeared holding the arm of the first washer-man. Munro stepped aside, let them go in and then shut the door. He stood outside, looking in, blocking the view of the other staff, letting them imagine the worst.

Immediately Tam started shouting. "Who are you protecting? Who killed Mr Chen? What did you see?"

Munro heard the young man make protestations of innocence, but Tam wasn't having any of it. He thumped the table and shouted questions again and again.

"Who killed him? Who did you see? Which gang is it? Answer me!"

Munro could see the washer-man quaking like someone with dengue tremors. Either he really didn't know or he was more afraid of the killers than the police.

All the staff were straining to see and hear, including the woman who'd vacated the office. She appeared to be hiding behind a steaming cauldron.

Munro opened the door and Tam stopped his barrage of questions.

"Thank you, Sergeant," he said, and tapped a cigarette from a pack. The washer-man accepted it and placed it in his mouth. Tam reached forward, causing the young man to flinch, but he lit the cigarette and stepped back.

In an even voice, Munro said, "Tell me what you remember."

"Sir, I haven't done anything wrong!"

"If you've done nothing wrong, then you've nothing to fear," Munro said, despite knowing it wasn't true. He smiled kindly. "I'm hoping you've had time to think. People often forget things and then remember them later. Small things."

The washer-man looked doubtful.

"Is there a gang involved?"

"I don't know. Honestly."

"We can protect you." Again it was a lie, but the man might fall for it.

The young man's eyes filled with tears as he sucked in the tobacco, possibly hoping it would ease his fears.

"You don't know?" Munro said quietly.

"I saw no one."

Munro waited. "But you heard something."

The man's eyes betrayed him.

Munro pressed on. "What did you hear?"

No answer.

Munro raised a finger and Tam responded to the signal. He exploded forward and banged the table so hard it could have been a clap of thunder.

The washer-man leapt backwards, shaking more than ever. At the same time, Tam shouted, "What did you hear?"

"Nothing. Honestly!"

Munro held out a flat hand signalling for Tam to wait.

A plate-sized clock on the wall ticked loudly. Munro heard traffic and people in the distance, but the office seemed like a cocoon, another world, isolated.

He waited. The clock ticked. The washer-man wasn't going anywhere until he told the truth.

"Daiyu," the man said. "You need to talk to Daiyu."

TWENTY-FIVE

Munro nodded despite having no clue what the washer-man meant.

"Who is Daiyu?"

"The office girl."

Munro nodded again. The anxious woman was watching from behind the cauldron. "What about her?"

"She heard something." As soon as he said it, the young man exhaled like he'd been holding his breath for minutes.

The truth, Munro decided. The young man was protecting the woman.

Seconds later, Daiyu was in the office, facing the detectives.

"Why didn't you come forward?" Tam asked gruffly.

"You know why." Her eyes were as hard and cold as the stone she was named after.

"Tell me."

If she could have spat without being arrested, Munro thought Daiyu would have. Or maybe it was just her natural demeanour.

"Police can't be trusted."

Munro waited for more and she obliged.

"My brother and cousin are serving time for things they haven't done."

"I'm sorry to hear that," Munro said. "We're not here to cause you trouble. We just want to catch Mr Chen's murderer."

"And what about Mr Lee? You have arrested him. He didn't do it."

Munro nodded. "I know. He has an alibi." From the woman's expression, he could see she knew about her employer's liaison. He had his hand out so that Tam knew not to interject.

She seemed to relax, her cold eyes less aggressive.

Munro said, "Please tell us what you heard."

After a breath, she said, "I think I heard him."

"Who? Who did you hear?"

"The man who let the girls out. I think one door was locked." She pointed at the ceiling. "The room above here."

"What time was this, Daiyu?"

She cleared her throat, sounding like a bullfrog as she thought. "About nine. Long before Master Chen returned."

Since she knew it was a man, he guessed she'd seen him. "Describe him."

"It was dark of course. And he was wearing black." She paused. "But it was him. I'm sure."

"Who?"

"The man who came earlier."

"The white man?"

"Yes."

"How can you be sure if it was dark?"

"Because of his size and shape. I am sure it was him because of the girl. She was there too."

"The Chinese girl?"

"Yes, I saw her clearly as she passed the window."

Munro smiled. "This is good, Daiyu, really good." So the white man had come earlier then returned when Chen was out.

She continued: "I was leaving anyway and was intrigued. I saw them all run away in the direction of Bonham Strand and I thought: Good they have got away from that horrible scum of a man."

"What about later?" Munro asked. "Did he come back?"

"I had gone home for the night."

"Yes, but did anyone else see anything?"

She looked out through the glass window, maybe for reassurance, but Munro believed her when she looked back and told him no one knew anything else.

Munro said, "Mr Lee said he remembered the white man and the girl. Did anyone else see them?"

"Everyone. We all talked about it later because it was odd. We thought perhaps he was a buyer, but then again he had a Chinese girl with him, so maybe he was a seller. It was strange that they were together because he looked like a gentleman and she was a poor worker."

Munro called the others into the office one at a time and got very sketchy information from each of them. They all agreed that the man had been white with a white shirt and cream or tan-coloured trousers. Most thought he had dark hair. Three couldn't remember facial hair. The first washer-man said he had a moustache and one of the women said it was a beard.

"What do you think?" Sergeant Tam asked as they left the laundry. "Could the white man be our killer?"

"What would the motive be? And we don't know he freed the girls. The only witness was the office woman and she guessed it was him because of his shape and size."

"Why free the girls?"

"Good question," Munro said. "Why indeed. The theory of a father rescuing his daughter is unlikely if he's white, that's for sure."

Tam grunted. "A red herring, I think. The rescuing of the girls might not be connected to his murder. This is still most likely a gang killing. Undoubtedly a man like Chen had lots of enemies. And I like the theory that the gang took the girls rather than rescued them."

"All right," Munro said. "We'll continue with the theory that it's a gang." However, even as he said it, Munro sensed there was more to the white man who had been seen in the alley.

Munro went back to the statements and was working through them again when his counterpart in Kowloon called with bad news regarding the address on Ki Lung Street. Later, Munro had to pass it on to his sergeant.

"We can't go, not yet anyway," he told Tam over a pint of beer at the Wellington Inn. Both men had a taste for the warm pale ale favoured by the colonists. The tavern smelled of sawdust and hops. A thick layer of cigarette smoke hung in the air, and the occasional raucous shouts meant they had to raise their voices to hear one another.

They were discussing the cases, frustrated that they had no suspect for the cold storage room murder or Chen Chee-hwa's killer. Too many white men fit the description of the gentleman who visited in the afternoon. All of the doctors had alibis and were either at work or home. Which left their only lead. The address on the mainland that had been provided by the prisoner, Chau Hing.

Of course, the Kowloon police knew about gangs—particularly around the Sham Shui Po district. However, his counterpart had told Munro that he didn't have the resources for a general investigation. They also couldn't provide men to support CID on the island.

"It's rubbish," Tam groaned. "They don't want us to usurp them."

"Good word, Arthur."

"I have even better words but you wouldn't approve."

Munro took a sip of beer. He could see the frustration on Tam's face.

"Look, Arthur, all we have is the word of a convicted felon. If we had something more substantial—"

"I could get something more substantial."

Munro shook his head. "Don't do anything foolish."

Tam said nothing.

"And don't go to the mainland investigating without the Kowloon CID's support. Is that understood?"

Tam drank his beer.

"Understood, Arthur?"

"Yes, sir," Tam said. However, Munro had known him long enough to read his face. He'd have to keep an eye on the young man, make sure he didn't do anything foolish.

He should have gone home, but Munro knew he wouldn't sleep, so he returned to the Victoria police headquarters.

He worked through the reports on his desk, checking the cold storage room workers' statements and the pathologist's report. Then he made a call to the hospital.

It rang for three minutes before being answered and connected to the morgue.

"Working late?" Yeung said.

"Something bothers me. The girl from the cold store—"

"Yes?"

"Strangled by strong hands."

"Big strong hands, I'd say."

"How many thumbs?"

"What?" Yeung laughed. "Two, of course!"

"Definitely?"

"Without a doubt. Both thumbprints are clearly visible."

"I thought so. Thanks."

That ruled out his best suspect. Fung, the pig storage room manager had a thumb missing on his right hand. He couldn't have strangled the girl, and yet there was the problem of the key. Who had access to the locked room?

"And another question, Fai. This one's about the squeezed-heart case. Might the victim have been poisoned?" Munro was thinking about what the prisoner Chau Hing had said.

"Alcohol in his blood, yes. Poison? No."

"I thought not," Munro said, and thanked his friend before ending the call. The lead Hing had given them was nonsense. The man had guessed and therefore knew nothing.

Munro would tell Arthur Tam in the morning.

TWENTY-SIX

Tuesday evening was a race night at Happy Valley. The crowds weren't as deep and the upper classes didn't attend. In fact, it was the first time Balcombe had been there dressed in a casual suit. He spotted a few boaters, but they were worn by Chinese men presumably emulating the Europeans. However, there were still plenty of white faces. Maybe one in four or five.

Despite the differences, the smell of the earth and horses was the same. The distorted electronic Tannoy announcements were the same and the cheers from the crowd were just as enthusiastic as a Saturday afternoon here.

Roger Toogood was a gambler. Balcombe had seen that in his rooms—from his books, but mostly from the newspaper cuttings. Racing form and odds were in his blood, that was obvious. Which meant he would come to the races.

Balcombe hadn't seen Roger on a Saturday, but then he wasn't looking for the boy then and there were thousands of punters. He didn't expect to see the boy tonight, but he did expect someone to recognize him.

There were ten bookies in the betting ring. Until the next race started, people were five or ten deep, placing last-minute bets. Suddenly they dispersed, dashing for the railings to watch their favourites compete.

Balcombe took this brief respite to approach the first bookie in the line.

"Good evening, Billy."

The man showed his surprise at Balcombe's presence at a Tuesday meet. "Good evening, sir. Who do you fancy?"

"Not tonight, Billy. I'm looking for someone." He handed over the rugby photograph and pointed at Roger. "Do you know him?"

The bookie pursed his lips and scratched his head. "Seems familiar, but can't place him."

Balcombe barely heard the man above the crescendo of noise as the race concluded.

People started to rush to claim their winnings. Billy was distracted as he checked the result and prepared for the tickets.

"If you spot him—" Balcombe called above the noise and saw the bookie nod before focusing on the punters.

At the next bookie, Balcombe had more luck. The man remembered Roger as a Tuesday night punter, sometimes laying big bets and winning more often than not.

Balcombe heard a similar story from three other bookies, and one called Tom was relieved that the boy hadn't been for a couple of weeks.

"Got the luck of the Irish, that one," the man said, and Balcombe realized that Tom had the hint of a Belfast accent.

"Meaning?"

"A bit like you," Tom said. "You go for the long odds and lose as often as I'd expect. This lad wins more often than not. Although last time"—he chuckled—"he lost big time."

"When was that?" Balcombe asked.

"Not here. It was on a Monday—a week last Monday in fact."

Balcombe had to wait ten minutes while Tom paid out and took bets for the next race.

"Not here you say?" he asked when there was an opportunity.

"Racecourse number two. I don't work there, but my lad does." Tom patted the head of the young Chinese man who was working for him.

Balcombe waited for an opportunity then showed the photograph to the assistant.

"Yes, that's him. Lost a bundle." He smiled.

"How much?"

"Two hundred," the young man called out as he took bets.

Balcombe waited for more and was rewarded during a respite.

The Chinese boy said, "And he wasn't happy. Had an argument with the other chap, he did."

Balcombe pushed closer and handed Tom a few of the notes that Denis Toogood had given him. "Just for a minute. I need to talk to your boy."

Tom nodded reluctantly and stuffed the money into his money belt. "Just for a minute. Literally."

Balcombe pulled the lad aside.

"Tell me about this other chap."

"Similar age, similar height. Brown hair."

"White skin?"

"Erm… possibly. Perhaps mixed blood."

Damn, thought Balcombe. He'd hoped it was the same person mentioned by the Chinese medicine shopkeeper. Then his breath caught.

The boy said, "Oh, and I noticed his left ear was missing."

TWENTY-SEVEN

Inspector Munro had a message on his desk from the morgue when he arrived. He'd wanted to clear his backlog of paperwork that morning. Little hope of that.

Before leaving the office, he called for Sergeant Tam.

"Not shown yet this morning, sir," one of the clerks said.

"Damn!" Munro said under his breath. "Get me Kowloon HQ."

A minute later he was talking to his counterpart across the water.

"I think my sergeant may be on his way to find the chap I mentioned yesterday."

"The tip-off from a prisoner?"

Munro could hear irritation in the other man's tone.

"Right. As I said yesterday, he might be a lead in a murder investigation here."

There was silence on the line for a while. Finally the man said, "We'll keep our eyes open, Munro. No promises. As I told you before, I can't provide support and he damn well better not stir up anything. We already have enough on our hands with squatters on Bishop Hill. Immigrant trouble."

Munro calmly thanked his colleague despite suspecting that the Kowloon division could do more. He would have liked to send a handful of his own men over to support Tam, but he knew the Chief would be angry.

He tried not to worry about Sergeant Tam as he hurried off to the morgue. He found Fai Yeung filing paperwork when he arrived.

"Good morning, Babyface," his friend said without enthusiasm. "Another knifing I'm afraid."

"Same technique as the squeezed-heart case?"

Yeung picked up a cup, slurped tea and then set it down again. "Come and see."

The body of a girl lay on a table.

"Japanese," Fai said unnecessarily as he pulled back the sheet. Munro saw his friend looking at him, wondering.

"I don't bear grudges if that's what you're thinking... except for the soldiers who killed my Yan."

Yeung shook his head with sadness.

"Tell me about the body, Fai."

"She's five five and early twenties. Sexually active. Never had a child."

Munro looked at the girl's grey face. She was pretty. Very pretty perhaps.

"A prostitute? Where was she found?"

"In a nice house at North Point. Had money though. She was in very good health."

Munro knew what his friend was saying. The Japanese prostitutes operated on and around Wellington Street, and by their twenties their health would start to suffer.

"Stabbed," Munro said, looking at the puncture wounds on the girl's torso.

"Five punctures with a sharp object. This one"—he pointed to the one over the heart—"was the death blow."

"A lot of blood then?"

"Not as much as you'd expect if the stab to the heart was last. I'd say it was perhaps the second or third blow. And there are no defensive wounds."

Munro looked at the girl's neck on the off chance there was a puncture wound. There wasn't. Her neck was blemish-free. So it wasn't like the squeezed-heart case. The girl hadn't been paralysed first. Which usually meant one thing.

"She knew her attacker?"

Yeung smiled. "You're the detective, Babyface."

"Right."

Munro leaned in and studied the puncture marks. "They look unusual. Can you tell me about the knife?"

"About four inches long. Almost an inch wide. Not sharp though. And these"—he indicated discolouration at either side of one of the slits—"suggest a short handle. Very short. Although not necessarily to protect the attacker's hand since the blade was so blunt."

Munro thanked his friend.

"You know," Yeung said as they left the morgue, "I was going to ask about your pig-girl case."

He was referring to the strangled girl found in cold storage. However, Munro sensed what was coming.

"You were?" he asked, dubious.

"And now a Japanese girl. It reminds me of the question: What kind of karate do pigs do?"

Munro sighed. "I don't know."

"Pork chops!" He gave Munro a nudge. "Get it?"

"It's not funny."

"You know your problem, Babyface? You have no sense of humour. In this job, it's what keeps me going."

Munro stopped on the way out.

"What?" Yeung asked.

"Your bad joke—it's just given me an idea."

There was still no news of Sergeant Tam when Munro got back to the office.

"Question the pig-man again," he called to another sergeant.

"Pig-man?"

"You know, the manager at the pig storage place… the strangled girl?"

"Ah. All right."

"Find out who he supplies. That business isn't just about storing pig carcasses," Munro said, thinking about the pork chop joke. "There will be a butcher involved."

TWENTY-EIGHT

Detective Inspector Munro watched the men carry pig carcasses more than a hundred yards from the docks to the cold-store room. He would have liked Sergeant Tam to have been with him, but the man still hadn't shown for work. So instead, Munro had his junior sergeant by his side.

The pigs weighed about the same as a small man and he figured he'd be able to lift one. But he wouldn't be able to walk far with his bad leg.

These hard men carried two at a time. They weren't big men but they were strong, that was for certain.

"I read through your statement," Munro said to Fung, the manager of the cold storage room. It was late and the man looked tired as well as nervous tonight.

Fung said, "I hope you aren't looking to stitch me up with a minor offence?"

Munro smiled. He liked that Fung was uncomfortable. The man definitely knew something. But what?

"Why would I charge you if you're innocent, Mr Fung?"

"Because that's what the police do."

Munro waited a beat. "Tell me something."

"I know nothing."

"You had the only key, so you opened the storage room doors, carried the body inside and locked it again." Munro tried to sound convinced, although he knew Fung wasn't the killer due to the missing thumb.

"I don't have the only key—well, I mean access to the key."

Munro nodded. Fung hadn't had an answer before; now he'd had time to think about an explanation.

"Go on," Munro said, smiling.

Fung swallowed, uncomfortable. "The key hangs up just inside my office door. Someone could have reached in and taken it when I wasn't looking—or reached in through the window and taken it."

"Someone who knew where it was," Munro said, cocking an eyebrow.

"Yes," Fung said, happy that Munro was buying his story.

Munro said nothing and watched the manager's face change as thoughts went through his mind. The change was gradual, but it went from confidence to doubt to fear.

Munro finally nodded. "This isn't your only business, is it?"

Fung cleared his throat. "I just manage this cold room."

"And where do the carcasses go after?"

Fung didn't answer immediately, and Munro saw something in the man's eyes. This was what he hadn't wanted to disclose.

"The butchers," Fung said quietly.

"And the butcher would know where you hang your key?"

Fung's mouth was dry. "Yes."

After being pressed, he then gave Munro the address of the butcher's shop, and ten minutes later, Munro was banging on a door.

"What?" a voice barked.

Munro stared at the man wearing a traditional butcher's apron. His features reminded Munro of the cold storage room manager.

"Name?" Munro asked after his sergeant showed his police warrant card.

"Haoran."

"Not your given name."

The pig butcher shrugged. "Fung."

Ah, that's why there was a resemblance. "Your brother runs the cold-store room."

Fung grunted.

"I'll take that as a yes." Munro and his sergeant walked inside. It was a small room with a pig carcass hanging at the back and various cuts of chopped meat.

"I didn't do it," Fung said as they looked around.

The sergeant said, "Didn't do what?"

"Kill the girl." He smiled confidently. "And before you challenge me, of course I know about the girl found strangled at my brother's place."

"Does it bother you?"

Fung struggled with the idea. Finally he said, "I'd only worry if she was mistaken for a pig." He laughed. "Can you imagine it if I chopped up some immigrant girl?"

Munro stared at him, waiting for the man to wonder about what he'd said.

"What?" Fung said.

"How did you know she was an immigrant?"

Fung swallowed and said nothing.

"Arrest him, sergeant," Munro said to the junior detective. "I think we have our killer."

TWENTY-NINE

Cat Street was buzzing with anticipation. The Chinese shopkeepers were either excited by the upcoming Christian religious celebration or they enjoyed encouraging the Europeans: whip up the enthusiasm and reap the financial rewards. Balcombe decided it was probably a little of both.

He'd spent an hour with Barbara McGowan, who'd arranged to use a friend's room for their rendezvous. She'd wanted the same thrill as before, insisting he squeeze her neck.

She has no idea how close I came to killing her.

This time, he controlled the strangulation. For her, the pleasure seemed the same. For him, it was just going through the motions. As he walked past the street vendors, ignoring their calls for his custom, he decided that it was time to end the relationship. Barbara McGowan certainly presented the risk, but the excitement was diminishing fast. He needed a new lover and knew he wanted it to be Grace Toogood.

But where was Roger?

After freshening up, Balcombe strolled to Central and queued on Star Ferry Pier.

The morning arrivals were packed with workers. The returning ferries were less than half full and Balcombe found himself on the *Polar Star* talking to an insurance broker. During the forty-minute chug across the strait, he discovered that the ferry firm had originally been established by an Indian merchant who loved Tennyson's poem 'Crossing the Bar' so much that he renamed the business Star Ferry. The insurance man recited the poem, which he said was about crossing over to the afterlife. Then he laughed and said that going to Kowloon was Hell compared to the island's paradise.

Balcombe thought this hyperbole was founded on misguided first impressions.

From Victoria, Kowloon appeared low-rise except for an imposing clock tower. Arriving at the public dock, passengers discovered that this fine building hid a railway terminus. To the left was a bus depot with grimy Customs buildings and the police headquarters behind. The road swept around, and the long stretch of quays with godowns and docks provided nothing but a functional and ugly view. There was none of the opulence of Hong Kong Island. It was as though the wheat had been separated from the chaff—and this was the chaff.

However, he wasn't here to see the sights, he was checking the passenger records. He asked a Customs officer and was directed back towards the terminus to Middle Road, where there was a block with shipping companies. Balcombe found the Orient Line Company and had to show fake credentials from the Special Investigations Branch before the manager, called Smyth, reluctantly let him check the records.

"From Whitfield Barracks?" Smyth asked, curious.

"North Barracks on the island." Balcombe felt a frisson of excitement. Did this chap know the military police here? After a smile, he added: "Colonel Stanford-Jones. He's the CO."

"I've heard the name."

"A good man," Balcombe said, although he himself had only heard the colonel's name in passing. Elaboration added depth to his deception—providing the shipping manager didn't know the colonel, that was.

He didn't, and it took Balcombe less than ten minutes to confirm Toogood hadn't been on an Orient Line steamer. They'd had two cruise ships at the port. On the 16th there was one en route to Japan and on the 18th one bound for the Philippines.

"If I were you, I'd be checking the commercial ships," the shipping man said.

"Why's that?" Balcombe had dismissed them because no gentleman would hitch a ride on a merchant boat. But then again, a desperate fugitive would find any means of escape.

"Well, you're the investigator. Don't let me tell you how to do your job, but I heard the last AWOL from Whitfield Barracks caught a cargo ship to Singapore. Passed himself off as a ship's hand."

If this was true then someone must have found out. Otherwise Smyth wouldn't know about it.

Smyth grinned. "I have a couple of friends at Whitfield Barracks—in case you're wondering how I know."

"How did they find him?" Balcombe prompted.

The man shrugged as though it was obvious. "Still need paperwork—unless you're a stowaway. Just like a passenger list. If someone's joining a ship to work their passage, their details are still taken down."

Minutes later, Balcombe had Orient Line's paperwork for people joining the boats. Ten ships, thirty-five men joining them, but all with Chinese-sounding names.

Smyth watched him the whole time. "No luck then?"

Balcombe shook his head.

"Do you know how many other merchant shipping companies there are? And where they have offices?"

"No. I'm hoping you'll tell me."

Smyth sucked air through his teeth. "Too many, but I have a proposition for you."

Balcombe expected this from the man's behaviour. "Yes?"

"I'll get you the list. But it will cost you ten dollars."

"How do I know it's worth ten dollars?"

"Because it will save you a day's work at least. And I know who to ask and where to look."

"How long will it take to get it?"

Smyth looked unsure, although his eyes glinted, knowing he'd hooked his fish. He knew how long, he just didn't want the job to sound easy. "A day or so."

"Are you working on Christmas Eve?"

"And Christmas Day. No rest for the wicked."

Balcombe agreed on the basis that he had all the names of men joining a boat since the 14th of December.

He travelled back to the island on the *North Star*. Halfway across, the clouds burst. The ferry was older than its sister, the *Polar Star*, with tired paintwork. Smoke from the stack stung his eyes, but at least the fair condition of the awning kept the rain off.

Albert was waiting for him under the shelter on the Star Ferry Pier and seemed to recognize Balcombe's disappointment. No words were exchanged except for him to be taken home.

Balcombe decided to let the rainstorm pass and to think. He was missing too much information. As an

MP, when tracking a missing man, he would try to put himself in their shoes, to think like them. But Balcombe couldn't understand Roger Toogood. He had too little information.

Unless he hadn't recognized the clues when he'd found them.

From the cover of the rickshaw's hood, Balcombe dashed to his building's entrance. Then he stopped.

Standing in the foyer were two men. One white and one Chinese. And from the look of them, they were plain-clothed police.

THIRTY

Two hours earlier, Inspector Munro had learned something very interesting. An old hag operating a shop close to the Japanese girl's home gave him a name and address.

Six other witnesses said that they heard a woman shout for the police. Seconds later, a man came out of the Japanese woman's home and down the steps. From their description of the white man, it was the same man who'd left his calling card with the old hag.

Munro was now at the man's address opposite the Connaught Hotel on Queen's Road. With him was Detective Constable Reece, a young Englishman whose father was a government official. He'd been educated at a minor private school that Munro had never heard of, and had passed his School Certificate. However, Munro suspected he'd had a lot of help because the boy had less intelligence than an ocean sunfish. Munro smiled at the thought because it was the boy's secret nickname in the department due to his blotchy white skin and thick lower lip.

Munro would have preferred someone smarter at his side—in fact, anyone other than the sunfish. However, it was departmental policy. When questioning a

149

European or US citizen, a white policeman needed to be present. No, it was more than that. The white man had to be seen to lead the interview. It was referred to as *showing respect.*

"It's bullshit, that's what it is," Sergeant Tam had said on more than one occasion. Munro had to agree, although he kept the opinion to himself.

He was just wondering when he'd hear from Tam when Charles Balcombe opened the door and shook rain from his hair.

Munro assessed the tall man as being fit and intelligent. Beneath Balcombe's clothes he could see a slim man, and his movements showed control and agility. *Perhaps he is one of the few Englishmen who do tai chi.* He had a thin moustache that made Munro liken him to that swashbuckling film star Errol Flynn. He had the actor's bright, questioning eyes and charming smile as he spoke.

"Good afternoon, gentlemen."

"Charles Balcombe?" Reece said.

"That's me."

"Could we have a few words, sir?" Both detectives held out their warrant cards and Balcombe nodded without studying them. He'd guessed who, or at least what, they were.

"Of course."

"May we go upstairs?"

They knew his rooms were on the third floor, but Balcombe smiled again as he shook his head.

"No need."

He asked the concierge for a meeting room. It seemed there was one off the foyer for such situations.

"So, how can I help you, gentlemen?" Balcombe asked once they were seated.

"On Monday, around five thirty," Reece began, "you were at North Point."

Balcombe smiled. "That's right."

"May we ask what you were doing there?"

"I went to the fair."

It was either a good lie or he was telling a partial truth.

Munro said, "And before the fair?"

Balcombe considered for a moment. "Look, I think you should tell me what this is about."

"A murder," Reece said, and Munro could have slapped him.

Balcombe's eyes widened. Genuine surprise or covering himself?

"A murder you say?"

Reece said, "A Japanese girl on Marble Street."

Munro saw Balcombe swallow.

"Marble Street. Yes, I know it. Runs parallel to King's Road."

Reece said, "I'm sure there's an easy explanation but—"

Munro interrupted. "Please explain why you left your calling card and were asking questions about Toogood."

Balcombe nodded, presumably accepting that they knew more than they were saying, although Reece had almost played their cards.

"I'm looking for him—Roger Toogood."

Munro nodded, waited for more then said, "Why are you looking for Mr Toogood?"

"Because he's missing and I heard that he might have visited Marble Street."

Reece said, "Why did you tell us that you went to the fair?" He pulled a smug smile that Munro could have wiped off the kid's face.

"Because I went afterwards. I went to the fair. I was looking for Roger Toogood, didn't find anything useful and had a walk around the fair. I got some popcorn."

Munro said, "Tell me about the Japanese girl, Mr Balcombe. Why did you visit her?"

"She was Roger's teacher. He's learning Japanese and she was his teacher. I wondered if she knew his whereabouts."

Munro nodded. "Why didn't you say this straight away?"

"Should I have?"

"We mentioned the murder of a Japanese girl on Marble Street."

"Was that the teacher?" Balcombe's eyes widened again like they had when Reece had said murder. This time it's definitely fake surprise, Munro thought.

"She was very much alive when I left her. What was the time of death?"

Reece opened his mouth to say, but got the message when Munro nudged his foot with his own.

Munro said, "She called 'Police'."

"She said she would call the police if I didn't leave," Balcombe said calmly.

"Why?"

"I don't know. She didn't like me asking questions."

"And now she's dead," Reece said.

Balcombe said, "I walked around, went to the fair, got popcorn and then decided to try again. You got my address from the *Money* shop close by. The shopkeeper recognized the boy's name, I'm sure, that's why I left my calling card. If I had killed... or planned to kill the girl, I wouldn't have done that, would I?"

Munro said, "Witnesses said you ran from the girl's house. You didn't walk around, you ran. Why do that, Mr Balcombe?"

Balcombe considered before speaking. "I saw someone watching. They had a dark blue suit. White skin and short brown hair. I would estimate five foot eight, ten or eleven stone in weight and maybe early twenties."

Munro said, "And you ran because you saw this person?"

"No one else mentioned this man in a dark blue suit." Reece added.

"If you ask the waiters at the terrace bar or the candyfloss and popcorn vendors, they might remember him."

Munro said, "You went back. You spoke to the girl again?"

"Yes. The second time, she was more accommodating, although I still learned nothing about Roger's whereabouts."

"And what time did you leave her?"

"About six thirty. I didn't check the time."

"Did you return?"

Balcombe's eyes flashed. Munro realized there was too much time between his visits and the time of death.

"No. Afterwards, I came home."

"Any witnesses?"

"Just the rickshaw boy."

"The concierge?"

Balcombe shook his head. "He finishes at six each night."

Munro had his chin in his hand, studying the Englishman. Balcombe was their only lead and his story appeared genuine. The mysterious man in a dark blue suit was intriguing but would lead nowhere. Munro didn't have the resources to send men to North Point fairground just hoping someone could verify

Balcombe's story. Even if they did, it wouldn't tell them any more than they already knew.

Reece stood up and offered his hand.

"Well, thank you for your time, Mr Balcombe. I hope we haven't inconvenienced you today."

Balcombe returned the handshake and said he was happy to provide any help needed.

"One more thing," Munro said before they left. "You said you were looking for Roger Toogood. Is that a service you offer?"

"Not really."

"Then why?"

"Because a friend asked me."

"And who is that friend?"

Balcombe hesitated before replying. "His father, Denis Toogood."

Outside, the rain continued to pelt the street.

"Coincidence?" Reece said as they jogged for shelter.

"Of course not," Munro said.

"Back to the station, sir?"

"No, Reece. We're going to pay Mr Toogood a little visit."

THIRTY-ONE

Balcombe was on Marble Street at North Point again. As soon as the detectives had left, he hurried outside and told Albert to take him.

Sheltered by the rickshaw's hood, Balcombe was dry enough and the rain stopped before he arrived.

He wondered if he'd find police outside the housing block where the Japanese girl lived—and died. But there was no evidence of a crime except for the DO NOT ENTER ribbon tied across her door.

He'd climbed the steps less than twenty-four hours ago asking questions about Roger Toogood and now his Japanese teacher was dead. Coincidence? Unlikely.

He put gloves on, ducked under the ribbon and let himself into her rooms.

She can't have been dead long before she'd been found. Even so, in the tropics, the smell of death often quickly pervades a house. As he stepped inside, he smelled only expensive perfume.

There was one main room and then a small bathroom. The living area served every function including a bedroom. A futon was made up with silk sheets and soft cushions.

The sheets were pulled up, but he guessed they had been done so hastily. He closed his eyes and visualized the events. The girl had been in bed. It wasn't an intruder because she'd got up and straightened the sheets. She'd answered the door and let the killer in.

Beside the bed was a bloodstain; irregular, as it had pooled around her body and been disturbed by the people who had taken it to the morgue.

A clean and well-presented room. No sign of a struggle.

The killer had come in and taken the girl by surprise. Struck her? Blunt instrument attacks were usually to the head and resulted in tell-tale blood splatter. This was unlikely, based on the blood. Not a head injury. A stabbing then. Multiple blows to the body he surmised.

Why kill her?

What did she know?

He looked up and into a round mirror. Had the killer stood here and looked at themselves in the mirror? Had they been calm or panicked?

Four expensive-looking pictures hung from the walls. All of them in the Japanese bamboo painting-style with pinks and greys—flowers and pagodas and bridges. He could imagine Emiko staring at the pictures and dreaming of home.

Apart from soft furnishings and a futon, there was a chest of drawers and a wardrobe. He opened the latter and noted fine clothes and an array of shoes.

In the drawers, he found folded clothes but nothing helpful. No diary or address book. Nothing.

Which was odd. Unless the police had already taken them.

The bathroom held nothing of interest, just a cabinet with make-up.

He was about to leave when instinct made him check the futon. He pulled back the sheets and confirmed what he'd thought. She'd been in bed before getting up to answer the door and then straightened it. Nothing else, he thought. But when he lifted the pillow he found a book.

The Haunted Hills. The byline said: *Shep Sherman, tenderfoot, rode a spectral trail of death that even seasoned cowboys shunned.* A western. A book that Roger Toogood would surely read. *Had* surely read. Balcombe thought back to Toogood's bookshelf. It had been dusted recently but he'd been sure a book was missing. And since Balcombe was a betting man, he bet that this was the book.

What had the girl told him? She couldn't remember when she'd last seen Roger. *He had a few lessons a while ago.*

Roger Toogood had been here recently, of that Balcombe was certain.

★

The man in the dark blue suit said, "Balcombe went back to the housing block on Marble Street."

"Where is he now?"

"I don't know. He rushed off."

The big man bristled. "You don't bloody know?"

"I'll find him, Captain."

"You do that, Davey." The big man paused and looked at the Union flag as it fluttered in a gust of wind.

"Sir?"

"Don't just find him, Davey. Get him. This Balcombe… his time is up."

THIRTY-TWO

Inspector Munro told Reece to park outside the bank.

"Shouldn't we make an appointment first?" the boy asked, his eyes wide with nerves.

"You want to be a proper detective, Reece?"

"Of course, sir."

"Then this is how it's done."

"But—"

Munro was already out of the car and walking around the monolithic structure to the entrance. He heard the boy scamper up behind him. He was right about protocol, but following the rules to the letter didn't catch criminals. Not that he thought Denis Toogood was a criminal, but catching the man off guard could pay dividends. They might actually learn something rather than warn him in advance.

After a ten minute wait, a young man—who described himself as Mr Toogood's assistant—took them to the back staircase. Their shoes echoed on the marble steps and Munro noted that Reece tried to step more lightly.

On the fourth floor, the assistant turned right and led them along a corridor. Obscured glass doors had names and impressive job titles stencilled across them.

When they reached Denis Toogood's door, the assistant led them inside and they found themselves in an anteroom followed by another door. The young man asked them to wait, picked up a telephone and announced their arrival.

He replaced the handset. "He's available now, but you only have ten minutes."

Toogood's office was north-facing with a view across the square and then Victoria Harbour. Munro admired it while Reece introduced them.

Toogood didn't stand nor did he offer his hand.

"What's this about?" he said abruptly after his assistant closed the door. "It's most unseemly to have two policemen visit me at work."

"Sincere apologies," Reece said.

"It's unavoidable, I'm afraid," Munro added quickly.

"Why?" Toogood asked. He didn't look at Munro but rather kept his eyes on his fellow Englishman.

"Murder," Munro said.

Toogood's eyes flicked to him and then back to the detective constable. He sighed.

"Sir?" Reece said.

"What about *murder*?" He gesticulated with both hands as he emphasized the word, like he was performing some amateur dramatic production.

Munro started to speak.

"Let the young man tell me," Toogood said.

"There was a murder last night, sir," Reece explained. Munro could hear the nerves in the boy's voice. He could have been insulted by Toogood's attitude, but there was no point. Someone like Toogood would expect to be dealt with by a white policeman. After all, that was why Reece was present.

"A murder, you say?" No dramatics this time. "Where and why should I be interested?"

159

"North Point. Marble Street."

Munro saw a twitch at the corner of Toogood's eye, although the man said nothing.

Reece said, "I'm afraid your name has cropped up twice concerning the woman's death."

"Twice?"

"We have just come from questioning a man who was observed talking to the woman."

Toogood's eyes narrowed. "Woman, you say? Who? What's her name?"

Munro said, "Emiko Sasaki."

"Pardon?"

"Emiko Sasaki," Reece said, and provided the girl's address.

Munro said, "You knew her." He fired it as a statement to watch Toogood's reaction.

Toogood's face was set, expressionless, as he looked at Reece. "How did you get my name?"

The young detective said, "The man we questioned said he was working for you."

"His name?"

"Charles Balcombe. Is he working for you, sir?"

"Yes, he is."

"He said he was looking for your son Roger."

Munro cleared his throat expressing his disapproval. Reece should be holding back such information and getting it first from Toogood.

"That is correct." Toogood took a breath. "Are you telling me that Balcombe has had something to do with this... this murder?"

Munro shook his head and Reece spoke. "No, sir. The timings don't work. Mr Balcombe visited the young lady late in the afternoon whereas the murder took place during the night. We understand that Miss Sasaki was your son's teacher."

Toogood looked uncertain.

"She taught Japanese."

"Ah, right, that must be it," Toogood said, and Munro wondered if he hadn't known about his son's lessons.

"You said *twice*. My name had come up *twice*. I presume you don't mean from Balcombe and someone else about my son."

Reece said, "You own Miss Sasaki's house on Marble Street. Your name is on the deeds."

Toogood nodded slowly. "That's correct. I have a portfolio of properties."

"So Miss Sasaki was a tenant?" Munro said more abruptly than he'd intended.

"Correct. But don't think for a minute that I knew her. I have an estate manager who handles the properties."

Reece asked for the man's name and promptly wrote it in his notebook. "Thank you for your time, sir."

Munro bristled. The interview wasn't over. "Where were you last night, Mr Toogood?"

"At the club." By which he meant the Hong Kong Club, of course.

"And what time did you leave?"

Toogood waited a beat then slowly met Munro's gaze.

"I stayed all night." He broke the contact and looked back at the younger detective. "I was working late at the bank and needed an early start. I often stay over, especially after..." Toogood raised his right hand as though holding a glass.

"That's understandable," Reece said.

"Who should we approach for an alibi?" Munro asked.

"What?" Toogood's jaw tensed and his pale skin reddened. "I don't need a bloody alibi, man! Who do you think you are?"

"Detective Ins—" Munro started.

Toogood didn't let him finish. "This meeting is over. I'm a busy man. Good day, gentlemen."

THIRTY-THREE

Racecourse number two was more of a practice ground with stables. They had races on Mondays, Wednesdays and Fridays. The best horses didn't race here because there was no official prize money. Although plenty of money changed hands.

When Balcombe saw Tom's assistant—the one who had recognized Roger Toogood yesterday—he asked, "Any more thoughts? Remembered anything else?"

"Sorry, no."

Balcombe worked the line of bookies like he had at Happy Valley but got no luck. No one recognized Roger's photograph or the description of his friend. Or at least was willing to admit it.

The Chinese medicine shopkeeper had said no right ear. Tom's assistant thought it was his left. The former had said a white man. The assistant had said probably mixed blood. The unreliability of witnesses!

There were a few hundred punters at the meet that evening. Most of the faces were Chinese. The bookies were a mix of Chinese and Indians. Balcombe spotted only a handful of white men.

He approached each of them and showed Roger's photograph. Each time, they shook their heads. It appeared that Roger wasn't a regular here. Neither did they know the one-eared young man. But then he struck lucky. A Chinese man overheard the conversation and pointed to the stable block.

"He sounds like one of the stable boys."

The stable block was in two sections: horses which were visiting for the races and those which were permanently stabled there.

Balcombe wasn't allowed near the horses preparing for the races but managed to speak to a few people who would give him the time of day.

"Missing an ear?" a trainer said, looking curious.

"Yes, and either white or mixed-race."

The man nodded. "Sounds like Barry."

"Barry?"

"I don't know his surname. Senior stableman." He pointed at the other section and laughed. "One of his ears was bitten off by a horse."

At the other block, Balcombe went into the office.

A manager looked up from his ledger. "You're looking for Barry?"

"He works here?"

The manager squinted, curious. "Yes."

"Where can I find him?"

"Why do you want to—" He looked out of the window and tracked someone leading a horse into a stable.

"Is that him?"

Balcombe saw from the man's eyes that it was. He ducked outside just as the stableman bolted the stable door.

"Barry?"

The young man looked at him and froze. They were thirty yards apart. Balcombe started walking. A horse trotted between them, and before it passed, Barry was running.

He ran to the end of the shed and disappeared through a gap. Balcombe sprinted after him. On the other side, he hoped to see the young man running straight for the road, but he wasn't. Balcombe swung around, searching. The young man had gone left or right around the rear of the stable block, circling back. Balcombe ran left thinking Barry would get away from the racecourse, but he hadn't. When Balcombe reached the office he finally spotted a running figure.

Barry had run for the crowds rather than try and get away.

Balcombe went after him, but the young man soon disappeared into the throng, and when Balcombe got to the body of race-goers, he was nowhere to be seen.

Balcombe worked his way along the side of the course, checking to make sure the fugitive hadn't slipped past. At the end, he worked his way back. Then he found a spot, midway and thirty paces out, where he could observe.

He watched and waited as one by one the punters filtered away. Then the last race finished. The light was fading fast as the crowds dispersed. Balcombe kept watching until the final few men left.

Frustrated, he returned to the stables.

"Did he come back?" he asked the office manager.

"What's this about?" the man said defensively.

"I'm looking for someone and think Barry might be able to help."

The man thought for a minute. "All right," he said eventually.

Balcombe waited.

"Barry's the senior stableman here. He's very good at his job."

"I understand," Balcombe said. "You don't want him to be in any trouble."

The office manager nodded. "He's good with the horses. A natural, which is surprising for a Greek. His real name is Demitri Baros but everyone calls him Barry." The manager looked over Balcombe's shoulder. "Excuse me."

The man jumped up and called out to a boy leading a horse. They exchanged words and he came back and wrote in his ledger.

He looked up at Balcombe. "Why did you say you were looking for Barry?"

"I'm looking for a young man called Roger Toogood. Do you know him?"

The man shook his head slowly as he watched another horse pass by.

"He's missing," Balcombe said. "Might be in trouble."

"I can't help you I'm afraid."

"Can you tell me where Barry lives?"

"No." He gave Balcombe an honest look. "We don't worry about such things."

"Cash in hand," Balcombe said, guessing how the operation worked. Minimal staff on the books. Maybe just the office manager on the official payroll.

He handed over his contact details and ten dollars. The manager's eyes bulged with delight.

"I'll let you know as soon as Barry's back to work."

Balcombe walked out. Beyond the stable's lights, the night was rushing in fast.

He'd left Albert at the main Happy Valley entrance but hoped she'd have followed and found him.

There was no sign of her so Balcombe headed back to the main road. He was halfway when he saw a man walking towards him. A man in a dark blue suit.

And the man was holding a gun.

THIRTY-FOUR

"You had the audacity to accuse the vice principal of the bank!" Chief Carmichael barked at Munro.

Munro stood impassively in the Chief's office in Victoria police headquarters. Denis Toogood had called Carmichael and complained and now the Chief was giving Munro a tongue lashing.

"What were you thinking?"

"I was doing my job, sir."

Carmichael shook his head. "I've read DC Reece's report. He says you asked Mr Toogood about his ownership of the property and he directed you to his estate manager." The Chief waited for confirmation.

"Yes, sir."

"And he thanked Mr Toogood for his time. The meeting was at an end."

Munro waited a moment before saying, "So it appeared."

"The protocol is for the"—Munro knew Carmichael was about to say *white man* but the Chief paused before continuing—"to show the appropriate amount of respect."

"I had one more question."

"About an alibi, for God's sake, man!"

"It seemed reasonable."

"Not to me, it doesn't. Mr Toogood is not a suspect."

Munro looked over Carmichael's head. Why was Toogood not a suspect in Carmichael's eyes? Because he was a white man? Munro didn't like coincidences. Toogood owned the property. His son was being taught by the Japanese girl and yet the bank boss claimed he didn't know her. He didn't know the motive, but that usuually came later. Opportunity was often the key to finding the perpetrator and opportunity meant whereabouts. Was Toogood at the Hong Kong Club all night?

Carmichael said, "Whatever you are thinking, Munro, you will not be going to the Hong Kong Club. You will not ask them to vouch for Mr Toogood. Understood?"

"Sir."

"And anyway, discretion would prevent them from telling you who was there. Police or not, they wouldn't break a confidence." Carmichael waited until Munro looked at him. "And I hear you questioned another Englishman as well."

"Charles Balcombe."

"I don't know the name."

"He's a friend of Mr Toogood."

"Oh bloody great!" Carmichael shook his head. "Do you know who else is a friend of Denis Toogood?"

"No, sir."

"The Governor, no less."

Munro said nothing and looked out of the window over Carmichael's head again.

"Do you have any other leads, Munro?"

"Not yet, sir."

"What about the pig-girl case?" He was referring to the girl found strangled in the cold-store room.

"We have a suspect. A butcher and the brother of the storeroom's manager."

"So, has he been arrested?"

They'd found sacking at the butcher's shop, like that used to wrap the girl's body, and neighbours suggested the butcher was a womanizer. Treated them roughly. But it wasn't enough to get a conviction, Munro explained to his boss.

Carmichael tutted. "So, he's still out there? Get him locked up, man."

"I'd love to, but the charges won't hold!"

"Is he guilty?"

"I'm sure of it, sir."

"Right then. Find the evidence. You know what I mean by that, Munro? I just need him charged and in prison before the end of the year. Can you do that, Munro?"

Munro understood. The Chief was asking him to plant or fabricate evidence.

Carmichael's eyes pierced Munro until he spoke.

"Yes, sir."

"Good. And the man at the laundry?"

Munro wanted to mention the tall white gentleman with the Chinese girl, but thought Carmichael didn't need any more white suspects.

"Still working on it, sir."

Carmichael looked down at his clenched hands for a moment. "How long have you been a detective inspector?"

The Chief knew the answer but Munro played along anyway. "Three weeks, sir."

"The most senior Asian detective."

Munro said nothing.

"Well, you are lucky that for the time being you will remain an inspector. Demotions can happen faster than promotions, Munro. Remember that."

"Yes, sir."

"Don't annoy Mr Toogood or his friends again. Understood?"

"Yes, sir."

"Good. I don't want to hear any more complaints about you. Ever."

Munro waited to be dismissed but the Chief had something else on his mind.

"Where's that sergeant of yours?"

"Tam?"

"He's didn't report for work yesterday or today. Is he sick?"

Munro tried to read Carmichael's face. Did he know more? Had he received a complaint from the Kowloon division?

Munro considered lying but was saved by the Chief continuing.

"Manage your men, Munro. Your workload is too big to have your men taking time off for sickness. Especially if it is booze-related. Christmas or not. Understand? Manage your men otherwise I won't think you're up to the job."

"Yes, sir."

"Don't give me a reason to demote you, Munro. Now get out there and arrest some criminals."

THIRTY-FIVE

The man in the dark blue suit pointed his gun at Balcombe and waited for him to approach.

"Who are you?" Balcombe asked.

"It doesn't matter who I am," Blue-suit said. "You're coming with me."

Balcombe noticed the car parked on the road as Blue-suit gestured towards the exit. He also spotted Albert close by, pretending to be asleep on her rickshaw.

He walked towards the car. Blue-suit followed a little too closely. Balcombe didn't look threatening, but he was fast. Rock climbing developed fast muscles. He knew he could whip out his knife before Blue-suit reacted. Alternatively, he could spin and disarm the man. It would be over in a second.

Albert glanced up and Balcombe shook his head.

Don't do anything.

The girl's head dropped again, although Balcombe was sure she was watching.

"In the car," Blue-suit said, and Balcombe obliged. He got in the back and the other man followed. The driver didn't turn his head, but started the engine and pulled away as soon as the car door shut. Again the gun was too close. He could disarm and take control.

But he didn't. He wanted to know what was going on.

"Where are we going?" he asked casually.

"Up here."

"Are you the police?" Balcombe asked, even though he was sure the man couldn't be. He'd met two detectives and could recognize the look. Their suits were grey or brown. Dark blue was too stylish, Balcombe decided. And yet the man had a gun. Guns were illegal without a warrant, and that meant police or army. And this young man wasn't in the army.

Which left him assuming an illegal weapon held by a gangster. A white-skinned gangster. Which was intriguing in itself.

After a short distance, they came to gates on Caroline Hill. The car drove through. Lights streamed from a large house at the end of the drive.

"What's his name?" Balcombe said.

"You're full of questions, aren't you," Blue-suit said. "You'll get your answers in a minute."

The driver didn't stop by the front steps but drove around the back to the staff entrance. At least that's what Balcombe expected. However, the rear of the house had a conservatory and patio. He could see a flagpole and two ship's cannons. And he could see a large man smoking a fat cigar.

Balcombe got out and strode towards the man with the cigar, ignoring Blue-suit and his gun.

"Mr Balcombe," the man said with a slight accent, Possibly Dutch or South African, Balcombe thought. "Welcome to my humble abode."

"Nice spot," Balcombe said, relaxed and friendly.

"Better in the daylight. Excellent views of the harbour and Peninsula Bay."

Balcombe nodded towards Blue-suit. "There's no need for the gun."

"Put it away, Davey."

"Yes, Captain."

"Captain?" Balcombe said. "Are you navy?"

"Jardines."

Balcombe had heard the name. The company Jardine Matheson were one of the original trading houses on the island, a *Hong*. They fired the noonday gun each day from their building at East Point, and Jardines Lookout had taken the company's name.

"Private militia," the man explained, "with a special warrant to bear arms, in case you were wondering."

Balcombe nodded. "Any other special... powers?"

The man smiled. "Not really. It's all just for show these days." He held out his hand and Balcombe shook it. "Captain Paul Van Ness."

"And you know who I am."

"But what are you doing and why?"

Balcombe thought to ask why Van Ness would be interested, but he was already forming an opinion on that.

"Looking for someone," Balcombe said.

"Who?"

"Roger Toogood."

"Any luck in finding him?"

"None."

Van Ness stubbed out his cigar and sniffed the air as though assessing whether fresh air or tobacco smoke smelled better.

"Why was your man at North Point?" Balcombe asked.

"Following you."

"Because I'm looking for Toogood?"

Van Ness didn't respond. He pulled another cigar from a breast pocket, lit it and sucked until it glowed brightly. Then he blew out a long plume of smoke.

Balcombe said, "I left my details at a shop below Toogood's rooms on Spring Gardens Lane." He paused, thinking. "You were watching his house."

Van Ness said nothing, but his eyes gave him away. Balcombe was correct.

"Why are *you* looking for Roger Toogood?"

"I brought you here. I'm asking the questions," Van Ness said, his voice edged with annoyance.

Balcombe nodded. "Of course, but we're both looking for him and we can share information."

Van Ness pondered.

Balcombe said, "He's missing. His parents have commissioned me to find him."

"They don't know where he is?"

"That would be the logical conclusion."

"Would you tell me if you found Roger Toogood?"

"That would depend on why you are interested in him?"

"He owes me money."

"Two hundred dollars?"

Van Ness looked surprised. "How did you know that?"

"It's how much he lost on a horse."

Van Ness shook his head. "Do you gamble, Mr Balcombe?"

"One can't live in Hong Kong and *not* gamble."

"True." Van Ness took a long drag on his cigar and blew out the smoke. "What else have you found out?"

"Nothing."

"Oh come now, Mr Balcombe… Tell me about the girl at North Point."

"The Japanese girl on Marble Street was his teacher. He was learning Japanese."

"Did she know where Toogood is?"

"No."

"She's dead. Killed the same night." Pause. "Did you kill her, Mr Balcombe?"

"No."

"As an investigator of sorts, what's your theory?"

"I don't believe in coincidences."

"So who killed her?"

Balcombe locked eyes with the other man. "My current theory is it was someone else looking for young Roger."

Van Ness snorted. "You think it was us?"

Balcombe said nothing.

"It wasn't."

"Who else would be looking for him?"

"That's a good question," Van Ness said.

"But you aren't going to hazard a guess?"

Van Ness stubbed out his cigar and did the sniffing thing again. Maybe it was a ritual or habit.

"All right. You are free to go, Mr Balcombe. Remember, we are watching. And make sure you let me know if you discover any news of our young friend."

THIRTY-SIX

The Toogood's gates were closed. Balcombe pulled the bell for a second time before a man introducing himself as the butler came hurrying out.

"I'm here to see Mr Toogood," Balcombe told him.

"He's not expecting you, sir." It was a statement, not a question.

No, he wasn't. Balcombe had been to midnight Mass and given it a lot of thought. Now, despite it being Christmas morning, Balcombe wanted to talk about the dead Japanese girl and what he'd found in her room.

"He'll see me," Balcombe said.

"I'm afraid not, sir."

Balcombe looked past the man at the house. For a moment he thought he saw movement, perhaps someone watching from an upstairs window.

"It's important. I need to see Mr Toogood."

"Not today, sir." The butler looked uncomfortable. "Perhaps tomorrow?"

Balcombe took a breath. The man was a gatekeeper. Literally. Balcombe wasn't getting past. Not without causing a scene.

He'd had a long night, partly because of the revellers outside the hotels last night and partly because he'd been thinking: a dead girl who'd seen Roger Toogood recently and lied about it. What else had she lied about?

What was the real reason Denis Toogood hadn't wanted to involve the police?

The butler waited patiently, making no eye contact.

Eventually, Balcombe said, "Please tell Mr Toogood that I called and will visit again tomorrow morning."

"Very good, sir."

Albert had been waiting outside and took Balcombe back home, where he changed and packed his climbing things. After paying her and offering Albert the day off, he walked to Star Ferry Pier where he caught the *Polar Star* to Kowloon.

At the far dock was a crowd of people bigger than he expected, and they weren't queuing for the ferry. It appeared there was something of interest in the water and the police were keeping people back.

Balcombe didn't feel the need to investigate. He knew that if a man pointed at the sky, most of those around him would look up. Human instinct. It didn't mean there would be anything of real interest.

He caught a taxi from the rank and asked to be taken to Lion Rock. The hills were only three miles north of Kowloon and the fare was exorbitant for the short journey, but the ride was more comfortable than a rickshaw bench.

Lion Rock reminded him of some of the hills in the Peak District back home. Maybe Crinkle Crags, although he figured the tallest hill in Kowloon was half the height of those he'd climbed in the Peak District. The rock was supposed to look like the head of a lion, although Balcombe couldn't see the resemblance.

When he said he was a climber, the taxi driver didn't understand. Europeans came out here to hike rather than climb the rocks. However, the man pointed to a track and Balcombe set off.

The trail took him up to Beacon Hill and he found the rocks were much more challenging than they looked from a distance.

Above him a black kite wheeled and shrieked in the warm air, possibly confused by his presence.

After three exhausting ascents, he stopped for lunch and enjoyed the view. Then he trekked east to Lion Rock itself. Here he found sheer faces with even less obvious routes to the peak. He climbed the shaded east face until he slipped. He'd gone for a high jam using a high foot smear to increase his reach. But it had been too far. One second his fingertips were reaching into a crack, the next he was dangling from his other hand.

Heart pounding, he hung eighty feet up. With only ringlock with his weaker hand to hold him, it would have been so easy to fall.

This is what it's all about!

This is what he'd been looking for. Digging deep, he swung his other arm and lunged. His fingers found purchase, and although weak, they managed to hold him.

Afterwards, he lay on his back and screamed at the sky.

"I'm still alive!"

He didn't want to analyse himself but he was certain a psychotherapist would say something about cheating death. And he'd probably be right.

Balcombe's index finger on his left hand was badly twisted from holding his weight. It would take days to heal but the pain had been totally worth it.

He came down from the hills via a different path and didn't recognize the area when he reached the streets. There were no taxis or rickshaws and so he began walking south. However, a boy soon spotted him and five minutes later he was on the back of a rickshaw.

"The Orient Line Company building on Middle Road," he told the boy, and they set off.

After a hundred yards the rickshaw boy said, "Jewellery?"

"No, just the docks."

"Girls, sir?"

"The docks."

The boy turned off the main road. "This is a quicker way," he said before Balcombe questioned him.

However, after another turn, he knew something was up.

"All right, stop!" Balcombe commanded. As he climbed from the bench, three men appeared from twenty yards ahead. They'd expected Balcombe to be brought closer, probably intending to jump him aboard the rickshaw.

Balcombe could have run. He might even have got away, although his legs were still suffering from the day's punishing exercise.

The rickshaw boy scuttled away, leaving the four of them. Three against one.

The Chinese men were young and slim, maybe very fit, although Balcombe suspected they were undernourished rather than toned beneath their dirty clothes.

"Give us your money," the man in the middle said.

He looked tough and Balcombe guessed these men knew how to fight—street fighting anyway. They spaced out, one straight ahead and the other two moving to Balcombe's sides.

He stepped towards the rickshaw so the one on his left had an obstacle.

And that's when the leader pulled out a knife. It looked menacing, with a jagged edge, which told Balcombe a lot. This was about a show of strength rather than intent to kill. If they wanted to kill him the knife would have been thinner and smaller. Quick. A jagged blade would snag on clothes. It would be slower to wield. It would be less likely to slice or pierce—unless he'd been incapacitated. And he wasn't incapacitated.

Balcombe could have simply paid them. But then again, he couldn't. It was a matter of principle. Just like the fact that he wouldn't have run even if his legs weren't tired.

"Give me your knapsack," the leader said. Balcombe could hear a nervous edge now. The man was starting to wonder why this Englishman wasn't terrified, why he wasn't immediately begging for his life.

"No," Balcombe said. "But I will give you a chance to walk away."

This brought laughter from the other two and a shake of the head from the leader. He wasn't backing down. He wasn't about to lose face.

"All right," Balcombe said.

He eased the knapsack from his shoulders, one strap at a time. Slowly.

The man on his right reached out. But Balcombe stepped towards the leader.

The knife lowered as he instinctively went for the bag. And that was all Balcombe needed.

Like a sprinter off the blocks, Balcombe exploded forward. The bag swung towards the knife. The other man reacted, but too late.

Balcombe struck him in the throat. Not hard. He didn't want to kill anyone. He didn't want to attract the attention of the police—certainly not after they had only just questioned him.

So he struck hard enough to incapacitate, not hard enough to break the man's larynx.

The leader went down choking.

He dropped the knife and Balcombe snatched it and turned in a single movement. The other two assailants had only just started to move. The shock attack had left them stunned and slow.

As their brains registered that Balcombe was now in possession of the knife, they stopped. Another second for them to look at one another and then they were off, scuttling into the nearest buildings.

"It's your lucky day," Balcombe said to the man on the floor. "Ordinarily, I'd have killed you."

The Chinese man's eyes were on the knife.

Balcombe smiled. If he hadn't had the rush of adrenaline from rock climbing, he may have wanted this man's blood. Lucky for both of them, then.

Balcombe picked up his knapsack, tucked the knife in his trousers and walked away.

Fifteen minutes later, after disposing of the knife, he was outside the office on Middle Road.

Smyth was there and grinned when he saw Balcombe walk in.

"Happy Christmas," the manager said.

Balcombe returned the greeting, then: "Any luck with the names?"

"Not luck," Smyth said. "Hard work." He patted a bundle of paper on his desk.

As Balcombe parted with his ten dollars, he doubted there had been any work involved at all. Maybe Smyth had had the list all along.

Balcombe went through page by page as Smyth told him how many ships there had been and how many names. Balcombe estimated a hundred names in total but he found only ten that didn't sound Chinese and four that sounded English.

Not one of them was Roger Toogood.

"A shame," Smyth said. "Sorry you didn't find him."

Balcombe nodded. But not finding something eliminates the possibility. Toogood didn't book a ticket, nor did he work his passage from Hong Kong.

It looked more and more likely that the boy was still on the island. Hiding, not fleeing.

THIRTY-SEVEN

Inspector Munro went through the reports on his desk. Chief Carmichael's pressure to get more arrests was working. Unfortunately.

Munro knew what was going on. The Governor put pressure on the police to crack down on crime—which was undoubtedly rising—and Carmichael wanted results.

But these were the wrong results. They needed to catch real criminals with real evidence which would lead to appropriate punishment. Not a handful of days in jail.

He looked up. There was excessive noise in the office. Granted it was Christmas, but the men should still behave respectfully.

"Quiet!" he shouted.

It wasn't like him to bellow like that, and it shut them up. Faces turned. But he didn't see contrition. He saw concern.

"What's happened?"

Men came forward looking uncomfortable. His junior sergeant said, "It's Tam."

It's funny how a tone can say so much. Although this wasn't funny at all.

Munro cleared his throat, giving himself time to say the words without a croaking voice.

"Is he dead?"

One of the clerks was pushed forward and he stood awkwardly in front of Munro.

"Well?" Munro prompted.

"I've just taken a call from Kowloon station, sir."

Munro waited.

"Sergeant Tam was found in the water this morning."

"Drowned?"

"Murdered, sir. His throat was slit."

"I heard the news," Chief Carmichael said when Munro went into his office. "Damned sad. That's three this year. And on Christmas Day too!"

It's not about the number, or the date, Munro thought. However, he said nothing.

"What was Tam doing in Kowloon?"

"Following up on a lead."

"With your approval—one of your cases?"

Not really, Munro thought. It had been a wild goose chase, looking for someone who might use a knife, might kill in the way the fat man, Chee-hwa, had been killed. Sliced under the heart for access rather than have his throat slit. Asking the prisoner had seemed like a good idea at the time, but it had been a mistake. And now Tam was dead.

"Well, Munro?" Carmichael said impatiently.

"Yes, he was following up a lead with my approval."

"Alone?"

Munro nodded, desperately trying to think of a valid reason, but Carmichael spoke first.

"Then why didn't the Kowloon station know about it? You know the policy, Munro. When we're over there, we use their help."

Munro nodded. Gangs were a problem on the peninsula and the Kowloon office knew them better. Everyone knew to avoid the Walled City with its Triads, but the other areas were less obvious. Kowloon officers knew the current no-go areas. They knew who they could trust, who was a snitch. They didn't want Island boys blundering into their operations.

"Munro!" Carmichael was getting more irate at his inspector's hesitancy.

"I don't know why, sir," Munro said. "Perhaps he intended to but didn't get that far."

"Right. Assuming everything is in order then Tam's family—he was married I suppose?—will get the compensation."

"He was tortured," Munro said after a pause. He'd spoken to his friend Yeung and been told the detail. Tam had had his throat slit, but only after he'd suffered broken bones and extracted nails.

"Who did it?" Carmichael asked.

"Chau Hing."

Carmichael squinted. "I know that name."

"He's at Stanley on death row."

"What!"

"I know—"

"Let me get this straight. You're telling me that someone on death row managed to escape and kill Sergeant Tam?"

"His first name was Arthur," Munro said quietly. "Arthur Tam."

Carmichael shook his head as though hearing nonsense and Munro regretted speaking out. Pointing out Tam's full name was a distraction.

The Chief said, "I want you to solve crimes, Munro. Remember the conversation we had only yesterday? Charging someone who couldn't possibly have committed the crime will make me look like an idiot. In fact, now that I think about it"—he fished in his desk drawer and pulled out a piece of paper. Munro noticed the letter heading was from the Governor's office— "Chau Hing is on this list."

"List, sir?"

"The Governor's New Year's clemency list."

Munro's eyes widened so far he thought his eyes would fall out. He shook his head, unable to speak.

"Imagine what that would look like, Munro. Not only couldn't he have killed our man, but it would look like we were deliberately countering the Governor's wishes. It wouldn't look good at all, man!"

"No, sir."

"Find out who did this, Munro. Find out who killed Sergeant Tam, but don't go telling me it's someone already in prison. Understood?"

Munro left the Chief's office wondering what he could do. He was certain Chau Hing was behind it. He'd directed them to someone called Ng Yim at an address on Ki Lung Street near Boundary Street.

Munro had already confirmed with the Kowloon station that Tam hadn't involved them. If he had, they'd have warned him about the area. Ng Yim wasn't a specific person, it was a code. Sergeant Arthur Tam had blundered in there announcing he was a policeman.

A gang member will have picked him up and tortured him. They'd have wanted names of snitches. Names he didn't know.

Chau Hing didn't kill him directly, but he was just as culpable.

Munro had gone into the Chief's office thinking he'd get permission to question Chau Hing again. The prisoner must know who was at the address. He must know the gang. But now Munro couldn't. Upset Carmichael again and he'd be demoted in a flash. Maybe he should do it. Maybe principle was more important than a job and income.

In the meantime, he called Kowloon CID and discussed a raid on the street. They'd already told him the killer and the gang would have moved, but Carmichael wanted action, and occasionally—very occasionally—a wild goose chase caught a goose.

THIRTY-EIGHT

Balcombe was sitting in his favourite chair with a book and tumbler of whisky when there was a light knock on his door.

Grace Toogood had on a black cape and evening dress, as though dressed for a formal event. She smiled with a mischievous glint in her eyes.

"I didn't expect—" he began.

"Aren't you going to invite me in?"

He stepped back, suddenly feeling awkward. "Of course."

She removed the cape and handed it to him. At her neck was a diamond necklace. She had more jewellery on her wrists.

His eyes appreciated her.

"This way?" she said, walking past him into his living room.

"Would you like a drink?"

"What are you having?"

"Whisky."

She nodded. "That sounds perfect."

While he poured her a glass, she looked around the room, taking in the ornaments and photographs.

"The books and pictures are mine, the rest came with the rooms."

"Ah," she said, presumably thinking that the taste in décor didn't suit him. And she'd have been right.

She touched his left hand as he handed her the glass. "You're hurt."

He turned his hand and flexed the finger that had bruised between the knuckle and first joint.

"Silly climbing incident," he said.

"It looks painful." She kicked off her high heels, sat in his chair, sipped her drink and looked like she enjoyed the burn of the liquid down her throat. He waited, desperate to ask her why she had knocked on his door.

Finally, he said, "It's Christmas Day."

"Yes, it is."

"Shouldn't you be with your husband?"

"Denis has gone to the club. I thought we were going out tonight, but he's been off all day. In fact, he was in a foul mood when he came home from work yesterday."

Balcombe sipped his whisky.

"I needed a friendly face." She reached over and touched his leg. "Someone to cheer me up."

He said, "I haven't fulfilled my part of the bargain yet."

She laughed lightly. "You make assumptions!"

"Seemed reasonable. You're here, in my rooms. Your husband is away."

"Let's talk," she said.

"What would you like to talk about?"

"The obvious. I have no idea how you are getting along with your assignment. Have you made progress in finding Roger?"

"Not much."

She waited, looking at him until he elaborated.

"I've checked passenger records and people working passage on ships. Roger wasn't on them."

She nodded.

"I've been confronted by some men who suggested that Roger owed them money."

"How much?"

"Two hundred."

She frowned. "That isn't a lot."

"For most people it would be, but not Roger, I'm guessing. He appears to have gambled it on a horse."

She nodded. "I hate gambling, but you'll have seen it was one of his hobbies."

"Along with cowboy novels and the Japanese military."

She nodded again.

"Did you know about his teacher?" he asked.

"From England... his school?"

"From here. He had a Japanese teacher."

Grace shook her head. "He didn't mention it, but it doesn't surprise me."

"She's dead." Balcombe said it quickly and watched her face for the reaction. Was Grace Toogood surprised by the news? He couldn't tell.

"Oh dear."

And then he struck like a cobra. It had been troubling him. Ever since he'd found the paperback book in her bed.

"Did Roger kill the Japanese girl?"

Grace knocked back her drink and blinked as the liquid burned her throat. "Did you really just say that?"

He said nothing and waited.

"How could Roger have killed her? He's been missing for at least ten days."

Balcombe shook his head. "If he didn't catch a boat then he's either in hiding..." He let her finish for him.

"Or dead," she said quietly.

"And my starting assumption is that he's alive."

She breathed deeply, perhaps still feeling the burn in her throat. "All right, but I don't..."

"You don't think he could do that—kill someone?"

Firecrackers went off in the street and she looked outside. When she looked back, her eyes had lost the shine he'd noticed when she arrived.

He said, "Who knows what anyone is capable of. Motive can often drive the most unexpected behaviour."

She studied his eyes as though trying to comprehend.

"If I knew the reason for Roger's disappearance, Grace..."

She looked away and didn't speak.

Balcombe said, "Did Roger run because he killed someone else? Is that why Denis couldn't involve the police?"

"Drugs." Her voice had a tremor. "No, I told you it was about drugs... we think... Not just using them."

Balcombe nodded. At last the truth. Denis Toogood wouldn't want his son arrested as a drug dealer. Not only would it mean a custodial sentence for Roger, but it would also undoubtedly tarnish the father's reputation and standing on the island.

Was Denis's status more important than his son's wellbeing? Balcombe resisted asking Grace because she seemed on the verge of tears.

"I've had a few bad days," she said. "Denis..."

Balcombe placed a comforting arm on her shoulder.

"I came here thinking... I'd hoped you'd cheer me up, but the mood..."

She met his gaze.

"I thought you wanted me," she said, her voice suddenly gently husky.

"I do. But—"

"There's a *but*?"

"I have a rule. Never here. Never in my home."

She said nothing for a moment, perhaps trying to read his eyes.

"What's your name? You never told me your name."

He blinked at the statement. "You know my name."

"Charles?" she said. "You don't look like a Charles."

His heart skipped a beat. Did she know he'd changed his name? Could she possibly know about his past, about BlackJack?"

She smiled. "You look more like a Max."

"Max?" he said with a laugh.

"Max Jacks, secret agent." She leaned forward and kissed him, her hand back on his thigh.

"Rules," he said.

She withdrew the hand, but the cheeky glint was back in her eyes.

"And what about you, Grace?"

"Grace? Oh no, I'm not a Grace. I'm Scarlett. Scarlett O'Hara."

She stood, looked at him seductively and he wanted her.

"Meet me at the Connaught in twenty minutes," she said. "And ask reception for Miss O'Hara's room."

He never fell asleep after sex with a lover, but he realized he must have been because Grace wasn't in bed when he opened his eyes. At first, he saw the empty bottle of champagne on the side table. Then he rolled and saw her standing at the end of the bed, pulling on her black dress.

"I didn't mean to wake you," she said.

"I didn't mean to fall asleep."

"It was endearing."

He groaned. "I don't think I've been called that before."

"I've got to go. Denis will probably stay out all night, but… you know."

He pulled back the sheet. "Come back to bed. I'm sure there's time."

She grinned and shook her head. "Next time, Max."

"So there will be a next time?" He reached for her, but she backed away with a hand raised.

"Down boy. You need to behave or I won't be able to control my urges, and then we'll be in real trouble. I'll arrange somewhere more discreet next time. I know a place." Her face became serious. "You will keep your end of the bargain?"

"To find Roger."

"You must keep looking."

He smiled. "Now that I've sampled the goods, I'm even more motivated."

"Good." She blew him a kiss and was gone.

Despite falling asleep in the hotel, when he returned home, Balcombe lay awake. Or maybe it was because he'd slept for two hours already.

The sound of revellers in the street outside didn't help, and he found himself pondering the case.

The Japanese teacher had been murdered after he'd visited. Had she known where Roger was hiding? Did Balcombe lead the killer to her door?

He was frustrated that Denis Toogood hadn't been honest about the drugs. That would have helped him understand the money situation. As a drug dealer, Roger would be a buyer and seller. Payment for product would be in advance. If he was sensible he would only spend money he'd earned from sales. But Roger was a gambler. He will have become greedy and overstretched himself.

He'd borrowed money from Van Ness, the Jardines militia man, but had then lost it at the races.

Who was the drug supplier? Roger will have owed him the money. And he will have been looking for Roger.

That was the logical conclusion. But Balcombe's theory was turned upside down when he met Denis Toogood the following morning.

THIRTY-NINE

Summoned to the Toogood house, Balcombe couldn't help wonder whether the husband had found out about last night.

There was no butler this time, nor did Balcombe see Grace Toogood.

Denis let him in and walked solemnly to the front room where they'd originally met.

Christmas presents were still under the tree, and instead of feeling festive the atmosphere was solemn. Toogood's face was grey and tired.

"Mr Balcombe," Toogood said.

"You asked to see me, sir?"

"There has been a development." Toogood stared at the wall, although Balcombe thought his eyes seemed unfocused.

Balcombe waited.

Finally, his host swivelled his gaze back to him. "You know about the Japanese girl?"

"I do. The police questioned me."

"Because you visited her and... and she was murdered."

"Yes. There must be a connection."

"I don't see how."

"Whoever is looking for Roger killed the girl. I led them to her. She knew him."

Toogood looked thoughtful before he said, "All right, but that's not the development I need to tell you about."

From his pocket, Toogood pulled a large box of Swan matches. He swallowed hard then held it out.

Balcombe took it.

"Open it."

Balcombe slid open the box. At first, he saw cotton wool, and then something bloody, about half an inch in length. A fingertip cut off at the first joint.

Their eyes met and Toogood blinked away tears.

"You think it's Roger's?" Balcombe asked.

"It came with a ransom note."

Toogood took back the matchbox, his hand shaking. In his other he produced a piece of paper. It had Chinese writing on.

"Have you had it translated?" Balcombe asked, thinking that he could show it to Albert.

Toogood nodded. "It says they have Roger and demand twenty thousand dollars."

Balcombe said nothing. It was a considerable sum that even he would have trouble funding.

Toogood said, "Of course, they threaten they'll kill him if I involve the police."

"What do you want to do?"

Toogood breathed in and out, took the piece of paper back and stared at it. "There's only one thing I can do."

Balcombe waited. Toogood was going to pay the ransom.

"And I'd like you to be the courier," Toogood said. "I trust you, Balcombe. I can count on you."

FORTY

The note instructed Toogood to deliver the money on Saturday at nine.

Tonight.

Eleven hours.

The address for the drop was on Ki Lung Street on the edge of the Sham Shui Po district. The name rang a bell, and then Balcombe remembered seeing something in the newspaper. The police had raided a house there yesterday, following up on the murder of a policeman, the man found in the water at Kowloon docks.

Of course, the note also said that the police shouldn't be informed.

"What are you going to do?" Toogood asked him.

"Surveillance initially."

Toogood shook his head. "We'll pay this and walk away."

"Of course," Balcombe said. "But I'm not going in there blind."

"They'll kill him if you don't play this straight."

"They might kill him anyway," Balcombe said. "Or they'll keep him and ask for more."

Toogood shook his head again. "They're asking for a fortune. They wouldn't—"

"They would, sir," Balcombe said. "Trust me. I've done this sort of thing before. I know what I'm doing."

"Do you have a gun?"

"No. And I don't want one." Balcombe trusted his knives—if it came to confrontation. Go in with a gun and escalation was much more likely.

They went around and around over the argument with Toogood finally accepting the plan. If he hadn't, Balcombe would have walked away. Despite his promise to Grace.

He would go to the area immediately then return. Toogood said the money would be ready by three o'clock. He would meet Balcombe outside the bank with a briefcase.

"It'll be locked," Toogood said. "Don't give them the key until they release Roger."

Balcombe knew it wouldn't work like that. The gang wouldn't release their hostage until they'd checked the money was all there. However, he agreed. They were wasting his surveillance time.

He saw no one else at the house and, as he left, he wondered again where Grace might be. Did she know about the ransom and finger?

Albert said, "I'm coming with you."

Balcombe started to disagree but she interrupted.

"With respect, master… you got into trouble yesterday."

"You being there wouldn't have helped."

"Not as a translator, but as your rickshaw boy."

"You operate here."

"There are plenty in Kowloon who will happily take your money and lend me the carriage. But I have a cousin at the docks and we can trust him."

And so, ninety minutes later, Albert was sorting out the rickshaw as Balcombe checked into The Peninsula hotel. The ferry didn't run at night and he needed somewhere to stay after rescuing Roger.

Albert was waiting for him, sitting proudly on the saddle of a trishaw when he emerged from the hotel.

"Faster and easier," she said with a grin. Hand-pulled rickshaws were preferred on the island around Victoria because of the hills. The only large flat area was the racecourse. The peninsula was ideal for the cycle version.

They headed north up Canton Road, passing Whitfield Barracks on the right and then the naval repair yard on the left. The godowns and lesser wharves continued along the coast and the housing became more densely packed. The further north they went, the poorer the streets became. They crossed Prince Edward Road. The next major parallel road was Boundary Street, forming the boundary between Kowloon and the New Territories. Ki Lung Street ran north across it a few blocks to the right, and Balcombe said he'd walk the rest of the way.

There was a death house on the corner. He could smell the incense and hear the chime of their gongs.

"You'll be too obvious," Albert told him. "People are already looking as you pass. You are better off in the trishaw with the hood up."

Balcombe reluctantly agreed. Besides, the death house had strangely unnerved him. Taking a risk was one thing, but he was entering an alien world here.

The plan was for Albert to take him up one street and down the next, passing both ends of the target road.

The streets here had Chinese names. Most of the properties along the first street were shophouses. The side streets and alleys weren't formally identified as slums, but they had crowded properties that looked run-down. It was a poor area despite being almost a mile from the docks.

Clotheslines ran across the alleys. There were hardly any vehicles—the odd taxi and van—and the streets were full of people.

Some glanced at the trishaw but Balcombe shrank back and felt invisible. Ki Lung Street was one of the widest and, after a circuit, Balcombe instructed Albert to go down it. Towards the end was a more substantial block of houses and then a restaurant with tables outside and more than twenty men passing the time.

The address in the note was next to the restaurant.

Balcombe took a long look at it. There was a green wooden door that reminded him of the one next to the laundry off Jervois Street—the one where he'd killed the fat man. There were three floors and six dark windows. They might have been blackened by curtains or barricaded, he couldn't tell. Everywhere else was teeming with Chinese people. The target property on the other hand was still and silent.

Albert didn't slow down, and at the end of the road, Balcombe whispered "Don't stop. Turn left. Keep going."

Albert followed the instructions and Balcombe directed her back past the death house and then south, two blocks.

Balcombe saw a café on Anchor Street. Under its red awning he saw office workers and junior clerks. Europeans. They would live in the houses between Canton Road and Nathan Road. Basic accommodation that was beneath the whites on the island but far superior to the crammed properties used by most Chinese.

He sat outside and watched a man in a purple turban. The owner, he guessed. Affable and welcoming.

The skies suddenly burst and Balcombe realized why his seat had been free. He was exposed. Hurrying inside, he received a frown from the turbaned owner. Perhaps because of his appearance, Or more likely that the inside seats were premium. Balcombe guessed he didn't look like someone who would spend much money. However, when he ordered a large lunch the owner smiled. When he later asked for more tea and a cake, the turbaned man even gave him a respectful bow.

"You are a stranger," the owner said.

"Here for the climbing," Balcombe said when the man expected an answer. He hoped it would explain his casual clothes.

"But you don't have any equipment."

"I climb without ropes."

The owner shook his head not comprehending.

"Do you like the cake?"

"It's very good."

"My wife makes them."

The man bustled away and Balcombe returned to a newspaper, reading about the police raid on Ki Lung Street yesterday. The coincidence troubled him.

When the rain stopped, Balcombe returned to his outside seat and the owner brought him another cake.

"On the house."

"Thank you." Balcombe thought for a moment then decided to say, "Terrible about that policeman."

The owner nodded. "But he was never in Ki Lung Street. If they killed him there, they would hide the body, not dump it in the water near the police station."

"But they arrested the gang?"

"On Ki Lung Street?" the man huffed. "There are lots of gangs, especially in Sham Shui Po, but not there."

"Where are they?"

"Gangs? Why are you interested?"

Balcombe shrugged with his hands, giving the impression he didn't care. "Just need to be careful."

"Yes, you do. A white man alone on some streets will invite trouble."

"Which streets?" Balcombe pressed. He had a theory. It was unlikely that the kidnap gang would take the money at the same site where they held the boy. He would be nearby. Close enough to reach quickly and for communication but far enough to be safe in case something went wrong.

The turbaned owner continued as though he hadn't heard the question. "To survive in Kowloon a man must know which roads to avoid. But this is not the problem. The problem is immigration. There are too many people. They come with nothing. They live in squalor and are desperate. The police should deal with them and not the petty thugs, because the Triads will expand from the Walled City."

Balcombe knew the Walled City. It was the site of an old Chinese fort. Within Hong Kong's state boundary but outside of its legislation. Officially a Chinese enclave, although Triad law prevailed.

"What about Sham Shui Po?" Balcombe asked, still thinking about distance and the district's dubious reputation.

"Generally avoid the north," the owner said.

"Any streets in particular?"

"Well, you'll know you're there because the streets have no names. They did once, but they've been removed. I suppose it's to confuse the police."

"The nearest with a name?"

The owner's turban wobbled as he considered. "There's Fuk Wing and Fuk Wa. The north end of those will lead you to trouble." He raised an eyebrow. "Avoid them."

This place will be ideal, Balcombe said to himself. He thanked the man, paid for his meal and added a good tip.

Once back in the trishaw he instructed Albert to take him to the ferry.

"And meet back here at sundown," he said. "I'd like a map of the whole of Sham Shui Po including the properties on either side of Ki Lung Street."

"There aren't any."

"Draw one."

"I'm not an artist."

"Do your best," he said. "Meanwhile, I'm going back to see Mr Toogood."

FORTY-ONE

At three o'clock, Balcombe was in the square outside the bank. He watched the last customers leave and the security guard lock the doors. A few senior bank staff left, driving away their cars parked in the square. It got to half past three with no sign of Toogood.

Most of the cars were small and black. Toogood's burgundy Daimler stood out. He was still here.

Heavy clouds darkened the skies and rain began to fall. Big drops bounced off the tiled concourse and drummed on car roofs. Balcombe sheltered under a tree next to the temporary PRO building and watched more staff dash for the tram and ferry.

The rain cooled the air with the fresh smell of vegetation on the hills.

He checked his watch. Toogood was forty-five minutes late.

Not good. What was the man thinking? His son was in jeopardy and he was presumably putting his work before his son's life.

Five minutes later the security guard opened the main door and Toogood stepped out. He pushed up an umbrella, glanced around and strode purposefully towards Balcombe's tree.

His left hand gripped a black briefcase. His face was set, looking tense.

"You're late," Balcombe said.

"I know, I know!" Toogood snapped. He put one foot on the low wall next to Balcombe and placed the briefcase on his thigh using it like a table. After a glance over his shoulder, Toogood flipped the clasps and opened the case.

Balcombe couldn't see inside and watched as Toogood pulled a tan leather bag out, placed it on the lip and relocked the case.

"Take it, Balcombe."

"What is it?"

As soon as he felt the heft of the bag, Balcombe knew what it was.

"I said no guns."

Toogood glowered. "He's my son. I want him back. You take the gun."

Balcombe continued to hold the bag and accepted the briefcase in his free hand.

"The key?"

Toogood shook his head. "It's a combination lock."

Balcombe looked down and saw the three dials beside each clasp. He waited for the code.

Toogood said, "Here's the plan, Balcombe. Roger will know the code. The case doesn't get opened until you have Roger back safe. Understood?"

Balcombe looked again at the briefcase. It was black leather over wood, he figured. It was about as secure as a loose belt on a slippery snake. The locks wouldn't delay anyone without the code for more than a second.

"Understood?" Toogood said again.

Balcombe nodded. "I'd better get going."

Whether or not Toogood registered that the ferry wasn't close to the dock, Balcombe couldn't tell. But he did have to hurry. He had an illegal gun and needed to leave it before crossing the strait.

"Get my son back!" Toogood said louder than was necessary.

Balcombe began to respond but Toogood took a step away, spun and walked off. Fast.

FORTY-TWO

The rain continued as Balcombe crossed over to Kowloon. First, he went to the hotel and changed. He entered the luxury hotel in casual clothes and drew a few disapproving glances as he left wearing a black roll-neck top, black trousers and his rubber shoes. What they imagined, he could only guess. A circus performer, perhaps. Although just why he was carrying a briefcase must have been a mystery.

In his belt he carried lock picks, a black balaclava and his knives. Although he hadn't argued with Toogood the second time, he wasn't about to carry the gun. He'd already been questioned by the police about the Japanese girl. If the police found him with the service revolver that Toogood had given him, he'd look even more suspicious.

He'd guessed the girl had been stabbed, but the newspaper reports had been silent on the method. That had intrigued him. Newspapers normally relished the gruesome descriptions of a murder. He doubted it could have been a gun based on the lack of blood splatter. But why withhold detail. Could there be something unusual about the weapon?

He was still thinking about the girl's death when he arrived at the café on Anchor Street. The red awning thudded with rain like a bass drum and he darted for its shelter.

"How was the climbing?" the café owner asked Balcombe.

"Not good. The rocks were wet."

The purple turban nodded as though the owner had first-hand experience of the perils of free climbing rocks. Which he probably didn't.

"And that's why you've changed?"

Balcombe smiled. "Easier to climb in these clothes."

"Although it will be dark soon." Now the owner gave a wily smile, an eye half-closed like a partial wink. Did he suspect something? Not a circus performer, more like a cat burglar, Balcombe started to wonder.

He was starting to think he'd made a mistake selecting the man. However, he was relieved when the owner changed the subject.

"Are you here for more of my wife's delicious cake?"

"No, but I will pay you for it," Balcombe said. "I have a favour. Would you hold onto my briefcase?"

"While you go climbing?"

"Yes."

The owner smiled and nodded. "And how long will that be for?"

Balcombe checked his watch. "It could be a couple of hours. It could be much later. Is that all right?"

"If the café is shut, knock on the side door. Someone will be up."

Balcombe pulled out ten dollars. "I'll give you another ten when I collect it."

The owner shook his head. "Twenty now and twenty later."

They settled on two fifteens, although Balcombe guessed there would be more negotiating when he returned.

"Stay safe," the owner said as Balcombe departed. "Watch out for those slippery rocks."

"You drew a map of the area?" Balcombe asked Albert when she picked him up.

"Yes." The girl passed it behind as she started to pedal. "The whole of Sham Shui Po."

"Perfect," he said as she passed it back to him. She was no cartographer, but it appeared comprehensive to his inexperienced eye.

They went along Boundary Street and turned north, crossing over into the New Territories. The rain had stopped and the clouds made the day bleed into night. In the tropics, daylight fades quickly after sunset, and by half past seven, burning torches were being lit.

There were more people around than he'd seen during the day. The local shops were open for most of the night and the bars and mah-jong clubs that did an active trade were just waking up.

Despite the number of people, Balcombe saw no policemen in the district. Night shifts used fewer men than the day shifts. And they didn't patrol residential areas at night, he figured. They were at the docks and warehouses protecting commercial property.

As they went north, Balcombe saw squatter housing on Bishop Hill to his right. On the other side of the hill, he knew the housing improved. On this side, to his left he could see the streets become narrower and the properties more run-down. The further in they went, the worse it got. Near the northern end, Balcombe got Albert to turn and cross the top of the district.

He shrank back in the trishaw and looked through the hood. He watched people and places. He looked down alleys and passageways as the trishaw splashed through puddles. The café owner had said there were no street names and Balcombe saw none.

At the western end, Albert stopped. "People stared at us."

"You were uncomfortable?"

"Yes."

"I thought you were invisible. That's what you told me, Albert."

"Most of the time." She glanced back and he knew she didn't want to ride through again.

"We'll circle," he said. "I want a sense of the whole thing."

She started pedalling again.

At nine tonight Balcombe knew he would be walking into the lions' den. Before that he needed two things. Every military strategist knows that a plan should include escape. Balcombe needed the map in case something went wrong. Which way would he go? Where should he avoid?

Now he was thinking about the hostage. If Balcombe could work out where Roger was being held he could operate plan A. Paying over the ransom was his plan B.

Rescuing Roger was plan A. However, he knew the odds weren't great.

They circled the district and then cut through on one of the few named streets. Balcombe noted arrogant-looking young men. They watched the trishaw pass with eyes that warned them not to stop. Most of the region was a slum but sections were better, rows of brick-built properties.

When Balcombe spotted a passage with metal sheeting across the entrance, he was sure of what he'd found: a gang-controlled street. He saw a man sitting in a chair close by. He would be a guard. Maybe one of two who controlled the barrier. They'd be armed with guns, probably. No one would enter that alley without gang authority.

Once passed, Balcombe had Albert loop around to the other end. Eventually they found it. Another metal sheet barrier. Two empty chairs and guards this time.

Albert kept going until she met the eastern boundary.

"Learn anything?" she asked.

"Not enough," he said. "Feeling brave?"

"What do you want me to do?"

He pointed along the line of shop fronts. "About halfway along. See if you can get through to the back— to the alley."

He thought she might turn down the request but was relieved that she didn't hesitate. While he found a place to hide, she hurried along the road and then disappeared.

Twenty minutes later she reappeared carrying an empty paper bag.

"What took you?"

"You owe me five cents for fruit," she said, showing him the bag. "I couldn't get through to the other side. It looks like the rear exists are blocked."

"Where's the fruit?"

She smiled. "I used it to ask questions."

"All right, what did you learn?"

"That apart from not getting through these properties, there's no way you're getting past the guards at the ends of the lane."

He'd hoped to identify where Roger was being held, but it wasn't clear and there wasn't time. Plan A had always been a long shot.

FORTY-THREE

Cloud cover made the heavens black. There were pools of darkness on Ki Lung Street, but it was lit well enough for people to see him clearly. A white man in Chinatown. He'd look out of place like a fox in a dog pound.

Not only would he be exposed, but if he walked down the street to the address, he'd have no control.

With ten minutes to spare, Albert dropped Balcombe on the road behind. He knew where the back of the restaurant was. Even in the dark, he could see smoke from the kitchens. Beside it was the property where Balcombe was to deliver the money. He kept going until the next door.

From the street, he stepped into dim light. Thick air smelled of damp and dirt. As he moved lightly down a corridor, past curtains acting as doors, he heard Chinese voices—normal, everyday chatter—mostly women and children.

He kept going to the end and realized his mistake. The buildings didn't go all the way. The property was much narrower with no access beyond. He slipped back to a door on his left, midway along.

A child screamed and a second later the closest curtain moved. A woman hurried into the corridor, calling. She spotted Balcombe, missed a step then shook her head and continued, darting into the next room.

Balcombe had his knife in his hand, prepared. The child's crying subsided. He heard other voices but no alarm in them.

Watching for movement, he turned his attention to the door. It was locked but was easily picked and he was soon into the property directly next to the back of the restaurant and behind the target property.

He was in another corridor with curtains, the mirror image of the house next door. The sounds were the same too: general everyday chatter, although louder than before.

This time there was a door at the end of the corridor. It wasn't locked and he found himself in a stinking well between properties: a dumping ground for food waste from the restaurant, he guessed. Possibly also used as a toilet. He held his breath and made for a door ahead and to the left. After testing the door handle, he was soon inside.

The place was wrecked. It had probably looked similar to the other houses until recently. Now curtains were torn and either hanging from doorways or on the floor. Other detritus was scattered around: clothes, broken furniture, empty bottles.

And there was an eerie quiet.

He could hear distant chatter and figured it came through the walls. This place was empty.

Which was odd.

If not meeting inside the building, then the exchange must be outside.

He quickly confirmed that Roger wasn't tied and gagged anywhere before heading for the door that opened out onto Ki Lung Street. To his left was the restaurant.

There was a woman serving tables outside. She stopped suddenly like she'd been turned to stone. Customers set aside newspapers, stopped their card and mah-jong games and watched him.

Balcombe saw Albert on her trishaw opposite the restaurant. She'd be a distraction rather than a getaway vehicle.

She began to cycle up the street and passed a man sitting in a doorway, head down. To Balcombe's right were two youths chatting. Beyond them was a large group on haunches, playing a game. They didn't look up.

Balcombe checked his watch. Ten o'clock.

He turned back to the door and knocked just for show.

"Go away," a wizened Chinese man whispered then walked away.

As Balcombe wondered where he'd come from, the youths crossed the street. They walked towards him with confident strides. No hesitation. No uncertainty. No fear.

"What do you want?" the one on the right said.

"I'm here for the exchange."

He saw nothing in their faces. No recognition. No acknowledgement either.

"How much money have you got?"

"Not now," Balcombe said, trying not to sound frustrated. "I have a meeting."

He stepped left towards the restaurant tables.

"You're meeting us," the second youth said.

The first called out and another young man appeared on the street. He had a wide face with wide eyes. One eye was askance, making him look like he was a little deranged. He approached at an angle so that when he stopped and Balcombe turned to face him, a table was between them.

"Are you Zhen?" Balcombe said. It was the name Toogood had said was on the ransom note.

The man scoffed. "There are so many Zhens."

"I only need one."

"You have money?"

This didn't feel right. These weren't the kidnappers. These were thugs like the ones who had tried to mug him yesterday, after climbing.

Balcombe stepped away. "My mistake. Wrong place."

Wide-eyes sucked at his teeth as though thinking. Then he said, "All right, go."

He made a small gesture that Balcombe recognized: a signal for the others to attack.

Balcombe stepped sideways, pushed over the table and readied himself for violence.

He expected the men to draw knives, but before they reacted, a broom whacked loudly against the fallen table and a woman began screaming abuse. He didn't understand the words but the invective was clear. Balcombe stepped away and was surprised that the three men also backed off. The lady—who he now recognized as the serving woman—swept and crashed the broom handle down.

The restaurant customers stared.

Balcombe stepped back again and saw Albert pedalling fast towards him.

He sprinted for the trishaw, which Albert spun around, although Balcombe didn't get in, not until they were clear of Ki Lung Street. He glanced back and saw the woman berating the young thugs who now loitered outside the house opposite.

216

"She is angry at the boys for causing trouble," Albert said hoarsely.

"Stop and catch your breath," Balcombe said.

Albert continued: "The woman blamed the boys for ruining her business, making the area disreputable. She mentioned yesterday's police raid."

Balcombe understood. Business owners, like the woman, wouldn't want gangs or thugs operating too close. Gangs caused problems. They expected free services. They demanded money. They sometimes took over the businesses to look legitimate. Honest traders feared them, feared the consequences of a slide into criminality.

There had been lions in the den, but not those he'd hoped for. Despite feeling as though he could deal with whatever had arisen on Ki Lung Street, he had failed to make contact with the kidnappers. He couldn't be sure, but it was likely they'd been disrupted by the police raid.

From what he'd read, the people who knew about the exchange were now in Victoria Gaol. Which gave him a problem but also hope.

A problem, because he couldn't make them lead him to Roger. Hope, because they were a lot of men down.

"Go back to the restaurant, invisible, Albert," Balcombe said when the girl was breathing normally again. Give the woman this money and find out if she knows where someone is being held."

Ten minutes later, Albert returned grinning.

"You were right," she said. "It's that street in north Sham Shui Po—the one with the barriers. The woman said a gang holds people there."

FORTY-FOUR

The air was filled with cooking-fire smoke and the smell of boiled rice.

Half of the properties made up a shantytown, insubstantial and in a perpetual state of decay. The rest were two- or three-storey buildings, and the barricaded street had most of the tall properties.

From Albert's previous attempt, Balcombe knew he couldn't get through to the alley. Like before, he selected a property away from the presumed target, only this time he scaled a wall and got onto the roof. There were flat sections and people had stretched tarpaulin and old sails between poles as makeshift shelters. He saw women with babies and a few children but he also saw people sleeping. What he didn't see were any men. They were likely on the ground, playing games, gambling and drinking.

He pulled on his black balaclava and slipped past. A woman challenged him, presumably concerned for her family. It was dark and he hoped she'd only heard a noise. He kept going and she didn't follow.

The block was only fifty yards long, and he found a spot on a sloping roof where he could look into the narrow street without disturbing the rooftop residents.

Faint light spilled from windows and he saw two men smoking.

The grating sound of metal on stone made him look to the end of the alley. A man moved the barricade aside and a car turned in. As it squeezed along, the lights showed the two smokers disappear.

The barricade slid noisily back into place.

The car passed beneath Balcombe to the next building. A dog barked followed by a hundred other dogs, all close. Balcombe realized they were down in the alley, although he saw no sign of them.

Ten yards further, the car halted. Intrigued at how anyone could get in or out, Balcombe watched as the left-hand side doors opened. Then he got it. There was a recess in the wall, a space big enough to allow access to a vehicle.

Balcombe strained to see. An interior light had come on, but the angle showed him nothing.

A man got out of the front and another came from the back. Together they appeared to drag a third person from the back of the car before they disappeared inside the building. The car drove off.

Was that Roger?

Had they brought him here ready for the exchange?

Balcombe started to wonder whether the woman at the restaurant was in on it. Was he supposed to be redirected to this street in the rough northern end of the district?

The lane returned to darkness and the dogs went quiet.

Balcombe watched and waited. He saw movement across the alley from one side to the other but it was too dark to see whether they looked like shop workers or gangsters.

He waited another hour. Nothing happened below and the sounds from the roof suggested most people had settled for the night.

Time to move.

Balcombe went over the edge of the roof and climbed down the wall. The poor construction provided irregular stonework with plenty of hand and toe holds, although the darkness made it a challenge.

Dropping lightly to the ground, he hurried into the space where the car door had opened. Lights filtered through curtains.

He opened the door a crack then shut it again after glimpsing a man on the other side.

Ten yards back he found a window. The faintest of light came from inside and he figured the room on the other side was dark. Light came from deeper, beyond. He jemmied the latch with his knife and then froze.

The alley door opened.

Without time to climb inside, Balcombe flattened himself against the wall. If the man looked hard, he'd surely see him.

But he didn't. The door closed and Balcombe was alone once more. Moving fast, he squeezed through the window. Once inside, the first thing he was aware of was the rank smell of urine.

The faint light came from under the door.

Balcombe listened to it, heard nothing and eased the door ajar.

He was at the end of a passage. There was a door to his left, one to his right. The room on the left had two camp beds in it. There were two men at a desk in the one on the right.

Balcombe stepped to the door on the left. Through it he could hear a low moan. He turned the handle and slipped inside. At first he thought it was totally dark, but candles provided faint light. He smelled incense. He saw metal bars, like cages.

He shut the door.

"Roger?" Balcombe whispered hoarsely. Then louder: "Roger Toogood?"

No response except for the low moan of the distressed.

He closed the gap to the first cage. Wretched eyes watched him. A young woman—more of a girl—squatting in abject terror.

He went from cage to cage. Four of them, each holding a girl.

No young men.

No Roger Toogood.

Balcombe could have just left. Maybe he should have just left. But he couldn't. He needed to get the girls out of this fetid prison.

Click

An electric light went on.

A man yelled in Chinese as he raised his gun.

FORTY-FIVE

"Toogood." The police chief looked up from his book and set down his pipe as Denis Toogood approached.

There were eight leather wingback chairs in the Reading Room of the Hong Kong Club. Carmichael graciously pointed to one nearby.

"You're not one to frequent this little haven of mine," Carmichael said. Despite the lack of inflexion in his voice, he was intrigued. Why had Denis Toogood approached him? He closed his book on his lap, his hands resting on top.

Toogood hesitated before sitting, leaning forward and speaking conspiratorially.

"Forgive the rudeness, Derek, but I'd be grateful—"

"A police matter?"

"That's right."

"Please don't tell me my men have been bothering you again. I had a word—"

"It's not that."

Carmichael couldn't read Toogood's face. The man seemed awkward but maybe that was because he was talking shop at the club. There was an unwritten rule that work was left outside.

Toogood was still hesitant. Carmichael's hand tensed over the book cover. *Come on, man, out with it!*

Finally, Toogood said, "It's about my son."

Carmichael couldn't recall the boy's name and was glad Toogood didn't notice.

"He's been kidnapped."

"Pardon me?" Carmichael stiffened, a hundred thoughts cramming his head. "Kidnapped? Are you certain? Have you reported this at Victoria police station?"

Toogood surprised him with his calm response. "No, I'm just telling you." He raised a hand. "I have my reasons."

Carmichael sat back shaking his head. "You had better explain."

"My son, Roger, was missing. Has been for nearly two weeks now. Then two days ago I received a matchbox containing part of a finger and a ransom note."

"Roger's finger? Good God, man!"

"I assume so."

"And you didn't report this straight away?"

"I thought I could deal with it," Toogood said. "I hired a man."

Carmichael nodded. So Toogood had planned to pay the ransom without police involvement.

"They told you not to involve the police?"

"I didn't want to take the risk."

"And the investigator. He's this Balcombe chap my men interviewed?"

"Yes. He's the one. Allegedly an investigator. But he disappeared with the money and now I'm not so sure. His behaviour has also been… well, not quite right."

"Suspicious?"

"I suppose so."

"Where is he now?"

"I don't know. The last time I saw him was on Saturday after the bank closed. He took the money."

"How much?"

"Two thousand dollars."

Carmichael nodded slowly. A man might question his morals when handed such a princely sum.

He checked his watch unnecessarily. He knew the time because dinner had only just finished. "You will appreciate that I can't do anything for you tonight."

"Of course."

"Bring what you've got to the station in the morning."

"You'll check the matchbox for fingerprints?"

Carmichael nodded. "And we'll need a full statement."

FORTY-SIX

Balcombe was held at gunpoint until two more men charged into the room. He was frisked, relieved of his knives and lock picks, and after the end girl was moved into a cell with another, he was pushed into the vacant one.

He waited in darkness for about an hour until the light came back on and an older, weather-worn Chinese man came into the room.

"Who are you?"

Balcombe told him.

"What are you doing here?"

"I'm looking for someone—Roger Toogood."

The man shook his head, although his eyes never strayed from Balcombe's. "I don't know the name."

"I thought he might be here."

"Why?"

"I heard you had people." Balcombe nodded in the direction of the scared girls. "And I see that you do."

"But no boys."

"No."

"I'm a reasonable man," the Chinese man said smoothly.

"I'm sure you are."

"There's a release fee."

Of course there was. "How much?"

"How much can you pay?"

"Nothing while I'm in here," Balcombe said. "Let me go and I will return with a hundred dollars."

"Who knows you are here."

Balcombe considered his options. Tell the truth, that he'd told no one, and the man might just kill him. Tell the man about the briefcase full of money and they would just take it. He'd be killed anyway.

"My wife," he said, deciding that delay was the only tactic.

"Where is she?"

"At The Peninsula hotel."

The Chinese man's craggy face wrinkled even more as he considered the situation, then he issued instructions to one of his men waiting in the corridor. The man came in moments later bearing paper and a pen.

"You will write to her, asking for one thousand dollars. She must give it to my man. You will write something that will convince her it is true."

"It's Christmas and the weekend. The banks are shut."

"Then you have until Monday evening. No money by then and... well you can guess the rest."

"I don't think the bank is open on Monday."

"Then that's your problem," the Chinese man said with a chuckle.

Balcombe wrote a note to an imaginary wife and told the man his room number.

They left. The room plunged into darkness and it was just him, four terrified girls and the awful smell.

By morning, he barely noticed the smell. There were no windows in the room, but the door was open and grey light washed from the hallway.

During the night there had been many voices, chatter and laughter. On two occasions, men came to look at him as if verifying he existed. Or maybe they'd heard him testing the bars, vainly hoping to find a weakness. He hadn't.

And then, after almost eight hours of incarceration, the prisoners were brought a pan of rice.

A man came through the door, but he wasn't carrying the pan. It was Albert. For a second Balcombe was relieved, and then he realized his foolish mistake. She was one of them.

He hadn't known whether he could trust her.

She'd played him from the start.

She was the one who told him what the restaurant woman said.

She was the one who brought him here.

Albert didn't make eye contact as she spooned rice into bowls and handed it through the bars. She came to Balcombe last.

"I told them you don't have a wife," she said.

Balcombe didn't comment.

"I told them about the money." She still didn't meet his gaze. "Where is it?"

"The café with the red awning."

"Ah," she said, and was gone. The man sat on a chair with his eyes on the girls. A leer on his face suggested he fancied at least one of them.

Balcombe watched Albert go and heard chatter down the hall. She was telling his captors. Would they let him go after receiving the money? No. He knew where they operated. He knew about the prison and the girls. Perhaps they were the start of the trade, perhaps the middle, but they were trading in human misery whatever, and he couldn't walk away from that knowledge. They would guess as much.

He needed time. He thought he had until tomorrow night, but his time was up.

FORTY-SEVEN

Balcombe stared at the bowl of rice. Was this to be his last meal?

The girls had all devoured theirs and were looking at him questioningly. Maybe they hoped he wouldn't eat.

Like a mantra, the army teaches you to eat and rest when you can. And like all good mantras it can take your mind off the issue.

No point in worrying about something you can't change.

He dug his fingers into the bowl. And stopped.

There was something hard at the bottom, stuck with congealed rice. He pretended to eat and then felt for the object again. A little manipulation and he knew exactly what it was: his lock picks.

Half an hour passed and the guard returned and took the bowls. But he opened the cell door furthest from Balcombe's and took hold of the girl inside.

She screamed and struggled weakly against his tug, but she was out of the cell and then out of the room within seconds.

Even before Balcombe heard a door shut along the corridor, he was at the lock, picking it.

The remaining girls watched him like he was a magician, hardly able to comprehend what he was doing.

"I'll come straight back," he whispered, hoping they understood his tone if not his words.

Stepping lightly to the room where he'd seen two men at a desk, he found it empty. He could hear the Chinese man and girl in the bedroom.

Balcombe's blood started to boil. He pulled out drawers hoping to find a weapon and found nothing useful. He was just considering using chair legs as weapons when his eyes alighted on a box. Pay dirt. Inside were his three knives and a belt.

He darted to the bedroom door, his favourite knife at the ready, and barged in.

Time to release BlackJack.

FORTY-EIGHT

Balcombe was awoken by a heavy banging on his hotel room door. It sounded urgent. Maybe he'd required a lot of banging to wake him up. Or maybe not.

"Police! Open this door," a voice barked.

"I'm coming, I'm coming," he said, slapping his face to wake up. It was still Sunday and he'd only slept for a couple of hours. Pulling on a gown, he cracked open the door, just in case it wasn't the police.

There were three policemen fronted by a sergeant. The man nodded politely despite the earlier demand.

"Good afternoon, Mr Balcombe."

"What's this about?"

"Please would you accompany me to the station, sir?"

Balcombe repeated, "What's this about?"

"Please get dressed, sir. We need your help with some enquiries."

Balcombe hesitated, saw he had no options and requested a minute.

Three minutes later he was walking out of his room and out of the hotel. He'd accompanied prisoners many times in his career as a military policeman. That's what it felt like now: the sergeant ahead and the constables behind, off Balcombe's right and left shoulders. They were armed but relaxed, confident in their roles.

The walk was about three hundred metres and Balcombe felt eyes on him despite trying to appear casual.

"Can you tell me what it's about?" he asked the sergeant.

The man didn't answer until they reached the white block of concrete and windows. Functional and ugly, Balcombe thought. The exact opposite of police stations on the island.

★

Inspector Munro was thinking the same thing. He would rather have interviewed Balcombe at Victoria Police Station, but the man was in Kowloon and they didn't want to lose him. Transport him on the ferry and he might get away. They'd lost a prisoner last year because of the sloppy handling of the man in custody. He'd jumped overboard and swum to a small boat, never to be seen again.

Charles Balcombe looked both tired and surprised when he was escorted into the room where Munro and Reece were waiting.

"Good afternoon, Mr Balcombe," Reece said with more respect than Munro thought justified. However, he'd been told to let Reece lead. Englishman to Englishman.

Munro's starting position was the assumption of guilt: have a theory and try and disprove it. The official and judicial approach was the complete opposite. Despite what you know, assume they are innocent.

It was nonsense, and doubly so when white folk were treated with kid gloves. Were non-whites genetically more likely to be criminals? Of course not. However,

Munro did accept that hardship and desperation could lead people to commit crime. But theft of food was a million miles away from kidnap and ransom.

Reece shook Balcombe's hand and Munro forced a smile in greeting.

"So, Mr Balcombe," Reece began, "please tell us where you were last night."

"I walked. I had a few too many drinks and I went to bed."

"And overslept?"

"Yes."

"And you are in Kowloon because—?"

Balcombe's eyes showed suspicion despite him trying to appear neutral, Munro thought.

"It's part of Hong Kong last time I checked. I come here often." He paused. "For the rock climbing."

Reece seemed to accept this and asked some more general questions. Balcombe fielded them until a knock on the door disturbed the meeting. A man poked his head inside. Munro recognized the signal.

"One minute, please, Mr Balcombe," Munro said, and he left the room. Outside he was shown one thing that confirmed everything and another which surprised him.

He stepped back into the room and couldn't mask his smile. Both Reece and Balcombe saw it.

Munro had hoped the search of Balcombe's hotel room would reveal what they'd been looking for. It hadn't, but they'd found something else incriminating. However, he decided to hold that back for now.

"The briefcase," Munro said.

"Ah."

"We know about the ransom, Mr Balcombe," Reece said. "We'll need your fingerprints. I trust that won't be a problem?"

"First tell me how you knew about the ransom. Did Denis Toogood tell you?"

"He did."

Balcombe nodded, processing the information, then he said, "Fingerprints won't be a problem, then. I'm happy to explain."

As Reece took notes, Balcombe gave them a statement. He said Toogood had shown him a finger in a matchbox.

Unnecessarily, Reece confirmed they had the matchbox. Munro shot him a look, but the boy didn't notice it.

Balcombe continued, explaining that Toogood had received a ransom demand. Twenty thousand dollars to be delivered to a house on Ki Lung Street at nine last night. Balcombe had checked into The Peninsula hotel and checked the street and surrounding area before he'd returned. He'd met Toogood outside the bank and been given the briefcase containing the money at about quarter to four.

He told them he'd returned to Ki Lung Street at the allotted time but no one had appeared. So he'd returned to his room.

Reece appeared happy with the statement and surprised at Munro's challenge.

"You went to a street where there had recently been trouble—you must have read about the raid? About the murder of my sergeant?"

Balcombe said, "It seemed a big coincidence."

Reece said, "No one collected the money." He looked at his senior. "Could it be that we arrested the gang responsible for the kidnap?"

Munro didn't answer. Yes, it was possible, since the house had been on the same street, but there was far too much left unexplained.

"Let's be clear, Mr Balcombe. You, a white man, went at night with a briefcase full of money to meet gang members."

"Well—"

"Were you armed?" Toogood had mentioned a service revolver.

"I don't have a licence to carry a gun."

Munro shook his head. No, Balcombe didn't, but he was ex-military, that was clear.

Munro said, "Tell me about your army career."

"I can't," Balcombe said calmly. "However, I can assure you that I wasn't carrying a gun, whether legal or otherwise."

Much to his frustration, they hadn't found a gun in Balcombe's hotel room. Maybe he really didn't go to pay a ransom with a gun.

"So why take such an incredible risk?"

Balcombe said, "I didn't. I was about to explain. I left the briefcase at a café on Anchor Street."

"Where's that?" Munro knew but wanted to make sure Balcombe did. The way he answered might give a clue to his honesty.

Balcombe described it as at the top of Ferry Street running west to Cosmopolitan Dock.

Munro nodded. It was a reasonable description of the street in the Tai Kok Shui district.

"Toogood's plan had been for his son to disclose the combination to the briefcase once released," Balcombe continued. "I thought that unreasonable, so I would only provide the money after they proved Roger Toogood was alive."

Munro's mind kicked into gear. "You left the briefcase? Do you have a witness?"

"The owner of the café." Balcombe gave them the name.

If Balcombe was running a scam and intended to take the money for himself, he wouldn't have left the briefcase at a café.

"Thank you," Reece said. "We'll confirm that." He sounded like he was about to wrap things up, but there was the other thing. The thing they'd found in Balcombe's hotel room.

Munro said, "Did you get hurt?"

"Sorry," Balcombe said, uncertain. "Did I get hurt?"

"Tell me about the blood on your top."

He saw Balcombe's realization that they'd found a black top with blood on it.

"Nose bleed," he said after a pause. "I was anxious. I get nose bleeds when I get anxious."

"It's a lot of blood," Munro said. "So it's not Roger Toogood's blood?"

Balcombe almost laughed. "No, it is not! Would you like a blood sample as well as fingerprints?"

Reece said, "That won't be necessary, sir."

"How did you bruise your finger?" Munro asked, pointing to Balcombe's left hand.

"Climbing. I slipped."

"You mentioned that you climb."

"It's my hobby. I usually climb the Peak, but I was on Lion Rock on Christmas Day and got my finger stuck."

"You should be more careful." Munro smiled kindly.

Balcombe nodded, returning the smile.

"So where is the gun?" Munro asked quickly, hoping to catch the other man off guard.

"Gun?"

"You have a gun."

"No. I don't have a licence."

Toogood had mentioned a service revolver, but they'd found nothing incriminating in Balcombe's room apart from the bloody top.

"Where is Roger Toogood?" Munro asked.

"I don't know."

Damn, Munro thought, the man seems honest.

What was going on here? If Toogood Junior was just missing, this was wasting police time.

Munro wondered whether to tell Balcombe that the partial finger in the box was older than a few weeks. It had been disarticulated long before Roger Toogood had gone missing. It bothered him that Denis Toogood hadn't reported it to the police until after he'd handed money to Balcombe. Why was the British establishment so insular? Why didn't they trust the police? Did they think it would reflect badly on them to have a mostly Chinese body investigate them?

He felt like this was a distraction from real crimes. They would question the men from Ki Lung Street again. So far they denied knowledge of Sergeant Tam's murder. Of course they would, but Munro believed them, just like he was inclined to believe Balcombe. So, they'd question the men about the ransom and Roger Toogood, but Munro thought it would lead nowhere.

Denis Toogood would get his money back and Charles Balcombe could return to searching for the missing young man.

Reece was looking at him, his mouth open, looking more than ever like a fish.

"We're done," Munro said to Reece's unasked question.

Reece thanked Balcombe and took him off to be fingerprinted. After that, Reece would visit the café and confirm Balcombe's story about leaving the briefcase there.

Munro didn't bother waiting. He went out into the fresh air, took a lungful to clear his head and strolled towards the Star Ferry Pier. He was almost there when a constable ran after him, waving frantically.

"Sir!"

Munro frowned at the young man. "What is it?"

Waiting ferry passengers turned to watch the young man approach.

"Sir, there is an incident. Sir, I've been told to take you to Sham Shui Po."

"What sort of incident?" Munro asked, wondering why the Kowloon police would involve him—unless it was connected to the kidnapping and ransom. But it wasn't.

"Murders," the policeman said under his breath, probably hoping he wouldn't be overheard.

Munro was still unclear why they'd want him involved. That was until the constable said one keyword.

"Knifing," he said. "Lots of men have been stabbed."

FORTY-NINE

Inspector Munro was in the gang's property in Sham Shui Po with a detective called Bao. Munro reprimanded himself for his initial unconscious prejudice. Bao was reasonably intelligent despite his family coming from Qinghai.

Before they entered, Bao had confirmed that the civil Kowloon police had surrounded the building, making it safe. It was ironic that the inhabitants resisted an investigation into the deaths of their own.

"Walk me through what you found," Munro said. "Where were the bodies?"

"Let's go to the cages first," Bao said, and led Munro through the warren of corridors until they reached a room that could have been in Victoria Gaol. No, this was worse. The smell of sweat, piss and shit was strong. There were no obvious sanitary facilities. Each cell had blankets on the floor and buckets. The blankets for sleeping on, the buckets as a toilet.

Bao offered Munro a tub of Vaseline and the two men pushed some up their nostrils to block the stench.

"Who did they keep in here?" Munro asked, shaking his head, trying to dispel the image of people crammed in here.

"Girls, or so our informant tells me."

"Just girls?"

"Yes, for the sex trade. Most, if not all, will be immigrants, bought or more likely stolen."

"How many?"

Bao shook his head. "Your guess is as good as mine. Could be four. Could be more to a cell."

"And where are they now?" Munro asked, almost distracted by the thoughts rushing in. He pictured the face of the girl in the cold storage room.

Bao shrugged and stated the obvious. "Gone."

"All right, tell me about the dead men."

"We start at the door," Bao said, walking back through the warren to the exit that led into the alley. "One man in here"—he opened a door to a small room. There was blood on the ground and a white chalk outline.

"Stabbed, I understand. Throat slit?"

"One blow to the chest. Looks like he was grabbed from behind then bam!" He demonstrated a quick stabbing motion over his own heart.

They left the room, turned at a junction and came into another room. This was a living area with a large sofa and windows to the other side. It smelled rank. Alcohol and drugs, Munro suspected.

"Three men in here," Bao said. He pointed to the blood on the sofa and floor and wall. A lot of blood.

"A vicious attack," Munro said.

Bao nodded. "Very different to the first one. At this point we must think rival gang. These men were overcome by sheer force of numbers.

"Maybe," Munro said. "Then where?"

"Through here."

A side room had another chalk mark but less blood this time.

"Simple stabbing through the neck."

"A clean blow?" he said mechanically.

"Stiletto blade we think."

There was a door on the other side. When Bao retreated, Munro went for the other door. "Let's go this way," he said, and didn't wait for a response.

After a few turns and doors, they came back on the original corridor.

"That was lucky," Bao said. "Up here."

They took two more turns and were just short of the room with the cages.

Bao opened a door on the right and revealed a bedroom.

"Body number six," he said, "and the most gruesome. This one had his genitalia cut off, but died of a broken neck, it seems. The PM will confirm, but I'm pretty sure it was snapped, and you don't die quickly if your dick is cut off."

Munro took a deep breath. He'd removed the Vaseline and sucked in a lungful of the bad smell from down the hall. But his mind was spinning with this latest information.

Munro nodded. He looked in at a room with a desk and chairs—an office and a small storage room with a window.

He stood in each, looking closely and thinking. Then he went into the prison room. Bao offered Vaseline again but he declined.

"So, Detective Bao, tell me what happened here."

"Three or four attackers minimum," Bao said. "They killed the sentry—the man in the room by the door to the alley. Then went into the living area and killed the three. Then the man on his own. They came back and killed the man in the bedroom."

"A rival gang attack?" Munro said flatly.

"You don't think so?"

"I think this was the work of one man."

Bao scoffed. "Seriously?"

"There was a window in the room on the left—the storage room. The latch looked broken."

Bao looked surprised. "I didn't—"

"He came in through there. He killed the man in the bedroom first. Based on what you described, the man was being punished. He was either abusing a girl or he'd previously abused one. I suspect the former."

"So this lone man got the girls out."

"Yes."

"From here first."

"Yes, came in through the window."

"Then why kill the others? Why the men in the living room and beyond. Why not just the sentry?"

"Because he likes killing," Munro said, but even as the words passed his lips he realized his mistake. He thought about the squeezed-heart case. This was the same man. He enjoyed it, but he had a wider motive. He didn't know the girls above the laundry. He didn't know the girls in the cells. He was dealing out justice.

"How do you explain the different methods?" Bao said, interrupting Munro's thoughts.

"The broken neck, because it had to be quick—and not traumatize the girl any further. I think he then killed the sentry by the door. Again quickly but using his preferred method. Maybe he heard the men in the living area and decided he needed to get rid of them. The lone man was probably chanced upon—probably face to face—and needed to be dispatched quickly so that he didn't warn the others." Munro paused as he imagined the man making decisions and moving fast. "The men in the living area were probably out of their heads. They put up a fight and it got messier than our attacker would have liked. Only after he'd removed the threat did he lead the girls to safety." He paused and nodded to himself. "And only then did he go back and remove the genitalia."

"Why?"

"Because that's the way he thinks. The rapist needed to be punished."

"How can you possibly—?" Bao started to ask.

"Because I know this man. Well, at least I've seen his work before."

"All right," Bao said as they walked back to the exit. "So what next? How did your vigilante get the girls away?"

Outside, they looked down the alley. At each end there were barricades. The gang would have had sentries there.

Bao said, "If you're thinking he went down, you're wrong. The sentries at both ends saw nothing. Not just the girls, but no one. No gang. No vigilante. There's no way in or out."

"What about these doors," Munro said, walking to the opposite side of the alley. But he saw the problem straight away. All of the doors were barred.

Bao pointed and Munro saw his oversight. Ten paces away, one of the doors wasn't barred.

"Unlocked," Bao said.

"So they came through here—in and out."

Bao shook his head. "No. Odd that it was unlocked, but you can't get anywhere from inside."

Munro frowned. "Then they're still inside!"

It took the civil police under ten minutes to find them. Four girls were hiding upstairs in an attic space. But no vigilante.

The girls confirmed Munro's theory. One man. A tall white man had freed them. He'd picked the locks and killed the gang members. He'd also scaled the walls.

Like a mountain goat.

Or a rock climber.

FIFTY

Balcombe had failed to rescue Roger Toogood. Was the boy being held by a gang? Was the ransom opportunistic? It struck him that many people knew Roger was missing. Easy to claim you'd release him for money. But why not turn up at the address by the restaurant?

He knew he had to talk to Denis Toogood and explain what had happened but he was tired. Maybe that was why he delayed his return to the island. Maybe he wanted to delay that confrontation. So he booked another night's hotel stay.

In the evening, Balcombe visited the café on Anchor Street and spoke to the owner. He confirmed that the police had been and taken the briefcase. The man was very apologetic, as though he thought Balcombe would be disappointed.

Despite being told he didn't need to pay, Balcombe still gave the man the fifteen dollars they'd agreed and thanked him. In return, he was given more of the homemade cake.

Albert was waiting when Balcombe came out of the hotel on Tuesday morning. The young girl grinned at him.

"You had me fooled," Balcombe said.

"Which way? Thought I was really working for them?"

Balcombe nodded. "And thought you'd taken the money."

"I lied," she said.

"I know."

"Not to you. I lied to them. I told them the money was hidden at the death house. I suspect they searched for hours. Meanwhile, I slipped away as soon as I could." She hopped excitedly from foot to foot. "I'm good, aren't I?"

Balcombe was striding towards the ferry. Boarding had already begun.

"Yes you are," he said. "I'll up your wages."

"That's kind." She grinned. "What's next?"

"Next I face the music," he said solemnly.

Albert jogged ahead to fetch the rickshaw. Balcombe could have gone to the bank but decided to wait until Denis Toogood left for the evening. Prevaricating again, no doubt. He'd explain then. He'd also report that the police had taken the briefcase.

But before he reached the rickshaw, he spotted Blue-suit leaning against a car. The man appeared casual, not caring that he'd been spotted.

He opened the rear door of the car. "Mr Balcombe." It was said in a way that politely meant *come here.*

Balcombe walked over.

Blue-suit said, "Mr Van Ness requests your presence."

Balcombe didn't get in the car.

"It's in your interest, sir," Blue-suit said, and Balcombe believed him. However, he still didn't get in.

"I'll have my boy take me," he said, waving to Albert. "I trust that won't be a problem."

Blue-suit blinked as he tried to assess the response. It was as though he hadn't considered that option. Eventually, he shut the rear door.

"I'll let Mr Van Ness know you'll be there shortly."

Balcombe nodded. "I'll be right behind you."

Less than ten minutes later, Albert pulled the rickshaw along the drive that led to the Jardines men's clubhouse, or whatever it was. Balcombe noted the Union flag fluttering in the wind, although he saw no sign of his host.

Blue-suit was parked and beckoned him to an outbuilding. Balcombe had assumed it was a garage, but there were no cars inside. It was part workshop, part office, he assessed.

Van Ness was inside. He wore the same double-breasted blue jacket and cravat. He was standing next to a chair. A second man was standing on the other side of the chair. He wore a dark blue suit and white shirt, an identical look to the man who Balcombe called Blue-suit.

On the chair was a young man, not much more than a boy. He had brown hair, and Balcombe immediately noticed the boy's right ear. Just a jagged piece of flesh, half missing.

He wasn't tied up, but he looked distressed. Balcombe thought he hadn't been tortured, but the fear in his eyes said he expected it.

Were they just waiting for Balcombe to arrive?

Balcombe looked at Van Ness.

"We found Barry," Van Ness said unnecessarily.

"Why?"

Van Ness smiled. "Because you were looking for him."

Balcombe nodded. He'd made a mistake. Blue-suit saw him chasing someone at the racecourse. Balcombe had spoken to the stables manager. He'd left his card. He may as well have signposted that he was looking for Demitri Baros—better known as Barry.

Balcombe played the innocent. "That doesn't explain why you've picked him up."

Van Ness said, "You are looking for Roger Toogood. You are looking for Barry. Two plus two, Mr Balcombe."

Balcombe nodded but said nothing.

"I don't wish to hurt Barry, you see," Van Ness said. "Barry doesn't owe me any money, so it would be unreasonable, don't you think?"

"I do."

"So we will leave him in your hands and you will tell me where Mr Toogood is hiding."

"Why?"

"Because he owes me money."

"Two hundred dollars? You could approach his father. I'm sure he'll pay his son's debt."

"It's now four hundred dollars. Additional collection fees. But it's not about the money, I'm sure you understand."

Balcombe did. Moneylenders needed payment on time. And to achieve this they needed borrowers to appreciate there would be consequences otherwise. They needed to send a message.

"But hurting this boy won't achieve what you want," Balcombe said.

Van Ness placed a hand on Barry's shoulder and the young man shrunk beneath the grip.

"Except for the pressure on you, Mr Balcombe. You'll get Roger for me."

Balcombe shook his head. "If I find Roger, he'll come and pay up. And he'll apologize. That's all I'll promise."

Van Ness waited a beat then bunched up his hand and pulled Barry to his feet.

"All right, he's all yours."

FIFTY-ONE

Balcombe pressed close next to Barry on the rickshaw's bench.

He told Albert to take them down the hill to the racecourse. Balcombe hoped it would make Barry feel at ease. Psychology: take him away from the threat of the Jardines men to a place where he felt comfortable.

There were no horses, just the odd member of the racecourse staff, working. No one batted an eye as Balcombe had walked Barry over to the white fence. He leaned against them as though watching invisible horses.

"Where is Roger?"

Barry said nothing for a while. Eventually, Barry leaned on the fence next to him.

"They asked me the same question."

"They threatened you?" Balcombe said without looking at the boy.

"Said they'd cut off my other ear."

Balcombe nodded. The stable office manager had said Barry had been bitten by a horse, but teeth hadn't done that to the boy's right ear. It had been sliced by a knife—not a clean slice either. Balcombe wondered if Barry had been tortured before or whether it had been the result of a fight.

Barry said, "I told them I don't know where he is. And I don't."

"I believe you."

The boy sighed. "Thank you."

"I'm not going to hurt you. I'm working for his parents. They're worried about him."

Barry said nothing.

"You were friends," Balcombe said after a pause.

"Not really."

"Roger bet on the horses. He liked studying form. He liked to win."

The boy spluttered a laugh. "Doesn't everyone?"

"Some people *need* to win. Roger borrowed money from Van Ness but he needed more. So he bet large and expected to win."

Barry said nothing.

Balcombe figured he knew why. Roger expected to win because he had inside information. Barry gave him tips.

"How much did he pay you?"

Barry shuffled his feet in the dirt and said nothing.

"All right, I get it," Balcombe said, staring off across the field. "You'll get fired if anyone finds out."

Barry stopped shuffling. His breathing was loud, and Balcombe guessed the boy was wondering how he'd get himself out of this predicament. How could he save his job?

Balcombe said, "Tell me about the drugs."

"Drugs?"

"Roger needed the money to buy drugs. He was dealing. I think he had contacts in Kowloon and something went wrong."

Balcombe's theory was that Roger had taken the drugs but then lost them. Maybe they were stolen. He needed to pay for the original drugs or the replacement.

Maybe he had a commitment and needed cash urgently to fulfil it.

"There was no mention of drugs," Barry said.

Balcombe came off the fence and looked at the stableman. "What do you know, Barry?"

"He was a gambler. He wasn't into drugs."

"Maybe that was a gamble too." People gambled for different reasons. Some, like Balcombe, enjoyed the adrenaline rush. For other gamblers, it was more about the money: winning, and hopefully not losing. Businessmen could fall foul of that same rush. And the drugs business offered huge gains. But also huge risks. He could appreciate the urge to play that dangerous game.

Barry stared into the distance.

Balcombe had an idea. "Roger had an address book. At the back were girl's names and next to them were two columns of numbers."

"He never mentioned any girls."

"No?" Balcombe said. "Was that his code for the drug deals?"

"It wasn't drugs."

"What was he into?"

"There was a problem at work."

"The bank?"

"Yes."

"How do you know?"

Barry considered his answer before deciding to speak. "My friend told me. He introduced me to Roger in the first place. David works with him."

Balcombe studied the boy's face. "Was it David Jones?"

"Yes, that's him."

★

David Jones came out of the bank. As Balcombe expected, the young man turned left rather than walk through the square to a parked car. He wasn't senior enough to have a car, so he would either walk or take a tram home.

Balcombe was waiting with Barry the stableman. They'd been there for half an hour before Jones appeared. The young man came out with a stream of other workers, most of whom looked up at the sky, checking for rain. Jones carried a briefcase and umbrella. He tucked the umbrella under his arm and started walking towards where Balcombe stood.

It took a few seconds before their eyes met.

Balcombe saw the recognition. Then the young bank worker glanced at the boy standing beside him. And the expression changed from intrigue to panic.

Jones stopped, gawped and looked back the way he'd come.

When he didn't move, Balcombe strode towards him. Jones glanced behind again and took a step backwards. This gave Balcombe the impression he was considering returning to the bank but liked neither option. He didn't want to return or be confronted by Balcombe.

Quickly closing the gap between them, Balcombe said, "What's wrong?"

Jones said nothing. He swallowed hard, glanced at Barry and now looked as though he'd take flight.

Balcombe grabbed the young man's sleeve so that he couldn't run. The umbrella clattered to the ground.

People around them turned, looked but didn't stop.

"What's wrong, David?" Balcombe asked again.

Jones looked at Barry. He half-heartedly pulled against Balcombe's grip as though he knew he should run, but also knew it was pointless.

"David?" Balcombe said more firmly.

And that's when Barry said, "He's not David Jones."

FIFTY-TWO

Not David Jones?

"Who the hell are you then?" Balcombe asked.

The young man's mouth opened but no sound came out. He was like a child caught with his hand in the cookie jar, eyes bulging, skin pale and sweating.

Finally, the man pointed away from the bank, towards the pier. There were lots of people there, queuing for the next ferry.

Keeping hold of the man's sleeve, Balcombe walked with him onto Connaught Road. However, before the pier, the man steered them behind the Queen's Building. It was still busy here, but less obvious. Balcombe realized that the young man didn't want to be seen standing and talking. Maybe he wanted a screen from the bank, didn't want to be seen by someone there.

When they stopped in a doorway, the young man sighed and said, "Peter Wallwork. My real name's Peter Wallwork."

Balcombe said, "Then why the hell did you tell me your name was Jones?"

Barry made a grunting noise showing he now understood the confusion.

"He doesn't look anything like David."

"No," Wallwork said hoarsely. "I work with him."

"That still doesn't explain the subterfuge," Balcombe said. "I'm waiting."

"I was told to say that I was David," Wallwork whispered.

"Why?"

"Because David wasn't available." He cleared his throat and found his voice. "It didn't matter because we both know Roger Toogood. And... and I never actually said I was David. You assumed and I didn't correct you, sir."

Balcombe cast his mind back to their meeting at his apartment. Yes, he'd made that assumption. He'd said David Jones and the young man hadn't confirmed or denied it. He'd just said good morning and they'd briefly discussed why Balcombe was wearing his climbing gear.

Then Balcombe remembered something else. When he'd asked the young man about his job, about working for Denis Toogood, he'd seemed perplexed.

"What is it about your job?" Balcombe asked.

"Sir?"

"Why were you concerned when I asked about Denis Toogood?"

Wallwork blinked. "I said I work with Roger."

"You said you didn't work directly for his father, Denis Toogood."

"Er... yes I do, sir."

"You work for his father?" Balcombe clarified.

"Yes."

Balcombe blew out air and stared down the road. The ferry sounded its horn as it neared the pier. There would be children in the water, jumping in, cooling off—and probably playing chicken with the ferry.

He turned back and looked hard at Wallwork.

"Why did Toogood ask you to pretend to be Roger's friend."

"I am Roger's friend."

Barry said, "I've never seen him before."

Wallwork said, "Well, Jones wasn't available, and I could tell you what you needed to know. His father told me to do it and I thought it wouldn't matter."

"Where is Jones?" Balcombe asked. "Is that who you're worried about? Might he have been watching you leave?"

"What? No!"

Balcombe waited, the silence putting pressure on Wallwork to say more.

The young man said, "He's not been at work for over a week."

"Is he missing too?"

Barry said, "I know where David lives."

Wallwork sighed. "He's not there either."

"Is he missing too?" Balcombe repeated, gripping Wallwork's shoulder.

"No, sir!"

"You know where he is?"

"He's taking a holiday."

It was Christmas after all, but Balcombe sensed this holiday was about something else entirely.

"Where is he?" Balcombe asked, tightening his grip.

"If I tell you... Please don't say how you found him."

"That depends," Balcombe said gruffly. "I don't like being deceived. And it depends on what I find."

FIFTY-THREE

The real David Jones had darker hair than his imposter. They were a similar height and age but Jones had a stronger chin and Roman nose. If Balcombe had known the men he couldn't have mistaken them, just like Barry hadn't mistaken them.

Jones was staying at a hotel in Waterfall Bay. It was on the far side of the Peak and too far for Albert to take him, so Balcombe had bundled Barry and Wallwork in a taxi and taken them both to find the real Jones.

"I'm taking a holiday," Jones said, glancing at Wallwork.

Balcombe said, "Cut the nonsense, Jones."

Jones looked at Wallwork again.

Balcombe turned to the young bank man. "Go home, Wallwork. Don't say anything to anyone. Got it?"

Wallwork bobbed his head as though relieved at being released. "Suits me!" Then he hurried away.

"Shall I go too?" Barry asked.

Balcombe shook his head. "You are friends?"

"Yes," Barry said. "I know David and he introduced Roger Toogood to me."

Balcombe looked into Jones's eyes. The other man nodded.

Balcombe asked, "Why did Roger bet on the horses?"

"He liked gambling," Jones said.

"But he needed to win. He borrowed money from Van Ness—"

"I don't know where he got the money from."

"Jardines' militia."

Jones nodded. "Ah, that explains it. Yes."

"Explains what?"

"Why he told me to keep out of the way of the militia. Told me to say I knew nothing."

"What do you know?"

Jones took a breath. "I introduced Roger to Barry. Roger needed two thousand and Barry could help."

Barry was shaking his head.

Balcombe said, "I know Barry was giving tips on form. You were paying him?"

"Yes."

"So you aren't friends as such, are you? Barry takes your money."

"Just a share of winnings," Barry said. "Never big bets, because that would get me into trouble."

"And then Roger placed a two hundred bet—and lost." Balcombe paused and watched the other two nod. "So why did Roger run?"

No one spoke.

Balcombe said, "It wasn't about Jardines, was it?"

"No," Jones said.

"And it wasn't about drugs. Roger wasn't gambling on a drugs business?"

"No."

"He wasn't in bed with a Chinese gang?"

"We talked about it but no. It was too risky. Making money on the horses was a better bet."

Balcombe nodded. He waited for more but Jones wasn't forthcoming.

Eventually, Balcombe said, "Where is Roger?"

"I don't know. I honestly don't know."

"But you know why he disappeared?"

"Yes, sir."

"Well?"

Jones licked his dry lips, looked away and then back at Balcombe.

"It was work. He had to leave because of work."

FIFTY-FOUR

"Time for you to go, Barry."

The young stableman didn't move. "How will I get back?"

"That's not my problem."

"I need the taxi fare."

"Think yourself lucky that I don't tell your employer about your little arrangements with Jones and Roger Toogood. However, I suggest it's time to start looking for a new career."

Barry shrugged as though he didn't care about his job, although Balcombe was sure he did. Minutes later, Jones and Balcombe were alone in the young man's hotel room.

Jones's eyes darted left and right.

"What are you scared of?"

"Are you going to kill me?" Jones said. He tried to sound brave, but his voice quavered.

"I'm not going to kill you."

"Who are you really working for, Mr Balcombe?"

Balcombe shook his head. "I'm not going to hurt you," he said in as calming a voice as he could muster. "I just want to know where Roger is."

"Why are you looking for him?"

"Because his parents asked me to."

Jones took a long breath. "Mind if I sit down?"

Balcombe pointed to a chair. "Now, tell me about work. Why did he need to disappear if it wasn't about the money?"

Jones looked puzzled. Cleared his throat. "I didn't say it wasn't about the money. Roger needed money for work."

"What about work?"

When Jones didn't immediately answer, Balcombe mentioned the address book.

"There were numbers against girls' names. Like odds or a score, or something else."

"Something else."

"Explain."

Jones took a nervous breath. Sweat beaded his upper lip. "You know about arbitrage?"

"A little. I know what the word means."

"You will know that the Hong Kong dollar is tied to sterling."

Balcombe did know this. Malaya and Singapore were the same. One pound was fixed at approximately fifteen Hong Kong dollars. It made trade straightforward, without the concern for money exchange.

Jones dropped his voice. "So you'll appreciate that they cannot, under any circumstances, be switched into US dollars."

"Right."

"But such arbitrage is possible," he said, lowering his voice even further. "Money can be made by buying in US dollars and selling in pounds. Or vice versa depending on the movement."

Balcombe nodded. "Go on."

"Roger was doing this. Not too much, but he was making a lot of money. For the bank, you understand, not personally. But he wanted to look good, especially since his father was the vice principal. Roger wanted to prove himself." Jones took a breath. "Not me though, you understand. I didn't do it and I didn't know what Roger was doing until it all went wrong."

"He started losing money."

"Yes. The value of the dollar went the wrong way and he lost money."

Balcombe thought about the list of names and numbers. The numbers had increased. The balance had shifted.

"He lost more and he gambled more," Balcombe said. "It was the classic gambler instinct. Lose and gamble more to make up for your loss."

Jones nodded then shook his head at a thought. "Until it was a big hole. Two hundred thousand dollars."

"And he planned to recover this on the horses?"

"Yes. He needed to fill the financial hole before anyone noticed. He had a plan to do this over a few weeks, but the very first bet went south and he was in trouble. He couldn't go back to Jardines, and his father would have eaten him alive. Besides, who has that sort of money?"

"So, Roger had to run."

"Yes."

"Where?" Balcombe asked again, hoping to get a different answer this time. He'd been an investigator long enough to know it happened. Either the interviewee forgot their previous answer or rapport had been established and they'd opened up. However, Jones shook his head.

"I don't know."

"And you're sure he didn't look for other means of raising money. Drugs, for example?"

"No, he wouldn't."

Balcombe paced the room while Jones watched him nervously.

"You're his friend, right, David?"

"Yes."

"Who else was he close to?"

"No one. He was a little... a little strange. Not very sociable."

Balcombe thought about the murdered Japanese girl, Emiko Sasaki. He thought about the paperback book in her bed, a western. Undoubtedly Roger's.

"David, did Roger tell you about a girlfriend?"

"No." A shake of the head. "He didn't date anyone."

"He was learning Japanese."

"Was he? I know he was interested in Japan."

"Warfare. Japanese military and planes."

"Yes."

"And girls?"

"No."

"How can you be so sure?"

And then Balcombe saw it. The way Jones squirmed at the question. He knew the answer but couldn't say. And yet there had been the paperback in the girl's bed.

Jones finally met his gaze, but his lips were shut tight.

Balcombe said, "Where does the Japanese girl fit in? There was a girl at North Point. Emiko—"

Jones's eyes lit up with recognition. "Emiko Sasaki?"

"Yes!"

"That wasn't Roger's girlfriend." Jones almost laughed. "That was his father's mistress."

FIFTY-FIVE

"Thanks for coming," Munro said to his friend Fai Yeung. They were in the Wellington, where Munro used to drink with Arthur Tam. The air was thick with cigarette smoke and chatter.

Yeung sipped his baijiu. "I'm happy to drink with you, Babyface, so long as you don't expect me to drink the warm ale," he said.

They'd toasted Arthur's memory and Munro was starting to think it was a bad idea coming here. He wanted to celebrate the capture of Tam's killer or killers, but there was no evidence against the men arrested in Ki Lung Street. There was also the issue that Chau Hing, the man who had sent him to his death, was going to be released.

Perhaps his promotion had been a bad move, Munro thought. As a sergeant he hadn't been so concerned about the politics.

"You've been quiet for a long time," Yeung said. "Is this what your drinking sessions have become, my friend? If so, I think I can find better company for a night."

Munro sighed and apologized. "I've been wondering whether it's time for me to retire."

Yeung shook his head. "You're joking, I'm sure. The Babyface I know and love is obsessed by justice."

"The Chief wanted me to fit up a man for the cold-store room murder."

"Was he guilty?"

"The pig butcher—undoubtedly, but I haven't got the evidence for the courts. They'll throw out the case."

"And you can't plant evidence."

Munro sipped his beer. "No."

"Inspector Munro." Bao, the detective from the mainland, squeezed through the crowd to their table.

"Bao?"

"I was told you'd be here."

When Munro looked at him quizzically, the other detective pulled something from his pocket and held it out.

A watch.

Munro took it, turned it over in his hand and nodded. "Sergeant Tam's."

"Yes," Bao said. "It was on one of the bodies from that multiple murder scene."

"The one where the girls had been released."

Bao nodded. "It was on the wrist of the man in the office. I thought you'd want to know straight away."

Munro shook the detective's hand. "Thank you."

It meant they probably had Tam's killer. Either the one wearing the watch or one of the others found murdered.

"Learned anything more about the tall white man dressed in black?" The girls had given a simple description of their saviour—the man Munro thought of as the vigilante.

Bao nodded. "The girls told us he'd been captured but unlocked the cage in the morning. He killed the men then came back for them. Seems you were right about the sequence if not the timings. They don't know where he went after leaving them."

"Nothing more about the man?"

Bao thought for a second. "You know about the moustache? Film-star looks with a thin moustache they said."

"No, that's new." It matched what one of the laundry people had said. Not a beard, a moustache.

"Oh, and—I don't know if it helps, but one of his fingers was badly bruised. That's it I'm afraid."

Munro shook the other detective's hand again. For a man from Qinghai, Bao wasn't too bad.

"Since you're in a better mood," Yeung said after Bao had left them, "it's time to remind you of our bets. That's three for three in my favour. You've failed to solve a single one of those murders."

"Conviction and solving aren't the same thing, Fai."

"If you say so." Yeung grinned but Munro was being serious.

"I do. And I haven't given up on the squeezed-heart case. In fact, I think I'm getting closer. Much closer."

FIFTY-SIX

David Jones's revelation changed everything.

On the journey home, Balcombe thought about what he'd learned. Roger had committed an illegal act at work, leaving a financial hole. He'd confessed to David Jones, his only close friend. They'd decided the solution was to borrow money from the Jardine militiamen and then gamble on the horses using inside information from Barry. Safe bets they thought, but they'd lost.

Roger was now facing trouble from the bank and Jardines. One may have cost him his job and the other his life. Or at least a very painful experience.

So he'd disappeared and hadn't told Jones where he'd gone.

Where was he? It was a small island and his contacts appeared limited. Balcombe could have beaten Jones and was sure that Van Ness would have his men try and get Jones to talk, but Balcombe believed him. Jones didn't know where Roger was. Jones was also afraid and in hiding.

Not hidden half as well as his friend though.

And then there was the Japanese girl. Balcombe couldn't explain the paperback, but he believed she wasn't Roger's lover, but his father's.

Had she been killed because she didn't know where Roger was? Or maybe she did know. Maybe she had sheltered Roger for a while.

Maybe Roger had killed her.

Balcombe's thoughts went round and round. None of it helped him find Roger though. He was missing a piece of the puzzle, he was sure.

What was he overlooking?

When he arrived home, he found a note from Grace Toogood. It said she had arranged a private apartment on Ladder Street. She would be there at ten tomorrow and hoped he could join her. She'd addressed the note to Max Jacks and signed it Scarlett.

He smiled at the thought of her delicious body, her eyes and the smell of her. And she was still in his head when he fell asleep.

But instead of dreaming about their lovemaking, he woke up in the night and found his thoughts full of the problem. The kidnapping ransom bothered him the most. The matchbox with the finger. The money in the briefcase. The failed exchange, then the discovery of all those girls held prisoner and no sign of Roger.

He thought about the detective inspector and his white assistant. He thought about the fingerprints and was back to the matchbox.

After hours of lying awake, he got up and poured himself two fingers of whisky. He sat in his favourite chair and went back over everything. Especially everything that David Jones had told him. And also what Jones hadn't said.

As dawn turned the Peak into a golden cap, Balcombe had realized something. This wasn't about Roger. This was all about Denis Toogood.

FIFTY-SEVEN

"Where are we on the high profile cases, Munro?" Carmichael was pacing in his office. From his appearance and odour, it was clear he'd been drinking, and not just last night. Rumour had it that the Chief kept a bottle of something in his desk drawer. Maybe more than one.

"The recent murders?" Munro asked.

"And the kidnapping."

Ah, Roger Toogood. The disappearance of a white adult male was high profile in the Chief's mind.

Munro shook his head. "We've got Mr Toogood's money back."

"What about this Balcombe chap? What was his involvement?"

Munro explained that Balcombe appeared to be genuinely looking for Roger Toogood. They'd found no evidence against him, not even the illegal firearm they'd expected.

"What's your theory?"

"About the missing young man?"

"Yes!" Carmichael clenched his teeth in annoyance. "Of course, Roger Toogood."

"Is he a case, sir? My understanding is Mr Toogood reported the potential kidnapping and ransom payment." *But only to you*, Munro might have added. "There was no evidence of either. The pathologist says that the partial finger in a matchbox provided couldn't have been Roger Toogood's. It was too decomposed."

"So we have nothing?"

"As I said, sir, we have the money back and no evidence of a gang trying to collect it."

"Most odd," Carmichael said. "All right, what about those murders. Start with the Japanese girl."

Munro swallowed. "We're working on it. There is a coincidence—"

"Yes? Speak up, man!"

"Denis Toogood owns the property where she lives. That's why—"

Carmichael's eyes bulged. "And I told you to tread carefully. Don't go accusing Toogood without copper-bottomed evidence."

"No, sir."

"And the squeezed-heart case?"

"I'm intrigued that there is a connection between what we found on Sunday in the Sham Shui Po district and above the laundry. Both operations were dealing in girls, but probably within the law." Munro didn't need to explain the problem of proving that a girl over the age of fourteen was being held illegally. The men holding them often had documents proving they'd bought the girls from parents. "Although the girls found yesterday had been held in cages."

Carmichael nodded. "And this gets us where exactly?"

Munro took a breath. "I have a description of a tall man."

"Excellent!" Carmichael said sarcastically. "Go and arrest all tall men then. Surely you have something better than this? For Christ's sake, it's almost the end of the year. Can I have at least one good result from you?"

FIFTY-EIGHT

Ladder Street was a long series of stone steps staggering from Queen's Road to Caine Road. Balcombe knew streets like these were built to link up the higher roads and properties before the Peak tram. As he climbed, he noted the proximity to Toogood's house in the mid-levels.

The air was filled with the usual smell of cooking but he could also smell baking bread and his stomach rumbled with appreciation. He paused for breath and to admire the view of Kowloon—a view afforded the properties further up the street. He noted the transition from shophouse at the bottom to the large British colonial properties at the top.

The address Grace Toogood had given him was the third highest. It had stone balconies around each of the three upper levels. The large house opposite had wrought-iron railings. Both had uninterrupted views; no trees, just buildings staggering down to the harbour.

At some stage, maybe a hundred years ago, this had been a single property, but the building was now split into six properties. The stonework was discoloured and the paint was fading. He climbed to the third floor and knocked.

Grace answered the door in a sky-blue silk dressing gown. She held a glass of gin in one hand and a cigarette in the other. It was in a long holder and didn't appear lit.

She smiled coquettishly and posed in the doorway. She had bare feet and bare legs. He guessed there was very little beneath the gown as well.

"Why, Mr Jacks, what a pleasant surprise," she said using the fake name she'd given him.

Chiffon curtains wafted in the breeze behind her. She took a pace back, looking him up and down.

"You appear overdressed, Mr Jacks."

"Grace—"

She frowned then laughed lightly. "Oh, Mr Jacks, you seem uptight. May I pour you a drink to loosen you up?"

She spun and headed for a drinks cabinet.

"What will it be, darling?"

"Grace, we need to talk."

She spun back and the frown returned. "Oh don't be a bore, Charles! I thought you were supposed to be fun!"

"I've been set up," he said.

She dropped the cigarette. "Pardon me?"

"Your husband has been setting me up."

She flopped onto a chaise longue and he took a chair close by.

"You'll need to explain," she said after a sip of gin. "Have you found Roger?"

He shook his head. "But I'm certain he's alive and I believe Denis knows where he is."

She blinked and stared at him.

"The Kowloon gang and ransom was a set-up."

"I'm sorry, Charles, you'll need to start at the beginning. What have you discovered?"

"I found Roger's friend David—his real friend." Balcombe held up a hand. "I'll explain that as well, in a minute. David told me why Roger had run. He'd done something wrong at work—at the bank. He'd traded illegally and lost a vast amount of money. Then he borrowed from a moneylender in the hope of winning a lot at the races. But he didn't. He lost, and that's when I think he told his father."

"You think?"

"Denis deceived me. He sent someone who works for him to act as David Jones, the friend. The fake David told me nothing because Denis wanted me to divert my attention from the bank. He wanted me to think Roger was either hiding from Jardines—who he borrowed the money from—or maybe it was a bad drugs deal."

"But Roger was kidnapped!" she said.

Balcombe gave Grace a hard look. "You don't believe that. You couldn't sleep with me knowing that the boy was in danger."

She said nothing.

He said, "So Denis changed his plan, or maybe it was always his plan. He made it look like I was involved in the ransom demand. When he handed me my expenses, I thought he behaved strangely. It was as though he wanted it to look like a forced payment. He was playing to the gallery—to the bank security man in particular. Then he did the same with the ransom money in the briefcase."

Grace had been squinting as though trying hard to follow his argument. She took a sip of gin.

"Go on."

He said, "I thought it a coincidence that he sent me to the same place as that in the newspaper. I don't think he knew anywhere else in Kowloon where there might be trouble. But he was wrong. He expected me to be mugged for the briefcase. Maybe he hoped I'd be killed."

Grace stopped squinting at him and he saw the truth in her eyes.

"You knew!" he said.

"I suspected. The fingerprints…"

Balcombe thought for a moment. The police had fingerprinted him to compare with those on the matchbox containing the partial finger.

He said, "Did Denis tell the police that I touched the matchbox?"

"He said you did it deliberately. He said he suspected you and he were the only ones to touch it, so you were making sure your prints were there. He told the police that you were guilty if they didn't find any other prints."

But they hadn't arrested him.

She took a final sip of gin, set down the glass and said, "I wiped the box. They won't have found any fingerprints."

"So you knew all along?"

"Only when he talked to the police. I eavesdropped. He'd been acting off, so I knew he was up to something and he seemed so calm when he showed me the box with the finger."

Balcombe said, "It won't have been Roger's finger."

"No."

Balcombe shook his head at the audacity of the plan. Roger had lost money from the bank—too much for Denis to cover, so they would set up a ransom payment and claim Balcombe had extorted the money.

He said, "There won't have even been much money in the briefcase he gave me—certainly not the money he claimed. I should have checked it."

"You weren't to know."

Balcombe said, "I'll take that drink now. Whisky. Straight up."

She poured them both a glass and he knocked it back. He was delaying and he knew it.

Finally, after the burn in his throat had subsided, he said, "We should talk about the Japanese girl."

"The Japanese girl," Grace said slowly. Her eyes narrowed. "What about a Japanese girl?"

"Denis had one killed. She lived over at North Point. On Marble Street."

She said, "Denis owns property there. He owns this building too." She breathed deeply, her bosom rising and falling beneath the fine silk gown. "He had a girl killed?"

Balcombe watched her eyes. "His mistress."

"Oh my!"

Ironic, he thought. Here they were meeting for a sexual liaison and yet the thought of her husband having an affair shocked her. At least that's what he first thought.

"Of course I knew," she said quietly. "All those nights away. He'd had too long here without his first wife and then after we married. What shocks me more is that he'd kill her."

"More likely have someone else do it for him."

"But why kill his mistress?"

"He made it look like Roger had been there. It was more evidence of a trail. Maybe she was being difficult. Maybe she'd threatened to tell you about their arrangement. Whatever, he decided to kill her so that it looked like a murderer—or the Kowloon gang—were after Roger. It reinforced his story."

"I'm shocked."

"People do foolish things," Balcombe said. "Crime might seem straightforward, but most criminals make mistakes. It's the stress, the worry, the fear that they'll get caught. The thinking becomes confused. There was no need to kill the girl, but Denis was panicking."

She was nodding. "He is all about his job at the bank. Roger carrying out illegal arbitrage would be seen as a reflection on him."

"Denis didn't want to lose face."

She stood and walked to the open window. He joined her, looking out across the rooftops.

After a pause, she said, "What are you going to do?"

"The police need to know," he said, although he'd already had more contact with the police than he ever wanted. The more they investigated, the more likely they were to discover his alter ego. BlackJack had fled Malaya and Singapore. He didn't want to spend his life on the run. What he needed was for Grace to report the crime. And, as he'd thought during the early hours, the solution was the murder of the Japanese girl. If that could be pinned on Denis Toogood, then Balcombe would not be involved.

When they discussed it, Grace was very uncomfortable. She didn't want the police involved, but he could see no other way.

"Remember, he killed his mistress!" Balcombe said.

"Possibly," she said.

She was right. He didn't have the proof, but the police might find it. Then she said something that he argued about but eventually accepted.

"First we'll talk," she said. "Come to the house at four this afternoon and we'll confront him."

It was a delay, but reasonable, he presumed.

However, he'd never get the chance to talk to Denis Toogood, because five hours later the man was dead.

FIFTY-NINE

Albert dropped Balcombe outside the Toogood residence. The gates were open. When he reached the door, he found that open as well.

It took just three minutes to discover Denis Toogood's body. He was lying in a pool of blood on the kitchen floor. His once white shirt was a mess of blood and Balcombe guessed there were four or five stab wounds to his chest.

However, the blow that killed Toogood was probably the one to his heart. The weapon, a pair of scissors, was still there sticking out of his chest.

Footsteps in the hall behind made Balcombe turn.

"Don't move!"

It was Grace Toogood. Her voice was strained, her pale face streaked with make-up and tears. A gun pointed at his chest. A Beretta 418. Nice. Small and ideal for her delicate hand, he thought at the back of his mind.

She looked him up and down with disapproval. He was wearing his climbing gear rather than the formal attire she'd have expected.

But she didn't comment on his clothes. She simply repeated: "Don't you move!"

He held his hands out at the sides, relaxed and unthreatening.

She looked past him. "Oh my God! What have you done?"

Balcombe shook his head. "Stop the acting, Grace."

"You killed Denis," she said.

"You won't get away with it."

Grace said nothing for a few beats. Then something flitted across her face. A thought, perhaps.

She said, "The police are coming. You killed Denis. You tried to extort money from him."

He shook his head once. "The police have the ransom money. I returned it. The kidnapping was faked by Denis."

"Or by you. And the briefcase—they say they recovered it. Not returned by you. There's a subtle but important difference. They found you and collected the money. Not you handing it in."

"Tell me why, Grace. Why do this? Did you kill Roger too?"

She laughed manically but it was forced. He saw relief in her eyes. She was happy to delay, probably hoping the police would burst in at any moment. Grateful that it would be over and Balcombe would be arrested for the murder of her husband.

She was too far away for him to dive and grab the gun. Her hand trembled but he had no doubt she could pull the trigger.

He was in trouble but he needed to know.

"Why, Grace?"

"Because he was a bastard. I despised him. I shouldn't have married the old grump but"—she shrugged—"I suppose it was the money and glamour. A girl's head can be turned. But he treated me like a chattel. Of course, I knew about his mistress and his prostitutes. I was supposed to just accept the situation and be happy. Even his son came before me—and Denis didn't treat Roger well either."

"What triggered it?"

"Roger and his financial mess. We didn't get along, but he came to me first asking for a loan." Grace smiled wanly. "I didn't know the whole story. Didn't know it was about arbitrage and a loss at the bank. So, when I asked Denis he said 'no'. He was a man of principle—a man who believed money should be earned. He insisted that Roger earn his way in life and not rely on hand-outs. So Roger went to moneylenders and lost more."

"Then he came clean about the bank's loss."

"Yes. He was desperate then. It worked out beautifully. I was able to get rid of him—"

Balcombe shook his head. "So you killed him!"

"No, no! He's alive but out of the way. He hated me almost as much as he despised his father for not giving him money. Me, because I took the place of his mother. He thought his father favoured me, but in reality, Denis just looked after himself."

"Whose plan was it to set me up?"

She smiled. "Mine originally, but I let Denis think it was his idea. As far as Denis was concerned it was about him saving face at work, so a kidnapping and ransom could explain the missing money."

"I was supposed to get killed in Kowloon."

"He hoped so. The fall-back plan was to have you convicted for your involvement. However, the return of the money—"

"There wasn't much in the briefcase, was there?"

"Of course not. Denis couldn't lose twenty thousand on top of what Roger had gambled at work."

"But you wiped my fingerprints off the matchbox. Which told me you had an overarching plan," he said.

She raised an eyebrow, perhaps suspecting that he knew.

He said, "You killed the Japanese mistress, didn't you?"

"That's pure conjecture."

She cocked the revolver.

"You're going to shoot me?" he said loudly, surprised.

"I can't wait for the police."

There was a noise behind her. Footsteps.

"Too late!" Balcombe said.

And the sound of a gunshot echoed through the big house.

SIXTY

"You took your time," Balcombe said to Albert. She was standing in the hall, her face pale, her hands shaking.

He stepped over Grace's body and took the gun from Albert's hand.

"I've... I've never shot anyone before," she said.

The trigger command was *shoot me*. He'd told Albert to creep in and wait until he said it, but she hadn't appeared until the last moment.

Balcombe had realized Grace had been lying to him. Earlier, she'd said she knew nothing about the money when he explained it.

Roger carrying out illegal arbitrage would be seen as a reflection on him.

In the house on Ladder Street, he hadn't said *arbitrage*, she had. She knew. She'd been lying. And then it all fell into place. Money may have been a factor, but more than anything she despised her husband and his philandering. Her relationship with Balcombe was a pretence. She needed him to either kill Denis or be the patsy.

So he came prepared. He'd hoped to overpower Grace with his strength and speed, but she'd kept her distance. He'd relied on the aim and timing of a little Chinese tomboy. He'd told her to point the service revolver at the centre of her body. Harder to miss that way.

The bullet had passed through the back of Grace's neck. It tore a bigger hole at the front and blood bubbled from the throat and mouth. She sank to her knees, spluttered a few times and then dropped face first onto parquet flooring.

Which gave Balcombe a problem.

The police would be here in a moment and he had a stage to set.

SIXTY-ONE

The house had been searched by the first policemen on the scene. There were no household staff here and the only person they'd passed coming in was a coolie. They should have stopped the boy and questioned him. But by the time they realized there had been a murder, it was too late. The boy had gone and neither policeman could describe him.

"I heard you got a conviction: Fung Haoran, the pig butcher," Assistant Pathologist Yeung said as Munro stepped into the kitchen. "Congratulations then?"

"The murder charge was thrown out."

"Your chief will be upset."

Munro nodded as he looked from the bodies in the kitchen through the door into the hallway. The crime scene didn't make any sense.

"So you only got him for a misdemeanour?"

"Meat hygiene offence. He'll be out after three more days in Victoria Gaol."

Taking off his round spectacles, Munro rubbed at the lenses, placed them back and studied the scene.

Two bodies. One male one female. The male had a pair of scissors in his chest and a revolver in his hand.

The woman had a hole in her neck.

"Tell me what we have here."

"Preliminary assessment: the male has five wounds to the chest, inflicted over a short time with the final one piercing his heart." Yeung pointed to the protruding scissors and grinned. "You'll probably find that's your murder weapon."

"Time of death?"

"Less than an hour, I'd say."

Munro nodded. The first police were on the scene twenty minutes ago, responding to a call from Mrs Toogood claiming there was an intruder in her house. If she'd said someone with a gun they'd have been faster. If she'd claimed there had been a murder then Munro himself would have been there in minutes. As it was, it looked like they missed the action. But what went on here?

"Tell me about the scissors," Munro said.

Yeung said, "Oh, I must be slow today. I blame it on working the nights." He dropped his voice. "And the days setting up my farm."

"Well?"

"The murder of the Japanese girl last week."

"Almost identical."

"That could be the same murder weapon. Scissors would explain the unusual puncture marks I saw."

Munro nodded. Interesting. "We'll check them for fingerprints," he said. "Reece?"

Fish-faced Reece got up from sniffing the revolver and, wearing gloves, removed the scissors and put them in a bag.

"So what happened here?" Munro asked him.

Reece looked at the bodies. "She stabs him four times and then he shoots her."

"What about the blood?"

"She was in the hall when the bullet hit. So maybe she walks away thinking he is dead. He isn't, fires the gun. From the smell of the gun it was fired very recently."

Yeung was looking at Munro.

"The scissors to his heart will have killed him almost instantly—"

Reece said, "Yes that was the final blow. He shot her, she staggered back and stabbed him in the heart and they both died."

Munro said, "She was walking away. He shoots her through the back of the neck. She staggers back and kills him." He shook his head, looking at the assistant pathologist. "Tell me about her neck wound."

"Fatal."

"How fatal?"

"Again, almost instantaneous. She'd have choked on her own blood."

"And yet she managed to get back—what, five yards?—and have enough strength and control to force a pair of scissors into the man's heart?"

Yeung rubbed the back of his bull-thick neck. "You're the detective, Babyface. I just deal with the bodies."

SIXTY-TWO

Balcombe climbed the Peak long after the sun had gone down and the hill tram stopped running.

After moving Grace's body, he had wiped Albert's fingerprints from the revolver and placed it in Denis Toogood's right hand. He prayed Denis was right-handed because he couldn't remember. Odds were in his favour and there was always the chance that the police wouldn't think of it.

It would be much easier to accept that Grace had stabbed her husband, who had in return shot her. Easier than inventing a third party who'd staged the scene. Wasn't it? How diligent were the Hong Kong CID anyway?

He read the newspapers, he knew the pressure on the jails and the number of unsolved major crimes. Much easier to close the books on this. He hoped.

He'd sent Albert away immediately, worried she might be in shock and hang about. However, she'd been calm and eager to help.

As soon as he'd moved the bodies, taken Grace's gun and placed the revolver in Denis's hand, Balcombe left by the kitchen doors which opened out onto the garden.

Within minutes he was over their rear wall and hiking up the hillside.

He'd buried the Beretta and marked it with a large stone in case he ever needed a gun in the future. He liked the fact that it was so small. He might risk carrying a concealed gun—once the murder of the Toogoods was put to rest.

He kept climbing until his fingers and thighs ached. Then he regretted missing the last tram and trekked down the mountain on the rail track.

Albert was outside his building looking as casual as anything. She raised her hat so that he could see her smiling face.

"You had me worried for a second there," he said.

"I kept watch afterwards," she said. "I thought you'd want to know what happened. I also wanted to make sure… you were all right."

He grinned.

Albert said, "Two policemen arrived within five minutes. Did you see them?"

"No."

She nodded. "Ten minutes later two police cars arrived with sirens on. Then an ambulance. I knew you hadn't been found because the detectives and medics were all very calm. It was those same two you met before. The ugly white man and the older Chinese one."

"How do you know about them?"

She tapped her nose. "I saw them talking to you last Thursday."

He walked to his front door, wondering just how often Albert followed without him knowing. She was good.

"What now?" she said.

"Now I sleep."

"You didn't find Roger Toogood, so you won't get paid."

"No, I won't, but—"

"What about me? Will I still get paid?"

"Of course. And I have a theory. I think I know where Roger is."

SIXTY-THREE

Balcombe knew that Inspector Munro would want to interview him. It would be a formality. Balcombe's employer had been murdered. The police would talk to all of the household staff and anyone who worked closely with Denis Toogood.

He thought he'd have a few days, but when he stepped off the ferry from Kowloon, Inspector Munro was waiting for him at the end of the pier.

"Good morning, Inspector." Balcombe doffed the fedora he was wearing.

"Mr Balcombe…"

"Yes?" Balcombe faced the smaller man. "Of course, I heard about the murders. Terrible. I assume that's why you'd like to speak to me."

Munro waited a beat, his eyes bright behind round spectacles. "I'd like you to come with me," he said.

They started walking along Connaught Road, past the ostentatious buildings: Queen's, St George's then the King's Building. The detective kept them going, past Blake Pier and the P&O Jetty.

On the wharf, Balcombe said, "You're alone today? Where's your sidekick?"

Munro didn't answer immediately. After a few more yards, the detective said, "Tell me about Kowloon. Why were you there this morning?"

"I was working."

Munro waited for more.

"Denis Toogood employed me to find his son."

Munro stopped with surprise on his face. "And have you?"

"I thought he was dead," Balcombe said. "But he's not. He's in Japan."

"I'd like the whole story."

Balcombe started walking. "I don't think so, it's pretty dull." He'd thought Grace had killed him when she said she'd *got rid* of Roger, but that didn't make sense. Denis was in on it. He wasn't a caring father, but even he wouldn't have killed Roger to save his embarrassment at work.

So Balcombe realized the hiding place would have to be clever. In fact, Roger could never reappear.

Which was pretty much like Balcombe himself. He'd faked his death and taken the name of his old climbing buddy.

Balcombe had looked again at the rugby photograph. John Daily, Roger's friend had died of a broken neck playing rugby.

This morning, Balcombe visited the Orient Line Company building in Kowloon. He'd spoken to Smyth again and asked him to check for a John Daily on the manifests.

It appeared that Mr Daily had made a miraculous recovery from his broken neck. He'd caught a boat to Tokyo on 15th December and arrived there three days later—three days before Balcombe was hired to find him.

Munro stopped walking again and pointed to a door. They were outside an office building at the end of the wharf. It had twenty different company names on the walls and looked run-down. The windows were grimy. The peeling paint was so discoloured it was hard to know whether it had once been white or cream or another shade.

"Why are we here?" Balcombe asked.

"For a chat," Munro said, his face showing nothing.

Balcombe considered his options and decided to go along with the detective's request. Munro had a gun at his waist but he was smaller and Balcombe was both quick and strong. If the worst came to the worst, he would overpower the detective and take it from there.

Of course, there may have been more men waiting upstairs.

There weren't. Munro led the way up a narrow dusty staircase past office doors with windows too dirty to see through.

At the top, he opened a door to a room with nothing but creaking floorboards and a blurred view of the building next door.

Munro shut the door behind them.

"What's going on?" Balcombe asked.

Munro said, "I'm sorry about the room. We're here because I don't want anyone else involved."

"Involved in what?"

Munro raised a calming hand. "Don't react. I want you to hear me out. I want you to hear about the murders."

Balcombe judged the distance between them. Three paces. Munro's hand wasn't near his gun. If he made a move for it, Balcombe could reach him first. No need to pull a knife, not until after Munro was incapacitated.

Then the luckless detective would regret that he chose a private location for the confrontation.

Munro said, "The Toogood's didn't kill each other. The service revolver had been wiped clean of fingerprints except for Mr Toogood's." Balcombe opened his mouth but Munro waved his hand to stop him. "The fingerprints were too precise. You see, when someone holds a gun, they don't just grip it in one place. Their fingerprints will be all over the weapon. It had been wiped first. So my conclusion is that someone placed the gun in Mr Toogood's hand to make it look like he'd fired the shot that killed his wife."

"Listen, Munro, If you're—"

"Next we come to the problem of the timing. They were both killed pretty much outright, so how did a dead person—whichever one was first—kill the other? It's quite a conundrum, isn't it? My theory is that, based on the fingerprints, Denis died first, stabbed five times, the heart stabbing being the killer blow. But you see, he was dead and Mrs Toogood was walking away."

Balcombe watched Munro's eyes, trying to read him, but couldn't. He desperately wanted a drink of water to quench his dry throat.

Munro continued, pointing his hand as though imagining a shooter aiming from the kitchen to the hallway. "Bang! She's shot through the back of the neck by the dead man, falls to the ground—still facing away mind you—and then drags her body back to the kitchen."

Balcombe said nothing.

Munro pointed again. "You know, to me it seems the shooter was on the other side. She was facing the shooter who was in the hall. Oh, which explains why I found a bullet in the kitchen, embedded in the pantry's door frame."

Balcombe had glanced around for the bullet but hadn't had time to search for it. He'd hoped the police wouldn't question the crime scene too much. It appeared he'd underestimated them. However, there was still no evidence against him.

"Interesting," Balcombe said, "but I fail to understand why you're telling me all this, Inspector."

Munro exhaled loudly then pulled a brief smile.

"I'm telling you, Mr Balcombe, because I found your fingerprints on the murder weapon."

SIXTY-FOUR

Balcombe felt his hand twitch in anticipation of grabbing the detective.

After a breath, he said, "You're accusing me?"

Munro turned away and took a few paces.

He's out of range.

Balcombe stepped to close the gap.

Munro said, "But I don't think you did it."

"Explain."

"I don't think it's your style, Mr Balcombe. I think it's the style of someone else. Someone killing through passion. Someone killing without a real skill for taking another's life."

Balcombe nodded slowly. "I have to say I'm relieved."

"You see, there was another murder. A young woman called Emiko Sasaki."

"You asked me about her. She was Roger Toogood's teacher."

Balcombe had been thinking about Denis Toogood's Japanese mistress. Grace had a motive. The girl probably hadn't taught Roger Japanese. She might never have met Roger, although the boy knew about her, that was certain. His friend David Jones knew, and so it was likely Roger had told him. The western paperback in the mistress's bed had bothered him. If Roger hadn't been there then it had been placed.

After Roger disappeared, two people had visited his rooms. The shopkeeper had said they'd been upstairs for a while. They hadn't been looking for Roger, they'd been staging the place for when Balcombe checked it. They didn't want him following any trails except the ones they laid. They'd wanted him to talk to the fake David Jones and to believe it was about borrowed money, maybe drugs and then justifying the involvement of a Chinese kidnap gang.

Unknown to Denis, Grace had returned briefly to Roger's rooms. She'd placed the photograph of her and Denis there. Maybe it was to suggest their marriage was stronger than it was. She'd written the dedication in the Dostoevsky book, suggesting her relationship with Roger was better than it was too.

Then she'd taken the western paperback and left it at the mistress's home. She'd killed the girl and then coolly left behind a clue that Balcombe would follow. He'd think the girl had known where Roger was. He'd also think she'd been killed by a gang on Roger's trail. It was to make Balcombe realize the Japanese girl was important. Maybe because in Grace's mind she was.

But the overriding reason was that she wanted Balcombe angry that Denis Toogood had set him up. Not just about the money, but also about the murder of a young Japanese teacher.

Munro said, "What are you thinking?"

"How was Miss Sasaki killed?"

"The same way as Mr Toogood."

Balcombe nodded. "The scissors. Grace Toogood did it."

"Can you explain?" The way Munro said it made Balcombe think that the detective honestly wanted the answers. And so he told him his theory.

Munro paced, and as Balcombe spoke he kept a watch for the detective's gun-hand. At one point he stopped and listened to creaking floorboards in case the door flew open and police charged in. But they didn't.

When he finished, Munro said, "So you maintain that you didn't stab Mr Toogood with the scissors, nor did you kill Miss Sasaki."

"Right."

"Then how do you explain your fingerprints on the scissors?"

"I held them." He cast his mind back to meeting Grace in the garden. She'd asked him to snip the cotton from her blouse. "She won't have killed the girl and possibly not her husband with those scissors. There will be another, identical pair somewhere. She won't have risked wiping my fingerprints off."

Munro nodded. "I found them under the sink. She must have placed them there when you arrived."

Balcombe said nothing. The inspector was fishing for confirmation that he was at the crime scene.

"Oh come now, Mr Balcombe, you were there!"

Balcombe started for the door. "This conversation's over."

Munro flapped his hands, more animated than Balcombe had thus far seen him. "Stop!"

Balcombe hesitated, his hand on the doorknob.

"Hear me out. Please."

"All right."

"You were set up for the murder by Mrs Toogood. I understand that Mr Toogood tried to set you up for the ransom."

"Yes."

"So you had every right to shoot Mrs Toogood having discovered Mr Toogood dead."

He's trying to get me to confess.

Munro said, "But it isn't your style."

"What do you mean?" Balcombe asked, intrigued by the statement.

"You wouldn't shoot someone."

Balcombe was ex-army. He'd shot people before. He'd killed with a gun. However, he wasn't about to disabuse the detective of his mistaken belief.

After a pause, Munro said, "You would use a knife."

Balcombe said nothing.

"In fact, you are quite proficient with the knife, aren't you? A single cut, not multiple strikes."

Munro seemed earnest rather than accusatory.

Munro said, "There was a man murdered recently here on the island. A slice to the chest—almost surgical—although a hand around his heart was what killed him. He was a nasty man trading in young women."

Balcombe tried to keep his face neutral. He thought about opening the door and leaving.

"And then there was that incident in Sham Shui Po." He paused, watching for a reaction. "Five gang members were killed. All with a knife. All killed by someone with skill."

Five? Balcombe thought.

Munro smiled, reading his face. "Thank you for the confirmation. I should have said *six* gang members. No one saw the killer. He's a ghost. He dispatched six lowlife's—men the police would love to have convicted, who I would love to have convicted—and then walked away."

Balcombe said nothing.

"Who was he?"

Balcombe said nothing. He turned the door handle.

"I think it was you, Mr Balcombe."

Balcombe started to open the door.

Munro said, "Stop. I have a story for you."

"More fantasy?"

"A different story." And then Munro told Balcombe about the crime figures, about the focus on numbers rather than serious crime and about the soft attitude of the Governor and the Prison Commissioner.

"There is a man on death row who has been pardoned," Munro said. "He most likely had my sergeant killed as revenge for his imprisonment and now he's being set free. I can't prove it. I don't have the resources to prove it. There are bad people, like the gang you dealt with in Sham Shui Po, and they need to be punished."

"Are you finished, Inspector?"

"Mr Balcombe, I cannot prove that you are the skilled vigilante with a knife." Munro took a breath. "However, I have your fingerprints on a pair of scissors. I can easily create a media sensation with the story of how you killed your employer and his wife—your lover."

Balcombe's grip on the door handle tightened. Then he shut the door and faced the detective.

Munro said, "I'll wipe off the fingerprints."

Balcombe waited a beat. Then he said, "And what do I have to do in return?"

Munro smiled. "I have a job or two for you."

SIXTY-FIVE

Chau Hing walked through into the Print Room at Stanley Prison. There were only two reasons for a condemned prisoner entering the notorious room. When they initially entered, the prisoner's details were carefully documented, including fingerprinting. The second time was before execution. Their details were taken again and matched to the former. Of course, they always matched, but it was a fail-safe because the British wardens didn't trust that they would identify the correct man.

The prisoners talked about fooling the system, trying to get another to go to the gallows in their place. But it never happened. Not to Hing's knowledge anyway.

However, Hing never expected to be executed for killing that man. It was just a matter of time, and as far as he was aware, he was the first condemned prisoner in history to receive clemency. Named on the Governor's New Year's pardon list.

So when his details were checked in the Print Room, it was to confirm his release.

It's who you know, he told his fellow prisoners without explaining. Hing's uncle was on the Chinese Board of Trade. He had a close friend in the Hong

Kong General Chamber of Commerce. At least the man was described as a friend. In reality, Hing knew that the man must be in his uncle's debt. Whatever the reason, it didn't matter, because the Chamber of Commerce man had the Governor's ear. It was just a matter of persuading the Governor that the killing had been justified. They said the victim was a communist. Hing chuckled at the thought. His rival had been nothing of the sort, but the British authorities feared communism, had an extreme, irrational fear of the ideology. It was ridiculous. Hong Kong would never be communist. It was a bedrock of enterprise and capitalism.

Hing had been trapped by the conniving Sergeant Tam. If the detective hadn't tricked Hing into boasting what he'd done with the knife, Tam would never have found it. They claimed they'd matched his fingerprints to the knife, but he thought the police had faked that evidence too. Even though he had killed the other man, it wasn't right to be caught by trickery, was it?

Never mind, he told himself, *Tam got his just desserts*. He'd stupidly gone to the address in Kowloon and walked into Hing's trap.

Hing owed the prison warder for passing on the coded messages, and once he was back in control, Hing would ensure the warder was paid handsomely.

The man had also arranged for his transport. Or so he said.

The end of the second day of 1954, Chau Hing walked through the prison gates a free man and looked up at the night sky. The Milky Way stretched across the velvet blackness. The welcome of the heavens.

This is freedom!

Ten past ten precisely. Just as he'd been told it would be, but where was his ride? There wasn't a car waiting, not even a taxi.

There was no one about except for a sleeping coolie with a tatty-looking rickshaw.

"Boy!" Hing shouted, waking the boy up. "Have you seen a car?"

"No, sir."

Hing huffed and glared down the road, then at the prison car park and back down the road.

The boy said, "I think there was a problem. A landslide or something from all of the rain yesterday."

It wasn't monsoon season. Hing couldn't remember that much rain yesterday, but then he wasn't paying attention to the weather. Inside, the only thing that mattered was the heat and humidity.

"Can you get past?"

"Yes, where would sir like to go?"

"Kowloon." Hing chuckled. "The ferry in Victoria."

"Apologies for asking, sir. You have money?"

"I have enough money," Hing said coarsely, offended by the question despite its reasonableness.

The boy paused, possibly weighing up the length of the journey versus the money he'd earn.

However, he took too long. There would be taxis at Repulse Bay, Hing realized. "Take me to Repulse," he said.

"That's the blocked road, sir. I can take you to Tai Tam."

"There will be a taxi there?"

"Yes, sir." He gave an extortionate price and Hing tried to knock him down.

The boy shook his head firmly and repeated the price. He knew Hing's option was to walk or ride.

"All right," Hing said, and decided he'd only pay the boy half when they arrived. It was only about a mile. Maybe he wouldn't pay the boy at all because of his cheek.

Hing sat on the bench and closed his eyes. The air was fresher, more perfumed than he remembered.

This is freedom! he said to himself again.

He opened his eyes. "Come on, we should be there by now!" Red Hill was on his left. The idiot was going the wrong way around the hill. Much quicker to go inland.

"Hey, boy!"

The boy stopped.

"I'm not paying you for this!" Hing snapped. "Get me to Tai Tam now!"

The boy didn't look at him. He stepped away from the rickshaw and into the darkness.

"Boy!" Hing shouted, then tutted. He'd walk the rest of the way. Even though they'd gone the long way round, the town couldn't be much further around the bend.

He took five steps and stopped.

There was a shape ahead. Just the rocks? He laughed at his skittishness. Prison taught a man to be on edge, always watching for danger. Now he was free.

Hing took another step. The shape by the rocks moved.

A man appeared. Tall. He was dressed all in black and was hard to see except for bright, piercing eyes.

"Chau Hing?" the man asked as though curious.

"Yes?"

A knife appeared in the man's hand. It moved fast, much faster than seemed humanly possible.

"My name is BlackJack," the man said.

Hing looked down. Blood pumped from his chest. The starry sky blurred and shrank to a dot. It stopped there for a second... and was then extinguished.

BlackJack said, "That was for Sergeant Arthur Tam." He wiped his blade on Hing's body before tossing the man over the rocks and into the sea.

He whistled.

The coolie appeared with the rickshaw. "Take me home, Albert," Balcombe said. "Tomorrow someone else gets released from prison. Tomorrow we get the pig butcher."

He sat back and enjoyed the fresh night air. This had been fun, but he had a problem: Munro, the detective. Sooner rather than later, BlackJack would have to deal with him too.

Acknowledgements

First off, I must recognize Dr Samson Chan's help regarding the Hong Kong prisons and penal policy in the 1950s.

My editor, Richard Sheehan once again did a great job, providing insight during the editing process. I must also thank my unofficial editing team of my wife and Pete Tonkin.

Finally, I should like to thank you, the reader for your support.

The first BlackJack thriller took longer to reach the shelves than intended. Hopefully book two, Second to Sin, won't be too far behind.

BlackJack book 2 "Second To Sin" is available now

Good vs Evil. Can you tell the difference?

As Balcombe battles with his demon, he investigates the death of a young woman. Was it an accident or did she kill herself? At first he thinks it's straightforward but as he digs, other cases reveal an evil in Hong Kong.

One that could consume them all.

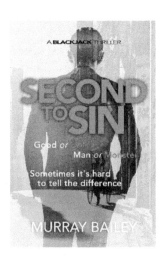

SINGAPORE 52

Ex-British military investigator, Ash Carter arrives in Singapore and finds trouble.

Caught between politics, the army and Chinese secret societies, he knows he must stop an attack.

Someone killed his friend.
And Carter may be next.

"Jack Reacher with a dash of James Bond, thrilling!"
Maggie Pagano, journalist

CYPRUS KISS

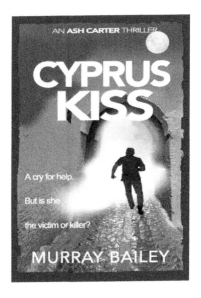

HELP ME!

Ash Carter receives a mysterious note from a missing woman.

In a race against time, Carter must work out the connection between a gang, the missing woman and the murder before it's too late.

"Twists and surprises abound!"
Roger A Price, author

THE KILLING CREW

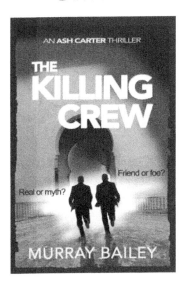

Israel 1948

Ash Carter and Bill Wolfe are hunting a group of British Army deserters known as the Killing Crew. Some people think they were a myth, others believe they were the most hated of British soldiers.

In the newly formed state that's at war with the Arab nations, hated by Jews and despised by Arabs, the two SIB officers think they face an uncomfortable task.

But when they become targets they start to realise this is more than just a job. It's life or death.

murraybaileybooks.com

IF YOU ENJOYED THIS BOOK

Feedback helps me understand what works, what doesn't and what readers want more of. It also brings a book to life.

Online reviews are also very important in encouraging others to try my books. I don't have the financial clout of a big publisher. I can't take out newspaper ads or run poster campaigns.

But what I do have is an enthusiastic and committed bunch of readers.

Honest reviews are a powerful tool. I'd be very grateful if you could spend a couple of minutes leaving a review, however short, on sites like Amazon and Goodreads.

If you would like to contact me, I'm always happy to receive direct feedback so please feel free to use the email address below.

Thank you
Murray

murray@murraybaileybooks.com

Printed in Great Britain
by Amazon